I0576141

The Great Illusion:
A STORY OF SELF-REVOLUTION

Part I: The Revelation

Written By
Phoenix Wise

Phoenix Wise
CO, U.S.A.

Library of Congress Control Number: 2020932222
ISBN: Ebook   978-1-7345769-0-0
ISBN: Paperback   978-1-7345769-1-7

Publishing Information: Phoenix Wise
phoenix.wise@outlook.com
Denver, CO, U.S.A.

For
My beautiful, wonderful, and amazing April.
You are my one and only and the love of my life.

Contents

Preface

I originally wanted to write a children's book to help counter all the lies that the kids are fed by their parents, the teachers, the religious leaders, the corporations, and the politicians. Then, I realized that most parents wouldn't let their kids read this book due to the cognitive dissonance and defense mechanisms that most people have to the truth and what is really going on around them and within them. After you read this book, you will probably agree that the book is more for adults. It may be the profanity and the progressiveness, but I believe that so many people are so brainwashed, so programmed, and so closed-minded that they would rather keep living their miserable and pointless lives than take some time to understand that they are not free and that they are living someone else's life. Unfortunately, they would rather their kids live an awful life like they do rather than change. It's sad but true. Instead of taking a few moments to accept that they are wrong and see the truth in what they are being told, people get offended and upset by what they hear or see that is different than the way they were raised and what they believe.

Well, I got news for these people. The truth hurts, and we were all lied to by so many people, who may or may not know that they were telling us lies. If you are a parent, I implore you to let your child read this book and let them decide on what the truth is, so they don't end up being a slave, being sick their whole life, dying an early death, living as a slave and doing things they would rather not be doing, killing helpless and defenseless animals, destroying the earth and its environment, and creating more misery and sickness for future generations. Even if you aren't a parent or don't want your kids to read this book, I still hope you read it, learn something, and start changing for the better.

We must get out of the cave, bubble, or prison that has surrounded us and trapped us by our family, friends, education, society, consumerism, entertainment, drugs and alcohol, other addictions, religion, and politics. Life is about experiencing things, learning things, creating things, having fun, and deciding what is best for us. You can't do that if you stay closed-minded and just believe what you were told and hold onto those beliefs in a stubborn and incorrigible way. That is a dangerous and futile way to live. You must accept the fact that you may be wrong, especially if haven't questioned why you believe in what you believe in or do what you do. How do you know that your religion is correct? How do you know that your politics are correct? How do you know that your parents, religious leaders, and politicians are correct? Have you heard the other side? Have you spent years listening to the other side like you have your side? Why do you have to have a religion or political position anyway? Humans make the huge mistake of only seeking out information that supports what they already know. In addition, humans hate to change and admit that they are wrong. Denial and irresponsibility are diseases of the human species. A lot of people would rather die than take responsibility and/or admit that they were wrong. Unfortunately, so many people and animals have died because of this stubbornness and idiocy.

Since I didn't want to mess with getting this book listed as a children's book, my hope is that the adults, young adults, and maybe even some teenagers will read it and learn a few things. As much as this book is a fictional book due to the story telling that I created with the characters and some of the events, it is mostly a non-fictional book based on actual things that have happened within my life. It is mostly auto-biographical due to the ideas, the dreams, events, attitudes, behaviors, the daily routines, and songs of the main character. Unfortunately, it's sad that a lot of people, who write biased and dishonest non-fiction or opinionated books, get to have their books categorized as non-fiction, but these so-called non-fiction books mostly consist of their distorted and erroneous thoughts that have no basis in reality or fact. Then, they have companies or organizations buy up all these fake non-fictional books, so it can be listed as the best-selling book on a disingenuous rating scale.

To me and even though I have to categorize my book as fiction, I consider it a philosophy and self-help book. I have spent most of my career in human services and helping people overcome many different problems. In addition, I have spent almost three decades reading and studying philosophy. With this understanding of philosophy, I have become pretty good at debating and logical thinking while identifying fallacious arguments, excuses, and irrational thinking. Therefore, I made this book very dialogue heavy with many conversations between the different characters and with the internal thinking sequences of the main character. It was more important to me to tell you what I think rather than spend time describing the environment of the characters. I would rather the reader use their imagination in creating the environment from their own experiences and creativity, so I can tell you what is going on in my head, which would have been more challenging for you to figure out.

From my human services experience, it's important to me that people are healthy and feel good. However, a lot of people don't understand the importance of not doing harm, so they find vices, such as drug and alcohol addictions, to try and make themselves feel better. Others may abuse themselves and others or focus on consumerism and materialism. There are also many other addictions, such as gambling, that people try to use to cope with their emptiness and trauma. Unfortunately, these vices provide a short-term fix, but they are riddled with many more consequences that definitely overshadow and negate any illusory benefit that they may provide. Therefore, it is important for us to be healthy, exercise, eat healthy, meditate, enjoy and be out in nature, and have healthy and clean fun.

Moreover, I have been a vegan for almost 25 years. This lifestyle has brought me so much joy over the years. I am a better human and being by being vegan. It makes me proud of myself and happy to not hurt another being just because others hurt and kill them, they taste good, I'm stronger than the animals, or I can't communicate with the animals. However, it has also caused me a lot of pain due to the horrible realities of the animal agriculture industry and watching people blindly do what the majority does. I hope that people will one day see the horrors for what they are, understand that they don't have to keep doing the evil deeds that the majority keeps doing or they were raised to do, and wake up and change for the better by realizing that they are the key to their happiness. The animals were not put here for us to exploit, abuse, and murder like we have done to other humans. They were here before us and will probably be here after we kill ourselves and make ourselves go extinct.

For the purpose of my goal to enlighten and free people with this book, I wanted to recognize and support the many oppressed groups in the world within this book. I feel extremely sorry and upset for the oppressed, the neglected, and the abused, especially women, the indigenous people who had their land stolen from them while being abused and murdered in the process, the gays and lesbians and all the LGBTQIA persons, minorities, immigrants and refugees, the vegans, the animals, and the earth. This book is my appreciation and love for all these groups. It's important that we promote and practice acceptance and equality through ahimsa, veganism, progressivism, environmentalism, sustainability, and renewable energies. All this division, separateness, judgment, hate, discrimination, and abuse need to stop. We will never know peace while we continue to engage in discrimination, inequality, and abuse.

I wrote this book to focus on the real societal issues and problems that we are facing today. I also wanted to provide some solutions too. The reality is that what we are mostly doing is failing. We are allowing the rich, the politicians, the government, and the companies to control us, manipulate and lie to us, and abuse us. It's a huge illusion. As long as people are taking on more debt and staying in debt, working most of the week, not taking care of themselves, eating unhealthy and processed foods, taking drugs and drinking alcohol, killing billions of animals a week, polluting and destroying the earth and its environment, engaging in pointless and destructive consumerism, focusing on mindless and trivial entertainment, avoiding responsibility, fighting pointless wars, and choosing to remain apathetic and ignorant, there is little hope for us now and in the future. We, and I mean you and me, have to change. We have to wake up and do better. We have to be smarter and see what is really going on with ourselves and the world. We are insane to think that we can keep doing what we are doing without any consequences. If you can't already see the consequences, you are a part of the problem and definitely need to wake up.

It doesn't seem like the politicians and the governments are going to change and deny the requests of and the money from the greedy corporations and the rich. The politicians and the governments are too corrupt at this point. They have been bribed and lobbied so much that they only work for the rich and the corporations. They have failed us. The rich and the corporations have failed us. The use of fossil fuels and all the pollution have failed us. The consumerism and capitalism have failed us. The classism and inequality have failed us. The animal agriculture industry has failed us. It's not okay that the people continue to allow the government, the politicians, the rich, and the companies to destroy everything in their paths. We must stop them before it's too late, and it may already be too late.

My hope is that this book will add to the revolution that is starting to happen and needs to happen. I started out writing this book after a tyrant and dictator was fraudulently, undemocratically, illegally, and illegitimately elected to be the President of the United States of America. Even though I was upset about many things before this incident happened, I needed to express myself to cope with the anger and hurt that I was feeling. After several months of writing, I ended up writing over a thousand pages. Therefore, I wrote three books from an idea to try and help wake people up from the lies and deceit. This first book is the first few chapters, or what I call episodes, of this story. For this book, I try to tackle certain issues surrounding cooperation versus competition, freedom and contemporary slavery, religion, politics, capitalism and the corporatocracy, and the separateness or division that so many people have that leads to abuse and discrimination of others, the animals, and the earth.

I hope this book wakes up a lot of people and helps them at least question what is happening to their poor lives, the poor animals, the poor earth, and the poor future generations. We must take a stand and start a revolution. We must change to succeed because what we are currently doing is not working. Things are getting worse, and we have to first accept that sad fact. I hope you thoroughly enjoy reading this book and the ones that follow. I hope we all find peace and love during this trying time. Please always question what you have been told and seek out the truth with facts and evidence before blindly believing it. Furthermore, it's always okay to say, "I don't know," "I'm not for sure," or "Let me check on that, and I'll get back with you."

I need to thank my beautiful, amazing, and intelligent wife, April, who has been extremely supportive of my creations and goals. She was instrumental in debating with me most of the ideas and concepts in this book. Her insights into her own psychology and why people continue to act like fools was very beneficial to me understanding why so many people would rather choose ignorance and apathy over progressiveness, evolution, compassion, and betterment. She helped me dig a little deeper into some of these controversial and provocative topics, so I could make a better argument for or against them and the alternatives and solutions that need to happen. More importantly, she has also been a great inspiration for my poetry and music. Thank you so much my love. You are my wife, my best friend, my lover, paramour, soul mate, and my confidant. I have always loved you and will always love you forever and ever. I owe you my life and all that I am. You are truly a special being in all this craziness. This acknowledgement is the least I could do for all that you have done for me.

Introduction

I wanted to write a brief introduction for the reader due to my decision to start the first chapter at the beginning of a dialogue between the main character, Emerald, and her friend and ex-coworker, Eric. As it so eloquently starts with some colorful language about them debating the benefits of competition, Emerald and Eric are sitting on a bench in a park engaging in some deep discussions. You will see that Emerald loves to think and talk about some major issues and is not afraid to be honest and tell others what she thinks about things. Nevertheless, she still tries to listen, question what she knows, and change her views when given new and compelling evidence that proves what she thinks is wrong. Throughout this book, I make sure to tell you more and more about this wonderful lady and her thoughts on so many different topics, especially societal issues and other important and controversial topics.

Emerald is a 45-years-old lesbian, an environmentalist, a progressive, a sexual assault survivor, a recovering drug addict, and a college dropout. She has been outcasted and neglected by her parents and family. She has been a vegan for over 20 years but was still very unhealthy for most of her life as a vegan. Over the past few years, she finally started getting her shit together, especially after she got arrested and almost lost the love of her life. She is very spiritual, but she is also anti-religion. She likes to discuss and debate provocative and controversial topics with herself, her lover, friends, and co-workers.

Emerald is also a singer-songwriter and loves to play guitar. She lives with her long-term girlfriend in an apartment in an undisclosed city and undisclosed time where she works part-time at a bookstore owned by a gay couple. After getting sober, she started questioning what she was told and taught to believe. Her struggles and conflicts relate to breaking through her denial and trying to figure out what is true or real and what is a lie. Emerald's goal is to affirm her suspicion that we have been lied to and that there is another option to consumerism and working full-time. She wants to live a happier, healthier, freer, and more spiritual life.

Episode 1
The Confrontation

◆

*The conflicts that we have with others are reflections of our own inner conflicts.
Therefore, facing your fears and your pain is inevitable to finding peace, love,
and happiness.*
You can't grow and evolve without learning from your mistakes and struggles.

"That's fucking bullshit. I don't believe that for a second," Eric piped up.

Some people walking nearby stared over at Eric in a shocked and offended way.

"Wow, I didn't think you would get so upset over a topic like this," Emerald calmly stated. "You're ruining the park's relaxing energy."

"It just doesn't make sense," Eric said in a lower voice.

"Well, you don't have to believe it for it to be true. There are lots of things that you and I don't believe that are true. And there are lots of things that we do believe that aren't."

"So, you're trying to tell me that there's nothing good about competition."

"Nothing at all."

They both paused for a minute and tried to enjoy the moment of the light breeze at the park as it rustled through the leaves and made a sound like waves gently crashing at a beach. It was a nice mild day with some beautiful plump white clouds.

"I can think of a few good things about competition," Eric said. "Competition is awesome. It's like the foundation to society."

"Like what?" Emerald asked. "Give me some answers."

Eric thought for a second. "It makes you better at what you are doing. You learn from others and your mistakes."

"Those are okay," Emerald said. "We'll come back to those. And…"

"Give me a second. You feel better about yourself, so you get confidence and a higher self-esteem."

"For whom?"

"The winner."

"What about the loser?"

"They get learned skills of what to do and what not to do next time."

"Anything else?"

"I think those are great. So, there are strengths, betterment, self-esteem, confidence, pride, and learning from mistakes."

"What about the negatives?" Emerald asked demandingly.

"What about the negatives?" Eric asked mockingly.

"We can't just talk about the positives without mentioning the negatives."

"But the positives far outweigh the negatives."

"How do you know? We haven't listed them yet."

Eric paused for a few seconds.

"Hurt feelings, sadness, and maybe shame," Eric reluctantly said.

"Not bad. That's a good start. What else?"

"I guess if you couldn't beat someone or win, you would get helpless or hopeless like you wouldn't be able to ever win. So, you might quit trying and give up."

"That's excellent and a great way to go into some insight with the loser. I'm impressed," Emerald said with genuineness.

"Hey, have I ever not tried to look at the other side of things?"

"We'll have to come back to that question because I can think of several times. You are a stubborn ass. Anything else?"

"That's all I can think about off the top of my head."

"That's a start."

"I'm sure there's more positives too. What do you have to add to both of those Em?"

"Well, let's see. Since I'm trying to justify that competition has no purpose, I'll start with the positives. Competition can create a learning environment for both parties, but it would need to be on a playing field of rules and fairness."

"So, you are going to immediately throw in some stipulations to minimize the positives?" Eric asked with some annoyance in his voice.

"Yes, we have to due to the fact that competition requires it. If it's not fair or even a remote possibility that one party or group can beat the other party or group, it's not competition. It's futile or dominance and what some would call a slaughter by the other party or group. In addition, that dominance might create an environment for the underdog to not want to compete or participate at all. They could also cheat or try to bend the rules to win."

"You could also say that the dominant or favored ones might already be cheating to have the upper hand," Eric said in an ingratiating way.

"That's good. Yes, that is what I'm saying."

"Okay, I see where you are coming from."

"For the most part, there's always going to be one party who has the upper hand," Emerald said. "However, it shouldn't be so much where there is no chance at all for the other party to not be able to win. Then, it wouldn't be competition. It would be biased or inequitable. So, let's focus on the underdog having some chance of winning. In that case, I would say some parties are learning, and that's about it for the positives."

"What?" Eric asked impatiently. "What about self-esteem, confidence, or even pride?"

"Well, that's fine for one party, but it doesn't hold for the other party. The positives should be for competition, which is about both parties and not just what one gets out of it."

"I don't know, but I'll stay with you since that might reduce the negatives too."

"The negatives of competition are separate from that rationale."

"How do you mean?"

"Well, if you use what's positive for one party and not the other party, then every positive for the party that won is a negative for the one who didn't."

"I got you. That makes sense."

"So, the only positive that I can think of is learning from what you did whether that was right or wrong. Do you have any more positives that you can think of?"

"I believe that's a big one and very important, but it's the only one that I can think of that is within our parameters." Eric thought for a few seconds. "Wait, if we are focusing on fair and just competition, then what about the benefit that they are giving to society? For example, people or businesses try to one-up each other to improve certain business products or services, especially technology."

"Yes, I would agree with you as long as the products, services, or technologies are not polluting the environment and contributing to other horrible problems or issues, such as discrimination, sexism, slave labor, tax evasion, and so on. Unfortunately, a lot of them have some or all of those consequences. People and companies also try to sell customers unhealthy and dangerous products. As you know, there are a lot of suckers and fools out there who will pay money to hurt themselves, the others, the animals, and the environment just because they saw it on an advertisement or they think everyone else is buying it too. The product may satisfy some immediate gratification, but it has negative effects. A lot of people don't think about the consequences, or they deny them. But I'm very pessimistic about capitalism and corporations, so I'll save that conversation for another day."

"I agree for the most part, but there is some good that comes out of businesses competing to have a better product."

"But they don't Eric. They are not trying to make a better product. That is a false ideal. That is what is supposed to happen in capitalism, but it doesn't. The competition actually hinders and prevents product growth and development as the companies are trying to make money, so they put less money into the product to make it cheaper and of less quality while trying to raise the price. The production of the product becomes a way for the company to make money and not create a better product for the people. The best examples are the numerous products that are absolutely horrible to our health and environment. You have pollution that is rampant and products that the companies intentionally make to break down after a short amount of time. Sure, I'll give you that there are a couple of good companies out there and some good products, but for the most part, companies aren't trying to find a way to help humanity. They are trying to find a way to make money and help themselves, which becomes a crime against humanity. It's a travesty. It's very upsetting. And if competition in business was such a good thing, then why do certain companies end up monopolizing most of the profits of an industry?"

"Sorry Em, I forgot how passionate you are about your convictions."

"No problem. I just hope you can see what I am talking about."

"I do. Unfortunately, I do."

"So, let's focus on the negatives. As long as we have a fair playing field for competition, I could see the negatives being what you were focusing on like feelings of defeat surrounding hopelessness and helplessness. However, I think those feelings could be dealt with in a healthy or productive way, but we don't know that. Therefore, those feelings and effects could be very unhealthy and detrimental to someone."

"That could be a positive then."

"If they are dealt with in a certain way, they could. However, we don't know that they will be. And, even if they are, some people learn to deal or cope with feelings surrounding certain situations in the past, but they continue to have difficulties dealing or coping with feelings surrounding similar situations in the present and/or the future. Therefore, they are still having problems. So, you can't say that it was a positive. We just don't know. Even with a guide, coach, or counselor, they may not get it or not be able to use the skills, so I wouldn't go as far as to say it's a positive. Either way, it would still fall into the positive category of learning from your experiences."

"Anything else?"

"Not sure. As much as I despise competition, it seems the biggest negatives surround the feelings of hurt and loss and low self-esteem, so the only other negatives I can think of relate to business competition, such as loss of money and financial consequences and the deleterious effects on society, such as discrimination, inequality, and pollution. You also have the lack of products and services if a company goes out of business and the other issue of a company raising prices."

"So, where does that leave us?"

"I still think that nothing good comes out of competition," Emerald said.

"What? You can't say that. A learning experience is an amazing positive."

"Yes, it is. However, do you have to have competition with all its consequences of hurt and loss to learn from your mistakes and weaknesses to learn or be better at something? Is there a healthier and better way to develop and grow without competition that doesn't have those serious negative effects? Can you still learn without engaging in competition? Can you learn more?"

"That is a good point. I would say that you could probably set up a better competitive environment to promote growth and development even if at a loss."

"But, is that also too idealistic due to the reality that a lot of competition breeds dishonesty, lies, cheating, bending the rules, and other unscrupulous acts? That is reality. So, I think we are at a place to say that most competition is unhealthy for us. There may be some that can be good, but that is debatable. It would be better to have growth and development in other ways such as with coaching or mentoring or even self-discipline."

"I guess I'm still torn. I see where you are coming from, but there has been some good to come out of competition."

"Eric, what is the opposite of competition?"

"Um…"

"What is competition?"

"Like a battle or game." Eric said reluctantly.

"So, it's like a conflict?"

"Yes."

"You have a rivalry to see who is better, to see who can win, or to see who has the edge. They are battling in a hopefully civil way, but they are still contesting each other. There is still conflict. To me, that just doesn't sound productive or effective, and it isn't, especially when you have significant feelings of hurt and loss on the table. And I do believe that people need to learn how to cope with these feelings and be able to accept loss and their limitations, but you can do that more effectively and productively with education, encouragement, and motivation."

"Well, when you put it like that, competition sounds hopeless. You better stop disparaging it, or you're going to hurt its feelings," Eric said sarcastically.

"It's like trying to say something good comes out of war, which is the extreme form of competition that has few rules. So, I'll go back to my question. What is the opposite of competition?"

"I guess it would be getting along with each other and working with each other."

"Yes, cooperation," Emerald said proudly.

"That's the word that I was looking for, but that sounds like some hippie bullshit. Like you said, the reality is that there is competition. You cannot stop that. It's there and happens every moment. People, groups, and businesses compete with each other all the time. And with that competition, there are all the negative consequences that go with it. We have to accept that."

"Yes, unfortunately, I have to agree with you. That is real. Nevertheless, competition is the opposite of peace and harmony, and as long as we have competition, it sounds like we will always have the consequences and problems associated with it. You are right. It would take a lot of change and work for us to overcome those patterns of belief that competition is a good thing, especially with the denial that it adds more value to a society. I strongly disagree with that. A lot of the competitions that we see are a scam. You have rigged contests and sports. You have athletes, officials and judges, and referees who are paid off to lose or throw games. You also have athletes using drugs and other performance enhancement products to cheat. From the business side of things, you have small businesses that are closing their doors for good because they can't compete with the larger companies, or they get overtaken by the larger corporations, who end up raising prices and/or offering lower quality products. We see companies pay low wages to the workers who do all the work. We see companies pollute our air, water, and land. We even see companies make products that are not utilized, not recyclable, and not sustainable. There are so many companies who make and waste food that is unhealthy and make billions of people and animals sick and die while polluting the earth with the chemicals that they use to make that food. All the while, there are just a few people getting rich in all this madness and what I would call a scheme. It's a very manipulative and detrimental scheme. You also have the companies paying off or lobbying politicians, so the companies can literally get away with murder."

"Okay Debbie," Eric said judgingly and jokingly.

"What?"

"You know. Debbie Downer. Depressing Debbie."

"Fuck you," Emerald said with some sass. "I'm not being a Debbie. At least, I have hope, and I'm not in denial about how horrible things are."

"Are you saying that I'm in denial?"

"About some things, yes. Especially how horrible competition is. I think Denial Debbie is way worse than a realist who accepts the horrors of a society gone wrong when they keep the masses asleep through materialistic and trivial means. It's absolutely atrocious. And, you know I love to have fun and enjoy life and laugh just as much as you do. But yes, I can get serious about stuff, and it's not bad to want the world to be different and better. I'm obviously not having an aneurysm over it. I still go through the motions of this sometimes pointless and consumeristic life that the government and the rich make us live. So yes, fuck you."

Emerald and Eric started laughing.

"I love how intelligent you sound during our debates and discussions, and then the foul mouth comes out to play when you get upset with my sarcasm," Eric said with a smirk.

"Well, you asked for that one. You know how I am."

"Yes, I do. I sure do miss working with you at the restaurant."

"It had its moments, and we met some good people. But shit, that was awful."

"What didn't you like?" Eric asked.

"You know."

"Yes, I guess I do know. The death of the animals, the overweight and fat fuckers, the mean religious customers, and all the sexual harassment from the young boys with their hormones raging."

"Don't forget that they only paid us a few coins per hour. Way below minimum wage. It was literally slave labor. The restaurants shouldn't get to use your tips as compensation for them to meet the minimum wage law. I don't know what rich fuck was able to get that law passed. Even with the tips, we didn't make minimum wage. Very unethical and should be illegal. What a horrible industry food service is. And yes, I'm glad I'm vegan and proud enough to not subject myself to a business industry that degrades and objectifies women. I know not all restaurants support or have those issues, but the ones that we worked at did. I have heard the same problems from other women who worked at a lot of other restaurants, and it gets worse when people are drunk and on drugs. It's unbelievable that they think it's okay to make sexual remarks to women and grab them without their permission, and the management doesn't do anything about it. Sometimes, they even participated or were the guilty ones. I guess they are just reflecting what our male religious and political leaders do. It's absolutely disgusting."

"Yes, as a man, it's very upsetting. I'm sorry for that. It had its moments though. A few laughs."

Emerald and Eric sat in silence for a few seconds and looked out across the pond as the sun and some clouds were reflecting on it. A few more people were out biking and walking at the park. Some squirrels were out running across the grass and climbing up the trees.

"Hey, I just thought of an idea," Eric said. "When we were just debating about competition, we were competing. I was taking one side, and you were taking another. We were having an intellectual competition. Right?"

"I can see what you are saying. Not sure. I think it would depend on the setting and the style of discussion. I don't think that either one of us was trying to beat the other one, but you could argue that we were trying to figure out the purpose of competition as to whether it had a positive or not. Our openness and acceptance that we might be wrong might challenge and discount whether we were competing. I think we were just rationalizing or brainstorming. There are definitely some similarities, and it could be a competition if we were trying to beat the other one or if someone was trying to be victorious over the other. I'm just not sure if that is the case here. What do you think?"

"Yes, it's close. I can definitely get competitive with some discussions and debates and want to win. If I did, I would shove it in your face too. You know. Some good ole fashion gloating."

"Yes, I know. That's one of the many things that I don't like about you and your jerkish ways, but it's important to accept that we are wrong. I do think there is something to be learned in the process of competition, but it just doesn't outweigh the negatives. It is good to learn from our mistakes and experiences but not at the expense of feeling hurt and loss and taking advantage of others. There are other more healthy and positive ways to learn from your mistakes and experiences. Either way Eric, you eventually have to come around and admit that you are wrong. You might go through all the stages of grieving or dying and death, which can be unbearable and agonizing. However, it can be very rewarding when you finally get to the acceptance stage. You would think after the many conversations that we have had over the years that you would be more aware of your response to new information that is correct or might be correct. Since this information challenges your old beliefs, you go right into the foregone response that so many humans continue to exhibit. Yes, I'm going to say it again. Denial. That's very immature of you."

"I listen and try to be open," Eric explained.

"Excuse me. What was your initial response to all of this discussion on competition? Wait. Allow me. You said, "That's fucking Bullshit. I don't believe that.""

"I may or may have not said that."

"What? Do I need a recording device to play back what you actually said, so you will believe it? That's the denial of the denial. Double denial. You are really fucked up now. You are going to need years and years of psychotherapy to deal with double denial. You know how you are. I think I already called you a stubborn ass. I may be stubborn too, but I try to make sure I get all the facts and evidence first before I make a conclusion about something. I still try to be open that my opinion could in fact be challenged by new information. As hard and difficult as it may be to accept the truth and have to change my beliefs, it is worth it for my own wellbeing and for others."

"Well, it's hard. Like you said, I guess a lot of people jump to conclusions or think they have to be right. It's like in our DNA or something. People are weird like that. It's interesting that denial is such a common response even to things that people didn't have any factual evidence to back up their original beliefs to begin with."

"You mean like religion," Emerald said in a suspenseful way.

"Oh, come on now. That's a hornet's nest of a discussion. You remember what happened the last time we tried to discuss religion."

"Yes, I remember someone being closed-minded, getting upset, and not wanting to face reality. Getting upset is in the early stages of grief and loss. It's not my fault that you want to stay in a place of tradition and debatable stories that have contributed to your beliefs."

"See. There you go. I could say the same thing about you. That you don't want to accept the truth that what has been passed down may be factual or truthful and that you are wrong."

"But isn't that the problem with debating history and stories is that we don't know? And, we should admit that we don't know. We shouldn't attach to things that evoke some emotional response from us or believe in things that a lot of other people believe in because you worry too much about what others will think of you. To me, that's dangerous, especially to blindly believe in something that you cannot prove otherwise. You only believe in it because you were told to believe in it. It could have been anything, and you would have believed it. It's conformity and compliance. It's not open-mindedness and acceptance. I would even go as far to say that it is not smart or intelligent. It's better to question the shit that we have been told and taught, even if it turns out to be true. It's better to be skeptical than not. There are so many things that we have been told by others that they fully believe in as true, but it is wrong and false. It's foolish to go along with the group that can't prove what they are saying is true."

"Well, we will have to discuss religion some other time because I get passionate about my beliefs and need something better from you to prove me wrong other than your opinions and logical thinking."

"That's horseshit Eric. I hate it when people say that they are passionate about something when they are really insecure and in denial about something and don't want to open their mind to the truth or even see something in another way. That's not passion. It's stubbornness, ignorance, and your own conflicted belief system causing you to act like an ass. Passion is about having a good cause, such as environmentalism, equality, or veganism. If you have real passion and are truly passionate, then your upsettedness is warranted and validated. Being passionate over something that you were told to believe in that you can't prove is not being passionate. It's being protective and obstinate."

"To me, my religious beliefs are a good cause, and I will go the grave with them. I have had many years of pondering my beliefs. I have pondered them more than you have. If I thought there was nothing to them or they were a joke, I wouldn't believe in them. I have a feeling, and they make sense to me. It would take a lot of arguing and debating for you to devalue them where I wouldn't believe them anymore. Just because you can't disprove something doesn't make it untrue."

"There you go with that asinine and ignorant thinking again. That is crap and a fallacy. Come on Eric. You are a smart man. Enough so, I hang out with you. Sometimes, I do wonder though, especially when religion or politics come into the discussion. If you can't disprove something, that doesn't make it true. You have to prove something to make it true. You have to have evidence. You are basically believing someone else's faulty thinking. It's okay to want to believe in something like a myth or a story that you can't prove, but it gets dangerous when you totally believe it as fact and have no doubt at all. It's a mental illness. You either have to not believe or say, "I don't know." You have to admit that you may not be right. If not, you are playing a dangerous game with your mind."

"Well then, I guess a lot of people are playing a dangerous game."

"Yes, indeed. They are. The world is definitely full of a bunch of morons. I would even go so far as to say that most people are stupid idiots who just go with the flow and believe what, for the most part, they are told."

"Are you saying that I'm stupid?"

"I didn't say that."

"Well, you are implying it."

"No need to get all upset Eric. You know I have some respect for you."

"Some?"

"You are just analyzing what I am saying too much and being too serious about our differences. We know we are different in those ways. Don't blow things out of proportion."

"Well, let's call it a day then on the topic of religion. It was fun while it lasted."

"Yes, we will continue this rough discussion hopefully in the near future."

"I hope not but maybe."

They both sat for a few seconds and watched a couple of birds fly over the pond and into a tree. The wind was still blowing the leaves and limbs in the trees and was making a nice and soft rustling sound. The wind caused some ripples on the pond. Some joggers and walkers passed by them.

Emily broke the silence. "How is your lady?"

"She is good. She is really enjoying her job at the construction company. As much as it's a guy's world there, she said that she got lucky it is with a good group of guys, or it may be that she makes sure everyone there gets paid."

"That's got to be tough to work with those guys and have some major responsibilities like that."

"Yes, but for some reason, she doesn't get stressed over stuff like that. I think she is preoccupied with us eventually having a baby. We are two months in now, so it's coming. It's going by so fast. It just seems like yesterday that we found out."

"Yes, crazy indeed. I can't believe that you both are having a baby. Good luck with all that mess. You breeder," Emerald said jokingly.

"Well, it wasn't exactly planned, but we did talk about it a couple of years ago. Just thought it would be longer, but I guess that's what happens..."

"When you don't use protection," Emerald interrupted and said with a smile.

"Absolutely. You never know what might happen. I'd like to think there are no accidents, but I may be making something out of nothing. So,

I'll stop on the baby issue. I know how you feel about people having babies."

"Yes, that's an argument waiting to happen. My passion will come out in a nasty way. It's so upsetting that the people can't take care of the babies and children that are already in this world. There are millions of them that are starving, poor, homeless, and dying. And, so many women are pressured and forced to keep having them."

"Calm down Em. What do you want me to do? You know we'll be good to that kid."

"You better. That's the worst. You have all these people having children because they think they should, and they don't love or take care of the kids. The kids grow up to be monsters with lots and lots of issues. It's a cycle that needs to be stopped. And..."

"Don't say abortion."

"Yes, the whole abortion issue has been shoved down everyone's throat with false information. How can you be pro-life and also be pro-war, pro-guns, pro-pollution, and also not care at all about the children that have already been born? Fucking hypocrites."

"Ok, let's move on."

"Sorry, I'll calm down. It's important to me."

"I know it is. Anyway, Christina is happy, and that's all that matters. It's nice to look forward to seeing someone after being away from them."

"I know. You guys have been married a while now. What? Five years?"

"Yes, it's not a super long time but enough to have some of the battles and arguments out of the way. Wouldn't it be nice to find someone and never fight?"

"Yes, but that would require both parties to have their shit together before the relationship starts. You may be asking for too much."

"How's Mary doing? I haven't seen her in a few months."

"She seems to be doing okay. We had a huge fight a couple of months ago. She is still wanting to get married. So, you know."

"Yes, I can already see how that conversation went, especially if it's anything like our conversations, but I can't imagine you two getting into a fight."

"You're right. Our version of a fight is a serious back and forth debate with some voices raised, but we try to stay tame. We do love each other very much. I've never been in a relationship this long with anyone. After 10 years, you've talked about so much, and you know what hurts and helps the other person. It's almost insane to think about the secrets you share. Good and bad. But yes, she continues to want to get married. She didn't at first, but I think with all this anti-gay bullshit she needs it or wants to do it to say we did it, which I disagree with. But it would be nice to shove it in their bigoted faces. I wouldn't mind doing a ceremony, but we shouldn't have to do something to let everyone know that we love each other. Do you know what I mean?"

"I think I understand, but what will happen if you don't?" Eric asked interestedly.

"Not sure. I think that's my point. It wasn't something agreed upon prior, and we aren't traditional people like most heteros. So, it's something she has decided she would like for us, but I don't need it. I am not afraid of her cheating on me or leaving me because we are not married. I hope she doesn't go down that road with thinking that I might do something stupid like that on her. I would never, but she still may want the marriage to feel better about that."

"There's the fear," Eric said.

"Yup, but right now, I don't feel that, but she might. I think we are totally one and committed like an old couple who has been married for 50 years. We are totally devoted to each other. I think even if one of us cheated on the other, which would be horrible, we would still stay together. I guess that's my point. It's our choice, but that's what makes a relationship hard is one party wants to do something and the other one doesn't. So, you have to talk about it and figure it out like mature adults. But, how much do you push the other person to do what you want before it's unhealthy, or how much do you give in to the other person before it's unhealthy?"

"Those are great questions or points. That's where the arguing and fighting come in or the domination and submission. I think it's good to compromise. Find a middle ground where both parties are happy. You might want to think about something you could do, even if it is some spiritual ceremony with you two."

"We'll see. But other than that, she seems to be doing good. We really enjoy our time together. I'm glad I found someone with some of the same interests and likes. That would suck if we had too many opposing interests. There's a few, but it's not bad. And, it's awesome that she doesn't smoke, drink, or do drugs, especially due to my past."

"Yes, I think Christina and I are half and half. We just try to not push each other on some of the things we don't agree with."

"That's what I always loved about Mary. She's not pushy, but she still expresses herself and respects me. The way it should be."

"Yes, sorry, you have to go through what you go through with society's…"

"And religious standards, and don't forget political ones too." Emerald said sarcastically.

"Hey, I was trying to show some compassion."

"That's the point though. Some of the same things that you believe in conflict with me and my life and who I am. It's not okay. As much as I like you and even love you and can see you care and are lighthearted for the most part, there are some contradictions with what you say and what you believe. And I know I don't have control over you, and you can do whatever you want to do, but you have to admit that you support the same institutions that have horrible and awful beliefs about homosexuality and other things. I'll say it again. It's not okay."

"Well, I'm not defending their hate, ignorance, and bigotry towards any of the LGBTQIA folks. We are all people, and I don't think it's okay either Em. There are religious and politically traditionalist people who are good and don't believe in hatred towards others who are different than them. You know that. Change takes time. You have the people at the top who are from another time who still hold traditional values and make it seem like the entire group holds those values. A lot of them don't."

"But a lot do, and they are the ones spreading the hate and passing the discriminatory and oppressive legislation. You should not be allowed to be in a position of power or authority if you believe in and practice hate, discrimination, and bigotry. It's terrorism to a lot of the population and citizens, and it's counterproductive to society."

"It's not good for you to generalize either. I guess I'm a progressive traditionalist, which I know sounds kind of weird. Maybe that's not the right term. That could mean that I am more traditionalist. Maybe there is a better term than that. Moderate traditionalist?"

"I don't know about the term. Maybe moderate traditionalist. But, either way, traditionalists, who don't believe in what your group is saying, should be speaking out against them instead of staying silent. Silence is consent. It's the same as going along with a murderer by not saying something to the murderer and letting the murderer murder. You have to try and stop the murderer. If not, you are an accomplice, and you are also a murderer. If you don't believe in what your group and your group leaders are saying and believe in, you need to either speak out, make a change, or leave the group. Hatred is an awful practice to be silent about."

"What do you want me to do? Go protest? That's a waste of time. Now, that's some hippie bullshit right there."

"Yes, it is. It makes me get all excited and want to take my bra off. Oh wait, I don't have a bra on now. I'm a hardcore feminist. It's unfortunate that we even have to wear a bra. The main reason that we wear bras is because men can't handle themselves."

Both Emerald and Eric started laughing.

Emerald continued, "But, silence is consent and revolutions and positive changes are based upon protesting. Freedom of speech has no point or is useless without protesting. If anything, protesting is the best thing you can do to companies and governments and other groups that are doing something wrong or bad. Without protesting, you just have compliance, domination, complacency, or even apathy, and that is not good when these groups are corrupt and evil and are trying to hurt others and spread hate. It's hypocritical."

"There you go again trying to imply that I'm a hypocrite. I would do more activism if I had more time. You could do more, but we have responsibilities and have to work. What, do you want me to quit my job?"

"Absofuckinglutely."

"Seriously?"

"Yes, that is some of the best protesting that you can do and the ultimate sacrifice to stick it to the government, the rich, and the companies. Your freedom is their loss. Your slavery is their power and income. It's an excuse to keep slaving away, especially at an evil and destructive company, and making someone else rich while you suffer and maybe get a few unimportant material things in your life. I do protest, and I make time to be an activist. That's why Mary and I live so minimally, so we can help the earth, the animals, and the environment."

"Some would say that you are just lazy and don't want to work."

"Some would say that you are a compliant slave who could be free but would rather choose consumerism, fear, and materialism over freedom."

"Well, that's just something you and I are going to disagree with. I choose to provide and care for myself and my family while accumulating things that I need and want, which requires me to work a certain amount of time per week. I am also helping the economy and the society while you are not. The rest of the time that I have outside of work is my time to use it how I want to. If I have time and I choose to, I might engage in something that I am passionate about."

"Sounds like you only do that around election time."

"I get to decide that Em. It's my choice."

"That's the point. Do you have a choice or are you a slave with the illusion of choice? You could be stuck in the system that some call the matrix and can't get out because you are afraid of the consequences. It's quite disturbing to hear someone talking about choosing when they have been manipulated or programmed to make those choices, and they don't even realize it."

"You are a part of the system too, even if you are trying to get out of it."

"You are right," Emerald said sullenly.

"And, your issues are not my issues. I believe in gay rights, but I'm not going to take extra time that I don't have to go protest someone, who I mostly believe in but disagree with some of their ideas. I care about your plight, but it's challenging in this time and in this life. I'll think more about that and what more I can do, but I'm not a hypocrite. And, if I was, I'm not trying to be. We all have things we can do more of. I don't see you protesting all the restaurants and animal agriculture farms because of your veganism. You are sitting here projecting your dislikes of the world onto me because I'm here and you are upset with a lot of things that you disagree with."

"Maybe, but I try to live my life everyday doing what I believe in. I can only do so much. I have to take care of myself first and foremost, and then give back. Still, I do a shitload more than most, especially you."

"What, is this a competition Em?"

"No. You know what I mean."

"Sounds like you are challenging me to a match of who can do more good things. Like I told you, I am comfortable with what I am doing. If I have more time to give, I will. You are the one who doesn't like how much I am doing, and that is not for you to decide. That is my choice."

"But that's what I'm saying. You think you are choosing, but you are not."

"Well, I could say that about you. That you are being brainwashed by the gays, the vegans, the pacifists, the atheists, the progtards, and all those books you read at that brainwashing bookstore that you work at for three to four days a week for 25 hours. You lazy ass."

"Sounds like someone is jealous."

"I'm not jealous of someone not doing their part to help out the economy. You are the reason that the economy sucks. The more cogs that are in the wheel, the easier it is for everyone else."

"That's fucking bullshit, and you know it."

"I disagree. Things are better when people are working and spending."

"Well, tell that to the poor and middle class, who both work over 40 hours a week and have very little to show for it, and then tell it to the rich, who own most of the wealth, don't work as much and as hard, and hoard most of the money in the economy. I bet you get two different points of view. It's another lie you believe with your blurry glasses. The rich love that you have bought into their manipulations and lies. You see the world a certain way that's been fed to you, and you fell for it."

"What? Now you are an economist?" Eric asked seriously.

"No, but I know enough to know bullshit when I hear it. I may not have the awareness and skills to run a smooth economy, but I do know that when the society is set up to feed a few people, who also influence the laws in their benefit while letting the businesses run wild and destroy everything in their paths, it is a disaster waiting to happen. Nothing good comes of it. For the most part, the economy looks good or okay because the government continues to borrow more and more money, but the debt keeps piling up, which will eventually lead to another recession and depression. It's fake. All the economic growth is fake. You can't keep borrowing money without consequences. In addition, people think they are okay, but they are not. They are just blinded by the idea of freedom, the fake success of the rich and corporations, and materialism. We also can't forget entertainment is a huge blinder for most people. The rich have enough money to change everything for the better, and they don't. They just keep on doing what they do best. They lie, steal, and cheat. We have to take it back. By force if necessary."

"I don't know about that. That's a discussion for another day. There is a lot of good that comes out of a capitalistic society. At least, we don't live in a dictatorship like a communist or a socialist society."

Emerald scoffed and said, "You have to be kidding me. You are not that stupid. Are you? I think that's the dumbest thing that I have ever heard you say, and you have said a lot of dumb things."

"What do you mean? There you go again calling me stupid, and that wasn't even implied."

"You don't even know what you are talking about. You are just throwing around terms that you heard by your beloved political party that have been distorted and manipulated as part of a propaganda to distract you from how awful and evil capitalism is. Those are traditionalist talking points. You just suck it up and believe it without questioning whether it's factual or not. A dictatorship is not communism or socialism. Communism and Socialism are the opposite of a dictatorship. Look it up and do some research before you start repeating someone else's lies. Furthermore, capitalism isn't even the opposite of communism and socialism. You can have capitalism in all those governments. Actually, a dictatorship is closer to a fascist, traditionalist, right-wing society than either communism or socialism. Have you ever read or done any research on any of those types of government? Tell me, what is communism or socialism?"

Eric paused for a few seconds and thought about the question and then said, "Well, I'm no expert in political science, but I think it's when the government owns or runs all aspects of the economy, and so the government gets rich and the people are left with nothing, which is why it's a dictatorship."

"Wrong," Emerald said obnoxiously. "It sounds like you have a lot to learn about both of those. I'm sorry you have been misinformed and don't know more about communism or socialism. They are not dictatorships at all. That's like saying a republic or a democratic society is a dictatorship because the leader or the rich make the laws and control everything. You know, like the country we are living in now. You can have a dictatorship and corruption in any type of government. However, unlike a republic or a democracy, the second that someone becomes a dictator, that is no longer a communist or socialist society. It's not a democracy either. The people have to maintain control for it to be communism or socialism. We have all been lied to in this country about those types of government, including what a republic or democracy is, due to the fact that the rich and powerful are afraid they will lose their money and power. It's a master manipulation by the rich few to keep you in check and working the machine for them."

"There may be some truth to that, but those governments have a bad track record."

"That's the point. They weren't communist or socialist governments. There's a lot to be said about the benefits of communism and socialism. If ran right, they are both ideal. Way more than our precious republic. You can also have democracy and elections in any of those governments, which I'm sure your brainwashers didn't tell you. You can have elections and capitalism in all of them. But, as with any society, no matter the political and economic structure, if you have greed, corruption, inequality, pollution, debt, high military spending, and a lot of the wealth in the hands of a few, you have a failed system. It will eventually fail. If it doesn't fail financially or economically, it will fail through a revolution by the people. All these different types of governments can work in a positive way, but to say one is superior to another is ignorant, especially if you don't know what they are and are just repeating what someone is telling you to say without knowing what they are saying."

Eric laughed and said, "Funny, I was going to say that you are spreading commie propaganda and trying to brainwash me into believing that something so horrible and awful as communism and socialism can be successful and good for us. Again, that sounds like some more hippie bullshit. Fuck that mess. There hasn't been a successful country that I would want to live in that has shown us that either one of those governments can be beneficial and helpful."

"Again, lies based on the fact that you think the countries who are so-called communist or socialist are actually communist or socialist countries. If you did some actual reading and research before you try and talk about something you know nothing about, you would see that you have been misled and even lied to. If something doesn't make sense, it's nonsense. And, you have never even left the country. You have no idea what goes on in those countries. You just blindly believe what you are shown and told and avoid the problems in the same country you are trying to defend. Damn the lying and bought-and-paid-for traditionalist media."

"That's funny Em. Traditionalist media. I love the shit that comes out of your mouth when we talk about politics."

"Well, it pisses me off that our education system has failed us in so many ways that it can't overturn years and years of lies by politicians and the rich, who support a corrupted capitalistic society where only a few benefit and everyone else either has to be a slave for most of the week or they starve and live in poverty. Then, the people who are starving and living in poverty are called lazy. With those and other lies and the truth of all the negative consequences and effects of capitalism being covered up, the brainwashed people end up seeing other options, such as communism and socialism, as evil and tyrannical governments that torture and kill people, which is exactly the opposite of what those systems do. It's crazy. Sometimes I think we are living in the dictatorship where all the stuff our brainwashed parents and leaders told us from their programmed and erroneous education just churns out and creates more idiots and ignorant slaves to do the bidding of the wealthy. It's false education with fake history. They teach us to memorize meaningless facts and information for tests. Then, this information is lost after we take the tests, and hardly any of the material is practical to real life. They should be teaching about relationships, communication skills, coping with feelings, health, diet, nutrition, happiness, exercise, and…"

"Don't say it," Eric interrupted.

"Meditation," Emerald said loudly.

"Damn you."

"We need to learn how to live and experience life. We need to create. We don't need to spend our lives trying to answer or live up to that bullshit question that they ask us. They ask, "What do you want to be when you grow up?" When you are young, you give these outrageous answers, which isn't reality, and the answers aren't practical. It's great to have dreams but come on. When you are young, you say, "I want to be an actor" or "I want to be an athlete." All that shit mostly never happens. It's like winning the lottery. It's a one in a million shot, maybe more. It's the exception to reach that dream and not the rule. For the rest, they fall into these mindless and sometimes pointless jobs that they might have some interest in."

"A lot of people like their jobs."

"I don't think it's as many as you think it is. If they had a choice, they would probably not be doing what they were doing. Oh, I forgot, they also end up going into huge amounts of debt by going to college because they were told and lied to that going to college is better for them. They think that's what they are supposed to do. There are some jobs that you need a college education, but for most, you don't. And it's not worth it anyway because of the debt you acquire and have to pay back, so you might as well not have gone in the first place. You would have made more money without going to college. It's a scam. And the most important thing is or question is, "What did you really learn?" or "How did the education help you in your career or life?""

"Are you asking me?" Eric asked.

"Not necessarily, but yes. What did you get out of your college education besides debt, drinking buddies, and possible STDs?"

"Well, Mizz know-it-all. My general business degree did have a couple of classes on marketing and advertising that helped me at my jobs. It was good to review marketing strategies and understand what other companies have done that worked and didn't. Not sure if it was worth it though."

"It's not. For the amount you paid for just the class, you could have easily bought over 150 books on that subject or just not spent anything and went to a library, or you could have gotten the information for free or cheaply some other way. So really, you didn't learn that much. Maybe some. You could have easily gotten that info in a lot cheaper way. Now, the question is whether the degree was worth it. They say you make more with a college degree, but is that true? How do they know? You can't go back in time and live your life differently, and it's not the equivalent to say that you probably would make less based on looking at the average of what people make with and without college degrees. On average, people do make more with a college degree, but some make less than people who don't have one. And some people didn't need their college to get the job that they have. It just gave them confidence. You can't ask, "How much would you pay me if I didn't have a college education?" You have to factor in the wasted time of you going to college and not getting experience. More importantly, you have to factor in the debt that you acquired while going to college. You may be making more than if you didn't go to college, but you have more bills to pay because of the debt. Therefore, overall, you may be making less than if you didn't go to college in the first place."

"I'm not sure. You bring up some good points. It is misleading to say that you make more with a college degree without factoring in the time lost not gaining actual work experience while you are attending school and the debt from the college education. Either way, it was worth it for me. I had fun."

"That's an expensive way to have fun. That's like having to take a loan out to go to a party. So, you have to ask, "Was it worth it?" I would say no. I'm glad that I dropped out when I did. It was one of the best decisions that I've made in my life. I am better for it, personally and financially."

"Not everyone has to pay for college," Eric said confidently.

"Again, that's an exception and not the rule. Most people do, but you are right. Education should be free. Somehow, it should be free, but I still think educating ourselves is better and cheaper."

"I think the fact is that most people don't educate themselves, so we need some kind of educational system. I agree with you, there is a lot of idiots out there. I think some are better off going to college and learning something. It teaches them things that they wouldn't have learned on their own and in real life."

"That's my point though. Is it worth it? Are they better off? I don't think so. College has many other negatives to it. There are the rapes, sexual assaults, and sexual harassments that are rampant, especially in the social organizations. These social organizations are a virus in the educational setting that condone discrimination and abuse. It is disgusting and appalling that the colleges do very little to deal with these problems. What are we to just accept that's what is going to happen to women and minorities who go to college? That they are going to get raped and abused and discriminated against. And if the guy is an athlete or a son of someone important or rich, they expel and push the victim out of the college, and the offender receives little to no consequences. The poor lady has to leave the school due to being harassed by the school and the supporters of the perpetrator like it was her fault. He gets to go on to be judge or a politician. It's very upsetting. This whole victim-blaming society makes me want to get violent. I'm getting upset, so we better stop."

"Yes, I'm so sorry Em," Eric said compassionately. "That's a tough one. I support you one hundred percent on that one. This misogyny must stop. It is unfortunate that there is so much rape and sexual assault in the various school settings. The schools should do a whole lot more to deal with that epidemic, and society in general should too. And, they do seem to support the male offenders more than the women and the victims."

"It shouldn't have to be a tough issue to deal with if they would just hold people accountable and support and care for the victims. They shouldn't let money, popularity, and politics get in the way of convicting the offenders. The world would definitely be different. No wonder victims of rape and other crimes don't want to report what has happened to them. They get called liars and other disparaging names. They are blamed to make them feel like it was their fault for where they were or what they were wearing or that they were drinking or drugging. They even charge the women victims with filing a false police report after they recant their claim or accusation that they were raped or assaulted because they were threatened by the perpetrator. That happens all the time. They don't do that shit to guys. They don't blame male victims, especially boys, for causing the horrible things that happen to them. It's a double standard. It's maddening. Sorry, I'll calm down."

Emerald took a couple of deep breaths.

"You don't have to apologize Em. We do need to do something about that" Eric started laughing. "Let's go protest. That is something I will definitely protest with you about."

"I hope you are not joking."

"Half and half. More on the not joking side."

"Women do need to stand up though. This patriarchy must be taken down, even if by force. It would be one thing if the patriarchy was ethical and moral, but it's not. I like to imagine what kind of world it would be if women were the majority in government and business management positions. Think about how different things would be. It would definitely be for the better."

"Yes, I think it would be better. I have to agree with you on that one. That being said, I'm going to get out of here. It was so good to see you. I don't think we had a comprehensive and diverse talk like that in a couple of years. Sounds like you have been waiting to get some of that out."

"No, Mary and I talk that deeply at least every other day. A few times a week. It definitely reflects the issues going on and tells me what's wrong with my own being. That's what is important. We see ourselves in the world and when we don't like it or can't change it, it gets nasty for us. So, we have to let go of what is outside of us and change ourselves."

"Wow, that is deep," Eric said sarcastically.

"Fuck off. It is deep and important and necessary for our health and well-being. We all have to get shit out and have to figure out how to cope with our feelings, or we would all be mental and maniacs. We would always be in a state of upsetedness because things are not the way we want them to be and people are not the way we want them to be. Just wait until you have that baby. You better understand equanimity before that happens."

"What's that?"

"Look it up you idiot. Don't you ever read?"

"Only if I have to at work. School burnt me out on reading."

"You should never stop learning Eric. You should always be reading a book, even if it takes a while to finish it."

"I'll try to remember that. Hell, I'll holler at you sooner than later. Maybe we can dive back into saving the world one idiot at a time."

"Sounds fabulous. Later Mr. Johnson. Tell Christina I said hey and thank her for letting me spend some time with you on a day that she had off too."

"Will do. She is good though. She enjoys some time without me. She can go shopping, which I hate. Tell Mary I said hey too. I hope you guys work something out with the marriage thing. Good luck."

Emerald and Eric hugged each other, and Eric walked off in a hurry. Emerald sat back down on the bench and tried to think about and process some of the things that Eric and her discussed. She was trying to find some peace with all the issues and problems with the world. For a few moments, she just looked across the paved path that bordered and ran along the pond. It made her feel better to just relax and listen to the breeze rustle through the leaves and limbs in the trees and watch how the breeze hit the water. She also loved to hear the birds singing and chirping away. She was going to miss the warmer weather as the climate in her area was getting into autumn. She still loved the changing seasons though and respected how each one had its purpose.

Her mind then raced back to some of the issues that they talked about. With how much time humans have evolved and become so-called civilized, Emerald was extremely bothered by how sexist people were and how society supported men sexually abusing women over the voices and accusations of women. She thought how crazy and insane that was. She started to really get into her feelings about being a victim herself and a survivor of sexual assault. She thought about how much she had blamed herself in the past for not trying harder to fight her 15-year-old cousin when she was seven years old. She did remember kicking him in the shins really hard, but it wasn't enough to get him to stop groping her and eventually raping her. While she was mad at herself for not doing more, she knew he was still going to do it.

Her anger was less at herself now and more at her dad, who didn't believe her. Since she was her parents' only child, her cousin was like a son that they never had. Her dad and her cousin had a close relationship, which was like a father-and-son bond. She was also upset with her mother for allowing her father to convince her mother to not take her to the hospital to get examined. She wasn't sure if they would have found anything, especially since he used lubrication and a condom, but they may have. The police may have also believed a seven-year-old girl over a teenage boy to at least start a police investigation. Since he used lubrication and a condom, Emerald felt like he may have done that before because he seemed like he knew what he was doing. It was all still very enraging to her after all these years. She felt a lot of guilt for not reporting it to at least a teacher or another adult.

It made her sick in the stomach to think about it again. It had been a while since she really thought about it, especially since there was nothing that she could do about it anymore, so she tried to focus on the now and enjoy life the best she can. However, all the talk about women's rights and the failure of law enforcement and the legal system to protect women and prosecute the offenders ignited the fire in her. She thought about all the cover ups with sexual assaults and rapes at the schools, colleges, and societies and how the rich and popular men didn't get charged or if they did, they didn't get convicted. For the ones that did get convicted, they just got the proverbial slap on the hand. She started to get upset again about how many people say adult victims are making up the allegations or trying to make money if the allegations are against a wealthy man, but Emerald knew for a fact that offenders and perpetrators lie. It's so rare for a victim of rape and sexual assault to lie, and it's so rare for an offender to tell the truth. Emerald wondered why women continue to allow society to discredit and silence them.

Emerald asked herself why someone would want to lie about being raped or sexually assaulted. It didn't make sense to her. There's nothing to be gained, especially with all the shaming and victim blaming that happens. A woman has everything to lose. The victim blamers make the victims feel like they are the ones who chose that to happen to them. It is crazy to think that someone would want to lie about something as horrible as rape and sexual assault while letting everyone know that something as horrible as those acts happened to you. Emerald would rather not anyone know that she was assaulted, and she was sure most women would rather not publicize to the world that something like that happened to them. It's very embarrassing and shameful, especially when you are young.

On the other hand, Emerald thought how important it was to speak up. You have to stop the evil men who would get away with anything, especially rape and sexual assault, if you let them. Now, her stomach started to grumble as she got anxious and more upset. Guilt started to set in. She always thought about confronting her cousin, who was a big-time manager at a retail store, but she was not sure how that would happen or play out. She didn't want to ever do something out of spite or for vengeance, but she obviously still recognized her issues with it. She took a deep breath and decided to use her energy of shame and regret to focus on a song she has been trying to get out of her head.

"That's it," she said out loud. "All this craziness leads to something, but it's the craziness that we have to accept. We have to recognize the issues and understand that when things are good, they are good, and when things are bad, they are bad. There is also some bad during the good and some good during the bad, and the bad can be good and the good can be bad. To make it, you have to adapt and accept the change, good or bad, and move on. It's your choice to live in misery or bliss."

Emerald got excited. She always loved it when she was thinking about something serious and was able to come up with a song. It was like it came together through her mind, body, and spirit into some creation. It was already there, but she needed something to happen. She needed her thoughts to be a certain way to affect her. Once her thoughts happened in a certain way, she would come up with a song or build upon an idea that she previously had.

She got out of the bench at the park and started to walk back home. She started humming the melody that she began working on a few months ago. She has been playing guitar for a while, but she spent the first several years playing other people's songs. She has never been in a band or performed professionally, but she would love to be in a band. She already had a name for the band. She wanted to call her band The Resistance. She really loved folk and rock music. A few years ago, she started writing her own music and putting different chords together, which she thought made her a better musician or guitar player. She really enjoyed progressive rock with its nice melodies and long instrumental periods. If done right, she liked words in songs, but she thought musicians and bands destroy beautiful melodies by not using the right words or singer. She also enjoyed psychedelic, stoner, and doom rock even though she stopped smoking marijuana and doing drugs. She got a hypnotic and trance-like feeling from some of that music. She thought it was very well written and beautiful music. She even thought it was ethereal to hear. To her, it was kind of like a music that sucks you in where you and the songs are one while you go on this ride and adventure together or travel through space and time.

She walked a little faster to her apartment. She was so focused when she got to her apartment that she didn't even think to tell Mary that she was home. After putting her keys down, she realized Mary was still working a shift at the local health food store. She walked past the living room, which had a guitar stand with a mediocre acoustic guitar, and went into her bedroom and grabbed the more expensive acoustic guitar. She brought it out into the living room and sat down on an ottoman to try and play the song that she had in her head.

She definitely wanted some darkness and emotion in the song, so she closed her eyes and thought about the pain of some of the issues that she was talking to Eric about earlier. She started playing the notes in an E-minor chord like an arpeggio, but she thought it sounded better on the seventh fret with the highest strings open. She played different notes of this chord instead of them all simultaneously. She played this chord for a couple of bars and then went to a D chord, then to a C chord, back to the D chord, and then back to the E-minor chord. It was a slower tempo but not too slow. Emerald thought there was something haunting about the song. However, it was also uplifting. With the open highest-note strings ringing with all the different chords, there seemed to be a nice connection to all the chords.

She felt like this song should be an instrumental song with no words. It was repetitious but powerful. She thought it was very simple but would sound amazing with a guitar solo over the chord progression that she was playing. She knew a bass line could be in there somewhere, but she wasn't going to mess with coming up with a bass line today. While she played the chords, she could hear the guitar solo start off slow in her head. She imagined some lighter percussions coming in during the earlier stages of the song and that the song would build and get louder and harder with all the instruments where it would reach a crescendo and then descend back to a quieter place.

She immediately thought of a name for the song. She called it "Prelude to Insanity." She continued to play. She started to hum the guitar solo that she heard in her head. It was definitely an electric guitar with a slight distortion but more of a clear and smooth tone. After going through a couple of chords, she started playing with some other sounds or notes like a guitar solo would. She really got into some high notes and some chords with her vocals and felt the crescendo coming on as she started feeling the drums and a more rocking and powerful moment of the song. She started playing the notes in the chords more together or simultaneously instead of picking the different notes. While she did that, she continued to hum the guitar solo with distorted higher pitched notes. To her, it was like a wild ride or a fierce storm blowing through, and then she felt like screaming at a higher octave than the chords. She started wailing really loud over the chords that she was playing as it matched the mood of the song's moment. Every time that she screamed, she would fade out at the end of each scream. She did that a few times and then thought that was the climax, so it was time for the song to wind down.

She lightened up on the chords and started picking the various notes of the chords instead of playing the notes together. She felt the guitar solo slowing down and the drums and the percussions slowing down and getting softer. She continued to hum a more mellow guitar solo with less notes. Emerald finally stopped on the E-minor chord. She ended the song by playing all the notes on that chord from low to high almost at the same time. When she stopped, she felt a rush of emotion. It was like some of the anger and frustration that she felt from the past trauma and the difficult issues that she was thinking about just left her body. There was a moment of clarity and peace that she was safe and would be okay. She felt some satisfaction with her creativity in writing such an emotionally charged instrumental piece of music. It was the first time that she was able to express herself through music without using words or lyrics in a song. It was like the music was speaking for her and expressing to the world what she needed to say about all the issues that she was discussing with Eric earlier. She even had some pride.

She looked over to the front door and saw Mary standing there staring at her in awe of what she just heard.

"Hey lady," Mary said. "That was amazing. I didn't know you had it in you to rock out like that."

"How long were you there?" Emerald asked self-consciously.

"Long enough to know how wonderful that was."

Emerald immediately got up and carefully set the guitar down on the sofa. She gave Mary a big hug.

After a few seconds of their warm embrace, Emerald pulled her head back, stared deeply into Mary's eyes, and said, "I missed you so much. I love you my one and only."

All glossy eyed and almost in tears, Emerald gave Mary an affectionate kiss. As they kissed more passionately, Emerald knew what she had to do.

Prelude to Insanity

Arpeggio, picking of notes
Em chord (7th fret A string, 9th fret D string; open G, B, and high E
strings) (8 beats)
D chord (5th fret A string, 4th fret D string; open G, B, and high E strings)
(8 beats)
C chord (3rd fret A string, 2nd fret D string; open G, B, and high E strings)
(8 beats)
D chord (5th fret A string, 4th fret D string; open G, B, and high E strings)
(8 beats)

Continuous throughout the entire song
Guitar solo comes in after a minute and plays throughout song.
Occasional vocalizing with other instruments, especially percussions
throughout the song

Episode 2
Controlling Freedom

Freedom is having choices and having choices is being free.
You are not free if you are afraid and living in fear.
Freedom is not about terrorizing, hurting, abusing, or neglecting yourself,
others, the earth, and the animals.
If you live in a society with laws and rules, you are delusional if you think you
are free.

Emerald woke up the next morning in hopes of feeling better, which she did a little bit. She woke up a couple of hours before dawn and heard some cars driving past the apartment complex. She realized it was a weekday and that people would be getting around soon and rushing off to work, which made her feel anxious. Mary was still sleeping, so Emerald gently got out of bed, left the bedroom, and quietly closed the bedroom door. She used the bathroom and splashed some water on her face. She was a little tired but not horribly tired. She decided to go ahead and make some breakfast, journal her dreams, and write down the song that she played the night before. She also wanted to squeeze in a stretch, a run, and a meditation session. She was going to wait to mediate until after Mary went to work, so she didn't feel rushed. Emerald didn't have to work today, so she wanted to make sure that she got a lot done but not stress herself out too much. She always tried to stay busy to keep herself out of trouble and away from negative thinking that comes with being bored or having nothing to do.

She made a raw, organic, and vegan whole foods shake, which had some diatomaceous earth and greens in it. It was also gluten free. Mary was allergic and very sensitive to gluten, so Emerald went gluten free for her a few years ago. She didn't want to get Mary sick from cross contamination, such as from kissing or touching and having the gluten and wheat products in the kitchen. Mary was also allergic to lactose in dairy, but since Emerald has been vegan for over 20 years, that wasn't an issue. Emerald thought how crazy and stupid it was that so many people are allergic to certain things, especially dairy and gluten foods, but they keep eating them. Most people are allergic to dairy and are lactose intolerant, but they would rather be sick and take medications that make them sicker than stop eating the foods that are making them sick. Humans are the only species on earth that consume another species' milk. If aliens showed up on earth, they would think humans are the weirdest, strangest, and most self-destructive beings in the entire universe.

A lot of people are also allergic to genetically modified organisms and foods and the massive amounts of poisons that they spray on them and use to make them. Emerald liked to call them genetically mutant organisms due to the fact that they are a science experiment to make a few people rich while the people who eat them get sick and live in ignorance and misery. These GMO companies are actually poison and chemical companies that decided to make poisoned foods. These companies have spent billions to bribe politicians and the consumer protection agencies. The government, the politicians, and these consumer protection or regulatory agencies have allowed these foods to not be labeled as such, so a lot of people don't know that they are eating them and how dangerous they are. They have also spent billions in marketing and advertising campaigns to convince the public that they are safe to eat even though they are not. There have been numerous independent and unbiased scientific studies proving that GMOs cause so many health issues, including but not limited to digestive problems, disruption of hormones, cancer, and death. Even without these studies, it doesn't take a genius to put two and two together since they use massive amounts of poisons to make GMOs. The poisons that are used in these GMOs have made so many people sick and have killed so many people. Emerald was so upset over the government allowing these harmful foods to be sold in her country, especially without proper warnings and labeling. It was an abomination and proof that our government doesn't work for the people. It was also proof that companies can do whatever they want at the expense of the people.

She grabbed some nut butter, a banana, an apple, and some fruit and vegetable juice. She started thinking about her dreams and how wild they have been over the past year. They have been very vivid while covering a lot of different people and places. She did not recognize most of the people in her dreams, and a lot of the places were unfamiliar. She has been having dreams of flying or floating across some fields and past some hills, which was weird since she did not think about those things. She liked the sensation of flying in her dreams, but she was not sure what it meant.

Emerald started thinking about how long she has been journaling her dreams. She thought it had been about several years, which was about a year after she stopped smoking tobacco and marijuana, drinking alcohol, and doing drugs, which were mainly prescription opiates and benzodiazepines. She was very proud of her accomplishment to be sober for so long but has felt so much shame and guilt for all the time and money that she wasted. She also felt a lot of guilt due to all the lies that she told Mary and the secrets that she kept from Mary. The deceit was very exhausting for Emerald and painful to their relationship. She was very surprised that Mary was still with her. She did not think that she would still be with Mary if Mary lied to her, kept things from her, and was killing herself with drugs and alcohol. She thought how awful that must have been for Mary to go through all of that and what Mary might have thought and felt at that time.

Emerald tried to not think too much about the past, especially the drug abuse days, because it made her feel so much regret and pain. It also blew her mind to try and think about all the times and things that she forgot or could not remember because of the alcohol and drug abuse. She was still bothered by all the arguments that she had with Mary. She remembered Mary calling her out on her lies due to missing money and Mary not knowing where she was. She also remembered acting funny and temperamental around Mary. Emerald would get very upset at Mary even though Emerald was lying and keeping stuff from her.

Emerald said out loud, "I was such an ass. So stupid. I just should have been honest with her."

She thought more about why she started drinking, smoking, and doing drugs to begin with. It made her think about being in high school and getting offered marijuana for the first time and feeling like she had to do it, especially from the peer pressure. She wondered what would have happened if she turned it down and said no. It was so strange to her how we think people control us, but they don't. So many people do legal drugs and think that is their right and that is what makes them free. It's like a privilege to them. Emerald bought into that thinking and the you-only-live-once mentality. She thought that doing drugs was actually what it took to have fun and enjoy life.

She snapped herself out of her trip down memory lane and journaled her dreams while she ate breakfast. After a couple of minutes of journaling, she thought how much happier and healthier she was now. She loved the feelings that she got when she abused the alcohol and drugs. However, like in her conversation with Eric about the effects of competition, the drug abuse was not worth the negatives and consequences that go along with the debatable positives of it. In retrospect, the positives weren't real anyway. They were an illusion. To Emerald, the feelings you get from drugs are fake as they create a chemical and biological response due to them messing with your natural neurotransmitters and their processes. In addition, the feelings that you get from getting drunk or high are like an idea that something is great, but when you actually experience it in its entirety, it's far from the greatness that you thought it was going to be. We remember things how we want to remember them. That's not what actually happened. When drugs and alcohol are involved, you remember the euphoria and not the stupid things you said or did or the physical, mental, and spiritual sicknesses that come from the drug and alcohol use.

Emerald's conclusion now was that so many people do drugs and alcohol because they don't know how to experience life sober and don't embrace life as you would a kid with all the curiosity, wonder, excitement, and awe of life and our being. We get channeled or focused on chores, responsibilities, finances, and work. These so-called responsibilities become very stressful, so we look for an escape or a quick fix. These thoughts about her abusing drugs made Emerald think about her abuse and trauma that she went through. It wasn't just about the sexual abuse. It also had a lot to do with the neglect that she had to endure from her parents and the teasing and bullying from the kids at school. The drugs and alcohol may have provided some escape and some temporary and illusory good feelings, but that's what it was. It was an escape. It did not assist in dealing or coping with the issues that needed to be faced and dealt with properly. You have to accept the pain and learn how to manage your thoughts and feelings in a good, positive, and healthy way. One of the secrets to life is how well you respond to adversity.

If only Emerald would have figured that out a long time ago, things would have been so different. It would have saved her a lot of time and energy. Maybe someone told her or mentioned it, but she never really heard it, or it never sunk in. She might have not understood what it meant to accept the pain and learn how to cope with it. It's very challenging and difficult to accept the pain. Most people run from it every chance they get. Emerald knew that she couldn't go back and change anything, which actually made her feel really good about where she was at. She was able to wake up every day feeling good instead of wasting time lying to herself and Mary and wasting time, energy, and money trying to find drugs. She hated lying to Mary almost every day about who she was with, where she was at, or whether she was high or not. She thought how horrible it was to have to live a life like that. It was very shameful to her.

"Oh shit!" Emerald said sharply. "I need to focus, it's getting late."

She redirected herself back to journaling her dreams. She had a dream about being in a building with a lady and a man. They were doing something, but she wasn't for sure what they were doing or where they were at. She remembered that they went to the top floor and then flew to another building, which was euphoric. She tried to think about what the dream might have meant and what was going on. Emerald tried not to take her dreams too literally. She tried to look at patterns or see that certain things, such as places, items, and people, may be symbols. She tried to look for hidden meanings in certain dreams that might be relevant in the conscious world. Even though she liked to journal and remember and analyze her dreams, there was still a little part of her that thought they may not mean anything at all. The dreams could just be some imaginative process of the brain and the mind while we sleep that uses some of our memories and experiences of the conscious world and mixes them in with the unknown or unrecognizable creative parts of the brain. The dreams do seem to incorporate some real-life people and experiences, but they could just be random thoughts that do not mean anything about anything.

Emerald thought about the times where she was worried or anxious about something, such as worrying about a sick friend or family member, and then she would have a dream about them within a day or two after thinking about them. This coincidence also made her think about another phenomenon where she would have a dream about a friend or family member and then within a couple of days that person who she had a dream about would contact her or someone would mention them. Emerald thought how bizarre that was since she had not thought about that person in a long time or had any recent contact with them. Those experiences made her think that there was something mystical or metaphysical to her dreams.

She thought about other dreams where she was late to something, such as school or a class or a test for class, and she was not prepared to go wherever she was heading. However, she had not been in school for over 20 years. She had these dreams about once a month, so they were occasional. Emerald used to be a good student, but she put a lot of pressure on herself and tried really hard in school, especially to be on time or punctual and to get good grades. She knew that this pressure she put on herself in the past was being reflected in the dreams she had. She also had some occasional scary dreams about trying to find drugs or hide them. These dreams were so vivid and took place in places that she never even had drugs in. She would wake up very upset and anxious from these drug dreams. These intense feelings were then replaced very quickly with a sigh of relief after she realized that they were just dreams. These dreams were like some effect from a post-traumatic event called drug abuse and addiction, which definitely did a number on her mind, body, and spirit.

"How strange this life is," Emerald said out loud. "So glad that part of my life is over."

Emerald finished eating and journaled the rest of her dreams. She had another dream about walking in a park at night, which was weird since she usually was asleep around dusk. She also couldn't remember a time where she walked in the park during the dark. Emerald put up her dream journal and grabbed her song book. She wrote out the chords and some of the ideas that she remembered from the "Prelude to Insanity" song that she played last night. She put up her song book and washed out her dishes. She went to the bathroom again and did a quick but thorough stretch. Just in case Mary woke up while she was gone, she wrote out a note for her that said, "Hey Beautiful, I'm out running. I hope you slept good. Very much enjoyed the sweet sweet loving last night. I'll be back soon. Love, Em." She drew a heart after her name.

Emerald walked out of the apartment. The traffic was picking up as people were driving to work. There was a paved trail that went all the way to another park that she liked. This park was different than the one that she was at yesterday with Eric. The sun was coming up, and she loved to watch the sunrise. While she ran, she thought more about the issues and problems that she debated with Eric. As much as she thought she had it all figured out, she wondered why things were not figured out and why so many people continued to allow themselves to be swindled by the government, the rich, and the corporations. Emerald felt like it was hopeless for some people to change but knew that most would finally rise up and deal with the corruption by the powers that be. Emerald felt sorry for most people as they are blinded by the lies and the distractions, such as materialism and illusory division, which is intentionally programmed into people.

She got to the park and ran around the backside of a field, so she could stop for a minute and enjoy the sunrise. There were some other runners out enjoying the morning too. She saw where the sun was going to peak at her over the hill on the horizon. She wished there were some clouds to reflect the sun's light and create some different colors. She always loved the dark purple, which was magic to her eyes, but the sky was clear this morning. There were some birds already chirping away and some squirrels rustling around. The temperature was almost perfect as it was slightly cool. Emerald didn't feel she would be drenched in sweat by the time she got back home. However, she hoped to sweat some. She was already sweating a little by the time she got to the park, which was a couple of miles from her apartment.

Since the sky didn't have any clouds, she noticed the chemical or chem trails from the planes and jets around the sun, which was almost about to pop up over the horizon. These chem trails pissed her off as she wondered about that issue and what kind of chemicals they were spraying in the sky. She heard the defensive argument a thousand times that they were just condensation trails or water vapor, but those reports are from the companies and the government that are doing it, so they are biased explanations. She didn't remember the skies looking like that a decade or more ago. It seemed to be a recent happening, which may relate to the global warming or climate change issue or some other conspiracy theory. Emerald didn't want to ruin the beautiful moment of the sunrise thinking about such a hot topic, so she redirected herself to drop that debate and enjoy the glory of the sun's magnificent light and energy.

As she waited for the sun to come up, she found a bench to sit down on. She thought about sungazers and how they swear up and down that watching the sunrise and the sunset give you some energy and power and help open your pineal gland or third eye. The sungazing is supposed to assist you with your circadian rhythm and other biological functions and cycles. Emerald hadn't done a whole lot of research on that issue, but she was fascinated by what the sun does for everything on the earth and whether there was something to the pineal gland. She remembered that some people have said the pineal gland is the gateway to the subconscious or the unconscious universe and that we need to be healthy and take care of ourselves to be able to access that plane or realm. However, she was still pondering those things but was slowly buying into it as she counted the years of being extremely healthy and not hurting her body, mind, and spirit anymore.

She was also sleeping a lot better than she used to, and she was feeling so much better than she did. She tried to go to sleep about the same time every night, and she usually woke up about the same time every morning even though she only got about six to seven hours of sleep. Even with that amount of sleep, she still had a lot of energy throughout the entire day, so she was not too worried about not sleeping a fully recommended eight hours. She usually woke up a couple of times in the night. She woke up to pee about halfway through her sleep and a couple of times the last one or two hours. She thought about going to a sleep doctor at one point just to make sure there wasn't anything wrong with her, but she refused to go back to a medical doctor due to them mainly wanting to dole out medicines, which don't cure the problem. If anything, medications make people's problems worse. It was upsetting to her how many doctors only deal with symptoms of problems and diseases instead of focusing on prevention and finding a cure for your ailments. In the doctors' defense, people are their own worst enemies though and would rather have someone else try to fix them than actually deal with or cure their problems. Most people would rather just take a pill that only acts like a bandage and actually makes them sicker. All people need to do is exercise, eat a healthy plant-based diet, have some health fun, enjoy nature, create, and meditate. Since she felt okay, especially with having a lot of energy and not having any mental and physical problems, she wanted to just keep monitoring herself.

She watched in awe as the sun rose above the hill on the horizon with a rich amber color. She could feel the warmth hit her face as gentle as it was. It was pure electromagnetic energy. She just sat there enjoying the gorgeous sunrise while she tried to take it all in. She felt a rush of enjoyment and excitement and was proud of herself for taking the time to appreciate and treasure this moment and others like it. In the past, she would have just rushed around to get to work, class, or an appointment. She used to be so stressed doing so many things. Now, she tried to be very structured and busy, but she did things that she chose, wanted, or even liked to do. She felt pressured to do a lot of those things in the past and didn't really want to do them. There is a huge difference between doing things you like and being made to do things that you think you like or don't like. More importantly, Emerald tried to be more spontaneous now. If something came up, she would accept it and go where it took her instead of fighting or resisting it. Life is more exiting and enjoyable that way.

Emerald got up, took a deep breath, stretched out her back and legs, and started running again. She ran down a paved path as she felt the cool morning air on her face, arms, and legs. She loved the feeling and rush that she got from running. It was like running was her drug now. It was her prescription. She loved the energy that she got during the run and how she felt immediately after the run and for the rest of the day, which was like a relaxed concentration feeling. She ran for about another mile past the park and then decided to turn back and head on home.

As she ran back home, she thought about her feeling of being free. It was a lot more now than ever. Even though she wished she could move somewhere else and work on an organic farm in a vegan pacifist community that was focused on being fully sustainable and off the grid, she still felt like she had a lot more freedom than a few years ago, and she definitely felt like she had more freedom than 10 years ago. Emerald felt like Mary and she needed to get situated in a better and more sustainable environment before the limited resources, such as coal and oil, become extremely scarce. Emerald thought how nice it would be to not have to deal with that panic and the suffering that this crisis will eventually cause. She thought how most people are so dependent on those awful and disgusting resources while the companies make billions off contaminating and polluting the earth, water, and land. This pollution has definitely had a significant and negative impact on the climate, especially due to the human overpopulation epidemic.

When the resources start running out, people will start freaking out and start worrying about how they will live and get from point A to point B even though scientists have been warning us for numerous decades and even centuries. Emerald hoped that Mary and she would be able to keep on living normally in a sustainable community. She scoffed at the rich and companies who lie about the realities of global warming and pollution, spread propaganda with "clean coal" rhetoric, and minimize the deleterious effects of using and relying on coal, oil, and natural gas. Fossil fuels are dirty, toxic, destructive, dangerous, and pollutants. Emerald thought their propaganda and lies were a bunch of bullshit and that people would have to really be stupid to believe that, but unfortunately, people do believe it, or they are ignoring the reality and pretending like there is not a problem. They are making so much money off that horrible industry and the raping of the earth that they are going to keep that money machine rolling until something drastic happens. Emerald wondered whether this event or turning point would be like a singularity, which could be good or bad. The changeover to renewable energies would be good, but the continuous use of unstainable and polluting fossil fuels would be bad. She had hope, but she thought they were running out of time. She felt like the people were going to have to revolt and take over the government to stop the corporations and the rich, especially since there were too many corrupted politicians already in the government who were not going to stop accepting bribes from these evil companies.

Emerald thought it was sad that people choose money over life and health and would rather support corrupt and deplorable politicians and businesses. It seemed to always be about money. It blinds people so much. You can't eat it, drink it, or breath it. To most, it's the most important thing in the world. So much, people will literally kill for it and destroy so many things for it. All the while, there are so many alternatives to both money and the limited and destructive resources that we are using. Money is like the carrot and the horse metaphor for people. It's a manipulation tool. It's like using candy to get a kid to do something, a treat to train an animal, or bait to catch a fish. Emerald thought how sickening money really is. It's just a fake reality or illusion of value. In most societies, how much money you have is a measure of how successful you are. In reality, the amount of money you have has nothing to do with success. Success is really about what kind of a person you are and how you treat yourself, others, the animals, and the earth. Most people who are rich and so-called successful were born into their wealth and affluence and inherited their money. Lots of people don't know that due to the facade that rich people create for their deceptive image. There are some exceptions to that, but it's not the rule.

She wondered why we don't live in a society where people can cooperate and work together to create things that we need and do away with slavery, inequality, materialism, and money. People would be so much happier. Because people have a false sense of happiness due to the brainwashing and programming from a capitalistic society that money and material items make them happy, most people are empty inside and are not really happy. Unfortunately, they may not ever be.

As she continued to run, Emerald thought about her reflections a couple of years ago when she really started to understand happiness and finding joy in life. She concluded that any external items that make you excited or happy are an illusion and finding happiness in external sources really says a lot about your own emptiness or your lack of ability to create your own happiness. You have to enjoy life as it is. You can't expect or want something external to fill the void of emptiness or sadness or fix your problems. You have to deal with your issues and problems internally and with a lot of self-reflection. You have to create your own happiness and not be fooled by the fake happiness that you get from external sources, such as material items and money, that are of someone else's creation and manipulation, which is really to control you and get you to do things.

Emerald thought that most people think that it's just easier to look outside of themselves to solve their problems. Drugs and alcohol and other addictions become the solutions too. People look for things outside of themselves to make themselves feel better. If it's not a drug, it's still acts like a drug. It may seem to help on a short-term basis and it does create some immediate gratification and seemingly good feelings, but when that external thing that you are using to make yourself feel better or deal with your problems stops or is gone, you immediately start to feel the real feelings of emptiness, sadness, hurt, pain, anger, and so on. The external coping skill was just a bandage hiding a mess of unresolved issues. You can't run from pain or expect it to go away magically with a pill or quick fix. We spend many years and sometimes decades screwing ourselves up and breaking ourselves, so it takes at least that amount of time and sometimes more to fix our problems and heal ourselves.

Emerald thought of all the worthless shit that Mary and she accumulated over the years. They bought most of it, but a good amount was from gifts too. At one point, they had to rent out a storage unit after filling up an entire bedroom with crap that they didn't need or were not using. She thought how ridiculous it was to hoard things that you didn't need or use. It wasn't just the closet in the bedroom that they filled up, but it was almost the entire bedroom that was full. While she continued to run, she started laughing at how ludicrous it was to have all this stuff that they never used and never appreciated but didn't want to get rid of for whatever reason. Sure, a few things were gifts and had sentimental value to them or were things that she thought she might use in the future, but Emerald thought of all the people in the world who had nothing or very little. This thought made her feel ungrateful and possessive. This ungratefulness and possessiveness can be very detrimental and destructive to a person and a culture. People need to share and donate all the things that they don't need or aren't using and stop buying new things and worthless shit. It's a whole lot better to be a giver and to share than to be a taker or hoarder.

Emerald finally got back to the apartment. She couldn't believe that her run went by so fast. It was probably due to all the thinking and processing that she was doing. She used to try to think of some songs while running, but either she couldn't remember what she thought of by the time she got back home, or it was distracting her from enjoying the scenery, environment, and energy of the run and her surroundings. She sweated a little, but it wasn't bad. She was out of breath though. She stopped in front of the door and took a couple of minutes to cool down and catch her breath. She took a few deep breaths and stretched her back out. She didn't want to wake Mary up if she was still sleeping. She quietly opened the door and walked into the living room. She did another stretch routine to loosen her up a bit and drank some water. She hopped in the shower to get clean. When she got out of the shower, Emerald heard Mary getting around. Emerald walked into the kitchen, and Mary was trying to make some tea and breakfast.

"Good morning my love," Emerald said in a welcoming tone.

Emerald gave her a big kiss on the lips and a brief hug as Mary seemed very focused on her mission to get some caffeine in her due to still being drowsy from waking up.

"Good morning to you," Mary said tiredly.

They both said that they loved each other at the same time. Mary took a drink of her still hot tea and ate a few bites of her banana.

Emerald didn't want to hover over her even though she was excited to see her, so she said, "Let me know when you are a little more awake and we can talk. I love you my intoxicating caramel colored goddess."

"Sounds good," Mary mumbled. "I love you."

Emerald went back to the bathroom, did some hygiene, and fixed her hair. She was getting hungry again, so she went back into the kitchen as Mary made her way to the living room sofa and turned on some upbeat reggae music.

"Great choice," Emerald shouted from the kitchen. "I love it. What a way to start the day. That'll keep my energy going."

Emerald made a mixture of nuts and seeds with some dried mulberries and cacao nibs. She added a little stevia and cashew butter to it. She grabbed a banana to smash into it. She made herself a glass of water. Emerald stopped drinking tea and caffeine a couple of years ago. She used to enjoy some of the flavors of tea but wanted to focus more on water and 100 percent fruit and vegetable juices if she needed something to drink. She thought all drugs, including caffeine and foods with added sugar, make us feel unnatural and think and behave how we are not supposed to think and behave. It was important to Emerald to be who she was supposed to be and not be someone or something else. She went into the living room to join Mary and the excellent music. She danced a little on her way to the sofa. Mary was starting to wake up and looked a little livelier.

"How'd you sleep my dear?" Mary asked.

"So so. Could have been worse. As always, I kept waking up about an hour or two after I peed. Very annoying, but I felt like I slept okay until then. It's very frustrating to keep waking up though. I feel great now after eating breakfast, stretching, running, and showering of course. How did you sleep?"

"Not bad. Seemed like it was pretty good. Just always need a little time right when I get up. Must have woke up while you were gone. The traffic was loud this morning."

"Oh, I'm sorry."

"That's alright. I think I was already starting to wake up. It was about that time. I wanted to see you anyway before I go to work."

"Shit, I knew that. I was hoping that we would have the day off together. I don't have to be a slave until tomorrow."

"That's cool. I have to work tomorrow too. We both get the day after tomorrow off together, so we can hang out then. Since I'm up so damn early, I still have a few hours before I have to go to work."

"It's not early for me," Emerald said jokingly.

"I know. You are an early bird. Makes me sick. Let me do some hygiene, and we can hang here or go somewhere."

"Sounds awesome. I'll think about where we might could go."

"I'll see you in a bit," Mary said while she got up out of the sofa.

Mary gave Emerald a kiss, washed out her dishes, and went into the bathroom.

Emerald knew the reggae song that just came on, so she grabbed her guitar next to the wall and started to play the chords that went with it. She jammed with the song for a few minutes.

Mary walked back into the living room and said, "Give me a hug lady." They hugged for a minute and Mary asked, "Did you decide where you would like to go, or do you want to chill here?"

"Let's ride our bikes down to the further park and relax and talk by that little waterfall. It should be nice."

"Sounds fabulous. Great idea."

Emerald finished eating, washed out her dishes, and used the bathroom one more time. They grabbed their bikes and headed out the door. They started peddling towards the park. It was mostly sunny, but there were a few white clouds to block the sun here and there. There was a light breeze to keep it cool too. It was a bit of a ways to the park, but they thought it was worth it. It was late morning, so the traffic already died down some and wasn't too busy. It was a nice day. They could hear some birds chirping along the way. They yelled at each other on the way like two kids getting excited to go somewhere because they have been wanting to go there for a long time. It was like they both had this buildup of excitement in them that was ready to bust. They even tried to race for a bit, but they were just playing and having fun. They got to the park and raced down the dirt pathway over the bridge. There were a lot more trees in this area. It was very green and lush.

"We are so lucky that we live in an area with nice rolling hills and lots of trees and water," Emerald said.

"Yes, we are," Mary replied.

They got to the little waterfall, got off their bikes, and found a place to sit down and rest.

"It's so nice to come here while most people are working," Mary said. "There's not too many people here. Nothing beats a quiet park with the wind blowing and the water trickling."

"It's fanfuckingtastic. I love it. You know I talked with Eric yesterday. He said, "hey," by the way. I think him and Christina might want to get with us here soon and do the couples thing."

"Sounds good. I like them. I know we don't agree on everything, but I can handle or tolerate them. They seem respectful enough. As long as you two don't start talking about politics and religion. What a disaster. However, it's nice to hear you put him in his place or make him seem like an idiot when he tries to repeat right-wing fascist propaganda that he heard somewhere."

"Yes, he started in on the capitalism versus the socialism and communism debate, and yes, I don't think he understood anything he was saying. He actually thinks capitalism is the opposite of those two governments and that people can't make any money. However, he was open to researching those concepts before we get back into that discussion again."

"Good. It's so frustrating and annoying when people say things that they know nothing or hardly anything about because they heard their lying and brainwashing pastor or politician say something about it. It's like someone put an idea in their head that seemed to make some sense to them, but they never questioned it or thought that it might be wrong. I guess they could have also watched a paid-for advertisement, which is what they call the news, and then they think that what they are hearing is factual information. It's also unfortunate how these biased and lying sources play on people's emotions to manipulate them and get them to believe what they are saying is true. So sad. You should always do your research, especially when you hear information from a politician or a religious or rich person. All the while, they are just trying to get rich off people's stupidity and ignorance."

"That's what I wanted to talk to you about. Eric and I talked about a bunch of shit yesterday. Mainly competition, but a few other topics came up. So, I was thinking on my run this morning about competition and all the topics and how so many of those issues revolve around the goal of controlling people in some way or another. Because, you know, I think a lot of people are a bunch of fucking idiots or absolute morons. Yet, some of these people are in very important roles in our society where they make important decisions for all of us. Like the politicians in government or the managers in the various businesses."

"You said it Em. I have no idea how they have gotten as far as they have, but then I think about what a lot of governments and businesses produce and get. Then, it all makes sense. An intelligent and awakened being wouldn't work for a government that says they care about people while the government and politicians kill innocent people in other countries and really only care about their companies and their money. Or, a smart and good person wouldn't be able to work for a company for very long that pollutes the earth and sells products that make people sick just to make money. Good people don't want to get involved with these entities and destructive organizations, so the evil, vile, and disgusting people walk through the door to be our leaders. They are okay with murdering, raping, stealing, lying, polluting, extorting, and bribing."

Emerald interrupted, "The money issue kept coming back into my head. People are so blinded that they would rather make money over being ethical and moral. At some point, they were willing to sacrifice their values and what is right, so they can get paid. Even though values and morals should be timeless and untouchable, in walks money as it chips away at their ability to reason properly about what is right and wrong."

"Like there is a price that you could pay someone for them to do something that they normally wouldn't do, such as murder, pollution, sex, or slaughtering of certain animals for food."

"That's very sad Mary. Don't make me cry. It makes me weep that there are these major game players, like the rich, who know what the weaknesses are for a lot of people, so they play on their excitement and their lust for money that they created in them to begin with. Since the day they were born. You even see that in the poor and struggling middle class people. You give them a certain amount of money, and they will do it. You get desperate enough, and you will do anything for money. So, that led me to think about the conditional bond that society, government, and businesses have on people and their idea of freedom. Are we free? What is freedom? People say they are free all the time, and our country and others claim to be free and that the people are free. It makes me think. Is that a manipulation tool to try and brainwash and convince people that they are free? Is it a type of control to get them to feel like they are okay, so they will keep doing the things that they think are helping them to be free? When in fact, they are not free and are under total control by the idea that they are free. I know it sounds crazy. Like some sort of conspiracy."

"It's not a conspiracy," Mary said seriously. "That is exactly what happens and what is happening."

Emerald continued, "I know that people in these countries that say they are free are freer than let's say a more authoritarian or dictatorship ruler, but instead of physically making people do what they want through force or threats, they use psychological or mind control. It's like a psychological dictatorship. People don't know they are being controlled because since the day they were born, their parents told them they have it good and they are in the free world. The rich and the politicians also push these ideas onto us by using the companies and lots of marketing and advertising campaigns to make people feel like they have all these choices. In reality, it's propaganda to control us through the use of lies, manipulation, and money. They really don't have any choices. The choices are manufactured and an illusion. They badger us with advertisements and give us money for certain things. This money makes us high like a drug, so we want more and more. We want more money and more stuff. It's programmed and intentional."

"The more you make, the more you spend," Mary said. "It's crazy. Poor kids. You would think that most of the adults would figure it out sooner than later, but nope. You got to go to college and get a job. No one asks why. Why do I have to do that? Why do I have to work for someone else and make them rich and keep them rich, so I can make a little bit of money and struggle through life while spending my money on food and stuff to make someone else rich? Why? It's insanity. There's a few that benefit from this maddening process, but most do not. Then, the rich, businesses owners, and paid-for politicians use a guilt and shame campaign to disparage people wanting out of this craziness by saying, "Well, you don't want to be lazy or a free loader. You have to provide for yourself and buy stuff to help the economy, or it's your fault the country is failing." But it's not really a country, it's a pyramid scheme."

"It is a pyramid scheme," Emerald said in agreement.

Mary continued, "It is so wrong for someone who is taking advantage of others to use guilt and shame to manipulate others to keep their money machine rolling. It's upsetting to others who don't have a choice to work either. You have stay-at-home parents, disabled veterans and other disabled people, retired people, people who choose not to work, and other cultures and societies who don't use money or a token economy. On the outside, these countries who use money seem to be more well off, but if you look closer, you will see the truth. You will see the crime, poverty, inequality, classism, discrimination, sickness, death, pollution, and the pain. Once you dig deeper into the problems and issues that are created with capitalism, it really makes you wonder whether this system is for the people and the masses or just for a few."

"You go girl," Emerald said in excitement.

"To make matters worse, you have astronomical spending on military that leads to government contracts to for-profit companies, which are owned by the politicians, their cronies, or the friends and family members of the politicians who approve the spending. You have to completely despise and disagree with nepotism, favoritism, and cronyism. It sets the stage for discrimination, corruption, and disaster. They also approve tax-payer subsidies to for-profit companies that already make billions in profits. These companies are also owned by the politicians approving these tax-payer subsidies, their cronies, or the friends and family members of the politicians. When people start to wake up, they start to ask if there is another way. Is there another way to eat, have clothes, and have shelter without being an economic slave who works most of your waking hours? Who was that fucker that decided that? For us to work most of the day, most of the week, and most of our lives is absolutely crazy. It's fucking crazy. I'm not totally sure, but I feel pretty good that is was most likely a man who came up with that. An already rich man."

"Oh, you know it," Emerald said while laughing. "I'm sure there are women today who believe in that and think that is what they are supposed to do, but they have definitely been bamboozled to see things that way. If you really want to spend your time making someone else rich and producing, for the most part, horrible products that either serve no value or very little value or do more harm than good and cause negative effects on the things and beings and the environment around them, you have to be nuts. You are definitely under their control. What's the saying? You go to work all week to pay for a home that you are hardly ever at, to pay for an automobile that you primarily use to drive to work, to pay for clothes that you primarily use for work, and to provide for a family who you hardly ever see."

"Totally Em. Hey, look at that blue heron over there standing in the creek."

"So cool. It's like it doesn't care that we are here. They are usually bashful and will fly away."

"That bird is free," Mary said. "He or she can do whatever he or she wants to do at any time."

"Yes. Freedom is being able to choose what you want to do at any time. That is true free will. You have many choices. You don't have to ask for permission."

"I think we do have freedom even in an authoritarian society like this one that claims to be a republic with a democratic process."

"What do you mean?" Emerald asked.

"Well, think about it. You can choose not to work and go wherever you want. However, you have to accept and face the consequences of that choice. I'm not saying it's fair, which is the problem. It definitely is a difficult and challenging choice, but it still a choice. It may leave you starving, homeless, and vulnerable, but if you don't want to be an economic slave, that is what is in store for you. Unfortunately, this capitalistic society made sure there were serious and severe consequences for people choosing not to work. Almost like a punishment."

"That is a good point. It would be very challenging to give up everything to actually be free. Are you free by quitting your job and surviving without that control or authority?"

"Good question Em. You would need to quit your job to be truly free. I would say that even though you have a choice to quit your job that you are not free while in that job because you are still slaving away. You are an economic slave. If you are in debt, you are even more of a slave to more people or companies. You are not free when you are a slave. Think about human slavery where people actually own other people as a property, which still exists even though some say it does not. Just because you could possibly run away from your owner or master and have a choice or opportunity to be free does not mean that you are free while you are a slave. Of course, there are more serious physical types of consequences, such as whipping, lynching, and/or death, to being a human slave versus an economic slave. However, an economic slave who chooses not to work still has a lot of consequences, which may also include physical illnesses, sicknesses, and death, due to poverty, starvation, homelessness, psychological distress, and disease. Those two examples may not be right on, but it still proves my point that just because you have a choice in your slavery doesn't mean you are free. It's an illusion of freedom still. I would say that the main slavery of today that we call slave labor or economic slavery is in fact a true form of slavery even though people could quit their jobs and face those consequences. While they are working, they are still slaves and are not free because they are being told what to do and if they had a choice, they would do things differently and be different, even in that job."

"Like what?" Emerald asked.

"Come in earlier or later, longer or shorter lunch, more breaks, get paid more, do a different type of job, not work as many days a week."

"Like me," Emerald said excitedly.

"Yes, like you. You lazy ass. I love that you have done that though. It's so awesome to spend time doing what we love and to be together. I love you."

"I love you Mary." Emerald moved her head over and gave Mary a big kiss on the lips.

Mary continued, "I'm sure a lot of people would love more days off and more paid time off, less rules, more overtime or less overtime, not being on call, or to do their job the way they want to do it instead of being micromanaged."

"On the other side of the argument, that's a choice or a contract that the employee agrees to and makes to be in that job or relationship."

"Most jobs are like that Em, but some are not. Some have more freedom, if we can use that word. However, most are a dictatorship, which I think is ironic considering that our country is supposed to be based on democratic processes. Most companies are ran like a fascist dictatorship where the employees have very little say, which is unfortunate considering how beneficial and awesome cooperatives are. Unions are also great to help diminish the dictatorship and fascist styles of certain industries and companies. For the most part, capitalism is a joke and a stab in the heart of the citizens in a so-called democratic country."

"I had an idea when we were talking about using money to manipulate people. You saying that companies are like a right-wing fascist dictatorship made me think that if someone or a company convinces you, entices you, or even manipulates you with money or pay and other benefits, and you end up taking the job where you have little choice and are under control and subjugation while you are working there, since it is your choice to accept the job and you have a choice to quit if you don't like the job, people think that is still freedom. I think that is either a very interesting point of view or a really fucked up point of view, especially since they have set up the society to force us into working to make money to buy necessities, such as food, clothing, and shelter. I'm not sure if force is the best word as it may be too harsh."

"It does sound forced Em. It does sound like these capitalistic societies have created a different and new type of human slavery, which I think we already have mentioned as slave labor or economic slavery."

"Yes, I love the play on words with slave labor instead of wage labor, especially if you look at all the inequalities involved within the company structure. The pay differences can be very significant and not fair or equal to the front-end, line, or entry-level workers, who do all the work anyway. Sometimes your direct supervisor can make double what you are making. Upper management and executives or the owners could be making 10 to 20 times and even more than the lower level or direct workers. And if you are a woman or a minority, you are really fucked. That's when you start to really feel bad about yourself and think you are a piece of shit. It's absolutely despicable. It is a true pyramid scheme, and it's a scam."

"Absolutely, and that is a model, if not one of the best, to keep the workers, I mean the slaves, under control by paying them just enough to get by where they can't save that much and can't quit because they need or have to work."

"What about the classic argument Mary? People still say, "If you don't like it then quit or find another job.""

"I think that's the point. We are in a position and a society to quit or find another job as challenging and difficult of a choice as that may be. Quitting your job and trying to survive or trying to find another job is easier said than done. And, finding another job that pays the same with similar benefits may be possible, but finding one that pays better with better benefits is the exception and not the rule. Even working less days and hours at your current job creates a lot of hardships and can challenge your ability to survive. We all know that pay stays about the same while the prices of everything continue to increase a lot faster than the increase in our pay. My conclusion is that they have set the society up to trap us into working while making it very challenging and difficult, if not almost impossible, to not work or not work that much."

Emerald thought for a few seconds, smiled, and said, "Let's not forget the debt issue too. Companies and the government spend billions in advertising and marketing every year to get people into debt. They start when we are children and continue to hound us throughout our lives. They try so hard to get us to go into debt. They are definitely doing it on purpose. All the loans and putting things on credit are scams. It's very evil and should be illegal. If you can't afford it, don't buy it. With the psychological manipulation at a young age with advertising, you feel like you have to have things. They even brainwash us in school that success is about how much money and shit you have. We even see that in the news with all the rich people who do whatever they want to do and get away with murder, drug offenses, and sex crimes. If you are not rich, you go to jail for that stuff. If you are rich, you mostly don't get convicted. If you do, you just pay a fine and go home. They make us think we have to have expensive automobiles, a big house, a boat, expensive clothes, new products, and other unnecessary material items. They make us think we have to eat out all the time, pay for entertainment, and spend lots of money on trips and games. They even push us into going to college, which is not worth the price at all. The more debt you have, the more of a slave you are. They know that, but most people are in denial about that or don't learn it until it's too late."

"Those are good points Em. People take out these loans and use credit and end up paying double and even more on the stuff they bought due to the interest. It's also very stressful to be in debt and owe money. Try not paying some of these companies that you owe money to. They will come after you and make your life miserable. They will sic their expensive and over-paid attorneys on you and even ruin your credit, which could negatively affect your job or finding another job too. They can even legally garnish your wages."

"Absolutely, It's awful. Some say that when we are born that we are already in debt of over several years of wages from a full-time job, and you were just born and probably won't start working for at least another 16 years. That's an insane amount of money for just being born. It just goes up from there as you get older and older, and it definitely goes up from there if you fall into the scam of consumerism and materialism by using loans and putting things on credit. So many people get manipulated into the desires of materialism and feel like they have to have things from societal and peer pressures, especially from advertising. So, we come back to the argument of whether we have a choice or is the choice made for us already by the rich, politicians, and businesses."

"I don't think we are free. We already have an obligation and are in debt as soon as we are born. To stay out of this trap and scam, we would have to know and understand all these issues and problems when we are children or at least in our early teenage years to avoid getting into debt and learning how to live minimally without having to work so much. That would require our parents to have an understanding of these issues too, and they don't. And, the education we get isn't going to teach us this stuff because the politicians, rich, and businesses decide the curriculum. They aren't putting that shit in there to teach us how to not make them or keep them rich. As much as our educational system should teach us about financial skills and fiscal responsibility in our adolescence, they don't. They do everything in their power to make sure we don't learn that."

"You are totally right Mary. It should be taught, but the powers that be and the citizens, who have bought into the scam and do not see it for what it is, would not like that too much."

"Not at all. They wouldn't like it. Freedom in a capitalistic society that doesn't deal with inequalities and discrimination and doesn't allow for significant amounts of free time and decent higher levels of pay is an illusion. You think you are free, but you are not. You are a slave. A slave to the system and the money and to your false desires and wants. You could be like that for a long time. Even your entire life. Most people are retiring now in their late 70s and some in their 80s and cannot even pay for their basic needs because they couldn't save enough, and they don't make enough. Most people are dead by the time they are in their 80s, but so many now have to keep working into their 80s because of the greed and corruption. For the ones that haven't died and can't work, they end up in these wretched, abusive, and horribly ran nursing home facilities where they are neglected and their family and friends hardly or don't ever go see them. That's where they stay until they die. A lot of them would probably rather just kill themselves instead of losing all their dignity in being in a place like that. People then ask themselves, "Was it worth it? Was there another way? Did I live my life? Did I get to experience life for what it should have been?""

"I would say no," Emerald replied. "You didn't get to live it to its fullest. You had to work too much for someone else, to make someone else rich, and at the expense of your own well-being. Don't worry. When you die, you will finally be free."

"You will. Death is the ultimate escape from slavery. No more government, rich, political, corporate, societal, and cultural control. Just pure energy."

"Don't forget how they use the societal and cultural control by playing with our emotions, such as fear. That is a major technique by them. It is huge. You were joking earlier about people who try to get out of the system by not working so much or at all, and they are called "lazy" or "good for nothings" or a "waste," which is funny considering that you and I think of those people as very intelligent and awakened or enlightened beings. They saw the truth, broke the illusion, and decided that they didn't want to be under control anymore. They decided that they were not going to be compliant and like a robot, who does just what they are told."

"Well Em, the first question that you hear when you are young in a capitalistic society is "What do you want to be when you grow up?" You get some amazing and fantastic answers. You get these very high-paying and prestigious jobs and positions, such as athlete, musician, actor/actress, scientist, astronaut, or doctor. You have a better chance of winning the lottery than accomplishing one of those positions. Some do and you should have dreams, but you have to be realistic too."

"Most or a very high percentage will not end up doing those things. Where do we get those ideas from? The media, parents, school, et cetera. Is that what they really want us to be or do? We gave those answers when we were young, but they didn't teach us how to be those things. School didn't really teach us how to do anything practical. Just to memorize a bunch of trivial and pointless shit."

"A lot of people will become criminals and drug addicts," Mary said sarcastically. "That's not on their list when they were young and looking forward to the future. A lot of people don't like their jobs. I would even say most people don't like their jobs and would have never guessed they would be doing what they are doing now."

"Sad but true. It's the pressure that we feel that we have to work and that there is no other option. We either have to be a slave to the system or we are called a failure or unsuccessful."

"The kicker is that it doesn't matter whether you are a good person or not. It only matters what kind of a job you have, how much money you make, and how much crap you can accumulate before you die."

"Disgusting," Emerald said slowly and judgingly.

"I would say that is emotional slavery too. They are programming people at a very young age to feel bad about not working, not making money, or not going to school. You are pressured to work and buy like a good consumer. People are even looked down upon for homeschooling their kids. That is pressure. That is control. That is not freedom."

"On top of that, they are giving kids false hope, so they end up disappointed and depressed when they finally realize that none of their dreams came true and that they are not rich and successful by society's standards. I realize that some, which is a very small amount, of people get into these high-paying and prestigious positions, but a lot of them got to where they were at because their parents were already rich and affluent and/or they knew someone. It's very political and biased. Do you want to know what the real question is though for those people who got lucky enough to get a high-paying job or become rich?"

"What?" Mary asked.

"Are they happy? So, you make a lot of money now. So, you are so-called successful. Are you happy? Are you satisfied? More importantly, are you doing something important? Are you helping others, the animals, and the earth? I would say mostly the answer is no. Even the medical career as a doctor is debatable due to what they are actually practicing. Most doctors don't cure and prevent diseases. They just cover up the problems and treat the symptoms. A lot of doctors make people sicker and into addicts. They are also salespeople for the companies who sale and make medical equipment, pharmaceuticals and drugs, and medical testing devices. A lot of those companies and products are pure evil. What a wasted career."

"I thought of a good one Em. It also doesn't seem like we are free if we have to live in fear and be afraid."

"That is a great point."

"We are not free if we live in a state of fear or worry about lots of things. You are never free if you are afraid. Anyone who uses fear or tells someone to be afraid, including the use of hate and judgment, is trying to control you through manipulation and emotional or psychological slavery. That is not freedom. Most so-called democratic societies do that. Our governments, politicians, and religions spread so much hate and fear. Mainly to divide us, but it also helps them keep their followers and supporters blind and in control or insecure, which keeps them giving money to them."

"It's so bad that they always pump all this fear mongering out to the public, but they are really just trying to make more money and make themselves rich. The best example is terrorism and the need for a huge military. They say that we are always in a state of being attacked by a terrorist, which is really just racism and a way to make themselves rich, but in reality, most of our wars and battles are internal or domestic. Not to mention that most of the mass shootings and bombings that have occurred in a country were done by citizens of that country. They were also a part of the majority race and most popular religion, which is why the whole terrorism thing is racism and hate at its core."

"Yes, the true terrorists are the ones who tell you to be afraid, hate, and judge and try to use fear to get you to do something or give your money to them."

"That's it Mary. They use the different institutions that they control to spread these messages to brainwash and program us. Like the media, school, work, debt, religion, consumerism, government, names, and labels. They use fear to control people in the church and within their religions too. They con people to give them their money by telling that they are going to go to some horrible and awful place if they don't give them their money, or they are not going to be saved if they don't give them their money."

"Don't' forget the other types of control, such as food and sugar, tobacco, drugs, alcohol, prescription pills, sickness, war, privacy violations, attachments and dependency, materialism, terrorism, guns, division, and other addictions, such as sex, shopping, video games, eating, gambling, and work. Wow, that's a lot. Did we miss anything?"

"That is a lot of ways to control people Mary. I think that's most of them. I'm sure there are things that we haven't even thought of. They are insidious fuckers who try to control us in so many different ways. It's kind of a given, but you can't leave out marketing and advertising and the use of the news and media. They spread a lot of false information on those platforms."

"They also get people worried about their crap and their possessions, so they make people afraid that someone is going to take all their shit. So, what's the answer to that or what's the solution to that?"

"Buy more shit," Emerald said smiling.

"Definitely. You have to protect yourself. You know, from the terrorists and the minorities. Even though the people, such as the politicians, religious leaders, and the rich, who are telling you to be afraid are the ones stealing from you the most. Nevertheless, they want you to buy one of the evilest things in the world."

"Guns."

"You are correct Em. You win a prize. It's so crazy that people think and feel they are safe and even more free with a weapon. They have no idea that they are actually doing exactly what the gun companies want them to do, especially with the billions that are spent on pro-gun propaganda and marketing campaigns to manipulate the public with fear and a false need for a gun or guns. Without saying it, they are saying make us more money because you are insecure, impotent, and a fool. They don't understand that they were manipulated and told to get a gun. They were brainwashed, so someone can get rich. It's also like an insurance policy that you pay a bunch of money for, but you never use. Just in case."

"Yes, the amount of money on advertising that is spent to sell a product is outrageous, and people fall for it. They have no idea that they were psychologically pressured to do something. Most people will never need or use a gun, and way more accidents and fatalities happen because of them. Too bad it makes men feel like they are more of a man even though it really means they are less of one because they can't deal with their problems in a mature, responsible, and civilized way. What's the saying? If you have to have a gun, you don't have one, and by one, I mean dick. What's the other one? With a gun in your hand, you are less than a man."

"That' funny. I got one that beats those. It's not as funny, but it's true. Guns are for cowards," Mary said with a smirk.

"It's true. Guns are for cowards, and you are not free if you think or feel like you have to have a gun to protect yourself, your family, your land, or your possessions. That is fear. Anyone who lives in fear is not free. They are scared and distressed. What do people do when they are afraid and distressed? They make irrational and impulsive decisions. They make mistakes and hurt themselves and the people around them."

"Freedom and safety are an illusion Em. It's an illusion that you own anything. At any time, someone could take your stuff, especially if it's on credit or loan. At any time, the government could take your land and things away from you and throw you in jail. They don't have to have any proof or reason. And, that's a traditionalist or fascist policy that was implemented to make us feel safe. Even with your guns, you can only do so much to protect and save yourself."

"I thought of another one. Even the borders around the countries or the nations are a control system. If you think you are free, try to easily and conveniently go to another country. You can do it, but it's not a feeling of ease and simplicity. For some, it's very challenging and difficult and can be impossible."

"Some are trapped," Mary interjected.

"All this talk about freedom and the illusion of freedom makes my head spin. I'm so glad that we can try and look at all of these issues objectively."

"You can thank our most amazing choice of not watching the media and paying attention to the brainwashing and programming advertising and marketing strategies of the rich, the companies, the politicians, and the government."

"I know. It's ridiculous. It's everywhere. The sad thing is that the powers that be know it works. People are so vulnerable and gullible. People just blindly believe what they are told. Some countries have strict laws on what people and companies can advertise because they know it's so influential and that the people and companies will use the advertising to spread lies and misinformation."

"That is the evilest way to control and get people to do things. It's one thing to force people with threats and weapons but using psychological manipulation with information and advertising is very wicked and vile. They mainly want us to spend money, but they definitely want us to do other things too. Most people don't ask whether the information or advertisement is true or not. People and companies lie all the time through media and advertising. So many people take it as fact and don't question it and research it, especially if it is a celebrity, someone who is considered successful, or a company that is considered successful. I can see people saying to themselves that there is no way that this person would say something that is not true. So many products that they advertise are so destructive and make people sick. The list is so long. There is alcohol, tobacco, herbicides, pesticides, plastics, GMOs, prescription drugs, over-the-counter medicines, sugar, vaccines, meat, eggs, and dairy. Of course, that is only a few of them. The companies spend billions to persuade people to keep consuming these harmful products."

"Don't forget that they use advertising as a distraction too."

"Absolutely," Mary said sharply.

"They keep everyone focused on trivial matters that entertain them, so the government and corporations can literally rob you."

"Yes, people are really distracted, especially by having to work so much, from what is really going on, such as war and mass civilian deaths due to war, government and corporate corruption, human trafficking, sexual assault and rape, racism and sexism, global warming, pollution, and other acts of discrimination. It's atrocious. They hear this stuff on the news and then a minute later they say, "Hey, my favorite show is on tonight." They don't care. They don't care that the politicians continue to give themselves raises, accept bribes from companies and foreign governments, and lower taxes for the rich and the companies but not the middle class and the poor. They don't care that another right-wing fascist traditionalist, who is of the majority race, shot up another school or church and killed a bunch of people. The don't care that companies, the rich, and our politicians are destroying and killing everyone and everything in their paths. If they did care, they would revolt and do something about it, or they wouldn't continue to elect the same corrupt politicians."

"We even try to call the citizens out on that intentional distraction of these very important issues. And, they call us crazy and that we are the crazy ones. They say that we are being extreme and radical. We are not crazy and are not radical, but most people listening to us having this conversation would call us crazy because they are so brainwashed, blind, programmed, and in denial. Their cognitive dissonance is off the charts. They don't even know what is real and true because they just believe what they are told and don't question it. Then, you have the ones that do know the truth, but they don't care. Their apathy is their demise. Isn't apathy crazy?"

"It is Em. It's a disease. It's a plague. It's worse than the plague. At least, the plague would kill you. We have to suffer through all this torture."

"It's crazy to be ignorant, and it's crazy to expect liars, thieves, and killers to change or do something different after numerous years of them engaging in these behaviors. That's insanity."

"They say that we have freedom of speech, but when you can't be honest or speak your mind because people get so offended, defensive, confrontational, and even aggressive because they don't agree with you, that is not freedom of speech. That is censorship and subjugation. A lot of people won't listen to reason on a differing point of view. They have been so brainwashed and are so blind that they can't see past the illusion. They are slaves and don't even know it. They keep repeating the rhetoric that they are free and that they believe in freedom, but they can't see that they are not free and that they are under control. They also only believe that freedom is only applicable to their beliefs and their behaviors, and if someone disagrees with them, they are the enemy, terrorist, or anti-patriot."

Emerald interrupted, "There are so many hypocrites out there who say they believe in freedom and freedom of speech, but to them, it's only okay as long as they agree with it. That's not freedom. And, what about freedom of religion? It's not freedom of religion if it only conforms or agrees with your religious beliefs. If you want to live in a free world, you have to respect diversity and differences. You can't have freedom and a free world in a controlled system where you are made to believe and do what a few want you to believe and do. What's next? Are they going to start controlling our thoughts here soon? Oh wait, they already do that. My bad."

"I hope they don't, but it seems like they already do. At this point, it's best to be skeptical, be open, be a minimalist, have no debt, and be independent while avoiding attachments."

"You are truly free when you have nothing and nothing to lose, you are flexible and accept change, and you are okay with not having attachments."

"True freedom is being able to say something, do something, or think something without someone stopping you. Even though we do have some choices and some freedom to some extent, there is a lot of room to argue that we are manipulated or enslaved into doing things, such as work and consumerism, because the alternatives are unbearable or lead to extreme suffering."

"On that note Mary, regarding freedom of speech specifically, you cannot have consequences to certain things that people may say, as horrible as they may be. If there are consequences, there is no freedom of speech. The only exception would be threats or harassment or other statements that involve fear and hate, which can cause emotional distress in people. As much as I want everyone to be able to speak their minds, unfortunately, there are some people who take that to mean they can be verbally abusive and threatening to defend their freedom of speech. Therefore, you have to have that exception even though it does limit the freedom of speech. You can say and do whatever you want to do, but you can't hurt others with your words and behaviors. You also can't hurt animals and the earth with your behaviors. That is not freedom. That is abuse. There is a big difference."

"That's a good point. You also have people who think they are free or think they are choosing, but they are actually doing exactly what the controllers want them to do. They are brainwashed and programmed by the media and the advertising. It's so dangerous that they don't realize they are under control."

"Especially when it comes to producing soldiers," Emerald added. "Don't forget fear, hate, supporting the killing of innocent civilians in other countries through war or unnecessary military strikes, pollution, sickness, guns, and addictions."

"There's a lot there for a society and its people to be aware of and deal with. It's crazy how we would be called crazy for talking like this even though we are the awakened ones who see through the lies and the deceit."

"Which supports our argument."

Emerald and Mary both took a deep breath and exhaled like all the negativity and problems were leaving their bodies. They calmly watched the glistening and pleasantly sounding waterfall. Some birds were chirping nearby, and some squirrels were rustling in the brush under the trees.

"Well, it's time for me to go and be a slave," Mary said.

"Got to love that. You do get a discount on some delicious organic foods though."

"Definitely. It is worth it. Let's roll."

They got on their bikes and headed back home.

"What a great day," Emerald shouted with excitement.

"It's going to get cold soon."

"Not if the polluters keep it up."

Emerald and Mary laughed as they tried to race each other back home. One would get in front, and then the other would.

"Hey, I think I thought of another song with those issues that we were just talking about," Emerald said excitedly.

"Awesome Em."

They got back home. Mary got ready for work. Emerald grabbed her better acoustic guitar out of the bedroom and sat down on the couch in the living room. She fooled around with some chords. She wanted the song to be mellow and like a folk song. She thought about the issues of freedom, control, choices, slavery, brainwashing, and programming. She started playing a C chord for 2 beats, then a G chord for 2 beats, and then an A minor chord for 4 beats. She played those chords over while trying to hum over them like she was singing a melody. After a few minutes, Mary was ready to go to work. She walked over to Emerald. Emerald got up and placed the guitar on the sofa. They gave each other a big hug.

"Can't wait to see you later," Mary said.

"I might be in bed and asleep by the time you get home. I'm exhausted."

"No worries. I'll see you in the morning. Good luck on your song. I can't wait to hear it. Enjoy the rest of the day. I love you my beautiful."

"I love you my gorgeous. Enjoy the work."

They gave each other a passionate long kiss.

"I'll miss you so much," Emerald said.

While Mary was walking out, Emerald said, "Will you bring home some more bananas, apples, and a couple of avocados please? Here, let me write it down. Bananas, apples, avocados, spring water, and reverse osmosis water. Here are the jugs for the reverse osmosis water."

"Will do sweetie. I love you."

"I love you Mary." Emerald made a kissing sound.

Mary left, and Emerald picked up the guitar and sat back down on the sofa. She started to play the chords again. She started to hum again like she was singing over the chords. Usually, that was how she was able to come up with the melody and the lyrics. She was waiting for some inspiration for the main theme of the song and some lyrics. She started with the chorus.

"What's wrong with me being free? Why do you gotta put these chains around me? I work all goddamn day. Sometimes I think I'm the slave."

She got a piece of paper and a pen to write down the chords and the lyrics while she played. She kept thinking about the oppressed and how pissed off she was that the politicians allow the rich and the companies to control them with money while their own people are getting sick, dying, living in poverty, being abused and neglected, and suffering so much.

What's Wrong With Me Being Free

C chord (2 beats), G chord (2 beats), A minor (4 beats); C chord (2 beats), G chord (2 beats), A minor (4 beats)
Repeat chord progression throughout entire song.

Verse 1:
I started out so innocent; Not knowing what I'd be
Thinking anything was possible; So many hopes and dreams
All my life I believed; That I would succeed
But now I'm the fool; All your lies and manipulations were your tools

Chorus:
What's wrong with me being free; Why do you gotta put these chains around me
I work all goddamn day; Sometimes I think I'm a slave

Why can't I just be free; That sounds okay with me
I got to work so much to just get by; I can't even live my life
I'm so tired when I get home; It's all I can do to rest my bones
Since you made me into this slave; I'm gonna have to work until I see my
grave

Verse 2:
When I was young; The world took me in
There was so much to learn; Didn't know what to believe
I can't believe how things turned out; I can't understand how
It was like a trap; All your money and things, it's all crap

Repeat Chorus.

Verse 3:
This stupid game that you made me play; This isn't a life worth living every day
It's like you wanted it to be this way; Are you happy that you made me into a slave?
I just want to see the world and be with the people I love; Do what I want, enjoy life, create, and have fun
I have to work to make you rich; And all I have is a bunch of shit

Repeat Chorus.

Episode 3
The Religious Dilemma

Religion is a man-made idea based on opinions, mistranslations, and misinterpretations.
The selling of salvation for a price is a scam.
Peace, love, and happiness can only be found within yourself.
Spirituality and philosophy are far more superior than any religion will ever be.

Emerald woke up the next day a little early. She was a bit restless from all the talk about control and whether people were all just made to play an awful game of existence to make someone else rich. She was feeling hopeless and upset, especially from the devastation that consumerism and capitalism has caused. She thought consumerism and capitalism have significantly and directly hurt and destroyed humanity, the animals, and the earth. She needed to clear her head, so she went ahead and got up and got around. She used the bathroom and did some light hygiene. She went into the kitchen and made some breakfast, so she could get her energy level up.

Emerald journaled her dreams while she ate and decided that she would meditate and get in a good stretch and workout after she was done eating and journaling. She made and drank her whole foods shake with diatomaceous earth and greens. She also drank some veggie juice, which she absolutely loved in the morning. The veggie juice with the tomatoes was so refreshing and rejuvenating to her. She made a fruit juice and grabbed an apple, banana, some nut butter, and her home-made chocolates. She took them to the living room and placed them on the table in front of the sofa. She went back to the kitchen and made a glass of spring water. She took that to the living room and placed it on the table too. She sat down on the sofa. She took a bite of her apple, grabbed her dream journal, and started to write about her dreams.

She couldn't remember a lot of details in her dreams, but she remembered being at a party at one of her houses that she lived in when she was younger. She remembered living in that house when she was about 15, which was almost 30 years ago. She thought it was night due to the lights being somewhat bright in the house, the dimness coming from the windows, and the feeling of lateness. She felt like she was older in the dream than when she actually lived there in real life. She felt like she was maybe in her 20s. She walked from the living room into the kitchen to make an alcoholic beverage. When she opened the refrigerator, she dropped some plastic bowls on the floor. They were all stacked together in a sleeve. She pushed them aside next to some plastic cups that were all stacked together in a plastic sleeve, which were on the floor too. She heard some celebrating going on outside. She had a feeling like it was New Year's Eve. She remembered feeling drunk and dizzy. She made a cocktail with some liquor and soda and took a couple of sips. She heard some unison counting outside by some people like a countdown to midnight, but it was still an hour away according to the clock on the kitchen counter. She looked over at the toaster and remembered feeling like she wanted to smoke some marijuana, which then appeared on the counter. She woke up after that.

Emerald didn't know what to think of that dream. It had been over several years since she drank alcohol or did any drugs. She felt like it was a flashback of her self-destructive days. She felt very unsure and anxious while engaging in those behaviors in the dream even though she couldn't help herself or stop herself from doing those things in the dream. She felt a lot of relief when she woke up due to realizing it was all a dream and that she didn't actually relapse. She was so glad it was just a dream. She hoped that those types of dreams would stop with the drinking and drugging, but they happened a lot more than she would like. They were a reminder to her that she shouldn't forget the past and must face the consequences of every choice that she makes for as long as it lasts. The dreams and the memories of her past shameful behaviors were a motivation for her to keep doing good and taking care of herself. She was trying to choose to feel better instead of worse.

She couldn't remember any other dreams even though she probably had a couple more. She wasn't for sure if she would remember them later. Sometimes she was able to remember them later in the day if something triggered them or happened that was similar to them. She thought it was strange how she would forget or not remember some dreams and then they would come to her later. Sometimes, she felt like there was something meaningful about the dreams that she could remember and recall.

Before she meditated, she washed out her dishes and used the bathroom. She went back into the living room and stood facing the window and closed her eyes. She stretched out her back by reaching her hands up and bending her back backwards as far as she could go without falling. She brought herself back up, so she was straight again. She took several deep breaths. Then, she mouthed some good positive thoughts and affirmations.

She said out loud, "I love myself. I'm in control. I promise to take care of myself and will try my best to love others, the animals, and the earth. No excuses. I am grateful and thankful for everything. We are all one, and I am everything. I love everything. Know thyself. I am healthy and successful. Positive, focus on the good, calm, relax, have fun, be wild and crazy, peace, compassion, ahimsa, love, caring, helping, understanding, happiness, smile, I can do anything, confidence, I am the one, everything is an opportunity, take advantage, take risks, learn, great things will come, have hope, do whatever it takes, take responsibility, be in the now, and be courageous."

She grabbed a mat and sat down. She sat with a very arched back with her legs crossed in a comfortable position. Then, she put her arms down with the back of her hands on top of her knees with her ring fingers touching her thumbs. She took several slow and long deep breaths. She tried her best to take in and enjoy the stillness and quietness of the morning. Since it was so early, the traffic wasn't noisy yet, so she was able to really focus on her breathing and her body. She let out several slow and long Om sounds. She then focused on various parts of her body starting with the top of her head all the way to the base of her spine. While she focused on the various spots within herself, she was also still focusing on her breath. After she focused on the various spots in her body by going back from the bottom or base of her spine to the top of her head, she just focused on her breath and her heartbeat. They worked in unison to give her clarity and focus. It was very peaceful. She liked to focus on her heart. It made her feel like she was learning something from it. Her heart talked to her and gave her guidance from its knowledge, wisdom, and energy.

She was very calm and relaxed and tried not to control her thoughts but tried to just be and accept everything as it was. She tried not to judge anything and just accept things the way that they were. Some thoughts came and stayed for a short period of time while others came and went very quickly. She knew and felt that she was going to be okay. She knew that she could respond to anything that was thrown at her in a responsible and healthy way. She felt the connection to herself and everyone and everything around her. She knew this connection was love, and it would overcome and be the final say so in whatever problems that she faced. She continued to meditate and be in awe of the opportunity to take the time to be aware, process things, find her peace, and recharge herself with purpose and strength.

When she came out of the meditation, it had been almost an hour even though it only felt like 20 minutes to her. She got up and stretched her back out by putting her hands on her lower back and bending backwards as far as she could. She thought how amazing it was that she could meditate for what seemed to be a short period of time, but almost an hour went by. It seemed like there was some sort of distortion in the space-time continuum or she was transported to another plane of existence or dimension. The time in the so-called real world or conscious reality went by faster than where she was at when she was meditating. The place where she was at when she was meditating went by slower. It was definitely a strange phenomenon to Emerald. She had heard other people experience this same distortion in time, so she wondered if people went to a similar place or if there were many other planes of existence.

She stretched out her back one more time and then stretched out her arms and legs. She got ready to do a muscle and upper body workout. She did some push-ups, pull-ups, crunches, and some planks. She did three sets of each of those while resting a couple to a few minutes in between each one. She felt really good mentally and physically while doing her stretches and exercises. She was very proud of herself for the gains that she has made with being able to do more push-ups and pull-ups and run harder, faster, and longer. She didn't even get sore anymore. When she first started getting back into exercising several years ago, she could barely do 20 push-ups and two pull-ups. Now, she was able to do over 100 push-ups and 10 pull-ups. To Emerald, it felt like yesterday when she first started exercising again, so she remembered how hard it was for her to get mentally motivated to do any physical exercise. Now, it was a part of her life. It was like eating, doing her hygiene, and sleeping. She didn't feel right if she didn't exercise. She just had to do it.

Emerald loved how she felt and looked. She thought that she looked amazing. Unlike before, she finally felt so good about herself. She used to be overweight, tired, exhausted, sick a lot, depressed, and self-conscious. Even though she didn't sleep all the way through the night and woke up a lot over the last couple of hours of sleep, she still slept a lot better than she used to sleep. She didn't feel like she needed that much sleep to have enough energy to get her through the day. She was rarely tired during the day. Even when she only got about six hours of sleep, she still had enough energy to stay focused and do what she needed to do without getting fatigued or tired. She also fell asleep about the same time every night and got up about the same time every morning without an alarm. She did get up a lot earlier than she used to get up. She didn't even get tired while reading a book or meditating.

"Yup. I've come a long way," Emerald said out loud. "And I do look amazing."

She finished up her work out and did another stretch routine. She got sweaty doing her workout, so she decided to go outside and cool off. She also wanted to see if she could watch the sunrise at the closer park before Mary got up. She wanted to take a shower, so she could tuck Mary out of bed. She jogged down to the park and found the bench, which had a pond in front of it. This bench was the same bench that she sat on with Eric while meeting with him the other day. It was a nice morning. It wasn't too hot or too cold, but it was cool enough to cool her down after her intense workout. The jog down to the park didn't even warm her up that much. She thought that the sunrise would be nice even though there weren't that many clouds. There was a slight breeze, and the birds were already chirping away.

She sat down and thought more about the conversations that she had with Eric and Mary over the past couple of days. She wondered if other people thought about these issues or if most people were just so enslaved with their lives, family, and work that they just went on with their lives without having deep reflections about societal and internal issues. She wondered if most people just accepted that their lives were just about working, family, eating, sleeping, chores, shopping, and entertainment. She imagined them thinking that they actually believed that was who they were and that was what they were supposed to do without realizing that there was more to life than those things. She admitted that a lot of people do go to church and may have hobbies, but Emerald didn't consider church directly related to spirituality and could actually be counterproductive depending on the church, the religion, what the preacher preaches, and what the person is getting out of it. In addition, the hobbies that people had could be a result of consumerism and capitalism to con people out of their money. A good hobby is something that sparks imagination and creativity and leads to spiritual growth for a person. They are supposed to make you happy and a better person.

All these thoughts made Emerald think if people were truly happy or if they get their happiness from external things, such as food, drugs, alcohol, other addictions, or entertainment. She thought it was interesting too that most of these things that people say make them happy are not just external things but things that cost money. She thought that it was definitely a scam. You shouldn't have to pay for happiness, but those things aren't really making you happy anyway. It's an illusion. It's a temporary or immediate feeling. The fake happiness doesn't last long, and you have to keep purchasing these things to keep that fake feeling of happiness going. It was important for Emerald to understand and practice that she could be happy with just herself and without attachments or external material items, drugs, or other entertainment that you had to pay for. The happiness had to come from within herself. She needed to focus on accepting that she could be okay no matter what the circumstances were.

The sun started to rise and peak above the horizon. A couple of clouds that were higher up from the horizon started changing colors to the colors that Emerald really liked. She watched as they started turning purple. She wasn't great at identifying colors as there were so many. She thought the color was similar to a violet or magenta or maybe even a maroon color. She watched in awe as the colors made her heart and soul stand still in the magnificence of nature's creation. There is not a human-made product that could even come close to what the earth and nature do every second of the day. Emerald thought that the sunrises and sunsets were absolutely brilliant. The color then started to turn more reddish. Emerald thought it was like a crimson or ruby. The purples were still her favorite even though the reds were striking too. It was very spectacular. She refocused on the sun instead of continuing to watch the clouds. She loved to watch the sun rise over the horizon when it finally reached that peak of a rich amber color. It was so amazing to her.

Emerald took in the beauty of the sun with all its power and energy. She also loved how much larger the sun was on the horizon. It was like a supersun, which was similar to a full moon rising or setting where people call them supermoons because they seem larger to our eyes or brain, but it's just an illusion. She remembered that she missed the last full moonrise due to it being totally cloudy. She loved to watch the moonrise too. She could hear the traffic getting heavier and louder as people were starting to drive to work, but there were some joggers, bikers, and walkers out enjoying the morning and the sunrise with her.

Emerald told one walker nearby, "It's beautiful, isn't it?"

"Absolutely," the lady replied.

Emerald watched for a few more minutes and decided to run back home as she had to work today. She didn't want to get too distracted. Sometimes on her days off, she would get into her groove where she was spontaneous and went with the flow due to not having a strict schedule, but she would lose track of time and could easily miss an appointment or be late for work. She ran back home and jumped into the shower. She was very happy that she took the time to go watch the sunrise. She did not plan on that, and it was worth it due to the colors of the clouds and the sun. She thought it was so cool that there were so many sunrises that were not the same. They were all special and unique in their own ways. It was like a symbol or meaning for diversity and change. Beauty comes in many different ways. Nature is a testament to that.

She got out of the shower and did some hygiene. She was excited to tuck Mary out. It had been a while since Emerald was able to crawl into bed before she got up. Mary usually got up and needed to eat and get her caffeine addiction going. Even if that was the case, they still made time for a prolonged hug and warm embrace. Emerald was so thankful and so happy that Mary stuck it out with her through her drug addiction and all the lying. She couldn't have asked for a better friend, lover, and companion to be with her through the craziness called life. Her hair was a little wet, but it wasn't too bad. She grabbed a towel anyway, so it wouldn't get the pillow too damp. She quietly opened the door and laid down in the bed. Mary woke up and turned over on her left side facing away from Emerald, so Emerald could spoon her. Emerald snuggled up to her and cupped Mary's left breast with her right hand.

"Nice," Emerald said. "Good morning my beautiful. I love you."

"I love you," Mary said tiredly in a low voice.

They laid there for about 30 minutes as Mary tried to wake up and probably fell back asleep a couple of times. While they were laying there, Emerald thought about how awesome it was to hold someone she cared about and loved so much. It meant a lot to Emerald to be in such a caring, safe, and trusting relationship where both people support and lift each other up instead of like other relationships that are dramatic, emotional, or even abusive. Emerald felt content in the moment and tried to enjoy it as she knew Mary would probably wake up soon.

While she laid there, Emerald listened to Mary's breathing. It felt invigorating to her. When they would both breathe or inhale and exhale at the same time and in unison, it was like they were one or connected. Emerald was actually starting to get aroused as she moved her hand down to Mary's thigh, which was smooth and soft. She could smell Mary's hair, which smelt like coconut. Emerald thought she might make a move to see if Mary would like to engage in some morning loving, but she knew Mary usually didn't like to have sex in the morning due to wanting to get something in her belly and take a shower. Mary liked to be right out of the shower and clean before she made love to Emerald. Emerald could sense that Mary was awake now, so she made her move anyway. Emerald started touching and rubbing Mary.

Mary turned over and laid on her back and said, "Oh, but I'm lying on my back to start. You will have to start off and do most of the work."

"No problem at all my love," Emerald said seductively.

After they finished making love, Emerald said again, "Good morning. I love you my dear."

"I love you my sexy. You beautify creamy white angel. That was a nice little treat before we go to work."

"My pleasure. I was thinking about how much I love you and appreciate you, and then when I laid down with you, I could just feel this connection to you and it just turned me on. Sorry if it made you a little uncomfortable. I know how you don't like to do it in the morning and like to take a shower first."

"Don't apologize at all Em. That was amazing and so worth it. It was out of my character though, but I thoroughly enjoyed it. I wouldn't take it back even if I could. Thank you."

They kissed passionately for a minute and held each other for a couple of more minutes. They both got up and used the bathroom and made something to drink and eat. They talked about their sleep and dreams. Since Mary barely remembered her dreams, which mostly focused on her work and stocking food on the shelves, Emerald told her about one of her dreams that she forgot about earlier but remembered while tucking Mary out. Emerald mentioned to Mary that she remembered having a dream about being at the beach again and seeing dolphins swimming and flying over the water.

"I would love for us to move closer to the beach one of these days," Emerald said.

"Yes, that would be awesome. This six-hour drive to the ocean is brutal."

"That's why it's been three years since we've gone. Let's talk about that some more some other time to see if we can make that happen one of these days."

"I'm game. I'm sure I can find a natural food store to work at, and I'm sure you can find something to do around the beach."

"I hope so. I love working at a bookstore, and there are a lot of people who love to read actual physical books, but you never know when those are going to be extinct here soon. Lots of people don't read physical books anymore, which is not good for their eyes and brains. You haven't lived until you have read a well-written fiction or non-fiction book that you can actually turn the pages. You know. One that sucks you in where you are experiencing the book the way the author experienced it. Those are the best. I wish I had time to read an entire book a day. It does something to me. It takes me to another place and time, and nothing else matters while I'm reading it. I can block everything out and be totally focused on the story. It's like a really good or interesting conversation. Where you feel like you are there and are experiencing the sights, the sounds, and if the author is good enough, even the smells and tastes. It's like you are getting all of this knowledge and energy from someone else's head and their ideas because it only takes you like a fraction of time to read it versus how much time it took the author to think about it and write it."

"I know just what you mean. However, I do like to watch a good documentary or live performance of a band that I didn't get to actually see."

"Shit Mary. Don't even compare. They are on different wavelengths."

"Not comparing. Just saying."

"A book on whatever documentary topic would easily be better, more educational, and more descriptive. The video of the live band would be a different type of comparison, so I can't disagree with you on that one. For everything else though, when have you ever heard that a movie was better than the book?"

"Good point. Just feeling lazy at times for not wanting to read a book, but you have to admit we have to have documentaries because so many people don't read. We need videos and other media to disseminate information to help people stay abreast of the issues in our world."

"Sad but true," Emerald said depressingly. "Oh fuck. I gotta get ready for work."

"Go for it."

"Thanks for getting all that crap last night at the store. I know that was a lot."

"No worries. I needed to get a bunch of other shit anyway. I got some more juices and some other fruits and veggies."

Emerald went to the bathroom to do some more hygiene, her hair, and her makeup. After some time, she got dressed. Then, she made and ate a quick meal and flossed and brushed her teeth.

"Well, I'm outta here," Emerald said. "I love you sweetie. Have fun at work and enjoy the rest of the afternoon."

"You too. I will. I love you. Thanks for the morning nookie. That was a special surprise."

Before Emerald left, they hugged and kissed each other. Emerald grabbed her bike, said goodbye, and walked out the door to head to work. She rode her bike to the bookstore where she worked. It was further in the city, but it wasn't too far from their home. The traffic wasn't too bad, but some were already taking off early from work to get lunch. Emerald was so happy to get bikes with Mary a few years ago and stop using their car so much. They have saved a lot of money and have been able to stay fit and in shape by biking to places. More importantly, they weren't contributing as much to the pollution of the earth and to global warming. They also didn't have to worry about the traffic as much and finding a parking spot.

She loved the freedom of running and using her bike instead of a car. It made her feel special every time she chose to not use their car. She was also proud of them when they got rid of Emerald's car, so they went down to only having one car.

They tried so hard to take care of the planet, which has taken care of them and humanity so much. It's unfortunate that so many people, especially traditionalists and business owners and managers, don't care about the environment and the earth. They just pollute and pollute some more, or they use products that are not biodegradable, such as plastics, that take forever to breakdown. There are a lot of people who don't recycle either. Emerald was enraged that people have allowed the government, their politicians, and the companies to engage in intentional and disastrous pollution practices. Instead of doing things the right and healthy way, especially to help protect our environment, the animals, humanity, children, and future generations, it has been about making money and a profit at the expense of all these things.

Emerald felt sorry for the children who were going to have to see and deal with the negative and deleterious effects of the greed and corruption from people wanting to get rich and the citizens who let them get rich at the expense of directly causing global warming, environmental devastations, animal and human sicknesses and deaths, inequality, and polluted air, water, and land. To Emerald, the future did not look good. She started thinking and getting upset about all the people who say they care about other people, especially children, but they are hypocrites who pollute and don't care about the environment and vote for politicians who let the companies significantly destroy and pollute the earth. You can't say that you care about babies and the children and still be a part of polluting and destroying the environment by using plastics, coal, oil, natural gas, genetically mutant organisms, and many other destructive products.

Emerald couldn't believe that we were still killing so many trees and wiping out our forests and rain forests without properly reforesting these places. It was very destructive and a complete abomination. It doesn't take a genius to find better and healthier solutions to these practices, but the powers that be won't do anything about it, especially since the people who could do something about it are the ones making money off the devastation. The kicker is that the better and healthier solution is probably cheaper and more efficient. However, the companies and the rich wouldn't make money or as much money off the alternatives, so they are going to keep raping the land and killing until the people rise up and make them stop.

Emerald got to the bookstore and walked in with her bike. She thought it was funny that she was talking about fear yesterday and not feeling free, but she made sure her bike was protected because she was afraid someone might steal it if she just left it locked or unlocked outside. She told herself that it probably wouldn't get stolen, but she did need it at times to get around. She would rather be safe than sorry for prevention reasons. If someone was going to steal it, they were going to steal it. She was just making it more difficult for them to steal. She made herself feel better about the fear by telling herself that if someone wanted to seal it, she would accept that and just move on with her life.

She walked inside the store with her bike and started feeling excited. There was a book signing tonight for a co-authored book, which she already read, on contemporary religions. She loved and really enjoyed reading it. She remembered taking an elective class on religion during her senior year of brainwashing and programming high school. This class focused on discussing several major religions in the world. As much as Emerald disagreed with organized religion and its attempt to manipulate and lie to people and extort them for their money, she thought the class was an awesome overview of the religions and their foundations. It really helped her explore the various religions, their similarities, and their differences. The class also helped her to understand the cultural, societal, and familial influences of people being raised on a certain religion and choosing a religion, which most of the time leads them to believe in that religion for the rest of their lives.

Most people don't understand that they do have a choice of choosing a religion and that familial and peer pressures and geographical location have a lot of say so in what religion you claim to be. For the most part, people don't choose their religion. They usually are told what religion to be or made to be a certain religion based on familial and/or geographical location pressures. It's unfortunate that most religious people are so closed-minded that they only believe in what they believe in because of how they were raised or where they grew up. You are basically your religion because you don't know about the other religions, especially the ones that created your religion. It's a very ignorant and careless way to go about your spirituality and belief system. If you are going to choose a religion, you should read all the other different religious texts before deciding on one. That is an intelligent and responsible way to live your life. Or, you could just be a good person and not worry about needing to base your belief system on someone else's distorted beliefs and theories.

"Hey Adam," Emerald said. "Good afternoon."

"What's up Em?" Adam replied. "So glad to see you so early. We are going to be busy tonight. It's going to be great to get some traffic and hopefully some good business."

"I know. I'm looking forward to meeting the authors. I also want to get a book signed and talk to them. I'm very excited."

"Totally."

"Is Don here yet?"

"He came in earlier. He ran out to get a bite to eat. He should be back soon."

"Cool."

"The authors aren't going to be here until five anyway."

"Sounds good."

"You can go ahead and start setting up. I'm sure some early bird customers will start coming in way before the authors get here. The boxes with their books in them are in the back. If you could start setting those up, that would be great."

"Will do!"

Emerald started walking towards the back with her bike leaving Adam to watch over the front of the store and the register. She passed by some bookshelves and then saw her co-worker, Beth, helping a customer.

"Hey Beth. What's happening?" Emerald asked.

"Not a lot Em. Good to see you. Should be fun tonight."

"Definitely. Can't Wait."

Emerald went to the back and set her bike against the very back wall. She checked out the boxes with the featured book in them by Brad Evans and Katy Lee simply called "World Religions: A Comprehensive Overview." She grabbed a copy for her to get signed later and then used the bathroom. After she used the bathroom, she found the dolly and used it to pull the boxes out to the open area in the store, which had some seats and a couple of tables. Luckily, there was no one sitting in the open area. All the customers were in other areas of the store. She rearranged the chairs and tables to focus on an area where the authors would be. She pushed the tables to the outer edge and lined up some of the chairs.

Emerald went back to the backroom and grabbed a longer fold-out table for the authors. She set it up and then grabbed some smaller chairs from the back. They didn't have a lot of chairs, but there should be enough for the people, especially any elderly or disabled, who needed to sit down. Everyone else would need to sit on the floor or stand. She remembered Don and Adam saying that the authors were going to talk a little bit for a few minutes but probably wouldn't take group questions as they wanted more one-on-one time with everyone. Adam and Don told Emerald and Beth that they were expecting a good crowd, so she wanted to make sure that the area in front of the authors' table was open.

She went back to the backroom again and made up a few reserved signs to put on the chairs closer to the authors' table for anyone who needed to sit down, such as the elderly or disabled. She wanted to make sure that the people who needed to be comfortable had some options. Emerald knew that she might be standing for a while, so she took a few minutes to stretch out her back. She arched her back backwards as far as it would go. She held that position for several seconds. Then, she reached down and put her hands on the floor and held that position for a few seconds. She finished the stretch by getting on the ground like she was going to do a push-up. She arched her back towards the floor and looked up to the ceiling. She moved her head backwards as far as she could go and held that position for almost a minute. She spent the rest of the time getting the chairs ready and helping a few customers find a couple of books. She never saw Don come back, but she eventually saw him up at the front with Adam.

She was so happy to be working for a nice gay couple. They have been together longer than Mary and her. Emerald loved how laid back they were, and they were so nice to everyone. She didn't think that they made a lot of money off the bookstore, but they loved reading, spreading knowledge, and embracing the imagination and creativity that comes from books. She thought it was great that they were letting the authors of a book on different religions come in to promote their book, sign books, and interact with their fans. Unfortunately, there were a lot of monotheists and people who believe in the most popular religion in the area who get insecure and offended by other religions. Emerald thought they were very pretentious, ignorant, and intolerant.

Emerald knew for a fact that Adam and Don also despised religion and thought that the world would be better off without organized religion due to so many religious leaders conning people out of their money with fake promises and lies. Most of the stories that they tell are either flat out lies or gross misinterpretations or mistranslations. She accepted that there would always be religion but thought how evil and disgusting organized religion had become. So many people have died and have been murdered due to religious or holy battles and wars. Technically, it's still happening today. She thought how ironic it was that religion condemns killing, but more people have been killed and murdered in the name of religion than any other reason. You can even argue that a lot of political wars with countries who are fighting each other are religious in nature due to the fact that politicians use their distorted religious beliefs to make and approve legislation and laws even though religion is not supposed to be a part of the political process for obvious reasons.

"What a mess." Emerald said out loud.

Don walked over to Emerald and said, "Looks good to me."

"Oh, hey Don. Sorry, I was thinking about something else when I said that. Just talking to myself. You know when you are so focused on an issue in your head and you forget everything around you and then you automatically start talking out loud not thinking that people around you can hear you?"

"Totally. Happens all the time. How's it going?"

"Really good. I'm very excited about tonight. Feeling good and can't wait for the authors to show up."

"Definitely. We are looking forward to the business too."

"That's what I was thinking about. I thought it was weird that you were okay with them coming and promoting a book on religions. I thought you guys were very anti-religion."

"We are, but we talked about it. Actually, we got a call from one of the authors, which was weird. The author, Katy, said she would like to meet at our place instead of the larger bookstore chain down the road. She said that they were trying to promote the book at smaller local businesses instead of the bigger chain stores to help them out. She was really nice and persuasive. She said that she was actually in here about seven years ago before you worked here. I don't remember her coming in though. Adam said he did, but I don't think he did. She remembered us being really helpful and having a book she was having a hard time finding at other bookstores. I believe the book was on ancient religions. Not sure what it was called. I think they were doing research for the book they are promoting now and used that book as a reference on a couple of things. She actually has an aunt who lives here, so she visits every few years. I think she felt like she owed us one too for helping her out. She mentioned that she likes to support the gays, which is always a plus. We need all the help we can get from the heteros, especially due to religion."

"True that. That's sweet of her. Score for us. Good job you two. You never know who you are going to meet. Huh?"

"Damn straight, but Adam and I started talking about Katy and Brad writing about spreading the knowledge and information on all the religions. They wanted to let people decide which religion is more their speed or in line with their values and morals and other beliefs instead of hearing one side of the story or belief system from one particular religion or their followers, which is very subjective and biased. Obviously, it doesn't tell you the whole story or paint the whole picture, especially since all the religions today have stolen all their distorted stories and beliefs from earlier or ancient religions. Supporters of one particular religion are very manipulative too. They try to suck you into their church and religion by focusing on your weaknesses with false hopes and promises. Some are even threatening or use fear to get you to buy into their church or religion. They conveniently don't tell you the downfalls and all the problems with religion."

"Well, I'm proud of you two. I totally agree. It is better to be subjected to all of them, learn about all of them, and then make a choice. However, what is great about life is that you don't have to choose a religion. You can still be an amazing awesome person without being a part of a religion. That's one of the biggest lies of religion."

"What's that?" Don asked.

"That you have to believe in a religion to be saved and go to this magical yet fictional place after you die. It's great if you want to believe that bullshit, but for you to say that someone else is not a good person, is a sinner, or is not going to be in a good place after their human body dies is a very pretentious, judgmental, and evil thing to say to someone. That's what I was thinking about before you started talking to me. It has been so crazy for humanity, the animals, and the planet that religion has existed. It has done some awful things to everyone and everything while becoming so corrupt and destructive. It's not okay to justify judgment, hated, and killing in the name of a god or a religion, especially when the religion itself says those things are not okay."

"Absolutely. Very hypocritical. I think it's good to have info on a lot of different religions. I wish kids had more access to that. So many parents are so brainwashed and programmed that they disparage and devalue other religions, so their kids get brainwashed and programmed too. It's not good for children to be told what to believe or only be exposed to a limited amount of information where they can't properly make a choice. That's not freedom. That is total control and fascist. They just end up blindly believing their parents or whatever church they end up in. There's something about the emotional aspect of being able to still go to a made-up paradise in the afterlife or fake promised land that is persuasive to people no matter how rational they are. They even think they are going to be saved even if they are awful people in this life as long as they believe in their imaginary god, go to church, and give money to the church. Very stupid. It's so crazy too that so many people in a particular religion think they are the chosen ones or the ones going to be saved while people who believe in other gods and religions are going to be damned. That's on the same wavelength of thinking as racists, nationalists, and aristocrats. It is totally illogical, baseless, and closed-minded."

"You said persuasive," Emerald said. "You mean manipulative."

"A bit of both. But yes, manipulative all the way. Have you read the book?"

"Definitely. You?"

"Adam and I read it a couple of months ago. It definitely made us feel good about our non-religious approach to life. Some religions talk about some good stuff. You know, the philosophies of life, which so many religious people don't follow but still think they are going to be saved because they believe in their imaginary god or false prophet. Most, if not all, of the historical and after-death claims are a bunch of garbage. It's complete bullshit and totally ridiculous. I guess we will never really know until we die, but it's not good to believe in something so blindly, especially if it comes from people and organizations who are known liars. I know some very religious people who seem very intelligent and rational, but it blows my mind that they have bought into the bullshit of a god watching over them or an afterlife. It's insane is what it is."

"That is so true. I thought the book was a good overview of the various religions. I believe that it's always a good idea to take an eclectic approach to beliefs in spirituality and religion. It is interesting to see the similarities in the different religions of how people should or are supposed to live even though there are still a lot of concepts, such as god and the afterlife, that have been defined and translated differently by the different religions. That's why I love to read about the ancient religions, which are where most of the major religions today get their teachings anyway, even though they have either intentionally or unintentionally changed the stories, names, and the meanings of what the ancients were trying to say."

"It is fascinating to try and understand or even grasp what cultures over tens and even hundreds of thousands of years ago were trying to understand in regards to human behavior and other spiritual concepts, such as god, our purpose, where we came from, or where we might go after we die."

"Great stuff. It makes you realize that there is no good or bad or right or wrong religions but only bad and wrong humans. No offense Don, but they are mostly men."

"No offense at all Em. I could qualify that with bad and wrong heterosexual men with some being in the closet and living on the down low."

Emerald laughed and said, "That's funny. Funny because it's so true."

"Well, we better get this party started. The authors should be here soon. Hey, if you and Mary want to get together after the event, we can talk more about religion."

"That would be awesome, but not tonight. I've been getting up really early, so I'll head on home to bed after we close. Mary's working late tonight anyway. Actually, I could stay for a little while. Let's see how I feel. If you all want to hang out after we close, that would be awesome."

"That might work. I'll ask Adam."

"Cool. Let's do this."

Don walked back up front with Adam. Emerald kept setting up the books and the chairs. She started feeling the excitement again. She couldn't wait to meet the authors and hear what they had to say.

After some time, some people started coming in. Some brought their own books to get signed, but a lot of them bought either a new book or a different book to get signed. Adam and Don had some free coffee and water out for the customers, but they also had some other beverages for sale. A lot of the customers browsed the isles and the various books on the shelves in the store. Emerald said hello to a few people that walked by her. She thought it was weird that she didn't recognize that many people. There were some familiar faces though, but no one that she really knew to chat with. Everyone seemed really friendly and in good spirits. She thought the store and the people had some good energy. The energy seemed to be enthusiasm, which was great considering the controversial topic of comparing and contrasting the different religions.

Emerald knew that a lot of people can't handle the topic of religion and get very anxious, nervous, and defensive. Their suppressed doubts about their own beliefs come out when they are confronted with information that conflicts with their beliefs. They start projecting their insecurities onto others through raising their voices, arguing, and making disparaging remarks. She thought about how people get so offended and upset when someone criticizes their religion or tries to challenge their religion's teachings or their beliefs as wrong or inaccurate. We should be happy and glad when someone is able to prove us wrong and show us the truth and what is correct. It's not good for us to use irrational and illogical thinking and be stubborn about our beliefs that have no evidence or proof to support them. We shouldn't immediately deny what others say or get upset with them, especially if they are making sense and have evidence and proof to back up what they are saying. More importantly, if you know you are right, there is no reason to get upset in the first place. To Emerald, that meant they knew they were wrong. If you are secure enough in your beliefs, it shouldn't bother you if someone else believes in something else.

We are a fallible species and have been wrong time and time again. Emerald thought about the fact that people have been proven so many times that they were wrong about ideas and beliefs that they had. In some cases, they arrested, imprisoned, and even killed people for not believing what the majority believed in at the time. People believed the planet was flat, the earth was the center of the universe or the solar system, and leeches and other superstitions could cure illnesses. Some people still believe these false ideas today. We are so ignorant and restricted to experiencing the universe with our limited senses and what we are taught, which is infinitesimal compared to all the information that exists.

Emerald saw the authors walk through the front door. Adam and Don immediately walked over to greet them. Emerald thought they were very uplifting and inspirational to see in person. She remembered seeing somewhere that they put 15 years of work into the book they were promoting. They spent a lot of time researching information and doing interviews with experts on the various religions. After it was all said and done, the publishing companies could have rejected it and blocked it from being released to the masses. She wasn't sure if they had enough money, connections, or resources to self-publish it. Either way, it's always a huge risk to put that much time and energy into something. She knew it probably still gave them pleasure even if the book wasn't going to be published or be successful. That reminded Emerald that she needed to always do what she loved even if it doesn't make her rich or pay the bills.

Adam yelled at Beth and Emerald to come over to meet the authors. They walked over to the authors, shook hands with them, and greeted them. Emerald felt like she was meeting a rock star. She felt herself getting giddy. She hadn't met hardly anyone in person who was famous or a celebrity. They engaged in some small talk, and Don told the authors to look for Beth and Emerald if they needed anything. More and more people kept coming into the store.

"Are we ready?" Don asked Beth and Emerald.

"Definitely. We are good." Emerald replied.

Adam continued to check people out with their books. Beth, Don, and Emerald walked the authors over to the table. Beth went to get them some drinks. Emerald thought the authors seemed very humble considering the high level of intelligence needed to pull off a book like that. It would take a high amount of intellect just to write in length about one religion. They were able to put together a masterpiece of comprehensive details on several major religions while also comparing and contrasting them. The book was almost like a thesis. Emerald thought it was very well written. It was easy to read and was not degrading to the religions at all. It seemed like one of the goals of the book was to just put the information out there on the religions and let the people decide. There wasn't any judgment by the authors in the book on who was right, who was wrong, or who was the craziest. The reader got to decide that.

Emerald told the authors, "I will try to stay nearby in case you need something."

"It'll be okay," Brad said. "We are looking forward to being here and relaxing."

"Thanks Emerald," Katy said. "We are already loving this venue. We haven't enjoyed the big formal stores. It's nice to be in a local store. It feels more intimate, and it's nice to help you all out. All the rules and policies of the chain stores are annoying anyway."

"We even had one store try to tell us what we can and can't say due to them not wanting us to offend some of their precious customers," Brad said mockingly.

"As sad as that is, I believe it," Emerald said. "Well, thank you both for coming. I'm glad that you are here, and it's a pleasure to meet you both. I loved the book even though I am very much against organized religion and the purpose of religion today. It seems you all put a lot of effort into the book. Great job."

"That's awesome to hear," Brad said.

"Yes, so glad to hear that," Katy said. "It was a challenge to figure out who are audience was going to be for this book as it could go either way or in lots of different ways. It seems like we attracted a lot of open-minded people who were not that into religion but enjoyed reading and learning about what the different religions had to say. Unfortunately, I think that the non-religious people get more out of the religious teachings, such as the philosophies and values or morals, than the religious people do."

"We didn't try to think about the audience because it was nerve-racking to do so, and you start doubting yourself," Brad said. "We just tried to look at it from a research and educational perspective."

"Well, you did it," Emerald said.

Beth came back and sat their drinks down.

"I think you all are up," Emerald said. "You may not need it, but here is a microphone. We have a couple of speakers spread out. It's not worth the trouble sometimes due to the feedback or the loudness."

"I agree," said Katy. "Thanks. I think we will be fine without it. If we need it, we'll try it."

Don came over to introduce them to the crowd. He yelled out to get their attention, and everyone quieted down. It was definitely standing room only. Emerald thought there were at least 100 people in the store. It was crowded and a little cramped but not horrible. Some people walked by outside, peaked in, and then left. Don introduced them and told everyone that the authors were going to speak for a few minutes and get right to the signing. He asked everyone to save any questions they had for their one-on-one time. Everyone remained quiet after he spoke like they were waiting in anticipation for an important speech.

Katy and Brad spent several minutes discussing how they decided on the book. They also discussed some of their biographical information that covered both personal and professional details. Brad grew up in a traditionalist and religious home, and Katy grew up more in an agnostic and pro-choice environment. Between them both, there was a good balance of perspectives for the book. Katy was always more fascinated by and attracted to religions that were more philosophical and about self-discovery and living a moral and ethical life. She didn't care much for religions that were about worshipping some external god or gods and putting belief in a highly debatable and questionable pre-life or post-life existence. Brad emphasized his love for religions and the importance to provide some guidance and morals for people, but he definitely expressed his discontent to use religion for fearmongering, profiting, political, and exploitive purposes. Katy and Brad separately read a few pages from the book but didn't spend a whole lot of time reading from the book.

"Religions have played and do play and important part in people's lives," Brad said. "They are held sacred to a lot of people and cultures. We hope people can continue to shape and develop their spirituality and focus more on the messages of how to morally and ethically live your life rather than fight over who is right or wrong about historical stories and myths, whether a god or gods actually exist, where we came from, and what happens to us after we die. We are all in this together and need to respect and love one another no matter what. Your beliefs are your beliefs, and you have a right to believe in whatever you want to believe in. If you think you can put someone else's beliefs down, then that gives them a right to put your beliefs down. What's really important is how you act."

"Exactly," Katy said. "If I tell you that your beliefs are wrong, that means that I am admitting that mine could be wrong because if I want you to respect and accept my beliefs, I have to treat you the same way."

"No matter the religion, love for yourself and others is what is important."

"We have to see the similarities of the various belief systems and focus on the messages of us needing to cooperate and love one another. Then, we can find a middle ground to become peaceful."

"We have seen so many offended and upset people on this journey of writing this book," Brad added. "So many have so much passion when they talk about their religion and their beliefs, but a dark and evil force comes out when they talk about other's beliefs and other religions or are challenged about their irrational or illogical beliefs."

Katy interrupted, "And the hate. People hating others that they have never met just because they are not their religion and don't have the exact same beliefs as them."

"The responses of hate, condescension, and pretentiousness are exactly the opposite of what the religions are trying to teach and say."

At that moment, someone shouted out, "You are going to hell! There is only one god and one religion, and if you don't believe in him and the book, you are dammed for all eternity. You should be ashamed of yourself."

Don walked over to escort the guy out of the store, but Katy calmly and politely said, "You have a right to your opinion sir, but if we let you express yourself, then everyone gets to tell you how they feel. And from the look of this open-minded and supportive audience, I have a feeling you are not going to win your argument. Don, he can stay if he can remain calm and respectful."

The guy stood there for a few seconds, and Emerald thought that he seemed to be contemplating whether to shout some more or just leave. The rest of the people just stared at him in disagreement. Some were nodding their heads in disapproval while others were whispering unintelligible remarks. Emerald thought she heard some people say, "What a tool," "So upsetting to hear in this day in age," "He doesn't have a clue," and "So brainwashed."

"We'll see," the guy said as he walked out the door.

After he left, the crowd erupted in cheers and applause.

"Thank you all for your civility during that episode," Brad said. "You wouldn't believe it, but that is the tamer of a few incidents that we have had. Most of them have had to be escorted out."

"We were afraid that some of these outbursts would turn into an all-out physical fight or brawl, but luckily, we haven't had any physical altercations yet," Katy said.

Brad continued, "Anyway, as we were saying…"

Katy guessed as to what Brad was trying to get back to and said, "Love."

"Yes. Love is the foundation and the cornerstone of any decent and respectable religion, so the differences in historical stories and the debatable and controversial concepts are of less importance."

"We are all one and in this together. We must embrace each other, learn from each other, respect each other's differences, and work together for the better good. Thank you all for your love and support, and I hope you got a lot out of the book. We sure did. We are forever changed."

"Absolutely. It has been so amazing to meet so many people and their diverse beliefs and backgrounds."

"Hey Brad, we should write a follow-up book just on the touring experience and what people have told us."

"Not a bad idea."

Katy nodded at Emerald that they were done with their speeches.

"Thank you all again," Katy said. "We are going to sit down and sign some books. Please try to be as brief as you can with any conversations with us, and we apologize if we rush you off after a bit."

"Okay everyone," Emerald said loudly. "We are going to let the folks up her in the front go first, and the rest of you can start a line behind them and these two chairs. Please be patient."

Katy and Brad sat down and started signing books and talking to the people. Emerald watched and listened to how professional and polite the authors were and how friendly the audience members were. The authors were very brief and courteous at answering some challenging questions. People were asking them about the holy places they visited, their favorite parts or most interesting parts of the religions, how their beliefs have changed, and their favorite books they read. It seemed like they had a lot of experience answering those questions. A lot of people probably asked similar questions on the tour, so their answers were well refined at this point. After about a couple of hours, they finally got through everyone. Emerald was the last one to get her book signed after Beth, Adam, and Don. Katy and Brad hung out for a few minutes to say goodbye. Before they left, everyone thanked each other and expressed support to each other on their individual journeys through life.

After Katy and Brad walked out the door, Adam said, "What a success. Best night ever. I never thought a controversial topic like religion and a book with so many different religions would be so positive for us."

"Great job team," Don said.

"And we did it with only four people," Beth said proudly.

"That was huge and very awesome," Emerald said. "We should do that more often."

"If we can, we will," Adam said.

"Totally," Don said in agreement. "Well, let's clean up a bit and close this mother down."

"Sounds good," Beth said. "I have a date to get to."

"You can take off if you want Beth," Emerald suggested. "We are going to stay and chat for a bit anyway."

"That's great," Beth said. "Thanks a bunch. Have a great evening. I'll see you all tomorrow."

Everyone hugged and said goodbye to Beth as she walked out of the store. They cleaned up the store and reorganized the tables and chairs. They all took their turns using the bathroom while the other two finished cleaning and organizing everything. They all grabbed something to drink and sat down in the chairs in the open area. After they sat down and in unison, they all took a deep breath and exhaled like they just did a physical exercise.

"That was great," Emerald said. "Thank you guys for doing that."

"No problem," Adam said. "I hope to do it again and hopefully not have an incident."

"Hey Don, I was hoping to see you get physical and beat some ass," Emerald said jokingly. "That poor ignorant guy. He picked the wrong place and crowd to pull that shit."

"Definitely," Don said with a smirk. "I didn't want to or expect to get physical, but I was ready. Adam and I actually talked about it for a little bit on whether a situation may come up tonight. We feel pretty good or safe in this city, but there is always some crazy lunatic who wants everyone else to think exactly like he does."

"I know," Adam said. "If he was so confident and secure in in his belief system, why would he care what anyone else thinks? Very insecure."

"He is probably very conflicted, but since he is so closed-minded, he doesn't realize it," Emerald said. "Most likely, he's the type of person where he's only happy if everyone else agrees with him, strokes his ego, and doesn't challenge his beliefs. Then, when people do challenge him, it shakes his whole world, and everything crumbles to the ground. Out comes the denial and the anger."

"The sad thing is that most never make it to the acceptance stage because they are so stubborn and brainwashed," Don said.

"Yes, the programming is scary and very unfortunate," Adam said seriously. "I can't imagine blindly believing something that I was told without asking, "Is this true?" or "What about that?""

"Are we all just saying the same thing but in different ways?" Don asked.

"Yes," Emerald responded. "I'm starting to think that every major religion or at least the contemporary ones stole, and I use that word because they didn't reference or give credit where credit is due, their stories from prior religions, lesser known religions, or other cultures' belief systems. People argue so much and debate over the mistranslated and misunderstood stories and miss the meanings of how they are supposed to live their lives. Who cares where we came from and what happens after we die? It's not worth fighting and killing over. If there is something after this life and if there is a god, it's about how good you are and how you treat yourself, others, the animals, and the earth. It's not about whether or not you believe in something that you can't prove."

"There are lots of suggestions that the ancient cultures and religions and their stories and texts are very cryptic and not literal in meaning," Adam said.

"Especially since some have gone through a few translations to different languages," Don added.

"We read it or hear it in our language today and that may not be the correct words and meanings used by the original source," Adam said.

"Even the word religion has been distorted and is totally misunderstood," Emerald said. "I believe the word religion can be taken in a few ways and can mean something like careful pondering, conscious scrupulousness, to choose, or consider carefully. To me, those terms do not even come close to meaning faith and acceptance of something you can't prove. I've also heard other meanings of religion related to respect or reverence, which seems more like humbleness, awe, or adoration of this amazing life, the universe, and everything in it. There are also suggestions that religion might mean to bind, yolk, join, or link, which imply that we need to cooperate, do some self-discovery, work together, and connect to make a difference and reach our full potential. So many religions and their supporters spend more time doing the opposite of those meanings. They judge, hate, and divide. It's crazy that there are so many different meanings and interpretations to one word."

"Even the word faith is misused," Don said. "Religious people really have belief in what they believe in. Faith actually means trust in the unknown or acceptance of the unknown. It's about not knowing and having total trust when you don't know, which is pretty scary if you think about it. If you believe something is going to happen, that is not faith. If you believe in something, you have a belief in that something. You have knowledge and understanding. That is not faith. I can't imagine all the concepts, words, and stories that have been accidentally or intentionally mistranslated and misunderstood by changing one single word."

"Yes," Adam said. "Like the halo archetype. So many religions use the halo to represent that someone was spiritual and was crowned by a god or assigned to wear or have the halo. It's almost like the person didn't get to choose that, but to me, it most likely represents energy from that person that they are not holy or not omnipotent but that they have done some hard work with self-reflection and self-awareness to achieve openness and enlightenment to be awakened and free of attachments and control by others and the external world. It could also mean that they have some amazing connection to the universe through their mind, body, and spirit, and they finally get that we are all one."

"Nicely said Adam," Emerald said. "I like that."

"I agree," Don said. "Well said. I haven't thought about that. A lot of people take a story from a religious text or a preacher to mean something specific and literal. Like that is what actually happened or that is what you are supposed to do, but that is most likely not correct or not accurate."

"That makes me think about the translation or mistranslation issue," Emerald said. "A long time ago, when these ancient cultures didn't have written language, they didn't write down what they believed in. It was just spoken or in music or a song. Over tens of thousands or even hundreds of thousands of years, they would verbally pass these stories and songs to the next generation or to another nearby culture. That was before written language. Eventually, they got written down. You know that over that amount of time without writing things down that words and terms got added, taken out, or changed. And depending on the person who wrote it down and their values and beliefs and their understanding of what was told or sung to them, it could have easily been misinterpreted, mistranslated, and/or distorted. Not to mention their translations were biased towards the powers that be at the time, the leaders, the aristocracy, priests, rulers, and other affluent people or groups. Some religions have been translated over several languages by now. You have to understand that what we are reading and hearing today in our language may not even be close to what they originally were talking, singing, or writing about. People who are so strict on believing something out of a religious text that has been translated and interpreted several times in different ways are very gullible, ignorant, and careless. It could even be considered dangerous and even just plain asinine."

"Don't forget the cryptic or symbolism arguments too," Don said. "The stories could have been just tall tales or fictional, but there's the strong possibility that would even make a believer's head explode that the stories from the religious texts were not about actual people. Even the main characters, such as the prophets or the saviors, were not real people. They symbolized something."

"I like to think that," Emerald said.

"Very interesting," Adam said.

"Since the ancients worshipped the stars and other celestial or astronomical bodies, which created the constellations and the ideas of gods, the people in religious stories were most likely not people at all but stars, planets, constellations, and galaxies," Don said. "The highest or most powerful god could also be the universe and everything. They may even represent the elements, such as fire, water, or wind, and different phenomenon, such as gravity or the weather, here on earth or in outer space."

"I think it's easier for people to understand that it was an actual person, especially to worship, rather than a star out in the sky," Adam said. "Most people have a hard time thinking in abstract and complicated ways. You know because they aren't that bright."

"Don't forget about the alien theory too," Emerald said.

"That god was an alien, or the gods were extra-terrestrials?" Adam asked.

"Yes," Don replied. "That's actually a good theory. It makes a lot of sense when you think about it."

"I'm siding with that one," Emerald said. "However, I do think that some of the characters were stars, planets, or other celestial bodies. From the stories, it just doesn't seem plausible that some of the gods were stars that never actually did anything. Now, if they were aliens from another planet, that would make more sense."

"Maybe," Adam said. "But that's a tough one to prove. It's more important that almost all those ancient religious stories are challenging if not impossible to prove. We are trying to get the meaning instead of validating the story. Right?"

"You're right," Emerald answered. "The message is the most important thing. I think that's why the image of a god and other gods or even prophets and disciples all had different purposes and did different things. For most of them, they were the messages of peace, love, and happiness or a moral to get to that realization if they did make mistakes or do something wrong and bad."

"Totally," Don said. "The fact that so many cultures have anthropomorphized objects and made them into almost all men and not included a lot more women is so egocentric and vein and shows the fallacy for what it is."

"It does," Emerald said. "What about evolution?"

"Oh shit," Adam said. "That's bomb waiting to go off."

"It's is crazy how many religious people don't believe in evolution, which has been scientifically proven over and over again," Emerald said. "You can even see evolution in your own lifetime."

"It is crazy and suspicious," Don said. "They don't want to admit that things evolve. However, they believe that a magical being created everything the way it almost is today in a matter of days, or that the earth is only tens of thousands of years old. That is more ridiculous than evolution."

"I'm no scientist, but I know evolution probably didn't happen exactly the way some scientists think," Adam said. "That's what makes them theories though. Religious people try to pass their beliefs off as fact and that you can't dispute it. If someone scientifically provides a better explanation to evolution, they change it. Scientists don't get mad and kill the ones who disagree with them or force everyone else to believe in what they believe in like some religions have done."

"So, the theory of evolution evolves," Emerald said.

"That's great Em," Don said. "Very smart. Ideas do evolve, which is proof of evolution."

"I'll be the first to say that I don't know exactly where we originated from, but I do know that we didn't just magically appear out of thin air by a god," Emerald said. "We evolved over billions of years from different life forms. I think that's the point. Most humans can't imagine or fathom tens of hundreds or even thousands of years. Let alone millions and billions of years. So many things can happen over the course of millions of years. We could have easily evolved from another species and life form."

"That's another great point," Adam said. "Hey, I thought of another issue that we have heard to help explain why a lot of people believe in what they believe in."

"What's that?" Emerald asked.

"Well, our belief systems are very dependent on where we are born, what our parents believe in, and what the culture or society around us believes in," Adam said.

"That is a good one," Emerald said.

"I agree," Don said. "That usually decides the religion you are primarily and mostly, if not one hundred percent, exposed to and decides what religion you will become. Not always, but for the most part."

"Most people choose the main or most popular religions too from like a peer pressure or anxiety response due to wanting to fit in," Emerald said.

"Don't forget the lame argument when you tell them that they would have believed in a different religion if their parents or culture believed something different or they were born somewhere else that had a different religion," Adam said. "Then, they ignorantly say that they would have found their way to the religion that they are, which either proves how stupid they are or how brainwashed they are or both."

"Yes," Don said. "Very ignorant, pompous, and pretentious."

"I think that implies brainwashing and programming," Adam said. "There is a lot of cognitive dissonance involved with that one when you think you wouldn't believe in something else if you were raised in a different environment."

"It could be gullibility and even fear," Emerald said. "Also, sometimes I think religion is like a fairy tale for adults. You know how we are manipulated into believing fairy tales as a kid, but you are eventually told they are not true. But with religion, your parents and other adults don't tell you that it is not true, so you keep believing in it."

"If you were raised and told to believe a bird was a turtle, you would believe that a bird was a turtle," Don said. "Then, someone comes by and says that is not true. You would deny and get angry and fight for your belief to hold onto it. It's up to you to finally see the truth even if you are completely wrong."

"They would go to great lengths to keep their beliefs," Emerald said. "They would even avoid listening to reason like a kid who puts his hands over his ears when he doesn't like what he hears to throw a tantrum because he didn't get his way and starts screaming immature things like, "Na, na, na, na, I can't hear you.""

"That's funny," Adam said while laughing.

"Sounds like you had some experience with that one Em," Don said with a smile.

"Yes," Emerald said. "I have. I won't deny it, but you have to take a minute when faced with new information and ask yourself if you are wrong. What's wrong with saying that you are wrong or admitting that you are wrong? There's nothing wrong with that. People should be able to say that they learned something and that they know better now. It's important for us to change, learn from our mistakes, or just say that you don't know something. Saying that you don't know something is one of the smartest and most intelligent things that someone can say."

"There is so much that we don't know," Adam said. "That's why science and the scientific method will always rule over religion, stories, and myths. It has a method to disprove something, and when you disprove something, you have to change and accept the new information or say that you don't know. The scientific method doesn't whine like a little bitch, cry, and throw a temper because someone threatened its false belief system and proved it wrong. Just because someone said that they are right and a lot of people believe in something doesn't make it true."

"I was talking with someone the other day about that erroneous thinking," Emerald said. "Just because you can't disprove something doesn't give it validity or truth. That's the ignorance fallacy."

"Unfortunately, that is a very common fallacy," Don said. "Not to keep bashing religion, but what about all the horrible and evil atrocities that religion has caused and been a part of. Religion speaks of peace and love but look at how many have been tortured and killed in the name of some of the most popular religions. It's insane. How can you kill in the name of a god or a religion?"

"Total hypocrisy," Adam said. "I think a lot of those atrocities were directed by tyrants, dictators, and aristocrats, but they did use religion and fear for their evil ways to get people to murder and do horrible things. However, it is crazy that there are so many traditionalist people who are very religious, but they are gun nuts. They are pro-guns, pro-weapons, pro-war, pro-destruction, and pro-military. That makes no sense at all. It is the definition of a hypocrite."

"So sad," Emerald said depressingly. "Which goes to show you how people and groups use religion for manipulation for their evil ways."

"I can't believe we haven't brought this issue up yet, but what about all the pedophilia and sexual assaults and rapes that occur by so-called religious people," Don said seriously. "It's a fucking epidemic. The priests are supposed to be celibate, and so many have sexually offended on children. Mostly little boys too."

"To top it all off, they are anti-gay too," Emerald said. "They even express their disapproval of homosexuality. They don't only rape little boys, but a lot of them are caught having consensual sex with men."

"That's hypocrisy," Don said. "The church doesn't even fire them either. They just move them somewhere else where the local people don't know what they did. They don't tell the new congregation either that he is a pedophile and has raped little boys and girls. They should have to report that to the police."

"That is a sad fact Don," Adam said. "Don't forget the hypocrisy of religions making fun of and discounting other religions when the religions were all founded on the same crazy and unbelievable stories. A lot of the times just the names were changed and maybe some of the story details. Your religion is just as nuts as the next one. It's all perspective."

"Don't forget about the hypocrisy behind the religion buffet," Emerald said.

"What's that?" Adam asked.

"That's where you believe in a religion but only believe in certain parts of it to suit your needs and wants. You only believe in what is convenient for you to believe in. You get to choose what you believe out of the religion and ignore all the contradictions and things that don't make sense or the things that you don't like."

"I can see that," Adam said. "That is very convenient yet still very hypocritical."

"It still upsets me that there is a good number of people using religion for hate," Don said. "What the fuck is up with that? That doesn't make any sense at all. We are all gay in here. Almost every major religion condemns homosexuality and the like, but they have also hated on women, other races, minorities, agnostics, atheists, and anyone who doesn't believe in what they believe in."

"Like the guy that was in here earlier," Adam said. "Saying we are all going to hell."

"That is a wild claim to make," Emerald said. "Sounds like he has been there, and we don't even believe in hell. Can you go somewhere that you don't believe in? I mean, there are a lot of good religious people, but something that has always bothered me was people believing in a god who created the devil, hell, evil, and misery. That just doesn't make any sense at all. It's stupid."

"If there is a hell, religious people who threaten and hate others will be going there," Adam said.

"Using fear, guilt, and hate is always wrong," Don said. "Guilt is a natural response to messing up, but you should learn from the mistake and not do it again. Someone who manipulates you to feel guilty so they can get your support and money is just plain evil. That makes me think about the institution of religion versus the beliefs. People having their beliefs is one thing, but religion as a company is a whole other monster."

"I just want to know why the religions need so much money, these huge and gaudy churches and temples, and expensive homes or mansions for the preachers," Emerald said. "You don't need money or any material objects to be religious or spread your religious message. You don't need a fancy church, and the preachers definitely don't need high-priced automobiles, homes, boats, or planes. It's obviously all about the money. You have to be blind if you can't see that. And if you don't give them some of your money, they make you feel like you are not a good person and that you are going to be damned. You are just making the preachers rich. The money doesn't get you into a better afterlife place. It doesn't please a god. Most churches don't eve use the money to help others. It's a total scam."

"Totally Em," Don said. "It is a business that targets emotionally vulnerable people. You can't buy your way into being saved or eternal happiness. You have to do that on your own."

"Yes, you do," Adam said. "They prey on people's weaknesses. The institution and business of religion is like a predator."

"They also prey on people's insecurities," Don said. "People need something to believe in because they don't feel complete in this consumeristic, slave labor, and materialistic life. Spirituality and religion help to fill that void. However, religion will suck more out of you than it gives. You have to become spiritual, not religious."

"I think it's fine to be religious and believe in something," Emerald said. "Just don't use it for hate, violence, discrimination, judgement, and bigotry. It's also not good to push or pressure your religious beliefs onto others. Even if you are being nice. I don't think it's even good to do that with your kids. You should give them all the options that are out there and let them make a decision. That is freedom. That is choosing. That is the right way to raise a kid. Most people believe in their religion because they don't know any other way and were told or pressured to be that religion. Religion is and always has been about peace and love. It's sad what it has become and what the preachers and church leaders have turned religion into. A money-making machine with so many lies and manipulations. They even use it to push political agendas too, which is absolutely disgusting, considering how corrupt and horrible politicians and politics are. The politicians pay preachers to tell their congregation to vote for them. Absolutely despicable and abhorrent. Life is not about being a religion or going somewhere when you die. It's about living a good, healthy, happy, altruistic, and enjoyable life. The most important thing is that you take care of yourself, others, the animals, and our precious planet. Love is my religion, and peace is my religion."

"That's it Em," Don said. "You nailed it."

"Love, love, and more love," Adam said.

"Shit," Emerald said. "It's getting late. Well, on that note, I gotta jet. Always great talking to you fine gentlemen. Thanks again."

"Thank you," Adam and Don said in unison.

They all stood up from the chairs. Adam and Don each gave Emerald a hug.

"Thanks again Em," Adam said. "See you tomorrow."

"Good night Em," Don said.

Emerald went into the back and grabbed her bike and said another goodbye while walking out the front door. She rode back home. It was getting dark. She thought on her way home about all the lies that we were told by a lot of different people and organizations and how we were able to overcome some of the lies but not others. At that moment, she remembered a melody that she was working on but hadn't been able to capture or complete the entire song. She had in mind a slower but resonating rhythm with different sounds that go with the guitars and drums. The song sounded hypnotic in her head. It was a darker or more doom rock like song. While she rode home, she made a "wah wah" sound that started out louder, repeated, and then faded out after two bars or eight beats. While that sound was going on, she imagined a bass line or lower rhythm guitar riff and some light drums that played with it. She thought that the wah wah sound could occur throughout the entire song. However, she might have it suppressed during the chorus. For the rest of the way home, she thought about how the verses, bridge, and chorus might go.

Emerald got home and put up her bike. She used the bathroom really quick. She was very excited about the song. She could hear it playing in her head with all the sounds and instruments. She went into the living room and grabbed her guitar next to the sofa. She grabbed her song notebook and a pen to write down the song. She sat down on the sofa. She started the song with an A minor chord and started writing some lyrics for the first verse and then the entire song came to her. She tried to fill in the chords while she hummed the sounds and sang some of the words that she came up with. After the chorus, she imagined the note holding or extending with like an electronic sound. It would go back to the A minor melody after the first chorus played, but after the second time the chorus played, the song would transition into a nice guitar solo.

"You were lied to," Emerald said out loud. "That's the title of the song. I love it."

She finished writing out the song while she played and sang. She was so proud of herself. It was rare for her to write an entire song in so little time.

She yelled out, "Fuck yeah!"

She was very excited. She couldn't wait to go over it with Mary to see what she thought even though Mary could be critical at times instead of giving her an easy general answer on whether the song was decent or not. Emerald knew songs take years to develop to get them right. Mary would be home late tonight though, so Emerald decided to play the song one more time before she got ready for bed.

You Were Lied To

(Wah Wah sound throughout entire song on each line that starts louder at the end of each line and echoes throughout next line while fading.)
(Am bass line)

Verse 1:
(Am) When you were young, you were (C) so vulnerable.
(Am) Then you grew up, and you were (C) so gullible. (Am)
(Em) You believed in the (D) things that you were told
(Am) You put your faith in ideas you (C) can't even prove

Bridge:
(Am) See (G) Now (Em) The (Am) Truth
(Am) You (G) Were (Em) Lied (Am) To
(Am) See (C) Now (G) The (Am) Truth
(Am) You (G) Were (Em) Lied (G) To

Chorus:
(Am) Open your (B) eyes and (C) see what's (D) real
(Am) Now is the (B) time for (C) you to (D) feel
(Em) See (D) now (F) the (Em) truth
(Em) You (D) were (F) lied (G) to (hold on G and "to), then back to Wah
Wah with Am bass line

Verse 2:
(Am) Religion is a scam just to (C) get your money
(Am) The government doesn't (C) want you to be free (Am)
(Em) Believe what you want ho(D)wever you should know
(Am) Ignorance and apathy are (C) just as evil

(Repeat Bridge and Chorus, but at end, hold on G and "to" and then to
solo with Bridge chords.)

Verse 3:
(Am) The history that you know is (C) not what happened
(Am) The education that you got was (C) manufactured (Am)
(Em) Addictions and enter(D)tainment keep you blind
(Am) Overpopulation and (C) pollution will end our time

(Repeat Bridge and Chorus, then back to Wah Wah with Am bass line.)

Episode 4
A Political Catastrophe

*When money, corporations, and religion influence politics and the government,
the people suffer.*
There will always be corruption when money and politics are mixed.
Politics is not about helping people, it's about the politicians helping themselves.

Emerald had to work the next couple of days. The bookstore had an unusually busy weekend. Some buzz got out about the book signing, and so people were avoiding the big chain stores to help support the locally owned business. Adam and Don asked Emerald to help them out and work some extra hours. Since Mary had to work anyways, she didn't mind helping them out. She enjoyed the bookstore and the environment. She still got to do what she wanted before and after work. She still woke up early, meditated, exercised, stretched, made some delicious vegan and organic food, and sang and played some songs on her guitar.

Emerald and Mary still made time for each other even when they both had to work. Usually, Emerald would wake Mary up a little early, so they could talk or do something, such as a bike ride or hike, before they had to go to work. They even enjoyed some cuddle time to feel and hold each other. They loved to just stare at one another while looking deep into each other's eyes. They always tried to make time to express how much they loved each other. That's what it was all about. To Emerald, it wasn't about running and racing around, worrying about what time it was or whether you were late for work, or cursing and screaming at the traffic. Emerald thought it would be a horrible life to live if you chose to live your life like that.

She thought the slavery of the alarm clock in the morning was one of the worst ways to be in bondage of the system. It was like your parents were still waking you up, but instead of your parents, it was a job or boss. Luckily, Emerald hadn't needed an alarm clock in over two years because she had been waking up so early. She finally felt free after all those many years of someone else telling her when to get up. She thought that waking up with an alarm clock would definitely take a few years off of your life, stress you out, and cause some serious health problems. It's never okay to let others have so much control over your life. It didn't matter how much they were paying you. It's not worth it.

On this weekday, Emerald and Mary made plans to meet up with Christina and Eric after a long time of not doing the couples thing. It wasn't because they didn't like hanging out with Christina and Eric. Emerald and Mary thought very highly of them and considered them a sweet couple, but Emerald and Mary really enjoyed their time together and were very selfish with the time that they had off together. They would rather spend time by themselves. Hanging out with other couples or spending time with friends and family was not something that was a priority for them. Even though Mary was a lot more extroverted than Emerald, they just didn't need that social interaction to be happy and enjoy life like some people do.

Emerald woke up really early again. She was alright with waking up so early because she wanted to make sure that she could get in her exercise and meditation routine before they went over to Christina's and Eric's home. She liked waking up early, so she could take her time and get all her responsibilities done without being or feeling rushed. She wanted to run outside and watch the sunrise again, but it was raining. She was a bit bummed out that she couldn't run outside and watch the sunrise. She ate some breakfast and journaled her dreams.

She couldn't remember very much of her dreams, but she wrote down what she could remember. She remembered dreaming about being in a store and walking around. She thought it was like a grocery or retail store, but she couldn't recognize the store or products they were selling. She didn't see the produce department, but she thought there was one. She wasn't sure why she was there or what she was looking for. She walked around the isles like she was looking for something, but she didn't know what she wanted. There were a lot of people in the store. That was about the extent to that dream.

She also remembered dreaming about driving in a country setting with Mary. It was daytime. She wasn't familiar with where they were at. She remembered driving while Mary was in the passenger seat. She saw some older homes on the side of the rode. She felt like it was out in the country, but she couldn't recognize it. She felt okay in these dreams other than feeling confused and lost.

Emerald washed out her dishes and went to the bathroom. She did some light hygiene and decided to go ahead and get her exercise routine completed. She did a stretch and cardio routine in the apartment. It was good they were on the first floor. She wouldn't have been able to do the cardio exercises if they were on a higher floor or had someone living below them. She did some running in place, jump squats, and some jumping jacks. She tried to do some jump squats once a week, but they were still very challenging. She didn't get overly sore from them, but she could definitely feel that she did them the next day. It was like her muscles were a little tighter the next day. She tried to do about three to five sets of about 50 jump squats. She tried to make the cardio last for about an hour. She was getting in pretty good shape, so she knew she could do it. It was probably more than what a lot of people would or could do.

"No excuses," Emerald said. "Know thyself. I have to take care of myself. Love myself."

For some reason, she felt very energetic and determined this morning. While she was exercising, she kept getting these rushes of elation regarding how responsible and healthy she had become. It made her feel really good about herself. She compared that feeling to what others call the autonomous sensory meridian response. She remembered learning about that concept and phenomenon a few years ago. She related it to when people get a euphoric feeling from massages, being whispered to, or getting affection from someone else. Emerald loved this feeling even though it was different when exercising, but she thought it was very similar. She would get a rush of energy from the back of her head that would tingle from her head down through her body. Sometimes, it would make the hairs on her arms stand up. She thought it was very weird and strange but a nice feeling. She felt spiritual from it. She wondered if it was a ghost or some presence flying through her. This rush or feeling would happen to her about once every other week, but no matter what she did, she couldn't make it happen on command. She wished that she could figure out how to make it happen when she wanted it to happen, so she could enjoy it more often. Either way, she saw it as a sign that she was doing something right or that she was on the right path.

Emerald felt like she was doing what she was supposed to do. To her, that was her karma. Everything that has happened to her, good and bad, has led her to where she was at, so she knew what she was supposed to do and would keep doing it. It was like the universe was giving her a sign that she was making the right choices, especially due to how awesome she felt. She knew she was supposed to be doing things to make herself feel better and not worse. She wished that everyone would try to take care of themselves. It made her sad to think how many people don't take care of themselves. They may help others, but they are really being inconsiderate by not taking care of themselves. Eventually, others will have to take care of them because they are not taking care of themselves. As weird as it sounds, it's very selfish to not take care of yourself.

She started to think about some of the talks that she had recently with everyone. They have been very intense and deep. The topics were very controversial. She thought about how she could be wrong on some of her views and stances and that she may be misunderstanding certain things. But still, she felt good about where she was at intellectually and spiritually due to her constant questioning and skepticism. She has fallen into the trap of being stubborn before and putting faith into the popular beliefs, such as religious views, major political positions, capitalism, materialism, consumerism, entertainment, working too much, and wanting to have a lot of money. She was upset at herself for falling into those illusions, especially with having to please others and having money or a certain job to be happy.

Emerald started laughing at how ridiculous those things are to her now. She thought about the control that these systems have over people and how most people don't even know that they are following someone else's orders. Then, when they are confronted about it, they deny it, get upset, and try to justify that what they are doing is their choice. However, they can't even give a good reason why they are doing what they are doing other than claiming that it's their choice, especially since the choices are so unhealthy and bad for them, other people, the animals, and the earth. They deny the consequences of their choices, and they can't explain the alternatives that they didn't choose, which would have been more of a choice since someone wasn't trying to sell it to them or manipulate them into it. The reality is that they went along with whatever they were doing due to pressure, fear, manipulation, ignorance, or guilt. All these thoughts made Emerald feel uplifted and free. It was like she broke out of that pressured thinking, so she could listen, be more open, be patient, learn from her mistakes, and make sure she understands things before she believes, commits to, or acts on them.

Emerald almost forgot that she had to go somewhere today. She had to go see her probation officer. She went every three months. Unfortunately, she got arrested a few years ago for prescription fraud or more commonly known as doctor shopping. She started to feel bad again about what she had done in the past regarding the drugs and how horribly she was treating herself and Mary. She immediately redirected herself on her exercising and reminded herself that she only had one more year left of probation. She would also be able to get her record sealed due to being considered a first-time offender. To not have a publicly available criminal case made her feel a whole lot better.

She finished up her work out and did a good stretch. She took a shower and did some hygiene. She went into the kitchen and made some lunch. She made a salad with some kale, avocado, tomatoes, seeds, herbs, spices, and apple cider and coconut vinegar. She also had some of her chocolates for dessert. While she ate, she looked over some of her songs to try and work on the lyrics some more. After she was done eating, she tried to tuck Mary out.

She laid down next to Mary and said, "I forgot I have to go see my P.O. this morning."

"No worries," Mary said tiredly but understandingly. "I think I'm going to sleep some more."

"Cool. Sleep good. I love you my beautiful."

"I love you."

Emerald got out of bed, left the bedroom, and got dressed. She left a few minutes earlier than she usually leaves. She had to take the car due to the rain, distance, and the time she had before the appointment. On the way, she thought how responsible she has been over the past few years. She had paid her fines and costs and had completed all her community service and counseling. Her biggest accomplishment was graduating from drug court with almost no issues at all. She never failed a drug test and met all her goals. She remembered her probation officer telling her that he wished he had a lot more probationers like her.

At one point, she asked the court to be put on unsupervised probation, and her probation officer even recommended it. The probation officer said it would have definitely helped them out since they have large caseloads, and it would have been good for them to focus on the ones who were not doing well, which was most of them. However, the prosecuting attorney objected to it, so the judge denied her request. The prosecuting attorney saw doctor shopping as a very serious crime even though the medical system is set up to get second and third opinions from different doctors as well as different prescriptions from different doctors. The prosecuting attorney even brought up an incident that happened while Emerald was attending drug court. She didn't relapse, but she knew about others who were using due to overhearing them one day. She didn't say anything about what she heard. When they got caught using, they blamed Emerald for not confronting them and bringing the issue up in group. Emerald knew that they blamed her to avoid and distract from their responsibility, but she was surprised that the counselor didn't see it that way.

Emerald's counselor even held her somewhat responsible, which Emerald thought was ridiculous. The counselor expected everyone to be honest even if it wasn't the person doing the bad behaviors. Emerald felt like the whole situation focused more on her than holding the ones who were abusing drugs accountable. She didn't even think that they really got punished. She was denied moving up a level at one point, so it delayed her graduating from the drug court for a couple of months. She thought that the prosecuting attorney was just looking for an excuse to keep her on probation so that they could keep getting a supervision fee from her. She's pretty sure they got a commission or a bonus for putting and keeping people on probation.

Emerald remembered that her counselor said that she was one of the most successful graduates that the counselor had ever seen. She still thought it was best that she kept her mouth shut about what the others were doing. She felt like they were just hurting themselves and not others. It was their business if they wanted to make poor choices, live an unhealthy life, and lie about what they do. They weren't pressuring her or others. They seemed to be minding their own business. If Emerald thought they were putting others in danger, she may have said something. She saw where the counselor was coming from, but the situation wasn't so black and white. Where do you draw the line with whether you are hurting or helping people by minding your own business and letting others do unhealthy things to themselves? Are you an associate if you find out someone is doing something illegal that is a self-destructive behavior without a victim and you don't say something to them or someone else? What if you felt scared to tell? What if you think that person would hurt you if you told on them? You never know. Some people try to do the right thing, and it backfires on them. It was a tough decision, but she made it through it.

Emerald thought about the phrase "no good deed goes unpunished," which has some truth to it, but it is a very apathetic and negative way to think. She felt like that phrase and that type of thinking allows evils of the world to blossom as people look the other way. Overall, she thought it depended on the situation, and she thought no one could judge another person's decision in a critical or serious dilemma. She knew there was a place to tell on someone and a place not to tell. She knew it would have been good to tell if those people who were abusing drugs had kids or they were hurting others around them, but she really felt like they were volatile. They could have easily hurt her for telling on them. It wasn't worth the risk. They were on drugs, and people don't make good decisions while they are on drugs.

Her biggest mistake was walking over to them one day after group to be nice to them and talk to them. That was the last time she tried to be friendly with any of the group members. She focused on herself and what she needed to do to stay sober and get her life back on track. Her recovery was not about pleasing others or trying to fit in. She spent the rest of the treatment program getting to her appointments right when they started and leaving immediately when they were done, so she didn't get involved with any of the other people's drama or their issues.

Mary was the only one that mattered anyway. Emerald knew it was hard to have a relationship with an addict. You never know if they are going to lie to you, relapse, steal from you, yell at you, or hurt you in other ways. Most likely, they have already done all those things, and so the other person tries to stick it out with them. That's a huge gamble to make. You are betting that they won't keep doing the things that they have already done to you. They have made so many promises that they weren't going to keep doing those awful things, but they have broken those promises time and time again. When is enough, enough? Emerald was just glad that she was almost done with probation.

She got to the probation office and checked in. She always had to walk through the disgusting smelling cigarette smoke and toxic vapor fumes even though there was a sign that clearly said don't smoke or vape in front of the door. A lot of people who smoke or vape are very disrespectful, which says a lot about how they feel about themselves. To Emerald, it made sense why they were abusing themselves anyway. Why would they care about anyone else if they don't care about themselves? The inside smelt just as bad. You could smell the body odor and the stale scent of cigarettes and vapor fumes. Even though she got there first thing in the morning and right when they opened, there were already about 30 people in the waiting area. Some were there for group, others were there for drug testing, and some were there to meet with their probation or parole officers. Since they had such large caseloads, she wondered if they double booked their appointments. That's the way you make some extra cash. Doctors do that all the time, which is technically fraud. There were so many times where she asked for the first appointment of the day, but when she showed up for her appointment, two other people were there to see the same probation officer. On a few occasions, the probation officer would see someone else before her. Emerald also hoped that she didn't recognize anyone while she was there. She hoped to not see anyone from her past or from the drug court group meetings. She tried her best to be avoidant and not look at people at the probation office. She couldn't wait until she didn't have to go anymore.

Emerald knew she was an addict and that she deserved the consequences for her mistakes, but she thought that she was stable and responsible enough to not need government supervision. It was a bit much at this point in her life. It would be different if she was still making mistakes or doing drugs. She tried hard not to judge the others there and not to see herself in a better light than everyone else there. She didn't want to get the attitude that she was better than anyone else. She had her problems too, and that just may be where they were at in their lives. Coming to the probation office was a crucial reminder of how she was definitely going down the wrong path, so she felt the feelings of guilt, shame, and regret. It was reminder of how horrible she treated Mary.

She waited for about 30 minutes, and her probation officer finally called her back.

"Good Morning," Emerald said.

"Good Morning," Tom said.

They walked back to his office. He always made her walk directly in front of him for security reasons. Emerald always thought that was weird because they didn't scan or check for weapons, but they weren't in a bigger city with too much crime. He told her to go down the hallway, take a left, and go into the second office on the right. Emerald walked into the office and sat down. It was a normal office setting, but there were papers everywhere. You could tell that the officer was overworked with cases.

"How are you doing?" Tom asked.

"Doing good. I'm staying out of trouble. Like always."

"Any problems that I need to be aware of."

"Not at all. Work is good. Just taking care of myself."

"Good. Any changes in your living situation, work, new address, contact information?"

"Everything is the same. No changes."

"Looks like you are doing everything that you need to do. You are almost done with your time. We just need to meet a couple of more times. As long as you keep up the good work, you will be done with all of this. Keep it up."

"Will do. Thanks."

"We need to do a drug test before you leave. Here's your next appointment."

"Sounds good."

Tom spent a few minutes documenting on Emerald. Then, Emerald and Tom went over to the drug testing bathroom, and she urinated into the cup for him. She passed the drug test, and Tom walked her out.

"See you next time."

"Have a great week. Thanks."

Emerald walked by the others who were waiting in the waiting area. The posters on the wall were almost laughable to her as they were focused on getting tattoos removed, not using technology while you were meeting with your officer, dressing appropriately and not wearing hats or caps, not smoking or vaping in the building, and making sure people don't bring their kids to their appointments. Emerald thought the no-kids rule was probably smart. She was sure they had some issues with that one before they made that one a rule. She walked outside where numerous people were smoking even though they were not supposed to smoke in front of the doors. Some of them stared at her, but she just tried to keep her head down and kept on walking.

On her way home, she thought about how most of the probationers were drug addicts or got arrested and convicted for drug crimes. It was an epidemic. It didn't seem like the businesses, the government, or society were doing much about it. If anything, they supported and sold addictive behaviors, especially to children, and then arrested people who became addicts. Emerald thought that was counterproductive and hypocritical. Most of the addicts and criminals at the probation office were also very young. Most seemed to be late teens and in their 20s. That seemed interesting to her. Due to that age significance, she thought that someone should have been able to figure out how to deal better with the drug problem that so many people had.

It was crazy to her how 75 percent of drug addicts return to using drugs after getting arrested and/or trying to be sober. That recidivism rate was very high. Obviously, something was not working. To Emerald, the high relapse rate was embarrassing not only for the drug addicts but also to the community and society. She didn't think that the addiction programs and the governments, including law enforcement, were competent enough or knew what they were doing when it came to them trying to solve the problem of addiction. She also thought there may be some conspiracy that they don't want to properly deal with it as people with addictions are cash cows and spend a lot of money. It was amazing to her how much money they make off people being addicted, but they put a fraction of that amount of money and resources into helping people deal with their addictions. She felt like that was the issue and problem with lots of other offenses, crimes, and problems too. It seemed to be okay to get rich off people's miseries and weaknesses instead of doing the right thing by helping people who need it and not selling products that hurt others, make people sick, and kill people. Emerald also thought how crazy it was that we didn't put more money into prevention. Almost all the money spent on trying to address societal issues and problems went to either intervention or postvention services, which was backwards. It was a reactive way to deal with problems, which said a lot about why the problems continue and even got worse. You have to prevent problems and not just put a bandage over them.

Emerald kept driving home and thought about what made her finally get her shit together and get clean and sober. For some, it was a loss of something, such as a loved one, job, home, money, or health. To others, it was facing death or a combination of things. She thought her main motivation was Mary but getting arrested and having to face her problems definitely helped. She knew that she would have continued to use if she didn't get arrested. It was the wakeup call that she needed. Still, those punitive consequences, such as being arrested and jailed, did not help a lot of people stop their criminal and negative behaviors. She really thought it was the realization of responsibility and choice. You can't make someone stop something. They have to choose to stop it. They have to want to stop. For a lot, there is nothing external or outside of them that is going to make them stop, especially when it comes to drugs and that euphoric feeling they get when they take the drugs or the fear or the feeling of getting sick when they don't have the drugs. Emerald probably would have been able to stop sooner if she didn't get so sick when she didn't have the drugs. That was a huge factor in her continuing to abuse the pills. She had an infinite amount of memories getting extremely sick with digestive issues, stomach pains, diarrhea, nausea, insomnia, ghost pains, night sweats, fatigue, rage, congestion, and anxiety.

All these reflections of Emerald overcoming her drug addiction made her feel very lucky as she could have easily kept on using after her arrest. She was in a small percentage of people who were able to stop that horrible cycle, which made her feel special too. She definitely thought society was doing a horrible and poor job of dealing with addiction. She believed that drug courts and counseling programs were more effective and far superior than arresting people and treating them like criminals or just locking them up with no rehabilitation efforts. Punitive consequences like the criminal justice system is like spanking your kid without educating or teaching them not to do the unwanted behavior. It is absolutely pointless to do that. You have to teach people and show them how to do better.

Due to the significance of addictions and how rampant the problem still was, everyone still had a lot of work to do. That reminded Emerald that a lot of people who were making a lot of money off addicts didn't want to deal with the problem. A lot of politicians, government workers, and law enforcement personnel get paid to look the other way. Even though drug addiction doesn't discriminate and affects every walk of life from the rich to the poor, drug addicts are still judged and looked at as disgusting and hopeless. They have a very bad stereotype, which could be a reason people turn their backs on them. You have to have a lot of support to get over any sickness, especially a mental health disease. It's extremely challenging and sometimes impossible to overcome an illness on your own.

Emerald got back home, parked the car, and walked into the apartment. Mary was getting up and around.

"Hey lover," Emerald said. "I was just thinking about you."

"Were you?" Mary asked. "I hope it was good."

They hugged and kissed.

"I love you so very very much," Emerald said heartfeltly. "Thanks for putting up with me when I got addicted and sick."

"Thinking about the past again, are you? No problem. Just don't ever lie to me again. We are in this together as a team. No secrets. If you think about killing someone, I want to know, so we can talk about it before you do it. Depending on who it is, I may want in on that."

"You got it gorgeous. I know my weaknesses and limitations now. I still can't believe all that happened. What a nightmare."

"Yes, it was tough."

"Well, are you ready for a fun time with Christina and Eric?" Emerald asked.

"Actually, yes. It would be great to just spend it with you, but we haven't seen them in a while, so it will be good to catch up."

"We have a couple of hours before we have to be over there. Do you want to do something in the meantime?"

"Let's just chill out and read. I know you have been wanting to get back to your book for a bit. It's been busy."

"Yes. We could do that. I think it's been a week since I read my book. Since the weather is shitty, that would be good."

Emerald went to the bathroom, and Mary grabbed her book and sat down on the sofa and started reading. Emerald joined her a couple of minutes later. They had some conversations back and forth with what they were reading but nothing long and elaborate. Mary was reading a book on morals and ethics from a philosophical point of view, and Emerald was reading a book about quantum physics, which made Emerald think a lot about reality and how the universe works, especially from our perspective as humans.

Emerald made a bite to eat while they continued to read. Emerald continued to blurt out statements here and there with what she was reading, but again, there were no real conversations as they both just listened to or agreed with what the other was saying. Mary's comments focused on how people seemed to be basically good in nature as an individual but certain societal and community demands and problems led people to make unethical choices to either hurt themselves and/or others through either greed, stress, unhealthiness, trauma, or survival. Emerald's comments related to how our minds actually make up the world and the universe that we see and perceive and that everyone's view of reality is subjective and based on their perspectives through their biology and intellect, especially regarding to how they were raised. Emerald really liked this viewpoint because it gave her more power. With this view, she was ultimately in control of what she was seeing and there was lots of room to interpret things differently and recognize how brainwashed and programmed we were based on what others, such as parents, teachers, preachers, and politicians, have taught us.

"It's time," Emerald said.

"Sounds good."

Emerald and Mary got ready to go over to Christina's and Eric's house. They were going to have it at their apartment, but they hadn't been over to their new house, which they recently bought. Emerald got the impression from Christina that she wanted to show it off to them. Emerald reminded herself to not say anything about how stupid she thought loans and debts were and to be happy and supportive of their home, especially since they would be having a baby soon. Emerald thought that she would be able to be tame and not make too many offensive and provocative comments.

Emerald and Mary left the apartment and drove the car in the rain over to the house. On the way, they talked about Emerald's problems with loans and that she was glad they were renting and had a paid-for car. Mary agreed but said she would like a house even if they rented it outside of the city. Emerald expressed to Mary that she would be okay with that. As much as they liked their smaller city with its amenities, they really liked the country a whole lot more. They didn't want to be too far out of the city though.

They drove up to the house. It was in a subdivision, which Emerald despised. She didn't like how cramped they were and all the things that go along with living right next to so many people. She didn't think it was worth the price. Temporarily renting in a subdivision might be okay, but Emerald didn't agree with buying in one. Their house was a standard three-bedroom and two-bathroom house with a two-car garage. Luckily, they had a fence, and the house was only a few years old, so it should be pretty maintenance free for a while. It was half brick with white siding and had a couple of columns on the front porch. It was nice and welcoming. They knocked on the door, and Eric answered.

"What's up ladies?" Eric asked.

Christina immediately came over. They all hugged each other and engaged in greetings and small talk.

"What do you all want to drink?" Christina asked.

"I'm good," Emerald responded. "I brought mine with me."

Emerald had a glass of spring water.

"I'm good too," Mary said. "I'll just share with Emerald if I get thirsty."

"Hey Em, do you mind if I have a beer?" Eric asked considerately.

"Not at all. Go for it. Thanks for asking. Just don't break out the painkillers."

They all started laughing.

"You don't have to worry about that," Eric said. "I'm not sure if either one of us has had a prescription like that in a very long time. Maybe not even since I was a kid when I broke a bone."

Christina went to the kitchen to get a beer for Eric and something for herself. They all sat down in the living room. Emerald thought it was a relaxing setting with the soft lights. The house was a comfortable temperature and felt cozy. The paint was an off-white color, which Emerald liked, and they had a few but not a lot of pictures and paintings, which were decent and not too bold for the setting. Eric put on some music at a low volume. It was instrumental jazz with a guitar, so it was mellow and nice on the ears where they could still hear each other.

"So, Christina, congratulations!" Emerald said excitedly. "Eric told me the good news."

"Yes, congratulations!" Mary said. "It's been forever since we have seen you. It's been so long that a baby is on its way. Congratulations to you too Eric!"

"Thank you both so much," Christina said.

"Yes, thank you," Eric said.

"I'm excited and worried at the same time," Christina said. "So much to do and learn. So little time."

"We don't want to be unprepared," Eric said. "So, we are going to take advantage of the knowledge that's out there already and the mistakes that people have already made."

"That's good," Emerald said. "It's always good to be prepared."

"We have already read four books and joined a local group for support," Christina said. "The group helps me understand and practice my breathing, stretching, and relaxation techniques. Great people too."

"I like the group a lot," Eric said. "It's nice to talk to others who are further along with their pregnancies, and once a week, they have people who recently had a baby come back after the birth to discuss their struggles and to give advice. It's really great that they do that."

"That's fabulous," Mary said. "I bet some don't like doing that, but I guess you would feel obliged after getting the support and wisdom from others during the pregnancy."

"Yes, they said a lot don't come back to help the people going through the pregnancy, but it's enough to get a lot of suggestions to them and help them understand the issues that may arise," Christina said. "The two facilitators are great. They have a couple of kids of their own. They are both women, but they have their husbands come in once in a while to encourage and help the group, especially the guys."

"The facilitators have heard a lot of stories too, so they are a wealth of knowledge just in case the new parents don't deliver," Eric said.

"Do you all have any gays or lesbians in the group?" Emerald asked.

"Great question Em," Mary said.

"Actually, there are two gay guys in the group," said Eric. "They are so funny. They are definitely the life of the group. It's like they have no fear and are 100 percent positive about their baby. They have a surrogate who comes in with them."

"That's great," Mary said.

"I still wish people adopted more," Emerald said.

"There's the Em I know," Eric said. "I've been waiting for your honest comments. A lot of people do adopt Em. I don't know if it's enough, but yes, there are still an enormous amount of people having kids of their own. Probably too much."

"I know we are having one of our own, but I promise you Em, if we decide to have another, we will adopt," Christina said.

"Way to go you all," Mary said. "Just be careful in the meantime."

"Oh, we are going to make sure we don't get pregnant again," Christina said.

"No, you mean…" Mary said.

"No way Eric," Emerald said. "I wouldn't ever think you would."

"I am," Eric said. "Probably before she delivers. I'm going to have a vasectomy."

Emerald got up and gave Eric a big hug.

"You better go through with it, or I'll do it myself," Emerald said.

"Emerald, don't be so crude," Mary said. "But I agree."

"Oh, don't worry," Christina said. "I'll help you do it too. Last thing in the world that we would want is another accident and then to have three, four, or five like some people do. Absolutely irresponsible."

"I'll take care of it," Eric said. "Your threat does help Em because I know you are good for it, and you will follow through with what you know is right and good."

"I will," Emerald said.

"She will," Mary said.

"I approve," Christina said.

"Seriously though, overpopulation is a huge problem and one of the biggest threats to this planet and the survival of the human species and many other species," Emerald said. "It took humans over a million years to reach a billion people on this earth, and now, we are at about 10 times that amount in only a couple hundred years. That's insane. We shouldn't be adding a billion people to the population every 10 years. That's careless and immoral. What are we a virus? A plague?"

"Unbelievable," Eric said.

"That's crazy," Mary said. "I think the mortality rate is increasing too though, and the population is supposed to start declining or remaining stable."

"Yes, I'm sorry that we have contributed to that," Christina said.

"It's okay Christina," Emerald said. "I know you two will at least love and spoil the heck out of that little one. Unlike most kids, who the parents don't want them to begin with and then neglect and even abuse them. So many mothers are pressured and forced to have their kids. Then, the kid turns out to be a menace to society. All thanks to this illusory pressure and expectation to have a baby."

"Even if it is a mistake, the parents still have a responsibility and duty to love and take care of the child," Mary said.

"Absolutely," Christina said.

"Definitely," Eric said. "As much as I don't try to think about the bigger picture, I can see the population becoming unsustainable eventually. Who knows when though?"

"It already is, and there are too many people starving right now," Mary said. "There is pollution everywhere. In our water, land, and air. The amount of resources for the population right now is not covering it. Time will tell when the so-called developed nations start to have food shortages, increased pollution, and other resource depletions. Even though we can already see the significance, reality, and devastation of global warming and climate change, the deniers and liars will finally admit to it and accept it. You can't ignore science and the facts of the temperature rising, the erratic and abnormal weather patterns, increased natural disasters from the fierce weather and storms, ice caps and ice bergs melting, increased pollution, lack of resources, rising of the sea levels, and the increased prices of goods and services due to these problems. We are just lucky and live in a bubble, which is probably why a lot of people deny what is really going on with this world. Most people are so out of touch with the rest of the world. All they care about is money, food, new toys and other material items, games, sports, their jobs, and entertainment."

"It's crazy how many people deny our impact on the earth and our surroundings," Emerald said. "It's nuts that people still deny global warming and climate change. They would rather believe a lying and corrupt politician, who is most likely traditionalist and only cares about money and profits, over tens and hundreds of thousands of scientists. We have to have population control. We have to act now."

"I'm afraid of what may happen to our children and the future generations if we don't do something and be more aggressive to deal with those problems," Christina said. "We can't continue to be careless and neglect the impact that we are causing."

"I agree," Eric said. "I can see some devastation ahead. Disease, famine, and more war. It's inevitable."

"I know you all don't want to hear it, but that's why birth control and sex education are so important," Emerald said. "People can take that pointless and tired religious and political abortion argument and shove it up their asses."

"It doesn't make sense," Mary said. "It's a fact that has been proven time and time again that the less access that people have to birth control and sexual education and the less access that women have to safe and legal abortions actually increases the number of abortions and also increases the health risks and mortality rates for women."

"Don't forget that so many of the pro-lifers only care about fetuses and making women have the babies," Emerald said. "After the fetus is born, they could care less about the woman or the kids due to their support for pollution, increased use of fossil fuels and unsustainable resources, deforestation, animal agriculture, guns, military, and war. They also are supporting sex offenders, poverty, inequality, discrimination, abusive parents, and unprepared and uneducated parents to have kids. To me, that is supporting the neglect and abuse of children. Most of the parents didn't want to have the kids to begin with. I don't want to even get into the fact that so many women who get pregnant were raped and sexually assaulted, which is horrible and traumatic enough. A lot were on birth control too and were trying hard to not have a child, but the birth control failed. They shouldn't be forced to have that baby when they were actively trying to not have one. Then, you have a group, who are directed by traditionalist and religious men, who wants to force pregnant women to have a rape baby because they don't understand gestation and biology. They only understand myths and false and misinterpreted religious information, and they only see the babies and children as money making machines for them. The more consumers and workers there are in the world, the more money they make. Sorry guys. I'll try to calm down."

"It's okay Em," Christina said in a comforting tone. "We know how you feel. I was looking forward to you getting some of that out with us."

"Well, you have all these religious freaks trying to tell others, who don't believe in what they believe, what to do," Emerald said. "However, they are being hypocritical though because they believe in and practice other behaviors that make children and adults sick and kill others. That's why they are not really pro-life. They are really pro-birth. After the baby is born, they don't care what happens. Some pro-lifers might, but it's probably just lip service. They can't back it up with their actions. Fortunately, abortion is legal in our country, but you have false information about women getting abortions too late into their pregnancy. That is rare if it does happen. So, you have these pro-lifers trying to ban abortion, but they neglect the real issues that are making so many people sick and killing people, the animals, and the earth. More people die because of food and health related issues and other problems, such as guns, pollution, opiate and benzodiazepine prescriptions, other drugs and alcohol, genetically modified organisms, the poisons sprayed on the food, accidents from automobiles, and suicides. Why aren't they trying to ban those things that are more significantly killing children and adults than abortion? It doesn't make sense. Then, you have these so-called pro-lifers who are okay with in vitro fertilization and embryo transfer to get pregnant but hide the fact that about 25 percent of those fetuses are aborted. Again, it's hypocritical."

"We do see your point, but there should be some restrictions and regulations on abortion," Christina said. "It's not good if women are getting abortions too late and killing innocent babies."

"Even if the life of the mother is at stake?" Mary asked.

"That's a tough one," Eric said. "That's a tough one to make a law or regulation for."

"It's easy," Emerald said. "If the fetus is going to threaten the life of the mother, you abort it. There's no debate there. If you want, you can add that it's up to the physician and the mother, which it should be anyway without any biased political and religious group with their unscientific methods telling medical professionals what they can and cannot do. The traditionalist talking point of abortion is all about patriarchy and misogyny. These men spend billions a year to spread false propaganda that women are aborting babies right before they are supposed to have them, which is not true, to get people emotional about the issue. When in fact, the true goal is to control women, control women's bodies, and to make money off more people in the world. It's disgusting. I don't know why people can't see through the lies."

"What if there is some gray area?" Eric asked.

"That's what Emerald is saying," Mary said. "That's up to the mother or the parents and their doctor to decide. It's a private issue. If the doctor doesn't feel comfortable, they won't do it. That's the doctor's decision. It shouldn't be up to a male politician who is pushing their religious views, oppressive and sexist values, and erroneous and unfounded non-medical claims onto women. Religion has no part and is not supposed to have any part in politics. There is also no place for religion in medicine and healthcare either. There is supposed to be a separation of church and state for a reason because religion is not based on fact and is not evidenced based, and so many people have different religious views and beliefs. You can't say that your religious views should apply to someone else. Then, that gives other people a right to force their religious views and practices onto you. How would you like that?"

"Some doctors are now using their practices to spread their religious beliefs," Christina said. "Some won't even prescribe birth control or emergency contraception, such as morning after pills, and since there is nothing controversial about or wrong with prevention, that doesn't make sense."

"Totally," Emerald said. "I adamantly disagree with health professionals using their practices to spread religious values and non-scientific or unfounded claims and opinions onto their patients or clients. That is a recipe for disaster. Their licenses should get revoked. Church is for religion. Church and religion don't belong in the doctor's office, the government, or the business world. It's a private matter. If a particular religion is influencing those institutions or organizations to manipulate and affect the citizens, we are definitely living in a fascist dictatorship. Moreover, if you let one religion express itself that way and influence things that way, you have to let them all do that. If not, you don't have freedom or freedom of religion. Again, it would be a fascist dictatorship even though it's also called a theocracy. You can't say it's okay for one religion to be forced or pressured onto people and not the others. It's better that none are. Keep it in the church or at home. Keep it to yourself and keep it out of the laws."

"They should just start a church or cult and not be using medicine or other healthcare services to spread religious dogma," Mary said. "Medicine and healthcare are supposed to have bases in research and evidence through the scientific method. If you are not using best practices or researched practices, you are being negligent, careless, and unethical, and hurting the people. It's more about you and not about them. Their medical licenses should get revoked."

"Either way, I love that some countries and nations are passing laws to regulate how many children people can have," Emerald said. "That is so awesome and responsible. It makes sense. They are actually thinking about the future and how to help people, the animals, and the earth."

"I don't know Em," Eric said. "That sounds overkill."

"What do you think anti-abortion laws are?" Emerald asked. "That's overkill and invasive. It's crazy that traditionalists don't want more government laws and regulations, but when it applies to pushing unnecessary, false, and unfounded religious beliefs onto people, they are all for extra government with extra government spending and additional taxation to accomplish those goals. It's hypocritical. It's the same as being pro-life while being pro-overpopulation, pro-gun, pro-military, pro-war, pro-punishment, pro-pollution, pro-fossil fuels, and so on. It doesn't make any sense at all. The only sense that it makes is that it doesn't make sense because it's really about money and profits and has nothing to do with religion or helping people. It's a massive campaign based on psychological and emotional manipulation with religious propaganda to distract from the truth of greed and corruption. It supports misogyny and continues the horrible patriarchy."

"I can see where you are coming from, but it's not as black and white as you are making it out to be," Eric said. "There are a lot of traditionalists who have progressive ideas and care about humanity's future and the environment, but they can see the dangers and concerns of us moving into a too progressive society, which can lead to chaos, anarchy, and a big tyrannical government."

"Well, we have to do something," Christina said. "I don't like the government sticking its business in our lives, but we live in a society that has to have some laws and structure. You are going to agree with some laws and disagree with others. We do need a lot of sexual education, which absolutely does not lead to increased sexual intercourse by teenagers and increased pregnancy. We do need access to birth control, emergency contraceptives, and safe and legal abortions, which actually do keep all abortions at a minimum and reduces the number of overall abortions as compared to societies who do not have access to safe and legal abortions. As a proud traditionalist, it is very upsetting to me to hear someone be pro-life and anti-abortion while also being against us teaching sexual education to children and adolescents and giving out birth control. It is negligent and irresponsible."

"It is Christina," Emerald said. "And since we are discussing overpopulation, it is extremely important that everyone move to a plant-based diet and to being vegans."

"Here it goes," Eric said.

"Damn straight," Emerald said. "It's a fact that with the increase in population, animal agriculture is totally unsustainable and is contributing to the exhaustion and overuse of fossil fuels, decrease of farmlands needed to grow real and nutritious food, waste of water and water shortages, deforestation, and significant pollution of the land, air, and water. Did you know that about 60 to 70 percent of the grains that we grow go to feeding animals and not humans, but there are starving people in so many places who could use that food? Most of the agricultural land that is available is used for animals to be on and to grow food for them. If we took half, most, or all this land and grew fruits and vegetables on it instead, which are astronomically more nutritious and would feed so many more people, we would have at least 200 to 500 times more food to eat. Did I mention that the food would be better for us too? It wouldn't be a dead animal that has diseases and carcinogens, is highly acidic and toxic to the human body, and has hardly any nutritional value compared to fruits and vegetables. Since they feed cows and other animals mostly soy and corn, which they are not supposed to eat, like we are not supposed to be eating animals, it's causing mass pollution and sicknesses due to the soy and corn being made through genetically modified means while being sprayed with tons of herbicides, fungicides, and pesticides, which are polluting the land, air, and water. That's not pro-life. That is pro-death. Being plant based, vegan, pro-reproductive rights, anti-overpopulation, pro-renewable energies, and anti-fossil fuels is pro-life."

"Well said Em," Mary said. "I hope the world and our societies can take population control more seriously before it's too late. We may not experience the negatives of overpopulation before we die, but the other generations will. A lot of the world is already experiencing it. Unfortunately, most people choose not to act on something important until it directly impacts them."

"Sorry for being so intense guys," Emerald said. "That's something I am working on."

"No problem Em," Christina said. "It's always great to hear you and Eric argue and debate. You are both very civil to some extent, and you do listen to each other instead of calling each other names or storming off in a temper tantrum like some of our leaders do. They are supposed to be role models too. Children and teenagers act better than our leaders. I'm just glad there is some middle ground where we agree, and we are not too different."

"Yes, we love you both and are happy to spend time with you," Eric said. "Differences aside."

"I have to say that you both amaze me with your thoughts and responses considering your political stance," Emerald said.

"Well, we are traditionalist, but we are progressive," Christina said. "Just a little more traditionalist than progressive, but not by much."

"In my head, I like to think of extreme traditionalism as a dictatorship, authoritarian, fascist, controlling, and oppressive," Mary said. "On the other hand or on the other side of the spectrum, I think of extreme progressivism as anarchy with no laws or rules, which is interesting since traditionalists talk about wanting less government but their policies support more government and control. Real socialism and communism would be more progressive or on the left than the right. However, if the socialist or communist leaders and government begin to rule as a dictator or an authoritarian, that is no longer considered a socialist or communist government and would immediately be called a traditionalist or fascist government. The same goes for a republic and a democracy too. Loosely speaking of course. However, it is interesting that civilian traditionalists see anarchy as scary but not fascism. We don't know what the effects of anarchy are as we have always been under some sort of rule, but we know what fascism does. It's brutal and abusive. It's never okay. I would choose anarchy over fascism any day."

"We do try to be open minded Mary, and we don't support fascism or a dictatorship," Eric said. "I don't support anarchy either. That whole socialism and communism debate is very confusing and frustrating. Christina and I do support lower taxes or less taxes and less government. I do think that less regulation of businesses is a good thing for free market purposes. It allows room for growth and healthy competition."

"How has that healthy competition and lack of regulation worked out for us?" Emerald asked. "It seems every time we turn around that we are in another recession and are facing another possible depression due to the unethical and unscrupulous politicians and businesses. The first chance they get they are committing fraud and conning and swindling citizens out of their money. They raise their prices, which increases inflation, while wages stay the same. In addition and to make some more money, the companies send jobs to other countries so they can pay lower wages, have less regulations, and avoid taxes. Thanks to these traditionalist business strategies, the economy eventually goes into the shitter, and the traditionalist government then raises taxes and borrows a buttload of money, which the poor and middle class have to pay back. Conveniently and since the companies end up failing and for some reason going broke after all this deregulation, the government and the politicians, who also own these greedy companies, use the borrowed money to help their companies and make themselves rich while everyone is struggling because of the choices that they made. It's a win for them and a loss for everyone else. You can also argue that they still get bailed out when they made a profit anyway, but for some reason, they say they are hurting. To top it all off, the citizens have to pay for everything and didn't want the companies doing whatever they wanted to do to begin with. Not to mention that the traditionalists are anti-welfare and anti-government spending. Yet, they are the ones approving and accepting the government handout, and all of it could have been prevented to begin with if the government did what it was supposed to do by regulating the conniving and insidious businesses. It's called checks and balances. You have to have regulation. That is my take. Did I miss anything?"

"What a great speech Em," Mary said. "I think you hit the nail on the head. It does seem like we always end up in a recession and on the verge of a depression after traditionalist leadership deregulates consumer protection agencies to let the businesses do whatever they want to do. It is interesting that the politicians, who own interest in those companies or who are getting bribed and lobbied with lots of money from these companies, let the companies run free and then have the taxpayers pay for their mistakes. After it's all said and done, no one is really held accountable. A citizen can be charged with a crime for doing something that horrible, but a company and its owners or managers get off free and clear. It's very upsetting. If no one is held accountable, it's going to happen again and again. That's the definition of insanity."

"It's sad the way things have gone, and the way things are," Christina said. "These governments, businesses, the wealthy, and the rich have enough money to change the world several times over and do some significant good. They could create sustainability, focus on renewable energy, create better and honest education, and have all organic farms. They could prevent crimes, drug addiction, pollution, poverty, inequality, hunger, sickness, death, and homelessness. So, what do they do? They focus on making money and doing horrible things to make money. That's how evil they are. Unfortunately, they are both progressive and traditionalist."

"They are both progressive and traditionalist," Mary said.

"We don't support illegal acts by companies," Eric said. "Not all companies are engaging in criminal acts or are being unethical."

"I think that's the point though," Emerald said. "Look at what the companies do when they are allowed to do whatever they want to do. It's not pretty to watch. You have to have regulation, especially when money is involved. People go crazy over money and so do the businesses. Following regulations shouldn't matter if you are being good and doing what you are supposed to be doing anyway. You have to have government oversight because it turns into them trying to make more and more money and a bigger and bigger profit at the expense of the workers, the environment, the other companies, the economy, the citizens, the consumers, and the nation or society itself. It's absolutely disgusting. It's like they have things that people want or need. They have a product that they could make really well, and it would be a great product. They put a reasonable yet profit-making price on it, but then they start thinking about how to make more money, so they decide that the product's quality needs to get watered down to increase profits. It's not enough for them to make millions, they want to make billions. They will do whatever it takes to do that even if they have to manipulate and pay off the politicians to either pass laws to protect them or to look the other way."

"Yes, I do have to say, maybe not always on the local level but almost always on the national or federal level, there is definitely a lot of political corruption with the businesses paying them off," Mary said. "It seems like the rich and powerful and their businesses bribe the politicians a lot. They call it lobbying or campaign contributions, but it's bribery and is not okay. It's crazy that the people have let the bribery, campaign contributions or donations, or so-called lobbying go on this long. We all know that the companies and the rich have more say than the general population does. They can give millions and billions to the politicians to do things, we can't. Even though we elected them and they said that they were going to do what is right and to help us, once they get into office, they do what is best for them, the rich, and the companies. It's like the companies are just paying the politicians to focus on laws to help them and the rich to make more money at the expense of the people. They even pay the consumer protection agencies to approve unsafe products or to look the other way while they destroy and pollute the earth. They also practice cronyism and appoint unqualified friends, family members, and business associates to political and judicial positions, which is very dangerous and has a long-lasting negative effect on so many things in society. It's all so disgusting and unfortunate. Why can they get away with all this corruption and bribery? It should be so illegal to do all these horrible things."

"It is unfortunate Mary," Eric said. "The sad fact is that both progressives and traditionalists engage in these horrible practices and allow themselves to get bribed by money. The crazy thing is that a lot of the same companies and rich people give a lot of money to both the progressives and traditionalists. It's like they want their bases covered in case the other party doesn't win, so they can still get what they want. It definitely influences the elections and the laws at the expense of the people."

"It's ludicrous how much money politicians are raising these days with their campaigns to get elected," Christina said. "It's insane. They could do so much good with that money. It's all wasted to make someone richer and to go towards a dishonest and manipulative advertising and marketing campaign. What a waste. I heard that a lot of money that the politician gets during their campaign is from rich people and companies. They say that it's from individual donors, but it's not due to the secrecy and shadiness of the campaign finance laws. Companies are not even supposed to be allowed to give to a politician, but they do. They just call it something else, such as a committee, which is supposed to be legal even though it's not. To me, a committee is not an individual, so how do they get away with that? And if you think the people within the regulatory agency that oversees the elections and politicians' campaigns haven't been paid off or aren't getting a piece of the pie, you are just as stupid as can be. It's interesting how wealthy the politicians are. They don't even come close to representing us. They make more money in a few years in office than we will see in our entire lives. They have regulations and laws to only allow citizens to donate so much money to a politician for a reason. It's not okay that they can bend the rules and create committees and let companies and the rich donate massive amounts of money to their campaigns and lobby them to bribe them to pass laws that favor them and not the majority of the population. It has to stop. There's no point in having rules, laws, and regulations if you are going to let the rich and companies bend them and find loopholes to still manipulate and influence the politicians to vote for and pass laws to help them out. It's pure insanity."

"Then, when the companies fail or get into trouble, the politicians, who were paid by those companies, bail them out," Emerald said. "But let's not worry about all the people who are poor and all the people who are struggling and living paycheck to paycheck to get by, which is most of the population. Donations, campaign contributions, lobbying, whatever you want to call it, are all bribes. Plain and simple."

"Since they are bribing the politicians, it's not surprising that the companies are allowed to get away with what they do get away with, such as low wages, pollution, low quality products and services, and lack of employee benefits or unsafe working environments," Mary said.

"Unfortunately, we have to accept that the government and the politicians are ruled by the rich and the businesses," Emerald said. "Their intentions are not to help citizens and the communities."

"That's a pretty bleak view Em," Eric said. "There are some good politicians."

"Really?" Emerald asked. "To me, the devil is either a salesman, attorney, or a politician. Who is sleazier and will lie more or do more for a certain amount of money is the debate. We do not live in a republic or democracy. It's more of an oligarchy. More specifically, some would call it an aristocracy, plutocracy, or particracy. You can also throw in a splash of theocracy when the traditionalists are more dominant in the government. We vote for politicians, but it's usually between two opposing candidates of two political parties. They are usually in the position that they are in due to being related to certain family members, being famous, having money and wealth, and/or having worked for certain businesses. You could also say that we live in a bankocracy and corporatocracy at this point as the politicians have a price, which is why they have the stereotypes of being liars and hypocrites due to promising one thing to the people or the citizens who vote them in and then they do something totally different that makes them richer, makes others richer, and helps the companies get more profits. Immediately after he is elected, you can spot a dictator and a horrible leader by how quickly he passes laws or signs executive orders to lower taxes for the rich and companies and deregulate the consumer protection agencies. These laws and orders were not supported by the people and were not approved by the other parts of government, which is necessary for checks and balances. It's tyrannical. Why don't they immediately sign executive orders to reduce and eliminate poverty, reduce and stop pollution, increase wages for people, stop discrimination and abuse, stop addictions, and stop gun violence and other crimes. He promised to help the people, but after he was elected, he does the opposite. If that happens, it is up to the people to rise up and start a revolution to forcibly remove him because the rest of the politicians will not as they will be getting rich off of his laws too. Even the ones who hail to a different political party will not stand up to him because they are getting rich and benefiting too. They may say they disagree with the dictator or tyrant, but they don't do much about it. It's not okay. It's just a matter of time before we have a rebellion and a revolution due to the lies and corruption. I'll keep voting, but elections are a joke. You also know you are living in a dictatorship and under the rule of a tyrannical government when they allow voting at churches. That is an absolute disgrace to the foundation of separation of church and state. A lot of the churches where people have to vote at even have their own traditionalist propaganda outside of the churches during election time. How is that okay? How is that legal? Why do I feel like I'm the only one who sees the corruption and problem with that? It should not be okay to have elections at a church. It's fucking insane. It's time to revolt."

"I would have to agree with you on that one Em," Christina said. "That one even blows my mind. There are many other non-partisan places to let people vote at. People could vote at libraries, schools, convention centers, and so on. I'm sure most of the traditionalists would not be okay with voting at an abortion clinic, renewable energy company, or vegan store."

"True that," Emerald said.

"Don't forget how political positions and elections are set up to attract wealthy and affluent people to get elected," Mary said.

"What do you mean?" Eric asked.

"Well, the problem with campaigns is that you have to raise a shitload of money to advertise, so that leaves out the poor and a lot of the middle class, which is most of the population. It's not a fair process, and I'm not even going to get into how corrupt it is to only have a couple of parties that most elected officials are a part of. Most candidates are usually well-to-do and rich people. Depending on the level or the political position, there should be a capped amount with how much you can raise for your campaign to make it fair for poor and middle-class people to run a campaign. The wealthy people are even allowed to use their own money. So, if you are a millionaire or billionaire, how is that fair? You could run a shitty campaign and hardly raise any money, but you can still be at the top of the polls because people vote for who they see from the advertisements and who they are familiar with. They may not even have the same values as the politician. They just know who they are. That's the problem with celebrities running for office. They have no experience and are probably going to do more harm than good, but people will vote for them over a qualified and more intelligent candidate because they are familiar with the celebrity."

"I agree," Emerald said.

"Don't forget that some nations have it rigged where the citizens have an election and vote for one person and then a smaller group of representatives have their election, which can overrule and vote for someone that the citizens did not elect," Mary said. "How awful is that? So, the citizens decide on a politician through an election process, then, another group of people can vote and elect someone else because the other candidate paid them more money. How is that democracy? It's not. It's awful. Those are truly illegitimate officials. They didn't win the election. I only recognize politicians who were voted in by the majority of the population and not a specific group of biased and unknown people who don't represent the general population."

"I'm familiar with that process," Eric said. "It does seem contrary to democracy, but it's supposed to assist with giving areas with less population or rural areas an equal vote."

"But it's not who actually won, and the representatives can be influenced and bought, which is not democratic at all and nullifies the general election and our votes," Mary said with passion in her voice. "It also leaves it up to only two main parties. Do you think these representatives are going to vote for someone who is different, doesn't have as much money to pay them, and isn't a part of the major political parties? To me, the election becomes a fraud when you have another paid-for group that can override the citizens. The election becomes a sham and does not represent what the people want. It is decided by the rich and wealthy. It's corruption."

"They are probably not going to vote for a different political party or a politician who is hailing to a minor or lesser known party," Eric said. "Some countries have been using that process since the they started as a nation. Most of the time, the representatives do choose the winner of the popular vote, but sometimes they choose the person who lost, which is suspicious."

"That's not good enough," Mary said. "We the people and the citizens do not need someone else who is bought and paid for to override our votes, so they can elect someone to make them rich and not help the citizens. It's time to change. I think the people voting is enough. The citizens shouldn't get overruled by a group of people we know nothing about. That's very shady. It's also shady that locally elected politicians can redraw local maps, such as gerrymandering, that include more citizens who vote for their party to keep their party in power longer. It's also shady that we allow them to purge voter registrations of mostly minorities and actual votes after an election by voters who voted for the other party during an election. All these behaviors are election fraud. It's not okay. They do that all the time."

"That's all shady," Christina said. "I haven't thought much about some of those processes. Those problems definitely need to be addressed. I thought of another issue. What about all the mudslinging and lies on the media by the politicians? That is out of control. It's definitely not democratic if politicians and groups spread lies and make stuff up about their opponents. They even do that in the primaries against their own party members. Even if they are my political party of choice, I can't stand watching a candidate or politician intentionally lie. I also can't stand watching their groups or associations intentionally lie about their opponents. It's sickening. I have stopped voting for politicians who say erroneous and disparaging things to others. I won't vote for them. I know it doesn't leave many for me to choose, but at this point, I would rather vote for a lesser known person from a minor party or who is an independent than one of the two major political candidates who are most likely going to win. We need to support the other minor parties and uncorrupted politicians."

"It is hard to watch," Eric said. "I wish they weren't allowed to do that. Very unprofessional and unethical. It's crazy how all professions have a code of ethics, but politicians don't have a code of ethics and don't follow an ethical code. The ethics committee in the government doesn't do anything and is a total joke. I think politicians should have to get licensed or certified and answer to a board and a code of ethics for them to be a politician."

"That is a great idea Eric," Emerald said.

"Man, they have been mudslinging for so long," Mary said. "It's like lying, manipulating, and saying mean and nasty things about your opponent is encouraged."

"You know why they do that don't you?" Emerald asked.

"So you get a bad image of the opponent," Eric responded.

"To some extent, yes," Emerald said. "In psychology, it's called avoidance and diversion or distraction. People who talk bad about others usually have a problem or issue going on with them that they don't want you to know about. So, by not talking about themselves or what they are going to do to properly address the issues or problems, which they probably have no idea how to fix anyway, they try to find something that can't be immediately or easily disproven about their opponent. It could be a flat out lie, a small issue that is blown out of proportion, something that is taken out of context, or an exaggeration, Unfortunately, a lot of people are stupid and gullible, so they believe it, especially if it's about the political party that they don't usually support. So, the next time you hear someone say something bad about someone else, they are really admitting that they have those problems and issues or something similar to them."

"They may have deep psychological issues, but they are still mean assholes and jerks," Mary said.

"Definitely," Emerald said.

"It goes to show you how impressionable and gullible people are if they believe that crap and get sucked into believing hateful and negative comments about others," Christina said.

"The power of repetition and hearing the same thing over and over again, even if it's wrong or false, is also very convincing," Emerald said. "The politicians know that too. They use that manipulation tool all the time on the suckers who don't question whether what they are hearing is correct or not. We have leaders at the highest level of our government right now who just keep saying over and over again that they don't and didn't do anything wrong, so their brainwashed followers end up getting manipulated and believing them over the facts and evidence that prove beyond a shadow of a doubt that they are guilty and did do something wrong and criminal. It shows you how gullible and stupid people really are."

"I can see that," Eric said. "It's the same with a company advertising a product, but instead of selling sweets to kids, the lies are the sweets and the adults are the kids. We are like kids getting manipulated into buying candy or other unhealthy food products. For adults, they are using dishonest political ads."

"It's the same with alcohol, prescriptions, insurance, restaurants, clothes, and other crap you don't need," Mary said. "The list goes on and on."

"Sorry Eric, but all that dishonest advertising and marketing by lying companies needs to be regulated somehow," Christina said. "The media companies need to take responsibility for letting the lying people and companies use their platforms to spread lies and misinformation. If you take money from a criminal and a liar and let them commit their crime through you, you are complicit and an associate. There has to be some accountability by the media for letting people and companies intentionally lie through their platforms. If you paid a person to lie for you, they would be guilty too. What is the difference between the two? Why can a company get away with not taking responsibility when an individual has to take responsibility and be held accountable for the same thing? The last time I checked slander and libel were illegal. You can't just make up stuff about someone. Unfortunately, people trust the media and news to report the truth, for the most part. There has to be some integrity with what we are exposed to. If you are going to say something critical about someone, you have to have proof or evidence with a source or reference. You also can't just put someone down when you are in an elected or professional position. That should get you automatically expelled, fired, or impeached by violating your oath to honesty, professionalism, dignity, and integrity."

"Proof?" Emerald asked. "Don't forget that so many traditionalist politicians have beliefs that don't have any proof or evidence. They don't believe in the scientific method of making sure you have evidence before you accept something as fact or possible. It's not surprising that they spout off so many lies as they don't think they need to have evidence to support their beliefs. I know some progressives do it too, but it's not as many as the traditionalists."

"I'm not even going to go there Em," Eric said. "That's a huge debate on who lies more, so all I will say is that it's sad that people lie and there are people who believe the lies. The citizens have to take responsibility too."

"What?" Emerald said. "For being idiots. You can't blame the survivors and victims of abuse. That is what you are trying to do with that statement. They don't know any better Eric. You can't blame the cult followers for the manipulation and lies of the charismatic cult leader. You can hold the followers accountable for engaging in bad, negative, illegal, or abusive behaviors that they engage in because of the cult leader but not for believing the lies that they were told. That's a thought crime, which is not okay, and avoidance of responsibility. Now, if the followers start doing illegal and abusive things for the leader, the followers should definitely be held accountable."

"I agree with Em Eric," Mary said. "Maybe you didn't mean it like that, and I agree to some degree that we have to hold adults responsible for being gullible to some extent and for not being too bright, but blaming citizens for getting manipulated by the awful and evil politicians is like being an offender supporter. You are taking the responsibility off the person or people you need to blame and hold accountable the most. You wouldn't say that to a rape survivor or a child who was abused. You wouldn't say that it's their fault for being abused because of what they were wearing, how they looked, or what they said. Oh wait, people do say those things to abuse victims."

"Maybe you are right," Eric said. "Maybe that came out wrong."

"It's not good to blame the cult members who were all manipulated to commit suicide by the charismatic, disingenuous, and conniving cult leader," Emerald said. "You have to blame the cult leader."

"I got you," Eric said. "I was just saying that's the downfall of a democratic society is that you get people who make their choice and vote. If the less intelligent or immature or impressionable voters, if you like those terms, have the majority and vote in an idiot, moron, greedy bastard, dictator, or tyrant, we all have to accept that and deal with it. Right?"

"Well said honey," Mary said. "Good comeback. We do have to take responsibility and work together to overcome that mistake and hopefully not make it again. Some say our leaders, as bad as they may be, are a reflection of the people."

"Still, it's not okay to lie, mudsling, avoid responsibility, blame, and give impractical, vague, or no solutions to the problems that we are facing," Emerald said. "Most politicians do not have a concrete and practical plan to help us. There is no real reason to vote for them other than we don't have any other choices and we have to choose the lesser of the two evils. Unfortunately, there is more reasons to not vote for them, but we have to vote for someone, or do we?"

"I think that they want voters to either be apathetic, not vote, or vote out of fear and hate," Mary said. "People don't make rational or good decisions when they are filled with those kinds of emotions. It's confusing and biased."

"They use that to their advantage," Emerald said. "The bigotry, inequality, sexism, racism, xenophobia, heterosexism, homophobia, and other discriminations are out of control. Most politicians are male, which is incongruent with the population, and the males call women names, such as bitches and emotional, and focus on their looks and what they wear to degrade them. The media lets the men do that too by saying what they said and focusing on women's looks instead of what they are trying to say and talk about, which is almost always better than what the male politician have to say. It's awful and disgusting. If men were treated the same way as women, they would be called worse names as they are more temperamental and emotional than women are, but people see that as aggression and confidence instead of bitchiness and emotional. It's also wrong that the traditionalists call the minorities names and make hate speeches towards minorities and women. It's not okay. The people need to stop supporting this misogyny, bigotry, and patriarchy."

"Unfortunately, it makes people not vote," Christina said. "I think about only half of the eligible voters actually vote. Sometimes, it's way less than that depending on the election or what positions people are voting for. Most elections don't represent what the people want. They only represent what the voters want, which may not be what the general population needs."

"So, you have these lies and manipulations out there to also play on people's fears, insecurities, and hate," Mary said. "These put-downs distract the public from what we like to call the major issues or the important issues, so everyone focuses on the non-issues or the minor issues."

"What do you mean?" Eric asked.

"Haven't you noticed that the politicians don't talk about real issues?" Mary responded. "Some even deny them, such as pollution, global warming, climate change, human's impact on the earth and environment, discrimination and inequality, rape and sexual assault, the negative effects of fossil fuels, and so on. If they do admit to them, they don't offer concrete solutions and plans to resolve or deal with them. They spend more time blaming, focusing on others, and putting others down. That is a sign of an awful and horrible leader, political candidate, or politician. You shouldn't ever vote for politicians who say mean things about others, deny and avoid the real issues, and don't talk about themselves and focus on the real issues with practical solutions to our problems."

"I can see that," Eric said.

"They do avoid those issues," Emerald said. "Pollution is a huge one. There are so many that they don't focus on. There is overpopulation, overcrowding in jails and prisons, crime."

"Healthcare, the economy, the nation's deficit and debt, poverty, sicknesses and diseases due to the unhealthy foods people are eating and their sedentary lifestyles, the horrors and destruction of animal agriculture, suicide, and the ridiculously high military budget," Christina said. "The military budget is so unnecessarily high. The politicians can't seem to find money to help the citizens and the people, but they can find billions to fund needless military and government contracts that conveniently go to the politicians' companies. So, they are basically getting rich while others suffer. They are abusing their powers. It's not okay that politicians, their family members, or their cronies can have ownership in companies that receive government funds. That is a huge conflict of interest. They do it all the time, and if they are not the owners, their friends, cronies, and family members are, which is favoritism. That is not okay either. How many contests have you seen where you cannot enter the contest if you or your family member is an employee or associate of the company who is putting on the contest? That is a rule because it prevents favoritism, fraud, dishonesty, and nepotism from someone cheating, but we don't have that rule for something as important as the government and society and the taxes that we pay. That's our money damnit."

"I do support the military," Eric said. "We do need some protection, but I'm not sure where the limit is to make sure we are totally protected. It does seem that the military budget is pretty high, especially if we are suffering domestically with ghettos, unsanitary living conditions, poverty, drugs, and high crime. The inequality, all the types of discrimination, and the sexual assaults and rapes really bother me too."

"Now, you're getting it Eric," Emerald said. "The government's priorities are all wrong. They say they are going to take care of us to get elected but look at what they actually do. It's not what they said they were going to do. They spend more time and energy putting money into the military, pushing bullshit and unfounded religious agendas, letting the companies do whatever they want to do at the expense of consumers and the earth, and reducing taxes for the rich and the companies. We have these huge cities and highly populated urban areas that need serious attention. And, it is totally racist and discriminatory that they neglect areas that have high numbers of minorities living there. The racists will say that those people want to live in those shitty conditions when it's actually because the government spends way more money on where the wealthier people live because they give more money to their campaigns. Again, it's not about helping people, it's about making money and helping the people who have the most money. There are so many other issues too like the inevitable depletion of fossil fuels and the pollution that comes from getting these fossil fuels, such as drilling, mining, and fracking. We have solutions for clean, sustainable, and environmentally friendly renewable energies, such as solar, wind, tidal, wave, and geothermal. It's ridiculous that we are not focusing on those sources 100 percent of the time. It's insane that we are not using renewable energies 100 percent of the time. We should have accomplished that a long time ago."

"Don't forget about the sad and pathetic educational system and the ever polluting and unsustainable animal agriculture industry," Mary said. "In addition and for the most part, the military and law enforcement are protecting the government and the companies and not the people and the citizens. That would suggest that we are being ran by an authoritarian government."

"That's a lot of issues," Eric said. "The more we talk, the more issues we bring up. I think we have created more problems than we can deal with at this point."

"The growing number of issues is proof of the lack of progress and that the politicians are not doing anything," Emerald said. "It's karma for us as a nation. So many countries and their governments already have so much negative energy flowing against and through them due to them revolting over the previous government and/or murdering, raping, and abusing the millions of natives that were on the land before they took it over and stole it from them. Our countries were created by abusing and killing others, so it makes sense that we will pay for those crimes."

"That is true," Mary said. "That is not good karma for any nation. The reality is that most countries and their governments are founded on horrors and unspeakable acts of crimes against humanity. The politicians and leaders try their best to avoid those issues. Our past is shrouded in horrors, shame, and guilt."

"So, what would they rather talk about?" Christina asked. "Instead of all those issues we have been talking about that are of the utmost importance and need to be discussed and dealt with, they spend all their time putting others down, which says more about them than the others they are focusing on."

"Some do talk about some of the issues," Eric said.

"If they do, they are either denying the issues or they give a vague recognition of them with an impractical plan to deal with them," Mary said.

"I think a lot of those issues are very controversial, so they don't focus on them because it would turn off a lot of voters," Eric said.

"I agree with you that you have to present yourself a certain way to get votes, but that goes back to the argument of the voters being impressionable," Emerald said. "If they are gullible and impressionable, you should be able to present controversial topics like ones we have been talking about in a way to deal with them in practical manners. It would be better if the politicians focused on the issues rather than spending time putting others down while focusing on non-issues, such as abortion, guns, homosexuality, terrorism, and immigration."

"Some of those are major issues," Eric said.

"Yes, I would agree that they are," Christina said.

"That's my point though," Emerald said. "They are symptoms and minor compared to the other issues that are not primarily focused on. If the major issues, such as inequality, classism, pollution, overpopulation, racism, sexism, heterosexism, homophobia, other types of discrimination, and slave labor were addressed and resolved, these non-issues would decrease. They are talking points and could be considered emotional issues that get people upset but do nothing to deal with our problems. They are problems but are not solutions. You can't just talk about the problems. You have to act and do something about them, which has nothing to do with increasing the military's budget, decreasing taxes for the rich and the companies, making the rich wealthier and the poor poorer, intentionally destroying the environment, polluting the earth, killing and abusing billions of helpless and defenseless animals every week, and continuing to let people get abused, raped, and sexually assaulted. Why do you think they mainly focus on those non-issues?"

"Because they don't know how to fix anything, and they don't want to look like an idiot when they are asked what they are going to do about the real problems," Mary said.

"Good one," Christina said.

"Yes, they don't know how to fix anything," Emerald said. "But there is a better answer. It's because they want to divide people. They want to divide and conquer. It's a political strategy that has been proven to help them win their elections. Unfortunately, you can lose an election by being the smart, tame, and cool candidate. However, you are more likely to win by being passionate, mean, controversial, and temperamental. By riling people up and angering others, you get a devoted base who will vote for you no matter what. Even if you are an idiot, lie through your teeth, cheat on your spouse, abuse people, grope and sexually assault women, steal people's money, obstruct justice, conspire with foreign governments, and screw everything up, you will have followers who will support you through all of that because you have the same views as them and they see themselves in you. However, if the politician or leader from the opposing political party even did one of those things, they would want them impeached and locked up. So, these idiots have some false connection with the moronic tyrant of a leader, and/or they think he is some chosen one by their god. They end up giving him a free pass to rape and murder without any consequences. Again, if it was a leader or politician from the opposing party, they would denounce and condemn him. That's how stupid people are. They would rather support and vote for a horrible, evil, and moronic human being who shares the same bigoted views as them but doesn't know how to help them rather than vote for someone who does know how to help them but they see them as different than them or like a tree hugging hippie."

"A lot of people do seem to hate tree hugging hippies for some reason," Eric said.

"It's unfortunate since they are trying to help so many people and things," Mary said. "Why do people hate others who are for peace and love? It doesn't make sense."

"It doesn't make sense, but it shows us how horrible people really are," Emerald said. "Since these non-issues, such as abortion and guns, are popular and controversial topics, they are used as a manipulation tool for fear and hate to get people out of the middle and on one side or the other. However, you will notice that as they may support a topic or issue that you agree with, they don't have a plan or any real solutions to deal with the problems that we are facing. These politicians usually don't accomplish anything that helps society and most of the population of the nation. Since they blame the other party and others for everything, their followers will always believe that it wasn't their fault as to why they couldn't accomplish anything or why the economy got so bad because the country went into a recession or depression or why drugs and crime are so bad or why there are so many white male traditionalists shooting and killing minorities and their own citizens or why health care and other needed goods and services are so expensive or why pollution is so bad. Their followers will always believe it was the other party's or politician's fault, or they will just flat out deny that these issues are happening. Even if that horrible politician and leader was in that position for a few to several years, his supporters will not hold him accountable. It's very misleading and manipulative."

"It is manipulative and very evil to play with people's emotions while lying to them and then stabbing them in the back," Mary said. "I wanted to add that most of these wealthy and affluent politicians are also not qualified to be politicians. A few may have some experience with the government or some experience from being an attorney, but so many are just charismatic and well-known people. So many are not even successful. Most rich people didn't bust their asses to make their money. It was inherited from their parents or other family members. So, they seem like they are successful or that they themselves made their wealth, but they didn't. They got lucky. So, voting for most of these politicians is like voting for the most popular kid in school. You know, the one who is not the best choice or the brightest of the bunch, but they are popular and put themselves out there, so people vote for them just because they are popular and present themselves well. Unfortunately, it's a front and a huge scam, and politicians who are or were business owners and managers are the worst. They only care about themselves and money. The proof that all these politicians don't know what they are doing and that they are a fraud is in the reality of what is going on with all these problems and issues that we have been spouting off. I'm not going to list them all again, but we have some serious and significant problems to deal with that they are not dealing with. I don't think they know how to deal with them, and they don't want to deal with them. Most don't even want to talk about them. And, don't forget that a lot of serial killers and cult leaders are charismatic, affluent, popular, charming, and manipulative. I think most of our politicians are also sociopaths and psychopaths. Did I mention that business owners and managers make the worst politicians? That also includes the billionaires and millionaires who try to be politicians. They are horrible politicians."

"Something does need to change, and something needs to be done very soon," Christina said.

"This political mess is definitely a monster that we have created," Eric said. "I would hope that if there was a solution that we would have implemented it, but it's very complex."

"It is complex, but it's not impossible, and we shouldn't try just because of how complicated and challenging it is," Emerald said. "It is going to take a multi-systemic approach on a lot of levels, but I think the fact that we have proven we are not living in a true democracy says a lot about why we have so many problems."

"And, it's not democratic for elected and non-elected or appointed government positions to not have term limits," Eric said. "Some are even life-long positions. What kind of shit is that? As a traditionalist, that doesn't even make sense to me. I do respect diversity and change. Not having term limits suggests and implies authoritarian and dictatorship rule with their position or department. They may not be the ultimate ruler or have the highest position in the nation, which definitely should have term limits, but the fact that so many politicians can be elected again and again until they die or be elected or nominated once and hold that position until they die is not democratic. It's important for us to have term limits for all branches of the government. I think anything more than several years is too much. Ten at the most."

"Totally," Christina said. "Some of our politicians are at least 70 years old. Some are 80 years old. That's ridiculous. I love old people and the geriatric population, but our life expectancy is about 80 years old with so many men and some women dying earlier than that. Something happens to you cognitively after you reach 60 and 70 years old and definitely when you are 80 years old. I love my parents and my grandparents, but I wouldn't want to ride in a car with them or trust them to drive a car. I definitely wouldn't trust them with running a nation or part of the government where people's lives depend on their judgments. There is even a lot of concerns that most of the politicians are alcoholics and abusing uppers, such as cocaine and amphetamines, and we all know that the elderly take a shitload of medications, which have many side effects."

"That is true Christina," Emerald said. "Great point."

Christina continued, "You are not in the right mind when you get to a certain age. People start to forget and misplace things, and they become temperamental. They don't have the best decision-making skills. We aren't even giving these politicians psychological tests to see if they are emotionally and mentally competent and able to do these jobs. Politicians have one of the most important jobs in the world, and we are just blindly trusting that they have it all together based on a couple of meetings, debates, and their shady advertising and marketing campaigns. They should have age limits too. If not, everyone, no matter the age, should have to take psychological tests every year to assess their emotional and mental competence. I think we should just do the tests no matter the age. I think we would find that many adults who are younger or in their 30s and 40s are not even competent. Before you even get to be on the ballot to be elected, I want to see your personal and businesses taxes, background check, drug test, psychological tests, and a recent physical or medical exam. That's what you have to do to be a public politician."

"Those are great," Emerald said.

"Well said," Mary said.

"You said it babes," Eric said. "It is also upsetting how taxed we are. The government needs to live within their means like they expect the citizens to do. The politicians seem to always vote for things that the citizens do not agree with. I do agree that there are a lot of traditionalists who say they are going to lower taxes and they don't. People seem to forget the politicians' campaign promises. They are manipulative. That would be great if there was a convenient place for voters or citizens to go that said what the politicians promised they would do, what they actually did or whether they accomplished those things, and the legislation that they voted on. I think a lot of people would see the hypocrisy and be appalled at what the politician actually voted for. Right now, it's too difficult to determine the performance of the politician. You are left with trusting their word and trying to figure out if they caused the good and the bad things to happen, which is hard to know sometimes."

"Since people are so enslaved with work, it's challenging to spend time to properly research politicians, so people just choose their political party of choice across the board," Mary said. "That is a horrible and dangerous way to vote. Those people should not be allowed to vote. Shame on those people. Just like a test, you shouldn't be allowed to vote if you are not prepared. They should have all that stuff you were talking about Eric on the election ballot with a resume that was verified by an independent and non-partisan third party."

"We need to be choosing the best person for the job," Emerald said. "Not the one who raised the most money, is a celebrity, is the most popular or wealthiest, or is a member of the two main or most well-known parties."

"That's true Em," Christina said. "Hey dear, what were you saying about the taxes? I don't think we hit on the taxation problem enough."

"There is just taxation everywhere," Eric said. "People are supposed to live within their means and can't create money out of nothing like the government does, but the government doesn't live within their means and creates money out of nothing because they can't get their shit together. Spending and borrowing are out of control. Most of it just goes right into the bank accounts of the politicians, their friends and family, their cronies, and the wealthy. The whole central, commercial, and privatized banking system is definitely a pyramid scheme. As much as I love capitalism, you still have to follow a budget and live within your means."

"Yes, the entire financial system is a mess," Mary said. "It's very corrupt and will lead to another recession or depression if they can't lower the debt and balance the budget. It's not hard to avoid a deficit. They are actively not trying to follow a budget and pay off debts."

"I do agree that we are setting ourselves up for another recession or depression," Eric said. "I think a lot of small businesses and some other businesses should be de-regulated and allowed to make some decisions on their own to help them develop, but there is something concerning and shady about the financial and banking industry. We have to keep an eye on them. They don't ever seem to make good decisions."

"Banks should be under a microscope," Emerald said. "They shouldn't be allowed to take a piss or shit without getting permission first. That is our money and everyone else's money. For them to be playing with our money by investing in risky trades is not okay. On the tax issue, it's enraging that citizens pay so many taxes and live paycheck to paycheck while the government takes or steals from us and puts it towards government contracts, such as the military, which the politicians make money off of because they own the companies who get the contracts. Then, the rich and wealthy and these profit-making companies only pay a fraction, if they even have to pay any, in taxes of what the poor and middle class have to pay. It's a scam. It should be the opposite. The poor and middle class should have to pay less than the rich and the companies. If politicians really wanted to help the citizens, they would lower taxes for the poor and middle class and raise them for the upper-middle class, the wealthy and rich, and the companies. No one needs to make millions or billions a year without paying higher taxes. They can afford it. Some companies make billions in profits and don't pay any taxes. How the hell does that happen? Who the fuck let that happen? They can and should have to pay a shitload of taxes. We do."

"Should a few be wealthy and everyone else be poor?" Mary asked.

"Eighty percent of people in a capitalistic society or developed country barely make it to the next paycheck and have little savings," Emerald said. "They may make money or have some money, but they are riddled with debt and have more debt than they can pay for. They may seem like they are doing okay as they have a bunch of shit that they don't need, but in a sense, they are poor due to the debt, credit, and loans that they have compared to what they are really making. Only a few are well off and actually saving money."

"Yes, there are so many people struggling," Mary said. "A lot of people have to work 50 to 80 hours a week or have to have more than one job to survive and live. That is abuse and shameful."

"I know," Christina said. "I would like to go back in time and beat the person, who was probably a man, who made us work five days a week for over 40 hours a week. It's very stressful and exhausting. It's a waste of a life. I know not all industrialized countries do that, but it's a lot."

"If people are working so much and paying so many taxes, why can't we figure out how to help the ghettos and high crime and drug areas?" Eric asked. "We shouldn't ignore the poor, poverty, crime, and drug problems because the people in those areas don't make that much money and don't have the money to bribe the politicians to help them."

"That is why the politicians from those areas should only receive a salary that is the average of what their citizens make," Mary said. "Why are those politicians filthy rich while the people they represent or are supposed to be helping are starving and poor and living in awful circumstances. The politicians should only get what the average income is for that area. Some politicians make double to triple and even more than the people they represent. That is not okay. There is no incentive for them to do anything or make things better, and it pisses me off that these traditionalist politicians complain about how big the government is and that they want to cut all these so-called socialist programs, but they are okay and don't say anything while they get all these government benefits, such as big salary, free healthcare insurance, and a huge retirement plan.

You are a fucking hypocrite and evil person to complain about socialism and make others pay for healthcare while you are receiving a salary, healthcare, and other benefits paid for by the citizens. That is socialism. You are a socialist, and you are a fucking hypocrite and liar."

"You are right Mary," Emerald said. "The politicians shouldn't get benefits and raises that they are not allowing the citizens to receive. That tells you what a piece of shit that they are. They want to tell us what we can and cannot have while they take, take, take. The rich shouldn't get to determine how everyone else lives. Revolution!"

"Don't start with that commie crap," Eric said with a smile.

"Hey, did you do some research on what socialism and communism are?" Emerald said.

"I did a little," Eric said. "To me, it just seems socialism and communism are bad ideas."

"How so?" Emerald asked.

"Well, I like the equality, the lack of classes, and that the workers have control of the companies, but it seems like communism has led to low productivity and poverty. Businesses need to be efficient, especially when it comes to making things that we need, such as food. It seems like the people are not motivated in that type of setting, and you get government corruption too. There needs to be motivation and incentives if you don't have a token economy in place. There needs to be some pressure from the leaders to get people to perform at their best. Socialism might work better than communism since there are wages, but then you have the government owning the companies, which again creates a lot of bureaucracy and low productivity. At least with democracy and capitalism, people are motivated and work harder to achieve more. They also have a chance at being wealthy. I'll admit that we definitely have our problems too, which seem to be numerous after our discussion here today, and I don't like it at all that most of the wealth ends up in the hands of a few. That needs to be dealt with sooner than later or like yesterday."

"I'm glad that you can see the problems Eric," Emerald said. "I think most of the problems are the same. It just depends on the leadership and politicians who are in place within the government. All governments face issues and problems related to corruption, poverty, and inequality. We need something in place to remove the corrupt politicians quickly and efficiently. The people shouldn't have to start an uprising and revolt to remove a tyrannical, corrupt, and/or abusive government, and since we can't rely on the other politicians to confront and deal with the problematic politicians, the people should be able to hold their own election to remove them."

"That is a good idea Em," Mary said. "The people do need a system in place to oust the bad politicians, especially since the military and law enforcement seem to protect the politicians, the government, and the companies when the citizens protest and revolt. Do the law enforcement and military not realize that they are our employees and we pay them to protect us? It always makes me so mad when you hear about the police arresting and beating peaceful protesters who are trying to stop evil corporations from polluting or engaging in criminal acts. I can't believe that the corrupted and bribed politicians accepted money and passed laws calling animal and environmental activists terrorists and criminals. You can get arrested and put in prison just for filming the inside of farms, CAFOs, slaughterhouses, and fossil fuel companies. You can also get arrested and thrown in prison for just protesting these industries. That shit is not okay. That's when you know you are living under fascism and a dictatorship. Freedom of speech and press my ass. That shows you that the government is just protecting the lies and devastation of the corporations over the citizens. The protestors are getting punished for trying to expose the truth about these awful companies, the government, and politicians. The law enforcement should be beating them and not the protesters."

"I agree," Christina said. "We are supposed to have a right to speak our mind and protest. The law enforcement and military should be helping us accomplish that and protecting us against corruption and abuse by the wealthy, the companies, the government, and the politicians."

"Oh, I almost forgot what I was going to say about the different types of government argument," Mary said. "I do agree with having the workers own the companies. Cooperatives are the best. If there are no cooperatives, unions and organized labor need to be in place. Those are the best options in a capitalistic society to increase productivity, protect human and worker's rights, and create high quality products. I think in a communist or socialist society the workers could easily come up with incentives and motivational strategies to deal with the past concerns of inefficiency and lack of productivity. I still don't agree that those nations who experienced that were true communist or socialist societies. They really seemed like oligarchies or autocracies. It's the same with democratic societies. The politician says one thing to get elected and then they do something else after they get elected. If the politicians or leaders are behaving like tyrants or dictators and not letting the people control the means of productions and the companies, that is not communist or socialist. The same goes for a republic and the democratic process, which is why most nations who say they are democratic are not democratic. If the people have very little say, it's not democratic, but you can still have capitalism in a communist or socialist society. It all depends on how you run it."

"I can see these systems working if the politicians who are elected into the government are not corrupt," Christina said. "I do think there is a lot of misinformation and flat out lies on communism and socialism. It's definitely a threat to the rich and wealthy. I can see the upper-class spending millions and even billions on anti-communism and anti-socialism propaganda to say negative things about those other types of governments and to fool people into believing that the way we are doing things is better. With all our problems, our government will fail eventually too. You can't keep doing what we are doing and survive. We are not successful just because we are still going. Look at all the problems that we have mentioned here today. It's disgusting. We should definitely be ashamed of ourselves. The horror. I think our nation just seems successful on the outside like a rich person. You think they are successful, but then you find out that they borrowed or inherited all of their money or they made their wealth off of horrible goods and services, such as foods that really make people sick and die, prescription drugs, real estate, poisons, guns and weapons, pollution, plastics, fossil fuels, or animal agriculture to just name a few. The success is just an illusion. The rich person could also be a horrible person who is sexist, racist, a bigot, sexual offender, or pedophile. Just like the nation that has so much crime, poverty, abuse, inequality, and unnecessary death and violence. That is not a successful nation. Our nation is like a bubble that is ready to bust or is already busting. We are not even financially successful. We are trillions in debt and just keep borrowing. A successful country would be sustainable and not have any debt, and every citizen would be well taken care of."

"We do have a lot of work to do honey," Eric said. "Those are some good points. Hey Em, after talking with you, I do see a lot of benefits to cooperation. I think it's just difficult for people in a competitive and capitalistic society with all of their egos to see and understand."

"Yes, you don't have cooperation in a dictatorship," Emerald said. "The tyrants who called themselves communist or socialist did not give those types of government a good name, especially since they were not communist or socialist to begin with. I hope we can combine the benefits of all these governments and create like a social democratic society or even a democratic socialist society, which both would include capitalism with cooperatives and/or unions and organized labor. However, the democratic socialist society would move more towards a real socialist economy where the people would have control over the economy, the goods, and the services instead of the rich and the greedy and corrupt politicians. We have to take an eclectic approach and be politically syncretic. I think we would be pleased. The makings are already there, but we would have to overthrow the rich and wealthy politicians in power and the corrupt ones who accept bribes by foreign governments and companies. Our country already has so many socialist ideals and practices embedded within it. These practices have also helped so many people who wouldn't have obtained assistance if it weren't for the government programs. Even the traditionalists and the rich rely and depend on so many government and socialist programs. They just deny it and don't talk about it."

"Like what?" Eric asked.

"A lot of retirement plans, government-based loans, healthcare benefits, tax breaks and deductions, subsidies, welfare, government contracts, social services programs, other social programs, and education," Emerald said. "There are probably a whole lot more too."

"I got you," Eric said.

"It is concerning to think about all the millions of people who wouldn't be able to live and survive if it weren't for the government and social welfare programs, which are based in socialism," Christina said. "Shit, so many wealthy wouldn't be wealthy or have what they have if it wasn't for the socialist programs. They would be suffering too. They just got lucky because, for the most part, their parents or grandparents or relatives in the past ripped people off to get rich, and their relatives passed down the wealth to them. They should be kissing the poor people's asses. The affluent and wealthy should help take care of the sick, kids, disabled, poor, the immigrants, the veterans, and the elderly. If it were up to the rich and capitalists, all these indigent groups would starve even more than they are and be without education and healthcare, so they would probably live more miserable lives and die a lot sooner than they should. The suffering would be worse than they already have to endure. A big part of me thinks that the rich and the powers that be would actually be okay with all of this suffering as they seem to be okay with it right now. All for greed. Absolutely despicable. It makes me sick."

"Man, if there wasn't government interventions and regulations, I can't imagine what it would be like," Mary said. "The rich would even put the children back to work, they would implement slavery again, and if they did pay a wage, slave labor would even be worse than it already is. The wages would be so low. The working and living conditions would be very unsanitary and so horrible. Poverty, crime, and disease would run rampant through all parts of society. The rich would have the military and the law enforcement protecting them like they already do around their gated and secured communities. They would have walls around everything to keep people out. Even though, we are the ones working hard to give them what they have."

"In a lot of countries, child labor is still very legal as is a lot of those awful things you mentioned," Eric said.

"As I'm more on the right in regard to traditionalist politics, it surprises and upsets me how many traditionalists don't care about minorities, children, the elderly, veterans, immigrants, and the disabled," Christina said. "It blows my mind how many elderly people and veterans vote traditionalist because most traditionalist politicians don't give a shit about them at all. They say they do, but their policies don't help the elderly or the veterans. Unless they are at least millionaires."

"I think the elderly and those other indigent groups vote for traditionalist politicians because of those non-issues that we were talking about earlier," Emerald said. "They manipulate them through their emotions on things like abortion, guns, homosexuality, other religious issues, and immigration. It's fearmongering. Progressives do it too, but it's not as much, and it's usually in response to traditionalists trying to manipulate and lie to the public. We all know that the older generations are more religious, traditionalist, closed-minded, racist, sexist, and more bigoted. It's not across the board, but it's a lot more than the younger generations. You can definitely get their fear and anxiety going with the fearmongering propaganda by the traditionalist politicians."

"I don't totally agree with you Em," Eric said. "The traditionalists try hard to protect values and make people safe. The also spend a lot of energy and effort in securing our financial futures while trying to keep the government's hand out of the cookie jar regarding taxes. However, the elderly does have a whole other set of values, which are unfortunately based on bigotry and discrimination."

"I just don't see the results of the traditionalist policies," Emerald said. "I think their policies are set up to just help the already wealthy. We'll have to agree to disagree on that one."

"I did want to get back to education as a socialist program," Eric said. "Even though public education is socialist, it's a mess. You all were complaining about how inadequate the school system is. That is because the government runs it. Privately ran schools are so much better."

"That's bullshit Eric," Emerald said. "The public education system follows a traditionalist-made curriculum of teaching meaningless, trivial, and easy-to-forget information. The progressives try so hard to fund art, life skills, and music programs only to get overridden by traditionalists who want compliant and dumbed-down soldiers and workers. If it was up to the traditionalists, the only thing we would have learned in public school would be religious lies and myths and how to shoot a gun. The kids would also be praying all day long to an imaginary and made-up misogynistic patriarchal symbol."

"The private schools are more structured and professional," Eric said. "The public schools seem to have a lot of issues with lack of progress and performance and high drop-out rates."

"I don't know Eric," Mary said. "I'm not an expert on the differences between privatized schooling versus public schooling, but I do know that the curriculum, for the most part, in both of these settings is not good. This mindless curriculum is mostly the traditionalists' fault. However, a lot of progressives have to take responsibility too as they have supported it without challenge. Both settings are problematic as they have to have the same type of curriculum, so the debate becomes which is the better setting. I think that just depends on the student, but you can't compare the two though as one costs parents a lot more than the other. The private school should be better because you are paying more for a better product. However, I haven't heard any students claim to be smarter or better because their parents were able to afford to send them to a private school. I think the students themselves determine their success from the tools they are given from both environments. The other difference is that you have people getting filthy rich off a mediocre education and curriculum. Parents, unless they are wealthy, end up spending their hard-earned money on a bad privatized education. Like I said though, I hope that the private school provides additional programs for the extra price, but they still support inequality in our classist society."

"What about homeschooling?" Emerald asked.

"What a joke," Eric said.

"Not true," Emerald said. "It's far superior to both public and private schools. Unfortunately, society has disparaged it, so the insecure parents are afraid to have their kids participate in a homeschool setting due to pressure, fear, and other judgments. The only major problem I have with homeschooling are the religious parents who just use it as a brainwashing and programming environment to push fake religious teachings onto their kids a lot more than if they had to leave the home to go to school. People also argue that homeschooled kids don't learn social skills, but there are lots of ways to teach social skills other than sending your kid to a brick and mortar setting. I could argue that social skills are actually diminished in some way in public and private school due to bullying, the class system, and peer pressure. You don't necessarily have those problems in a homeschool setting. You can still have a homeschooled child participate in extracurricular activities or other community groups to learn social skills. A lot of public schools will still allow homeschooled kids to utilize the groups, clubs, and activities that they provide. The only other argument I can think of is athletics, which to me, is a waste and an absolute atrocity to society. The athletic systems and departments are so racist, sexist, and abusive. It teaches kids to cheat, be overly aggressive, and hurt others. There is also so much favoritism and politics in athletics that it's shameful, and I'm not going to even start with the cheerleading issue. That is appalling and one of the most sexist and degrading things that girls can do. Cheerleading is like the reflection of sexism, the patriarchy, and the misogyny that is going on in the society."

"Athletics is basically a fundraiser and cash cow for the schools too," Mary said.

"Yes, so many kids learn the wrong things, get hurt and injured, and end up with low self-esteem, but who cares because the school is making money off of them," Emerald said. "Isn't that exploitation and child labor? The kids don't even get paid or compensated for it. That is so wrong on so many different levels."

"How many homeschoolers end up shooting up the school, which happens so much in all the schools, including colleges and universities?" Mary asked.

"Absolutely none," Emerald said. "Zero. All the kids who stole their dads' guns were traumatized from being in a brick and mortar school setting, so they end up killing all these teachers and other students because of how horrible the school systems are and the lax gun control laws. If that's not proof that something needs to change, I don't know what is."

"All of the school shootings and shootings in general are horrifying," Christina said. "How many kids have to go crazy and how many people have to get shot and die before they finally take action and do something about all these educational issues, especially the bullying and teasing, not only by the other kids but also the teachers? The schools end up making excuses for the abusers and bullies while they protect the asshole jocks who do most of the bullying. It's so upsetting. I don't even want to get into the whole gun control issue. That's a monster. While the politicians are paid off and bribed by the rich and wealthy gun industry and their associations, people are dying. People should have a right to a gun and to protect themselves, but it should be a privilege after you are screened and assessed to be safe and competent to own a gun while having to follow strict regulations on storing and securing your guns, so your kids or anyone else can't easily access them. In addition, if you are allowed to have a gun, you really only need one or two guns at the most. That's it, and there is no citizen that needs a semi-automatic or automatic weapon. It's not asking too much to do all that."

"You said it Christina," Mary said.

"I don't think there should be guns at all," Emerald said. "You can replace them all with tasers and stun guns. Problem solved. You can still protect yourself, and no one dies. Guns are an old barbaric tool to deal with problems, which are internal anyway. Guns cause more problems than they solve. Unless you are an insecure and impotent man. Then, you might need a gun to make yourself feel better than you really are."

"That's funny," Mary said while laughing.

"There are always going to be guns and weapons," Eric said. "We just have to find a middle ground to stop these awful shootings and deal with the root causes of them, which isn't the guns. We have a right to guns, for now. I agree that we do need better screening procedures. I just don't know what that is. Hopefully, they will keep working on that."

"We'll see," Mary said. "They are definitely not doing enough to deal with the gun problem, and that in itself is an additional problem to the gun problem because of how much the gun associations are paying off the politicians to not pass legislation that regulates and restricts gun ownership and use. Regarding the curriculum issue, it's also upsetting that the schools are teaching so many things that aren't practical to real life and what we have to face in society."

"The focus seems to be on meaningless data and information that we have to memorize," Emerald said. "Then, you forget it after the test. It's stupid and a waste of time and money. A lot of it to me is focused on the left-brain areas or for the masculine purposes to hinder our creativity, so we can't think for ourselves. It's like they are actively trying to make us into subservient beings for compliance and control purposes. They want us to be workers, soldiers, and slaves. If they can keep us from questioning and from being independent, that helps them accomplish their goals of making a profit off of us."

"I do agree about the grades, but I'm not sure about your conspiracy theories Em," Eric said. "Just because someone is smart or deemed intelligent in school isn't a measure of their ability to have common sense or be a good and honest person. If a kid really wants to, they can get good grades. It doesn't mean that they are smart or intelligent. They just temporarily memorized some stuff that may or may not have anything to do with life. There are lots of psychopaths and horrible people who got good grades in school."

"The school system is based on task orientation and memorization," Mary said. "It does seem like they are training us to be slaves. There is no openness, questioning, creativity, curiosity, imagination, or independence, and the kids who try to do that are shamed, punished, diagnosed with mental disorders, and medicated. If I hear them call one more kid attention deficit or hyperactive or bipolar, I'm going to shoot someone. A mental health disorder is a rare occurrence. Hardly anyone should have a disorder. The fact that so many people are being labeled as so is careless and negligent. Those kids don't have those disorders. That is who they are and what they are. If they were hurting themselves or hurting others that would be one thing, but I think it's great that kids can't pay attention and are hyperactive. Most kids, especially adolescents, are temperamental and have mood swings. That doesn't make them depressed and bipolar. The powers that be try to control them and put them on medications, which is a money-making machine. They want to suppress our creativity, independence, genius, and who we really are. That is not okay, and it's not okay for drug companies and the pharmacology industry and businesses to prey on children by paying off politicians and school officials, so they can profit off medicating kids for no reason at all other than pure greed."

"True that," Christina said. "They have to diagnose them, or the insurance companies wouldn't pay for mental health or medical services or for the medications."

"Yes, the medication issue needs to be addressed too," Eric said. "That is out of control. Parents need to say no to medications and not let the schools manipulate them or fool them into prescribing drugs for those behaviors and attitudes, so the school doesn't have to take responsibility and individualize their approaches to kids who can't sit at a desk all day and listen to trivial information. I think it's a mental disorder to be able to sit at a desk all day and not get bored and antsy."

"It doesn't make sense to teach things that have nothing to do with life," Emerald said. "The curriculum could easily include more arts and music with relationship skills, money management skills, and other life skills, such as laundry, hygiene, and home care or home improvement. Organizational skills are always great too. Instead of waiting for the kids to get into trouble or have a breakdown, they could go ahead and teach them coping skills for their feelings and behavioral management skills. Shit, even most of the jobs that people do will have nothing to do with the core subjects that they teach in school. They could have field trips to spend time at different jobs and with different employers, so the kids could figure out what they want to be when they grow up."

"It does make you wonder what they are really doing with our educational system," Christina said. "I don't know if I agree with all of your conspiracy theories either Em, but you may be on to something."

"I know there is something there," Emerald said. "We are being grown to be mindless workers, soldiers, and slaves. If they really wanted to deal with kids who they see as troublemakers or who they misdiagnose with those rare mental health disorders, they would teach meditation on how we can appreciate silence and concentrate better. They should be spending most of the time at school teaching about healthy plant-based diets, nutrition, exercise, healthy fun activities, meditation, nature, ahimsa, and stretching. Other subjects should include philosophy, psychology, and a primer in all religions, especially the ancient ones where the contemporary major ones stole their stories from."

"I do think they are making kids to be drones, obedient slaves, and soldiers," Mary said.

"As much as we need the military to some extent, that is a whole other matter of disappointment with them preying on young kids and adolescents to be soldiers," Emerald said. "It's upsetting how much money goes into and is received from the military, war, weapons, death, and destruction, but they can't seem to find any money to help their citizens. We don't need to put any more money into the military. It needs to be defunded. Defund the military! They expect companies and individuals to eventually be independent from government funding and be able to sustain themselves, but when it comes to the military, it's a hypocrisy of government waste, excessive spending, and unsustainable operations. It is so enraging that almost all of the traditionalists and some of the progressives support increasing the military budgets while justifying the cutting of social programs, which are actually helping people and are a fraction of the military budget."

"It doesn't seem like most of that money goes to the military anyway or for actual and useful military purposes," Christina said. "It seems like the politicians approve the funds for the grossly overbudgeted military because they or their friends, their cronies, and family own shares in the companies that receive the government contracts. Our taxes are actually just making a small group of people richer rather than keeping us safe and protected. It's very unethical and should be illegal for politicians to have any say so in where money goes when funds could or do go to their businesses or businesses that are owned by them or anyone close to them."

"I'm not sure if most of the military even protects us and keeps us safe," Emerald said. "The politicians declare war, which seems to be a front to invade and steal another country's resources, so we end up killing more innocent civilians than the other country's government officials or their military. Most of the wars seem religious in nature too. It's so upsetting how many civilians die in war. You would think you would have better aim with the high level of technology and weapons that we have and the amount of training that the soldiers get. It's like they are aiming for the civilians. They also end up bombing and destroying residential areas where the civilians are at. If you are at war with a country, you are at war with their government, their politicians, and their military. You are not at war with their citizens. It seems like they avoid targeting and going after the politicians and soldiers that they are at war with. Why don't they bomb and destroy the government buildings or their military compounds and bases? Why do they target and kill the residential areas and the civilians? It's very suspicious and upsetting."

"That is a great point Em," Christina said. "It also upsets me that the politicians or whoever can declare war but not fight. In the past, the leaders who decided to go to war and battle were also soldiers and were on the front lines because they had a responsibility to be a part of the decision that they were making. The politicians and leaders today are cowards and hypocrites. They make decisions on matters that they won't do themselves. They won't even let their friends, their cronies, and families fight in the wars that they support and vote for. Telling someone else to fight and die for you and your country when you won't do it is like a cult leader or dictator or bad boss who wants people to do their dirty work for them."

"I agree," Mary said. "They should at least have to be there to see the misery, suffering, and death of their decisions. I've also heard that most wars could have been prevented due to our politicians and our military approving the selling of guns and weapons to groups in other countries because our government isn't getting what they want from their government, such as access to natural resources, oil and coal, drugs, and money. So, they sell the weapons and guns to these groups and factions to help them overthrow the government, so we can get what we want. Then, after they overthrow the government, when the group that we sold weapons too doesn't do what we want, we call them terrorists or radicals and go to war with them. We were the ones who sold them their weapons and guns to begin with, and now they are going to use the guns and weapons that we sold to them against us. Tell me how that make sense. We created the so-called terrorists. We are the terrorists."

"Yes, lots of governments and politicians make a lot of money off selling weapons and guns to other countries and certain groups within other countries," Emerald said. "Most citizens and the public have no idea that we do that. We even sell our own citizens guns and weapons. Then, they kill other citizens with those same guns and weapons. It's absolute insanity."

"Oh Eric," Mary said in taunting way.

"Yes," Eric said reluctantly.

"I know you greatly support the military," Mary said.

"Yes," Eric said. "Unfortunately, it's a necessary evil, but we have to protect ourselves."

"We do," Mary said. "I think we all agree that we need to have a military to some extent but not as big as it is where we have to have bases in other countries where we are literally occupying other countries, making politicians rich off of unnecessary military government contracts, and selling guns and weapons to groups in other countries."

"All of that is so true," Emerald said. "It is so suspicious for us to have military bases in so many different countries all over the world. It makes us look like a bully or a tyrannical government."

"That's the question," Eric said. "How big is too big? How big does the military need to be to protect us? I'm not sure anyone can answer that question."

"You have to admit that our military is way over budgeted," Emerald said. "It could be cut in half and still serve the purpose of protecting us, especially with the technology that we have to look out for danger. A lot of weapons are automated now. Defund the military now!"

"We could cut it back, but you have to be careful," Eric said.

"You don't need that many soldiers, and with nuclear weapons, the military is almost irrelevant," Emerald said. "It only takes one nuclear weapon to be dropped at this point, and it is game over for all of us. That is the reality for us all at this point. The next war could be the last, and not very many people will live through it. It's very scary. That makes me realize how hypocritical our government is to say that we are a peaceful country, but we are one of the countries who has the highest budgeted military, biggest military, and most nuclear weapons. I think it's interesting that we are actively trying to tell other countries that they can't have nuclear weapons, or they can only have so many. If someone with a gun told me that I couldn't have a gun, I would laugh my ass off and tell them how stupid that statement is. Not that I would want a gun because guns are for cowards, but for someone to have something and tell someone else they can't have the same thing is the definition of a hypocrite and a tyrant. You can't say that you believe in freedom and peace as long as others aren't allowed to do what you are doing. You can't believe in freedom and peace and try to control others through bullying, guns, weapons, and threats."

"That reminds me of how many times our leaders threaten war and use of nuclear weapons onto other countries," Christina said. "That should be totally off limits, illegal, and an impeachable offense. Citizens can't threaten other citizens with violence. You can get arrested and go to jail, but it's okay for our leaders to do that to other countries, which actually could lead to war, death, and possible nuclear war, which I personally don't want to go through. I want to beat the shit out of our leaders and politicians who do that."

"Wow, those are some very important and serious issues guys," Mary said. "I was just trying to make a point to Eric about what we are talking about earlier. So, Eric, you do know that the military is a part of the government?"

"Yes," Eric said.

"The military is socialism at its core and a socialist program," Mary said.

"Damn you," Eric said. "I haven't put much thought into that."

"That's a good point," Christina said. "I guess we need socialism after all."

"That is something that most traditionalists don't think about with their anti-socialist ways," Emerald said. "A lot of our budget goes to the military and supporting veterans and their families. That is a lot of taxes and government funding. Socialism at its best. The military is pure socialism."

"Talking about all this traditionalist government military spending makes me think that the traditionalists are more socialist and communist than the progressives, but they say they are the opposite," Mary said. "Either they are in denial or are lying."

"Hypocrisy through and through," Emerald said.

"However, it seems that progressives support socialist programs to help people, but the traditionalists support socialist programs that make people rich and help the wealthy while mostly killing and hurting innocent people," Mary said. "War is not a business. It's pure macabre."

"Eric, it is interesting and suspicious that the capitalists, wealthy, and traditionalist politicians have spent billions over the years on advertising and marketing campaigns to manipulate the public and lie about a lot of things to get rich," Christina said. "I'm sure progressives do the same thing, but it doesn't seem to be as prevalent with the progressive agenda."

"I call it propaganda," Mary said. "Traditionalists say that socialist and communists use propaganda to spread lies, but that is exactly what they do. The capitalists and traditionalists are totally guilty of spreading propaganda that is so untrue that it's not even funny. They even spread anti-socialism and anti-communism propaganda that has no basis in fact or reality. We have already proven that so many traditionalists are actually more socialist and communist than the progressives."

"I agree with what we were talking about earlier in regard to the so-called socialist or communist nations not being those types of governments," Christina said. "I have been trying to wrap my mind around the manipulation, and the spreading of propaganda helped me understand the deception. I can see now that the capitalists and traditionalists have tried so hard to discredit and say how horrible communism and socialism are when these countries that they are degrading are not really those types of governments. They are autocratic, dictatorships, or authoritarian. They are actually more right-wing, traditionalist, or fascist. They may have sold it that way and manipulated the people with the communist and socialist jargon, but we don't even know if that was true because that is what we hear from the traditionalist propaganda and paid-for advertisements. The socialist and communist rhetoric or philosophy does sound good and makes sense for the most part, but these countries that they say are socialist and communist are not being ran that way. They are not in the hands of the people like those governments are supposed to be."

"I can see what you are saying," Eric said.

"In a sense, the capitalists lie about these fake communist and socialist countries who have fallen into tyranny and have either failed or had lots of issues like poverty," Emerald said. "So, the capitalists are doing the same thing with their propaganda that they claim the communists and socialists do to their citizens. They are so guilty of misleading, manipulating, and saying things that are not true. You can't take an awful situation like a government who abuses their country and citizens and say that it is something that it is not. It's an obvious attempt to confuse people about socialism and communism and dissuade them from seeing the benefits of these types of governments. All the while, our so-called free and first-class nation with its capitalistic and democratic processes is riddled with numerous problems, especially rampant inequality and poverty, which is not supposed to be and shouldn't be happening. People are suffering and dying while we speak. Absolutely disgusting. Our government and politicians should be ashamed of themselves."

"Exactly," Christina said. "It's very insidious and deceptive."

"Why would the rich and powerful, especially the wealthy politicians and business owners, want a communist or socialist society?" Mary said.

"They wouldn't," Emerald said.

"They would lose all their money and power," Mary said. "So, if they can lie, manipulate, and convince the voting citizens how bad communism and socialism are, it will keep them rich and powerful."

"Well, I see through the lies and know they don't want democracy either," Emerald said. "We live in an oligarchy or plutocracy. It is a fake or false democracy. It's an illusion."

"I hate you guys," Eric said sarcastically. "I always feel so confident in what I believe, and then I talk to you all and start to think and learn. I have to admit that you all have made some great points. There are some conspiracy theories in there that don't have the proper proof, but I can believe a lot of what you all are saying. However, we have to be careful of the government having too much control, and anarchy is not good either. You can have corruption, greed, and abuse of power in any society. So, where do we go from here?"

"Nature is anarchy, and it does just fine," Emerald said. "You get a lot of beauty and some disasters. That's just a part of it, but the good always prevails. It will even overcome the atrocities of man."

"I think we need to take a multi-systemic and comprehensive approach," Christina said. "We have to have checks and balances, which are lacking in our current society. I think Em mentioned earlier the need for an eclectic and politically syncretic approach to cover all the areas and deal with all the problems. All forms of government have their pluses and minuses. You could have a utopian society or a successful and wonderful republic, but if a corrupt or evil person or group gets into power, it could still destroy the wonderful society that was created. I'll say it again and again. You have to have checks and balances. You can't have capitalism without having government and regulations, and the government needs to be checked by the people. A traditionalist politician can't say that they don't believe in socialism and then get elected and work for the government, collect taxes, and receive government funding and benefits. Those are all socialist practices that they are participating in. Even though they don't want to admit to it or believe it, they are socialist and communist. It's preposterous for them to deny that. It's sad that citizens have been lied to about and manipulated into being afraid of different forms of government while the one they are in is so corrupt and has so many problems."

"Well said Christina," Eric said.

"Yes, great ending to a wonderful and productive conversation," Emerald said.

"Couldn't have said it better myself," Mary said. "I hope someone was taking notes. We made a lot of progress and hit on some great recommendations to fixing our challenged and concerning nation."

"I would like to see less government spending, especially with the military, but it's important, especially in regard to freedom, that companies be allowed to grow and progress without too much regulation," Eric said.

"That's the point Eric," Mary said. "If the people have the government in check and it's not corrupt with greed, money, and favoritism, all the people should control the companies and the government. As long as you have inequality, classism, and the pyramid scheme of a few people hanging on to all of the wealth, you will always have a disastrous and sick society, especially when it comes to capitalism and privately ran businesses. It's not okay that a few people are rich and most everyone else is poor and struggling and having to work most of the week or even all week. To avoid total socialism and communism and keep our capitalistic society, there has to be regulation and a separation of not only church and state but also a separation of business and state or separation of corporation and state. Politicians should not be allowed to receive any money from groups, associations, companies, or even people. There should be no lobbying allowed. Maybe they should all receive a certain amount or the same amount for their campaigns, or maybe they shouldn't be allowed to raise money at all for campaigns. They should all get to display their messages and platform in a convenient and public place, which is in the same location as all the other candidates. There should definitely be a separation of wealth or money and state, and the politicians shouldn't make more than what the average person makes in their jurisdictions. By taking away the money, you take away the greed and corruption. We also need to be able to vote them out or remove them a lot easier if they turn out to be corrupt and start engaging in unethical or criminal behaviors. There needs to be a central location to keep track of their promises, what they did, and what they voted on, so we can see their progress and success or lack of it."

"Those are great Mary," Emerald said. "We have to take care of this financial mess too. The government needs to be paying off the debt and living below or within its means. Since the debt is so high, they need to spend below what they are making to run a surplus to pay off the debt.

That's where cutting politicians' salaries and defunding the military and doing away with subsidies for companies who are making plenty of profits comes in. We can also raise taxes a lot for the rich and companies to help get us back in a better financial situation. We need to lower debts for the citizens and lower taxes for the poor and lower middle class, and the companies need to be forced to lower prices and live within their means too. More importantly, after the debts are paid for and settled, we can finally do away with the corrupt and destructive central banking system, which is a pyramid scheme anyway. Privatized banking is pure evil in disguise."

"I would like to see the educational system transformed into having lots of different types of art classes, more practical life skills, and less of the core curriculum," Christina said. "Everyone should receive free or very cheap healthcare. Companies, doctors, and other healthcare providers shouldn't be getting filthy rich of off people's sicknesses and health needs. You are supposed to be helping people, not taking advantage of them. If someone is sick, you help them. You don't see if they can pay first, and if they can, then you help them, but if they can't, then you don't help them. What do you think my love?"

"Those are all great guys," Eric said. "I think that the advertising and marketing issue is important. It's not fair to a lot of people who don't have resources and money who would make great politicians. They can't afford to advertise like a rich person can. You shouldn't have to be rich or affluent to campaign. Obviously, the rich and the powers that be are not doing what they are supposed to do, or they are incompetent. So, we need to elect and hire intelligent and competent people to deal with the problems that the rich have created. I think they should either restrict how much a campaign should be able to make, have a shared amount to give to all the candidates, or have a central location with the candidates' information with no fundraising or donations allowed. It is upsetting that so much money goes to lies, manipulations, and bribes. The candidates' campaigns and advertising should only focus on them and not others. They should be telling us about their ideas, what they are going to do, and how they are going to do it. They definitely shouldn't be allowed to bad mouth and talk negatively about others."

"Excellent," Emerald said.

"I think we just solved our country's problems," Mary said.

"Let's put it into action," Christina said.

"How so?" Eric asked.

"We could write up a manifesto on the importance and need for either democratic socialism or social democracy," Emerald said. "I personally like democratic socialism better as social democracy may still allow companies through capitalism to corrupt the system and the destroy the economy like they have been and are doing. That will definitely continue the problem of inequality and classism."

"It just sounds so radical," Eric said.

"But isn't capitalism?" Mary asked. "Look at all the problems. I don't understand why traditionalists consider equality, peace, and love as radical ideas, but it's not radical to destroy the earth through so much pollution, have the government trillions in debt, have a very small percentage of people own most of the wealth while most people are either poor or struggling, and let the companies corrupt the government and the politicians at the citizens' expense. People are suffering and are dying because of how radical and extreme right-wing fascism is. It's not radical for the people and the citizens to actually have a voice and say in how things work. That is what a democracy is supposed to be. And, those are just a few of the radical effects of capitalism and the way things are now. There are many more problems and issues. The reality is that things have to change. That is not radical. That is a necessity for our survival and for your baby's survival. Time has told us that this system is not working, so we need to change it. It's on the brink of a total collapse, and I don't want that. It's already bad enough."

"It's interesting that some political scientists and social philosophers always say that socialism is when capitalism fails, which is inevitable," Emerald said. "It's not a question of whether capitalism will fail. It's a question of when it will fail. Then, after socialism saves the day, the greedy capitalists come back in to corrupt and fuck it all up again with their lies and evil ways."

"I can actually see that Em," Christina said. "That is a good way to put it."

"Well, that was fabulous everyone," Emerald said while yawning. "I enjoyed it thoroughly, but I have to go to bed."

"No problem," Christina said. "That was some deep stuff, but it was great. I enjoyed it too."

"We love you both," Mary said.

"Yes, I love you Eric and Christina," Emerald said.

They all go up out of their seats and walked to the front door.

"It was great to see you and to have a deep conversation instead of talking about trivial matters, such as entertainment, the weather, sports, or celebrities," Emerald said.

Emerald and Mary hugged Christina and Eric. Mary opened the door, and they walked out.

"We love you guys," Eric said. "See you soon"

"Love you both," Christina said. "I hope we can get together sooner than later."

They all said goodbye. Emerald and Mary got in their car and drove home. It was dark and later than Emerald would have liked it to be, but she was so interested and into the discussion that she didn't want to leave. She always thought that she could have been a politician, but she was scared to think about getting attacked, shot, or killed because of her strong beliefs against the rich and the companies. She always thought it was so crazy that so many traditionalists say they are for rights and freedoms, but they are only for rights and freedoms that agree with their beliefs and way of life. If you believe differently than they do, they threaten, disparage you, attack you, and even kill you. Emerald knew that they were the true terrorists.

While on the way home, Emerald and Mary chatted about some of the topics that they all discussed earlier. Then, Emerald got an idea for a song in her head. She had come up with the melody a few months ago but couldn't get a theme or the lyrics to match it. She started making a bassline sound. Mary told her she thought it sounded pretty catchy. They got home and Mary jumped into the shower. Emerald grabbed her guitar that was in the living room and sat down on the sofa with her song book on the table in front of her. She titled the song "Political Corruption." She played some notes on the guitar that mimicked the bassline she was making with her mouth in the car. She liked the sound of the A note on the low E string. She started playing and writing the notes. As she played, she was able to think of the lyrics.

Political Corruption

Intro: Instrumental build up with guitar chords and drums. Slow and
dramatic.
A, B, C, F, E, E, F, E, D, C, B, C, A, A, B, G, A
Repeat 3 more times.

(Note: This song can also be played as a reggae song without the bassline
by just using the chords noted in the chorus and verses, primarily A
minor, to be played as a reggae song)

Bassline: starts on low E string, play twice before first chorus, it is the
bassline to play during chorus.
A (X7), C, A
G, A, A, G, A, A, A, A
E, E, D, C, D, C
G, A, A, G, A, A, A, A
A(X7), C, A
G, A, A, G, A, A, A, A
E, D, C, D

Chorus:
(Am) It's called political corruption, it's not about production.
(Am) It's all about destruction, of the society
(Am) It's called political corruption, it's causing a disruption
(Am) It's bound for eruption, due to greed and (D) money
(Am) It's called political corruption

Bassline: starts on low E string, play once before verses, it's the bassline
to play during the verses.
G, A, A, G, A, A, G, A, A, A, C, A, G, E
G, A, A, G, A, A, G, A, A, A, C, C, D
G, A, A, G, A, A, G, A, A, A, C, A, G, E
D, D, D, D, A

Verse 1:
(Am) You got the politicians telling you what you want to hear
(Am) They're out there on the trails and they're spreading fear
(Am) They're trying to draw a line between you and me
(D) It's all an illusion, man, can't you see, yeah
(Am) Getting your vote is what they're trying to do
(Am) And then they get elected, and then it's screw you
(Am) Cause all they really cared about is their companies
And now they're (D) sittin back laughing countin all their money

Repeat Chorus

Verse 2:
(Am) Did you ever wonder why all the politicians are rich
(Am) We work so hard every day, man, it makes me sick
(Am) They say they're gonna take care of you and me
(D) They only look out for themselves, it's all about greed
(Am) The people are the ones who voted them in
(Am) But the business bribe them, it's called lobbyin
(Am) The laws that they pass don't benefit us
(D) Open up your eyes, they threw us under the bus

Repeat Chorus

Verse 3:
(Am) The military budgets are out of control
(Am) Someone's getting paid, man, don't you know
(Am) They're sellin guns and weapons, just to get rich
(D) And then they turn around and call them terrorists
(Am) The foreign governments are their biggest fans
(Am) They got your politicians in the palm of their hands
(Am) The president picks the judges, so they don't take the fall
(D) A judge who's political is no judge at all

Repeat Chorus

Episode 5
Corporate Corruption

When companies are given rights and are not regulated properly, they become viruses in the society.
Companies are inherently evil when their number one goal is to make a profit.
A company's priority to make a profit will always be at the expense of the people, the animals, and the environment.
Allowing companies and religious institutions to have a say in legislation and influence politicians through lobbying, campaign donations, and bribes will always negatively affect the people and society.

Emerald spent the next few days thinking about religion and politics while she went through her days, exercises, meditations, and talks with Mary. She had a couple of days off in a row like she usually does, but they were very refreshing and reenergizing for her. She spent a lot of time with Mary and out in nature. On one of the days, they went on a long four-hour hike in the country. It was a little cool on the hike, but since the sun was shining and they were hiking, it was perfect. While on the hike, Emerald expressed her deep gratitude and love for Mary and how much she appreciated her. Emerald has told Mary a lot about how she feels about her but thought it was deserving due to her past neglect of Mary for so many years, especially while Emerald was abusing the drugs. She has felt so close to Mary and wanted to make sure she kept giving, which was nothing compared to what she has gotten from Mary. Emerald really enjoyed the time off that she had and wished that everyone's time off work was like that.

Emerald had to work today. She exercised every day over the past few days, so she promised herself she would take the day off and let her muscles and body rest. She got up very early like she usually does, but on this morning, she woke up about three hours before the sunrise. Emerald thought it was awesome that she was waking up without an alarm clock every day over the past couple of years. She despised waking up to an alarm clock, and she thought that using one constantly and every day to get up was definitely a sign that you were stressing yourself out and not taking care of yourself. Either you needed to go to bed earlier, exercise more, meditate more, eat better, stop drinking alcohol and doing drugs, eat different foods in the evening before bed, stop eating and drinking so close to bedtime, or do all the above.

Emerald was so proud of herself. She couldn't believe how much she relied on the alarm clock before, and it used to be very difficult for her to go to bed at a decent hour. She used to stay up until at least midnight. She knew that she had issues with her sleep due to drugs, alcohol, caffeine, tobacco, poor diet, and not exercising. Getting Emerald to go to bed at a decent hour and wake up on time in the morning was like trying to get a child to go to bed and get up. It was like trying to move a mountain. Mary would throw water on her about noon to get her up, so they could do something or so she wouldn't be late for work. Then, Emerald would get mad at her. She would even throw a temper when Mary was just trying to get her to be responsible.

"So Shameful," Emerald said out loud. "What a mess I was."

Emerald used to sleep a lot too. Before she got healthy, she needed almost 10 hours of sleep to get up and function during the day. She mainly needed that much sleep because she didn't sleep well. She would wake up a lot throughout the night while tossing and turning. She would also snore a lot and had sleep apnea. She still had times of waking up and tossing and turning, but it was not as bad as it used to be. She could even function on a few to several hours of sleep, which was a lot less than what she used to need to get up and around. Even on a small amount of sleep, she had tons of energy, especially if she exercised that day. She wouldn't even get a little tired throughout the day.

At first, she thought it was weird going to bed before the sunset with it still being daylight outside, but that's when she gets tired. She still felt strange though because she would go to bed so early on the weekends when people were just going out to eat and getting their night started. Emerald didn't feel good when she tried to stay up past when she normally went to bed or fell asleep. Since Emerald and Mary stopped eating out, drinking alcohol, and hanging out with friends during the evenings, they just stopped worrying about going out on the weekends or their days off. They didn't have a lot of money anyway, so they saved a lot of money not going out and trying to have a good time that way. Mary thought it was odd at first, but she has gotten used to it too. They still would go out once in a while, but it had to be for a really good band or something significant that they both really want to do. However, no matter how late Emerald stayed up, she still woke up about the same time, so it was best that she went to bed at the same time every night.

On this morning, she decided to eat a huge breakfast, journal her dreams, get a good stretch in, meditate for a long amount of time, and go watch the sunrise. She hoped that it wasn't too cloudy. She had to be at work at noon, so she wanted to make sure she didn't overdo it on her activities that she wanted to accomplish today. Beth and Emerald were running the store by themselves today, so Adam and Don could enjoy the day off together. They tried to do that for them as much as possible since they were such awesome bosses who probably paid them more than they should for what they do. Emerald thought they were always so generous to her, especially since they hired her with a criminal record. She couldn't wait to get the record sealed next year. She was almost done with that horrible part of her life.

She loved that she made a decent wage for only working about 20 hours a week. Some people had to work full time to make what she made. The bookstore was just part of what Adam and Don did. They were smart as they bought used things, such as furniture, and fixed them and prettied them up, so they could flip them at a higher price. Emerald helped them at times with this so-called hustle to make some extra cash here and there too. She thought Adam and Don could probably do this hustle full time eventually, but she was not sure that she could do something like that or pull that one off. She did find a used table one day at a thrift store or re-sell shop and asked Adam if she could sand it, paint it, and sell it through them since they had a good reputation and people looked at them as honest sellers in the community. They even let Emerald use their tools and paint. She ended up selling the table for about triple the amount that she paid for it. She wanted to pay Adam and Don some of her profits, but they refused. She thought they were awesome like that. Emerald even talked Mary into helping her find items around town to fix up and resale.

Emerald was very grateful that she met Adam and Don. She just happened to be looking for a job after her arrest and was having a hard time finding one. She was working at a big-box electronics or technology store when she got arrested, so they fired her the next day when she told them she was arrested. She always thought that was really shitty of them. She thought they did background checks, so she wanted to be honest with them before they found out. They used her honesty against her. Her supervisor even gave her a great performance review and evaluation a month before she was arrested. A couple of months before that, she was chosen to be the employee of the month. She thought she was a hard worker and one of the best employees. She didn't like that they didn't consider her performance and how she was doing as an employee before firing her. It was like they were judging and discriminating her based on a mistake that she made instead of giving her some credit based on the proof that she was a great employee. The charges didn't even have anything to do with her job either. It was very impulsive, unprofessional, and inconsiderate of them. She always wondered if they would have even found out if she didn't tell them, but she was glad that she did. She didn't want to work for a company like that anyway, so it worked out.

One day, when she was just riding her bike through town, she saw a now hiring sign in the window of the bookstore. She loved to read books, so she decided to go right in and ask about it. She wasn't necessarily looking for a job at that moment as she was just out for a bike ride, so she was not dressed for the interview and was sweaty. She walked into the store, took a deep breath, and with all her confidence, she asked a worker, who was Beth, if she could talk to the owner about the hiring advertisement. Adam and Don came over and introduced themselves to her, and she said that she desperately needed a job, loved to read, and had a criminal record. She thought they really loved the confidence, assertiveness, and genuineness. They told her later that they were actually thinking about hiring a lady from an interview the day before, but they didn't think she was as personable and friendly as Emerald came across. The really loved Emerald's attitude.

They ended up hiring Emerald right then and there with the sweat pouring down her face. They didn't even do a background check on her.

She was not sure they would have even done one, but she was glad that she was honest with them. She thought they probably sensed her genuineness. In the past, Emerald's dishonesty hadn't worked out too well for her anyway. If she was dishonest now, she knew she would show it. She would probably look nervous with a lack of eye contact, shaky voice, aloofness, and uncomfortableness. She thought that being honest probably helped with her being more relaxed and relieved, so she could communicate better and have a smoother interview. They loved that she was riding her bike too. They liked her dedication to stay in shape, save some money, and help the environment.

A couple of months after they hired her, Emerald told them that she was a lesbian and introduced them to Mary. They were very happy to hear that and to meet Mary, so they immediately disclosed to them that they were gay. Mary actually guessed that they might have been gay by the way Emerald was talking about them to her, but Emerald just thought they were good friends and business partners. They were very professional in the bookstore and didn't show affection towards each other at work. However, after they told Emerald that they were gay, she would catch them flirting here and there, but they may have started to do that in front of her due to her being comfortable with them being gay. Emerald thought they tried to not be in everyone's face about being gay, but she didn't care if they showed affection. She always wanted and encouraged people to be happy with who they really are and to show it off. Heterosexuals get to do that without judgment. Some traditionalists do judge straight people for showing PDA, but that is their problem. You shouldn't oppress and suppress feelings, especially love, just because you are uncomfortable with your own self or it conflicts with what your church or preacher brainwashes you to believe.

Emerald took a deep breath to focus on herself. She promised herself that she was going to not get so upset over things that she disagrees with or does not like. She wanted to be able to disagree and not have an emotional response like anger, upset, or discontent. She was starting to think that was bad or unhealthy for her mind, body, and spirit. It was allowing the negativity to get to her and have power over her, which was not good. So, she was starting to recognize when she was getting frustrated or upset a lot quicker. If she noticed these feelings, she would take a deep breath and focus on her body and heart. That kept her calm, so she could either keep discussing or processing what made her emotional or move on to something else to get her mind off of it. She thought it was crazy they don't teach coping skills like that in school or that parents don't teach things like that to their kids. Some probably do, but that is the exception and not the rule. Everyone should be taught coping skills for their feelings. A lot of fights and disparaging remarks could be avoided with some good parenting and teaching.

Emerald finished eating breakfast and got very full as she usually doesn't eat anything else the rest of the day when she doesn't exercise. She usually had some water for a couple more hours after she ate, but she stopped that too in the late morning. She found that she didn't need to eat as much when she wasn't expending so much energy. She might get a little hungry before she goes to bed, but it wasn't that bad. She thought how irresponsible and unhealthy it was that people eat so much. She thought most people eat too much and were very ungrateful for what they had and were able to eat. So many of these people don't exercise either, so they don't need to be eating that much. You can tell that they don't need to eat that much either as obesity and diabetes are an epidemic. She was so happy to be at a good healthy weight and not let the pressures of the food advertisements and others push her into eating more. So many people are manipulated by the marketing campaigns to eat this or that, and then the people pressure others into doing the same thing. Society needs to deal with that problem, but they aren't because there is so much money and greed wrapped up in overeating and medical costs from people getting sick from their food addictions. It made Emerald feel really sad to see overweight and unhealthy people, especially children.

Emerald washed out her dishes and went to the bathroom. She walked into the living room and did some thorough stretching. She did some chin tucks and neck stretches and stretched out her arms, legs, and back. She waved her arms over her head and from side to side. She rotated her ankles around a few times. She bent down and back up a few times like doing squats while she took some deep breaths as she slowly inhaled and exhaled. She lifted herself up with her toes a bunch of times. She stretched her back out backwards and forwards. She put the palm of her hands on the floor while she was standing, which she used to have a hard time doing. She then separately stretched both legs out behind her, in front of her, and to the sides of her. Lastly, she got on the ground like she was going to do a pushup, and she pushed her abdomen forward while looking upward to really stretch her back out. She held that position for a while as it really made her feel good to stretch her body and back out like that. She then got on her knees and took a deep breath and slowly exhaled it.

She grabbed a mat by the wall and laid it down, so she could sit on it. She got into a comfortable sitting position with her legs crossed and back straight up and down. She closed her eyes and started her meditation session. Emerald tried to focus her attention on her head at first and then slowly focused her attention down her body and back up again. As she focused on the top of her body, she tried to feel everything from her hair, head, face, eyes, nose, mouth, teeth, tongue, chin, ears, neck, and shoulders. Then, she let her attention flow separately down each arm to her elbows, hands, and fingers and back up to her shoulders again. She let her attention flow into her chest, heart, lungs, stomach, abdomen, and groin area. She kept moving her attention separately down each leg to her knee, feet, and toes and back up through her body until she got back up to the top of her head.

She went back to focusing her attention on her heart. She has been trying to give more focus to her heart while not thinking of anything. She would just let her breath go in and out while having an awareness on her heart. She found it was interesting that the more she focused on her heart that she felt the beating and rhythm more. While she was focusing on her heart, she would have a few random thoughts come through her mind. She would think about Mary, work, religion, and politics, but instead of focusing on them, she just let her mind do its thing. As long as she didn't consciously try to stop thinking about these things, these thoughts would usually just go away until she was in a state of nothingness. Surprisingly, she also felt like she was in a state of everything. The thoughts just came and went while she kept giving attention and awareness to her heart. She got very relaxed almost to the point of not feeling her body at all. It was like she was levitating or floating as she couldn't feel the floor or mat under her. Emerald mediated for about an hour and then opened her eyes. She took a big deep breath, stoop up, and stretched her back out again.

"That's how you start the day," Emerald said out loud.

Even without exercising, she still had a little time before the sun came up, so she grabbed her journal and her music notebooks, which had all her original songs in them. While she was meditating, she thought of a dream that she forgot after she woke up. She thought it was weird that she would sometimes remember a dream that she forgot while she was meditating. It was like she was accessing her subconscious mind that retains that information, but she had to be in a certain state of relaxation or focus to access, get, or remember it. It was like the dream was brought into her conscious mind or awareness through the relaxation, focus, and attention.

She wrote down that she was in a building. She thought it was day due to the amount of light coming in from the windows. There were others around. She thought she was with a man, but she was not sure who he was. They were on a high floor and waiting for an elevator, so they could go down. The elevator door opened, and they walked into the elevator. She tried to push the buttons, but it was confusing in the dream. The buttons were not labeled or numbered. There were a lot of them, and she didn't know which button was the floor that she was on or which button to push to get to where she needed to go. She actually had no idea where she was going. It seemed that there was some kind of writing or symbols next to each button, but Emerald couldn't decipher what they meant. It was like in another language. She didn't know what happened after that. She either woke up or couldn't remember anything else after that point in the dream. She thought the dream was odd. She felt anxious and frustrated from that situation. She wasn't sure what to make of the dream either or if it had any meaning for her. Since she forgot about it, she wasn't sure if she was supposed to forget about it.

She couldn't remember any other dreams, so she put down her dream journal and grabbed her music notebook. She read over a few songs that she was writing and came up with over the past few months. She thought how different the songs were from the songs that she wrote a few years ago. They were more passionate with the issues of society and the world and focused on rebellion and revolution. The songs were also heavier or more rocking than her earlier songs that she wrote, which were more about love and sounded more folky. She used to write a lot of love songs for Mary, but Emerald has had this fire burning in her regarding the problems going on with society and the nation. She read over the lyrics and tried to think of changing or adding to the lyrics. She read back over "What's Wrong with Being Free," "You Were Lied To," and "Political Corruption." She made some minor changes here and there but nothing major.

Emerald saw that it was getting lighter outside and felt the sun coming up, so she decided to stop looking over her songs for now and get ready to head down to the park. She went to the bathroom and got dressed. It was a little cool outside, but she didn't overdress. She threw on some thin pants and a short-sleeve shirt. She left Mary a sweet note telling her where she was, that she hoped she was sleeping well, how beautiful she was, and how much she loved her. She grabbed her bike and headed out the door. She felt a little rushed, so after she got outside, she paused for a minute to look up at the darkish bluish sky that still had some stars shining. She was trying to take more moments like that to check herself when she was rushing around and not enjoying life. She took a huge deep breath and took in the fresh cool morning air. She thought it was so nice. She got on her bike to take off. Right before she got to the end of their parking lot, Mary opened the door and yelled at her.

"Em, wait up!" Mary shouted.

Emerald heard her, turned around, and peddled back over to their apartment door. She saw Mary was dressed and had her bike.

"What are you doing silly?" Emerald asked.

"I got up to pee, and I heard the door close. I saw your note, so I got dressed as fast as I could to see if I could catch you. I thought I might have missed you. Then, I was going to try and track you down."

"Oh yeah? Where would you have gone?"

"To that park over there."

Mary pointed to the south.

"Well, you would have found me," Emerald said.

Emerald got off her bike and set it next to the wall. Mary did the same with her bike. They kissed and hugged each other, greeted each other with a good morning phrase, and told each other that they loved one another. The took off on their bikes to the park. The traffic was staring to pick up, but it was not too bad yet. They played like they were racing each other. Mary would get in front of Emerald, and then Emerald would speed up and get in front of Mary. They laughed a few times and made eyes at each other. They got to the park and found a bench. Emerald's favorite bench was taken by a couple, but there was another one close by that was still by the water where you could see the sun and sky reflect off the water. The sky was clear this morning, so Emerald was going to miss out on the colors that the sunlight creates by hitting the clouds just right. They were just going to have to enjoy the amazing and wonderful sun in all its glory. They got off their bikes and sat down. They still had several minutes before the sun poked its nose over the horizon, so they chatted a little bit about their sleep and Emerald's morning.

"How'd you sleep?" Mary asked.

"About the same. I fell asleep alright. I slept pretty good until I peed after midnight. I fell back asleep okay and slept good for a couple of hours, but I started waking up a couple of hours before I got up. That has been happening to me a lot. I start waking up and falling back asleep and tossing and turning the last hour or two before I get up. I finally just say fuck it and get up. I'm a little tired when I get up, but it's not horrible. I feel great now after eating, stretching, and meditating. It's also nice to get outside and feel the elements. You liven me up too."

Emerald leaned over and kissed Mary.

"That's sweet Em."

"What about you?" Emerald asked.

"Well, I'm up. It was good. Not as rough as you, but I probably didn't finish sleeping as much as I should have. I slept most of the night. I got home about nine and was out by 11. So, not too bad."

"That's great. I'm not sure if I should be worried about my sleep or not. I feel great when I'm up. It's just those last couple hours are brutal sometimes. It's bizarre that I do that."

"If it means anything, you look fabulous and are fabulous."

"Thanks."

"Just keep assessing your body and how you are feeling."

"There she is. See that." Emerald said as she pointed to where the sun was coming up on the horizon.

"Yup. So beautiful. I wish there were some clouds."

"I was thinking the same thing. That would be awesome. Just be glad there aren't any chem trails from them spraying the poisons in the air. Those bastards."

"Not only poisoning us but also uglying up the sky. So disgusting."

"Very colorful," Emerald said excitedly. "Look at that white yellow and the darker yellow."

"Oh wow. That orangish to almost reddish color across the horizon is amazing. Very spiritual."

"Just soak it in. Let it hit your third eye and get that pineal gland going. Very energizing. This is how you wake up in the morning and get the day started."

"I see why you try to get down here as much as you can. It's so invigorating."

"Absofuckinglutely," Emerald said with a smile. "Especially since some days it's too cloudy and rainy. It's good for me to try as much as possible.

You are always welcome to join me. I know it's early for you, and I do love the quiet and alone time, but it's great to share something as special as this with you."

"We'll see. Maybe once in a while."

"Great. Just let me know when you might feel like it and leave me a note, and I'll rustle you up."

"Sounds good."

Emerald and Mary took a break from talking for a minute and just held each other's hands on top of Mary's lap and watched the sun slowly creep up above the horizon.

"I love this," Emerald said.

"Me too."

"Do you want to walk the bikes around the park or just ride the bikes slowly around the park?"

"Let's walk for a bit, but I'm getting hungry."

"Cool. Just let me know when you are ready."

They started walking around the pond with their bikes.

"I wish we didn't have to work today, and we could enjoy each other all day," Emerald said.

"We gotta make that money somehow. Just enjoy the now, and if you are lucky, maybe we can have a moment when we get back. After I eat a bite though."

"Sounds delicious. I was hoping for some dessert, so that would be perfect."

"You know it. It always is."

"I love making love to you Mary. I mean that."

"I enjoy it too Em. It's like we were made for each other."

"I'm so lucky to have you in my life."

"I am too. I don't think you give yourself enough credit Em. Sure, you have made some mistakes, but we all have, and it's more about where you are at now and how you are doing now that matters."

"You are right. It will take me some time to feel humble about the shit I did to you and how I fucked things up for you and us."

"Well, unlike most religious folk, I forgive you. You know. Because they are supposed to be forgiving, but they are not."

"True that. Thanks. That means a lot. I just wish that we didn't have to work at all, so we could be totally free and enjoy this life to the fullest. I know that we would still have to do chores and take care of our responsibilities, but it wouldn't be like being an economic slave. Most people have meaningless and pointless jobs just to produce ridiculous and pointless products to make someone else rich. Most of the products that we make are pollutants to us and the earth. We also shouldn't have to pay taxes towards horrible and awful things like rich and corrupt politicians, wars, and subsidies for already rich and profitable companies that focus on destroying and polluting the environment and making people sick. There's no point for our taxes to go to companies that are already billionaires. It's like a slap in the citizens' faces of how corrupt the politicians are for these companies to bribe them with lots of money, so they end up giving them lots of money. Why doesn't someone do something about that? It's not okay."

"You are right Em. It's not okay at all. That's the problem with having rich and greedy politicians. The people who could do something about it are the ones who are benefiting from the scam and corruption. They also own and/or have interest in those companies."

"Well, we know who they are. Some of these companies make automobiles, airplanes, drugs, and technology, and some produce coal, oil, and aluminum. Don't forget the poison and chemical companies that pollute, poison, and infect everything around them by not only using poisons but also making genetically mutant organisms like corn, wheat, cotton, and soy. There's the despicable tobacco and alcohol companies too along with the disgusting animal agriculture industry. You also have the physically and sexually abusive dairy and egg industries. Why don't they subsidize organic farming and produce, renewable energies, and the arts? That would actually make sense and help us all. It's like they want us all to get sick and die horrible deaths, and they are actively trying to kill us all. At this point, it's very suspicious that these same companies are major contributors to pollution, environmental disasters and destruction, and global warming. Furthermore, they all could have easily been ethical and environmentally friendly companies by now by focusing on renewable energies, sustainability, organic processes, and the well-being of people, the animals, and the earth. Think about it. These are very evil companies that make billions in profits, so why are we paying them more money in taxes that they don't need? It needs to stop today."

"Settle down Em. I know those issues make you upset. I think the argument is that the subsidies keep the prices low and the jobs in our country. It's like a bribe to keep the company from abusing us even more, but you and I know that those are bullshit reasons because the purpose is for a few people to get very rich off our misery. It's called getting rich by making the rich richer. You scratch my back, and I'll scratch yours. It's politics. The wealthy help the wealthy in this country and not the people, the citizens, and the small businesses or at least the businesses who are trying to do good, such as organic farmers and renewable energy companies. It is crazy and unfortunate that they only give the enormous amounts of money to wealthy companies who don't need it and are already making millions and even billions in profits. It's even more crazy that people keep voting for these same politicians who are so corrupt and don't give a shit about the voters who vote for them."

"Well, most of the politicians own those companies or have interest in them. If not, they receive campaign contributions and lobbying funds, I mean bribes, from them. Their friends and family members may own them too."

"Yes, that is well put. The companies do bribe the politicians through campaign donations or contributions and lobbying."

"Sorry, I'll refocus. I don't want to ruin our lovely morning with my wonderful and beautiful Mary."

"It's okay. You know I like a good deep discussion, especially if it's bashing our corrupt and deplorable government, politicians, and businesses."

"You know I wouldn't mind working and paying taxes if it was like a community and there was actual production, sustainability, organic farming, and renewable energies. Wouldn't it be awesome to work in a cooperative or community type setting?"

"It would be fucking fantastic. We should start doing some research into that to see if there is something out there that we would fit into."

"That would be great. I just don't think I have the patience to hope that anything will change for the better in this country. The citizens are going to have to revolt at this point and fight a bloody and deadly battle to finally end the tyranny of our government, but since so many are so blind, ignorant, apathetic, brainwashed, programmed, and enslaved in the system, I'm not sure the revolution could be a reality or could happen. So many people would just shrug their shoulders or not think it would be worth it. I think they are for a revolution, but to actually be a part of one is a whole other story. Then, you have the vicious and dishonest marketing and advertising campaigns that the government would put out there to lie and make stuff up about the people revolting or threaten anyone who wants to be a part of the revolution. You know, because they own the media, and people believe what is on the news and the lying politicians."

"Hey Em, it is better that we take our lives into our own hands."

"I hate to give up though, but what can you do when there is so much corruption? We could die fighting for our own rights too."

"Some think that is worth it."

"I'll think about that more. If I'm going to die for a cause, it better be good. Overthrowing our non-democratic and authoritarian government would be worth it."

"With what we are talking about and how bad things have gotten, it would definitely be worth it. I know that we are not the only ones who see the truth or feel this way. There are others out there Em. We have to keep trying and speaking out. It's important. Terrorism is not just about making people feel physically threatened, but it is also about making people feel like they can't do anything or that speaking out and a revolution wouldn't do any good. It's like they want us to have free speech and freedom, but they really don't. That is how we terrorize the terrorists, who are our government, the politicians, the rich, and the corporations. We keep speaking out, we vote, we protest, and we revolt. They can try to censure us and shut us up, but we will keep screaming and fighting. Silence, apathy, and conformity are consent."

"You are right Mary. Revolution! I love you my dark and sexy everything."

"I love you too my beautiful creamy white open-minded lady. Let's get out of here."

"Sounds good."

Emerald and Mary gave each other a passionate kiss and watched the glorious sun one more time while holding hands. The sun was up over the horizon now, so it was more yellow. They both weirdly took a deep breath together like they were feeling the same thing in that moment. They took in the breath like they were breathing in the energy and strength from the sun and the universe. They both exhaled at the same time too like they were letting out all the negativity, pain, and suffering. They got on their bikes and rode back to the apartment. There was a lot more traffic out as people were headed to work, so Mary asked if they could take a longer route around the main roads. Emerald was okay with that recommendation. She loved it when Mary was spontaneous. Doing things on the spur of the moment helped Emerald stay out of a rut from being too scheduled and too disciplined. They took a road without a sidewalk, so they had to ride in the street. They headed south for a while, which was in the opposite direction of their apartment.

The surroundings gave way to some country and fields instead of the buildings and residences. There were a couple of pastures with farm animals on them. Emerald tried not to focus on the captured, abused, and neglected animals that people think they own. To Emerald, it was no different than human slavery. Just because animals can't defend themselves and communicate with us doesn't give us a right to do whatever we want with them. Since you cannot get their consent, it is abuse. Emerald knew in her heart that killing animals is murder. She was starting to get upset. She thought about how many people don't think about the evils of the inhumane animal agriculture industry and how animals are treated. They always say asinine things like they taste good or stupid religious arguments that animals were put here on earth for humans. Emerald thought how idiotic and moronic the taste argument was due to everyone adding fruits and vegetables to their dead animals to make them taste good. She also thought how stupid and ignorant the religious and speciesism argument was that they were put here for humans due to the fact that animals were here before humans existed. If anything, we were put here for the animals. Then, there are others who don't eat as many animals but justify the abusive and murderous animal agriculture industry by thinking that the animals are actually treated with respect and dignity.

Most people don't realize where their food comes from. People think farm animals live in these wide-open spaces, but they don't. Most animals are kept in small confined places and forced to live in unsanitary conditions while being fed foods they wouldn't normally eat that has chemicals, genetically mutant organisms, and poisons in and on them. They also shoot up most animals with medications and anti-biotics. If they didn't, the animals would get sick and/or die due to the chemicals and unnatural food they are given and the unsanitary and disease-ridden living conditions that they are forced to barely survive in. People would also get sick and die if they didn't medicate the animals because of these issues. They also have to rape and sexually assault the animals to make more animals or make the dairy and eggs. Having to go through this bizarre process to make sure your dead animal that you still have to cook thoroughly to avoid getting diseases from is a lot of effort and work just to be able to say that it tastes good. It would be a lot easier, cleaner, and healthier to just eat fruits and vegetables. Most importantly, all farm animals are neglected and abused. They are slaves. A lot of them are also tagged, branded, burned, and beaten to obey.

Companies spend billions to keep negative advertising of the animal agriculture industry out of the media and the positive, misleading, and dishonest ones in the media. This industry has also paid billions to bribe politicians to pass laws to make it illegal for animal rights activists, journalists, or others to take pictures or record videos of the horrible conditions that the animals are grown in, which is contrary to freedom of speech and freedom of the press. They have even found some of these heroes and patriots to be guilty of environmental terrorism when they were just trying to show the public the truth of where their unsanitary and sickening food comes from. The real environmental terrorists are the politicians who support this industry and the people in the animal agriculture business who kill billions of animals a week for food, clothing, and vivisection or scientific testing. That astronomical number is absolute insanity and disgusting. The pollution that comes from the animal agriculture business is a whole other atrocity and terrorist act as it directly and significantly contributes to global warming and climate change and pollutes the air, water, and land. It's all so much death and destruction. Emerald could cry every day thinking about this horror and these truths. Emerald stopped this thinking process for now and took a deep breath. She looked up to the clear sky and saw a half moon still shining bright to the west. She yelled at Mary to look up at the moon.

"It's beautiful," Mary said.

"Yes, amazing. So awesome."

They rode west on a cut off road for a little while longer and then started heading north back to the city and their apartment. A few automobiles drove by but not as many as they thought would have. Emerald thought it was a bit scary riding a bike or jogging on a road without a sidewalk as a lot of drivers are inconsiderate and always in a hurry. She knew some were just selfish assholes who think they were the center of the universe and even think other drivers should get out of their way. They tried to enjoy the rest of the journey and adventure. They raced as fast as they could passing each other while laughing. Emerald was starting to feel excited and happy again, especially after thinking about the animals. She knew she was doing her part. She just wished a lot more people would wake up and start caring more. She knew love was the answer.

Emerald and Mary made it back to the apartment. It was a longer ride than they had expected, so they decided to get clean right away. Emerald turned on some instrumental psychedelic rock to assist with the ambience. They wanted to spice it up, so they took a shower together, which Emerald loved as she was very physically attracted to Mary. Emerald thought she was the most beautiful woman in the world. She loved her darker and smooth skin. Mary was very sexy to Emerald. They both enjoyed a moment together in the shower, dried off, and went to the bed to finish making love.

After they pleasured each other, Emerald made them some lunch. She made her tasty organic, raw, gluten free, and plant-based guacamole salad with hemp and pumpkin seeds, pine nuts, herbs and spices, kale, spinach, chard, diced cherry tomatoes, and kimchi. She added some apple cider and coconut vinegar to liven it up. Mary made them a couple glasses of spring water. They enjoyed the music while they ate and talked about how their work was going. After they finished their salads, they had some frozen fruit and some of Emerald's delicious home-made chocolate, which she loved to make. It was also organic, raw, gluten free, and plant based. She would whip it up over the weekend in small batches to last them for a couple of weeks. She would make different kinds, but they all had some similar ingredients of cacao, cinnamon, stevia, pink sea salt, cashew butter, coconut oil, coconut butter, cacao butter, and vanilla. She would also make one with almond butter, another with pieces of cashews and pecans, and another with shredded coconut and coconut flour, which was like a macaroon.

Emerald thought the chocolate was absolutely delicious and way cheaper than the overpriced processed crap they sell at the store. Most of the ones from the store also have dairy and chemicals in them, which make people sick and cause them to have allergic reactions and/or stomach and digestive problems. The processed ones also have added sugar in them, which causes cancer, diabetes, and obesity. Emerald concluded that people who eat things that they think taste good but make them sick were absolutely stupid and asking to die an early death. To Emerald, it was just not worth it. It wasn't okay to make yourself sick while sexually assaulting, neglecting, abusing, and murdering innocent and helpless cows and other animals. It also wasn't okay to steal their milk while the abusive and murderous farmers take their babies away from them to either abuse or slaughter them.

Both Emerald and Mary had to work today, so they held each other after they ate for a while and then got ready to go to work. Emerald was looking forward to just working with Beth tonight. She hasn't had the opportunity to have a long conversation with her in a while. Emerald thought Beth was pretty cool. She was younger than Mary and Emerald, but she had a good smart head on her. Beth still had a lot to learn though. While Mary got ready in the bathroom, Emerald washed out their dishes and then grabbed her guitar out of the front room. She sat down on the love seat. She had to tune it a little and then started playing some chords. She had a tune rolling around in her head, but it was more of a sinister type rock song than she usually plays. She thought it would sound better on an electric guitar with some distortion. She imagined it being more related to doom rock, and it needed a wah pedal for some parts of it. She didn't want to drag all her guitar gear out, so she just tried her best to create it on the acoustic guitar. She imagined herself playing in front of thousands of people. She could hear this awesome sounding rock song about revolution and taking back what was stolen from us. When she played, she wanted everyone to feel where she was coming from and her feelings of angst and frustration with the powers that be. She tried to play a few notes and chords that go low and then high. The song sounded dark and mysterious.

Mary yelled to Emerald that she was done in the bathroom. Emerald wrote down a few notes and some ideas for lyrics. She decided to call it "The Reclamation." She wanted it to be about the oppressed and abused where they would rise up and take back what was taken from them. She was very excited about the idea and the sound of the song. She has come a long way from writing folky love songs for Mary and playing other people's music. Emerald went to the bathroom, did some hygiene, and got dressed for work. They both kissed and hugged each other before they left and said their goodbyes and how much they loved one another. Emerald grabbed her bike, and Mary grabbed the car keys. They both went to work.

On her way to work, Emerald kept thinking and humming the tune that she was working on before she left. She tried to work out the riff for the verse and the chorus. She wasn't feeling a bridge on this one in between the verses and chorus. She tried to think of some more ideas to come up with the lyrics. She started the song with like a wah sound that was evil or dark sounding. That riff would play for about eight measures before the lyrics would start. She wanted to make sure the lyrics were very powerful and meaningful. She imagined herself listening to some other deep and moving songs where the singer actually opened your mind with the words that he or she used. That's what she wanted out of this song.

She got to the store and Beth was waiting on her. Beth was ready to leave for a bit and get some lunch. Beth wanted to go ahead and take a break while they were slow, so she could get back in case they got busy. Emerald brought her bike inside the store, so she could park it in the back room.

"What's up Beth?"

"Hangin out. Doing good. How's it going with you?"

"Excellent. It's been a great day so far. Looking forward to chillin out and talking with you."

"You know what? Me too. It seems like it has been a while since we had more than two minutes of conversation."

"Absolutely."

"Do you mind if I go ahead and take off for about an hour?"

"Not at all. Go for it."

"Cool. So good to see you. There is no one else here right now."

They hugged and Beth left. Emerald walked her bike to the backroom and hurried back to the front in case someone came in. She walked around the store to make sure things were in order. She grabbed a book off the shelf on philosophy. It was a general book that covered some major philosophical thinkers over the past few thousand years. It was like a primer. She thumbed through it. Then, a woman and a man walked through the front door into the store. They had a low sounding electronic bell that dinged when someone would open the front door. She put the book back but tried to commit it to memory in case she wanted to look at it again later.

"Hello there," Emerald said. "Please let me know if I can help you find anything."

"Sounds good," the male customer said. "We're just browsing for now."

"Actually, where is your section on botany or specifically on trees or dendrology?" The female customer said.

"You got it," Emerald said. "It's right over here."

They walked over a couple of isles. Emerald showed them a section on botany and horticulture.

"Right here is actually a couple of books on dendrology," Emerald said. "I don't think I have ever heard that term before."

"Yes, it's becoming an interest of mine," the female customer said.

"Well, let me know if you need anything else."

"Thanks."

Emerald walked up to the front behind the counter. Adam and Don asked that at least one of them stand up at the front of the store when there was a customer there, so they could see the store better, just in case someone tried to steal something. They put in a security system, but there were a couple of blind spots. Emerald kept humming that song she was working on earlier. The two customers sat down in the open area with the seats, so Emerald thought that they might be a while. The male customer had a book too that he was looking through. It looked like the female customer grabbed both books on dendrology. Emerald quickly walked back over and grabbed that philosophy book. She brought it back to the front behind the register. She was pretty familiar with several of the philosophers and had a good idea of some their topics that they discussed, especially on morals, ethics, and human behaviors. Emerald has read several books on a variety of philosophers over the past 20 years. This book struck her interest as it had a few names that she did not recognize. Two of them were women, so she was very interested in learning about them.

Emerald started thinking how upsetting and disappointing it was that there were so many men noted and recognized in history and taught in school while the women were oppressed, neglected, overlooked, and forgotten. We have given so much fame and credit to men even though women have done just as many great things. Knowing how men were, Emerald knew that a lot of our history was a lie and has been manipulated and distorted to make men seem superior and more intelligent than women. When in fact, the women probably did most of the things that men got credit for. The men just stole the ideas from them. It made her wonder how many things, ideas, inventions, and major discoveries were actually from women. Their wives, girlfriends, or mistresses probably mentioned something amazing to them, and the rest was patriarchal and sexist history. She laughed out loud as there was probably more truth to that than anyone will ever know or say.

She read a little about how this woman philosopher discussed the old debate on inner conflict and insecurities of fear and self-hate projecting itself into the problems of society, such as war, pollution, abuse, neglect, and animal cruelty. The woman philosopher's theory was cyclical though. It wasn't just about the inner struggles that the individuals have, but it was about how over time and through generations the cultures and problems create just as many problems for the individuals as their own. So, it makes it more challenging for the individuals to cope with their own problems or even see that they are the problem because the external problems become the excuses and a distraction from their own problems, which they don't deal with. All these different problems become complicated and very challenging to handle. The philosopher went on to say how many people use these external problems as excuses, but the external problems are really just an illusion because the real problem is within the individuals. She used an analogy of someone who digs a whole but ends up at the bottom of the hole and has a hard time getting back out. So, the same person struggling to get out of the hole that they dug is also the same person who is doing the digging. You are your ultimate problem and have to take responsibility for making your life more miserable. Emerald thought about responsibility and not using excuses for difficult situations.

The woman and the man came up to the front to check out.

"We'll take these four," the male customer said.

Emerald was excited as she couldn't remember ever selling more than two books in one sale. She checked them out and took their payment.

They both said thank you.

"Thank you," Emerald said. "Please come by and see us again."

"We will," the female customer said as they walked out of the store.

Beth came in a couple of minutes after they left.

"I just sold four books in one transaction," Emerald said proudly.

"That's crazy. Since I got here this morning, I think I sold about 15. There must be something in the air convincing people to buy books today."

"We should ask for a raise," Emerald said while she laughed.

"Well, with it getting colder, we might have some good business and get a bonus."

"We'll see. As much as I hate money, they make it so damn necessary. It's like a trap."

"It is. Maybe one day we'll figure out how to get out. I'm just glad we aren't in a factory or doing hard, sweaty, uncomfortable labor for a low wage. You know, like how our largest and most profitable companies treat their workers in other countries."

"True that. It's hard to complain when things could be worse."

Emerald and Beth went to go sit down in the comfortable chairs in the open area where people would sit down for hours and read. They engaged in some small talk, and Beth told Emerald that she was seeing a new guy and that it was going alright. Emerald told Beth about her and Mary's adventures to the park and that she has had a lot of deep thoughts and conversations lately. Emerald confided into Beth that she was seriously thinking about moving sooner than later.

"I'm getting concerned about the apathy, corruption, denial, and flat out abuse and neglect," Emerald said seriously. "The government, politicians, and law enforcement are out of control. They are just letting the corporations run wild. It's an abomination."

"Totally. If I hear one more person deny global warming and climate change, I'm going to hit them in the face, and they are going ask me why I did that because it hurt, and I'm going to tell them that I didn't do it and it doesn't hurt. I'm going to tell them that me hitting them is not real and that they are just imagining that I hit them and that it hurts. Just like they are imagining that global warming and climate change are not real because they are too stupid to think for themselves, use common sense, and listen to reason and the truth. They would rather listen to a corrupted, dishonest, and paid-off politician, who coincidentally has a shitload of money wrapped up in or is being given a shitload of money by the fossil fuel, animal agriculture, and deforestation industries instead of listening to actual scientists and seeing the factual evidence. You would have to be a complete moron to not see that humans are significantly affecting and polluting the climate and the environment while depleting the planet's natural resources. I mean it's insanity that people listen to their religious and political figures and leaders over science and facts. What is up with that? It drives me crazy."

"That was an amazing speech Beth. You should write that down. Can I use that?"

"Definitely. Yes, I have rehearsed that one a few times. Not sure if I would actually hit someone, but that speech gets my point across. I'm definitely going to express that when I hear another idiotic statement that denies science and facts."

"Well, it's beautiful. The whole pollution, resource depletion, and the raping and destroying of the earth issues have me so concerned. I would rather live in a country that cares about its land, water, air, people, and animals. The avoidance, denial, lying, and manipulation are not okay. All so they can keep the money machine rolling."

"It's all about money Em. Money will kill us all. I know the earth goes through natural states of climate change and global warming, but without a significant natural disaster like a volcano erupting or a comet or big asteroid hitting the earth, the only reason for how quickly things are changing and how fast the greenhouse gasses, such as carbon dioxide and methane, are increasing in the atmosphere is from the direct impact of humans. For the planet to naturally do that on its own without the help of humans or a natural disaster would take tens of thousands of years. It wouldn't take less than a century where we can see the changes with our own eyes. And, the significant increase in these greenhouse gasses into our environment just happens to coincide with the industrial revolution of when we started to mine and use fossil fuels for energy and farm animals on a large scale with concentrated animal feeding operations. You have to be an idiot not to accept that, or you are just a liar and a greedy bastard."

"Since companies are also in the business of making money as well as polluting, you think they would accept climate change instead of looking like an idiot and denying it due to them losing lots of money on weather related issues that they are causing to begin with. Stupidity at its best. I guess they are willing to take a risk on making as much money as possible before the disasters hit them. I guess that's what insurance is for even though that's a scam."

"Unfortunately, I think the citizens and the people deserve the problems that we are facing. They deserve the future hell that they and their children are going to live in with plastic and trash everywhere, polluted land, unclean and chemical-laden water, toxic air, and so many overweight and sick people."

"It is very depressing. I am struggling with hopelessness Beth. It's like we have reached the point of no return. The government has to do something now, but they keep procrastinating and avoiding their responsibilities. It's both the traditionalists and the progressives. They seem like they are both corrupted. We should have become politicians or doctors, but then I think I couldn't sell my soul to make money off destroying things and making people miserable and sick. It's crazy how many politicians screw things up more than before they were in office, and it's crazy how many doctors just provide treatments and bandages that don't cure anything. They actually create more sicknesses from their methods instead of focusing on prevention and curing the problems. I can't believe that most doctors throw pills and prescriptions, which are mostly poisonous and toxic, at illnesses without doing any tests and proper diagnostics. It's careless and negligent. How can you prescribe a medication or treatment without knowing what the patient has, and how can you prescribe medication and treatment that doesn't cure the problem, which would be curable with a healthy diet, exercise, healthy fun, and meditation sessions? It doesn't make sense. I wouldn't prescribe any medications or drugs, unless you consider food and plants medication. I would focus on recommending a plant-based diet, lots of organic and raw fruits and vegetables, exercise and stretching, meditation, sunshine and nature, and having fun and laughter. I would spend time educating others on the different benefits of fruits and vegetables and responsibility. That is how you cure and prevent diseases and problems. People, society, and the world would be in such a better place. Unfortunately, I wouldn't make a lot of money though as people would get better and not need to have to come back to see me."

"You are right. Not too many would come to see us then. Almost everyone would be cured and have no problems. We would be starving doctors who couldn't pay back our insanely high student loans and way over-priced education. I guess that would be a good thing though. If you can fix problems and work your way out of a job, you did a good and fantastic job. Since people aren't fixing problems and creating more problems, they should be fired. Very shameful. You aren't doing a good job if problems stay the same or get worse."

"That is sad but true Beth. It's like people are being commended for being incompetent, and the citizens are okay with it. They would rather take a pill that causes a few other diseases and problems rather than change what they are doing that's causing their illness in the first place. If they would just eat healthy and exercise a little bit, they wouldn't have all these sicknesses. What a bunch of lazy pieces of shits. A bunch of sedentary asses."

"Totally Em. I'm with you. I don't eat raw foods that much, and I'm not vegan, but I mainly eat organic. I don't want to eat poisons and science experiments that they call GMO foods, which are poisons and cause lots of different types of sicknesses and cancer. I'm so pissed off at the government, politicians, and the consumer protection agencies accepting bribes to be paid off to look the other way. It's so upsetting that the politicians and government agencies have interest and ownership in the conventional farming companies that spray massive amounts of poisons on their already genetically mutant organisms that are supposed to grow without the poisons anyway. What is the point of a consumer protection agency if they don't protect the consumers from illegal, unethical, and evil practices of the businesses? The government and politicians are supposed to be protecting the consumers and citizens too. It's not okay for them to have a price and for them to be able to be paid to look the other way while these evil corporations poison us with their chemicals and genetically mutant organisms that they try to pass off as food. The only reason there are genetically mutant organisms is that the companies needed something to patent, so no one else can grow and make these types of poisoned foods. It's all about money and not the safety of the people, society, animals, and the environment."

"Yes, the poisons or the herbicides, fungicides, and the pesticides that they spray all over everything get in the food, the air, the water, and the land, so people end up getting sick. They also end up getting a host of diseases and even cancer. These companies then spend billions in advertising and false, biased, and erroneous research while paying off government officials by saying that they are not causing these diseases or any problems. Unfortunately, the citizens are stupid enough to believe them instead of using common sense to deduce that it's probably not a good idea to be eating poisoned and chemical-laden foods. People wonder why they are getting sick when the evidence is right there in front of them."

"People are idiots Em. They deserve to get sick. We don't, but they do. And, don't forget that the bugs and the weeds adapt and become stronger due to the poisons that they use. You know. Because evolution is real and a fact. The companies have to keep using higher concentrations and stronger doses and more of the poisons than they started with because the weeds and the insects become resistant to and stronger than the poisons. The weeds and the bugs grow faster and bigger. In addition, their overall yields of food are not that good. It's actually worse than organic farming, but they don't talk about that. So, you get increased and massive amounts of pollution, environmental destruction, bigger weeds and insects, increased sicknesses and cancer in the human and animal populations, increased death in the animal and human populations, and less food to feed everyone. Tell me how any of that makes any sense. It's complete insanity.

The rational thing to do would be for them to stop this madness and focus on organic farming, but that is too sensible. They also wouldn't have a monopoly on the seeds. Instead, they just spray more of the poisons and make and spray stronger doses of the poisons. All these poisons go directly into the land, our water, and our air. Even people trying to be healthy and eating organic are consuming these poisons because of the toxic runoff and the pollution. There are so many people, especially babies and children, who have been tested with high levels of these poisons in their bodies. It's making them sick and die. There's proof of that, but the companies deny that it's their fault, and the people keep eating their foods and making them rich. I can't imagine the long-term impact of this science experiment, which is really what it is with no proof at all that it is safe."

"Those are great points Beth. They also are destroying the farmlands that they grow these genetically mutant organisms on while spraying all these chemicals and poisons on them. Since they don't care about the soil, use poisonous and toxic synthetic fertilizers, and don't till the soil, the soil is unusable after they are done with it. Many of these conventional farmers have had to move to another field due to their crops dying off. It would take an organic farmer hundreds of years or generations to rejuvenate the soil to grow something in it. They basically destroy what was excellent farmland that could have been used indefinitely if cultivated organically, but they turn it into a wasteland. It's so horrible and not okay. People have no idea what is going on because these malicious companies are putting so much money into public relations and marketing by lying that what they are doing is a good thing, especially due to overpopulation. They say they are trying to feed the world, but they are really killing everyone by poisoning them. If they cared about feeding the world, they would let everyone have their seeds for free, so everyone could grow their so-called safe foods. They could also give food away, but they don't. Instead, they sue everyone who tries to use their seeds and cover up scientific evidence and proof that their genetically mutant organisms and poisons that they are using are causing people to get sick and die. They even do all those horrible things while polluting the earth. They also intentionally plant them on other farms who are not using them, so they can sue them for using them."

"Get that shit away from my organic food," Beth said in a sassy way.

"Absolutely! The other farmer should get to sue them for poisoning and tainting their crops with their science experiment, but good honest farmers don't normally sue every chance that they get. I don't think they even have the time or the money to do that because they are actually trying to do some good unlike the poison companies who are polluting our world with genetically mutant organisms and chemicals. You can't trust anyone who sues hardworking farmers, especially when it's the GMO companies' fault to begin with. That is a low blow. Don't forget these are poison and chemical companies first and foremost. How does a poison company get approval to make food? How does that make sense? How does that happen? That is unfuckingbelievable. I wouldn't trust an electrician to do plumbing, I wouldn't trust an astrophysicist to solve a biology problem, I wouldn't trust a politician, who only cares about himself and money, to fix our societal problems, and I wouldn't trust a doctor, who only cares about profits and money, to cure my affliction. You don't put your trust and support in people and organizations that make their money doing something completely different and then want to venture into a completely different field for only monetary reasons. No matter what they say, they are doing it to make money. They don't care who gets hurt and what the consequences are. If the oil companies wanted to get into renewable energy or if an animal agricultural company wanted to sell plant-based products, I would tell them to fuck off. They had their chance. It's an obvious attempt to exploit everyone in another way."

"It totally is Em. You go girl."

"It's actually worse to have a poison company make our food. Hell, they put poisons in and on the food. They make it with the poisons. How safe is that? How can a consumer protection agency deem that safe? It's not safe at all. You don't need a biased and paid-for research study to say that they are safe. It's not safe and will never be safe. It makes me question the intelligence of the population. Without saying it, they are saying that they are a poison company that also makes our food. Without saying it, they are also saying that they are just in it for the money and do not care about your health and that that they pay the government a shitload of money to let them patent it, so no one else can make it. They also pay the consumer protection agencies a shitload of money to look the other way and accept their biased and erroneous studies that say their foods are safe when they are not at all safe. They also put a fuckload of money into marketing and advertising to con the public that the genetically mutant organisms are safe while discrediting and discounting the factual, independent, and accurate scientific research that has proven over and over again that poisons and genetically mutant organisms make people sick, cause cancer, and kill people. Sugar, processed foods, and foods made from animals and dead animals also have these deleterious effects. The sad thing is that the consumer protection agencies know that these types of foods aren't safe and are a hazard to human health and shouldn't be eaten and consumed by anyone. Even the poor cows and other farm animals, who don't have a choice, have to eat these poisons and genetically mutant organisms that make them sick and die. Then, people murder and eat those poisoned farm animals. That is the definition of insanity right there."

"That was great Em. I couldn't have said it better myself. Instead of consumer protection agency, it is more of a consumer destruction agency. All these facts definitely show and prove the corruption with money from the businesses through the government and its agencies while covering up the truth with an insidious marketing and advertising campaign to mislead and brainwash the vulnerable and gullible citizens. Very sad indeed."

"Shit, I forgot something. That's what I was saying before, but I got carried away. These poison companies that make the genetically mutant organisms and try to pass them off as food pay off the politicians to allow them to patent food and their seeds, which blows my mind that they are allowed to do that. What are they going to patent next? Genetically modified water or genetically modified air? They already make genetically mutant animals. Are they going to make genetically mutant humans too? Where does it stop? It enrages me with what I mentioned earlier that the genetically mutant seeds, which the organic farmers don't want, blow over into their organic fields or are intentionally put there by the poison companies. It's very suspicious that the poison company even knows that the organic farmer was using their genetically mutant seeds. How did they know that if they didn't intentionally plant them there? Are they snooping around the organic farmer's land? Then, they sue the organic farmer and harass them. Since organic farmers are not that wealthy and some are just knee high in debt and are actually poor, they don't stand a chance at defending themselves from a billionaire corporation that is suing them. The organic farmer ends up filing bankruptcy or goes out of business. Not to mention that the poison company paid off the local judge to help them win."

"Yes, I have heard of that Em. Some say that it's a conspiracy theory, but it's as real as evolution, global warming and climate change, homosexuality and intersexed persons, black holes, dinosaurs, and the atoms and quantum particles that make up everything. It's even as real as the earth and the universe being billions and billions of years old. The corruption is happening right now as we speak. There is some poor farmer who is being bullied by money and greed. It's not okay. Why would an organic farmer want their sickening and cancer causing genetically mutant and poisoned seeds anyway? They wouldn't. Again, it doesn't make sense, so why do people believe it?"

"Well, we do have a lot of morons living on this poor earth. Lots and lots of morons. You also have the other issue too with labeling genetically mutant foods. The poison companies have paid billions to politicians to vote for laws, so they don't have to label genetically mutant foods as such. They don't even have to list out the warnings and dangers of these foods, especially since they have poisons in them, which have been proven to cause illnesses, cancer, and death. If the poisons were all by themselves in a container, they would have to label their poisons as dangerous, but they don't have to label the foods that are made with the poisons and have poisons in them and on them. Tell me how that makes sense. You can even test someone's blood after eating poisoned-sprayed food and genetically mutant organisms, and they will test positive for the poisons in their bodies. That's not safe and healthy. Since the poison companies don't have to label their foods, organic farmers and organic food companies have to spend a buttload of money that they don't have to label their food as organic even though that should be a given for all food. What kind of society do we live in where you have to pay money to label a product as organic and safe but not genetically modified or poisonous? If that isn't corruption, I don't know what is. It shouldn't be a given that foods are genetically modified, dangerous, and poisonous. It should be a given that they are organic and safe. Organic foods shouldn't have to be labeled. We might as well take the warning and danger signs off everything if that is the rationale."

A couple of customers walked in, so Emerald walked up to the front and Beth tried to help them. After they looked around and left, Emerald and Beth sat back down and continued their conversation.

"It is very upsetting that the politicians have supported the poison companies over the organic ones," Beth said. "Very upsetting. You are right. It is enraging. People have a right to know that their food is genetically modified, their food has poisons in them and on them, and the dangers of eating these foods that have poisons in them and on them."

"Let's not forget the price debate too. If I hear one more person say that they can't afford organic produce because the price is too much, I'm going to slap them. That's a stupid and ignorant thing to say too. Add it to the list of stupid things that we have to hear these days. Most people don't realize that their taxes pay for genetically mutant foods and lots of other horrible products to keep their prices down. Yes, our government subsidizes poison companies and conventional farming to help make them rich and keep the prices down but not the organic farmers and companies, who are trying to keep us and the environment healthy, safe, and sustainable. Why would you subsidize an unsustainable industry that does more harm than good while manipulating the consumers with lower prices and dishonest advertisements? Oh yeah, we already answered that question. Corruption, greed, and money. You would think government subsidies and our taxes would be better spent on organic farming and produce, renewable energies, and sustainability practices to help lower their prices instead of an industry that is destroying humanity and the world. I'm not even going to get into how that is socialism and that so many traditionalists are all for government subsidies and taxes going to their companies. Companies pay a lot of money to make sure there are no labels on their foods, so consumers have no idea how their food is made, where their food is made, and what their food is made from."

"Something needs to be done about all that. That is crazy. Are we crazy?"

"We are not crazy Beth. We are just awake. We know the truth and are tired of being lied to."

"The corruption is outrageous. Companies pay a lot of money to politicians and consumer destruction agencies to look the other way, say that what they are doing is safe and okay, and deregulate these awful companies. They don't properly oversee these wicked and destructive businesses."

"There's the revolving door syndrome too with government and business. We all know that a lot of politicians are shareholders and big business employees. They actually have that issue with the consumer protection agencies too. Sorry, I meant to say the consumer destruction agencies. That actually has a nice ring to it as horrible as it is. The consumer destruction agencies have a lot of employees that have been employed by the same companies that they are assessing or supposed to be regulating. Tell me how that is not a conflict of interest. That totally pisses me off that they allow that. Those employees of these government agencies should be unbiased and non-political, but they actually hire employees from these evil corporations that are destroying and killing us all, which makes sense why none of it makes sense. They are in some powerful and high-up positions in these consumer destruction agencies too. That is a huge reason why these companies are allowed to pollute so much and sell us unsafe and harmful products."

"That is a huge conflict of interest Em. Not okay at all. They definitely do not have our best interest in mind. That is the same conflict of interest with business managers and owners being our politicians too. Money, money, money. It is so unethical. People are suffering and getting hurt and killed, and they don't care at all. It's disgusting."

"Unfortunately, we have to have regulations and regulatory agencies for private businesses in a capitalistic society. For the most part, businesses are not good natured and do not have people's and society's best interests in mind. Their number one goal is to make money and profit. They will accomplish this goal at all costs. Can you imagine if we didn't have the laws and regulations that we do to keep them in line?"

"I don't want to think about that Em. It would be right out of a horror story. It's sad that we have to tell someone and a company to not do something abusive for them to abide by it, and some still break the law. Not to mention that hardly anyone ever goes to jail from these companies' criminal acts. They just pay a small fine and keep on being abusive. The atrocities would be endless if we didn't have government oversight for these businesses. There would be a lot more violations of child labor, low and slave wages, slavery, unsanitary and unsafe working environments, little to no benefits, little to no time off, verbal and physical abuse, sexual harassment, sexual abuse, rape, a lot more pollution, unsafe food and other products, high prices and inflation to the extreme, poverty and a lot more inequality, increased stress and health issues, increased amounts of suicide, decreased life expectancy, environmental destruction, and racism, sexism, and other discrimination. I'm sure there is more, but that's all I can think of off the top of my head."

"Great list of issues Beth. I'm impressed. I can't think of any more than that either. Yes, it always leads to disaster when deregulation occurs. It is also very problematic when employees of big companies infiltrate the government as politicians or employees of these consumer destruction agencies. I don't know how it became okay for that to be or for the companies to be able to pay the politicians and these regulatory agencies off. Not to minimize the other issues you mentioned, but we have to get on the problems of pollution, global warming, inequality, discrimination, and poverty. It's a crisis and a national and worldwide emergency. I don't know why the leaders aren't just taking action. They sure make time to give themselves raises, reduce taxes for the rich and their companies, and take months off at a time. It's very upsetting. Nobody gets that much time off. Children get to have a recess. Adults don't take recesses because it's immature and unnecessary. So, why do the politicians get to take a recess, especially a month-long recess? Who the fuck needs a month off work? They don't even do anything while they are supposed to be working. What are they children?"

"They sure act like it. We have leaders right now who throw fits, tempers, and tantrums like babies. It's ridiculous. They call people names and can't even properly defend themselves. These are grown men who say that women are the emotional ones. They are completely out of control and irresponsible to the max. It's also crazy that their companies are even allowed to pollute as much as they do. Because of overpopulation and increased consumer demand, the consumer destruction agencies and the government just allow the companies to increase the amount of waste and pollution that they can dump into the water, air, and land. You know. Because that makes a lot sense. Instead of them forcing them to make safer, sustainable, and environmentally friendly products and use biodegradable plastics and renewable energy sources instead of disastrous and awful fossil fuels, they just let them pollute and destroy even more than they already do. That's the definition of insanity too."

"You are right about that Beth. That's insanity too. Besides the pollution, there are the intentional faulty products that they make that go right into the trash because we make shitty products that don't last very long and break after a short amount of time."

"I know. When I heard about that business strategy of object or product obsolescence, I almost threw up at how vile and deplorable that is. That is an actual business strategy that most businesses have. They can intentionally create a product to break down after a short amount of time, so people will have to buy another one. They teach that in business school. What is wrong with this world for that to be okay to do to consumers and the environment? Products should be made with quality and last as long as possible. It shouldn't be the opposite."

"That was how the light bulb was originally made. It was a pioneer in product obsolescence. They intentionally made it to break, so people would have to buy another one. More money for them, less money for us, and more trash and pollution for the earth. That's the business strategy right there. Product pollution."

"That's a good one Em. Unfortunately, all this waste and pollution is catching up with us and is hurting us. The earth can only hold so much waste, trash, and pollution from us humans. Other than the atrocious plastic substances and products, which have to be in the running for the worst creations ever made, you have other non-biodegradable or toxic products being dumped into the water, ocean, and land. You have medications and drugs too. These companies pay billions to the media to cover up this reality and not focus on pollution and how our products and our foods are made. You have all these horrors going on, and they talk about craft events, the weather, programs and shows, celebrities, and sports. How is that news? They should have a program to focus on all that bullshit and another program that exposes the reality of what is really going on. Oh yeah, I forgot. The media companies are owned by the same corporations and politicians that are doing all these awful things."

"Totally Beth. The media is a douche bag. Freedom of speech my ass. It's more like censorship of speech or paid-for speech. That is what they should have called it. It's not the news either. It's entertainment and programming. They program you how to think. Did you know that we actually pay other countries to take our waste and trash?"

"No way. That is crazy."

"Some countries can't do that, but we do. It helps keep the people blind as to how much waste, trash, and pollution we actually have. We have so much, we can't even handle it. When we are not just dumping it into our already full landfills and the oceans, we pay lots of money for other countries to pollute their air, land, and water with our trash and waste. We are polluting and poisoning other citizens because it's not enough for us just to do that to our own citizens."

"We have to switch over to renewable energies Em. It's a given. We have to reduce, reuse, and recycle. You are a horrible human being if you use anything that is disposable when there are alternative reusable products, and it pisses me off that so many people still don't recycle. It's like they are walking around like an apathetic zombie. They just don't care. That's why I always say that I want to hit or slap someone. They need to wake up. Something needs to wake them up. You can't keep acting like everything is okay when it's not. You can't keep thinking that you don't make a difference. You can't keep thinking that the rich, politicians, the government, and the companies actually care about you and are eventually going to do the right thing. They don't care about you and us, and they are not going to voluntarily do the right thing. They have proven that time and time again. Quit believing the lies. You are the fool for falling for the same old tricks."

"True that Beth. It's amazing how many people just don't care and are okay with the way things are. They just don't even want to put up a fight or battle. That makes them complicit. They are also the problem, so they have to be held accountable too. Silence and apathy are consent. I can't wait until we start shooting trash and waste up into space, if we aren't already. That's when the aliens will finally show themselves and say, "Hold up now earthlings. You fuckers can destroy your own forsaken planet, but now you have gone too far. You aren't polluting the universe too. You fucking parasites. Die humans die." Then, they shoot this little laser that destroys the whole entire planet in one second. When all we had to do was make some easy changes and put health, safety, and sustainability over profits and money."

"That's funny Em," Beth said while laughing. "Good alien accent."

"I try. Mentioning the aliens and their possible power over us makes me think about the horrible animal agriculture and fossil fuel industry."

"It's very sad. You would be proud of me. I have been trying to go longer and longer on a plant-based diet. One of these days, I will just continue it indefinitely and then work on being vegan with my clothing and hygiene and cleaning products. I am addicted to cheese, but I am trying to focus more on the reality of them sexually and physically abusing and neglecting the poor cows and goats to motivate me to stop eating it all together. They make some good plant-based alternatives too, which helps a lot. It's so sad the way we treat animals. We will pay for that. Those conditions are wretched. I will never get those images of the slaughterhouses, feed lots or concentrated animal feeding operations, poultry houses, and disgusting dairy farms out of my mind. They are putrid."

"That's awesome Beth. I'm so proud of you. Yes, they are absolutely disgusting. It's so horrible for the animals to live like that and then die in so much pain and misery. The environments they are in are so unsanitary that they have to spray the animals and the places with massive amounts of pesticides, fungicides, and larvicides, which people end up eating and consuming. In addition, so many people have no idea that a lot of these animals are science experiments as some are genetically modified and are given massive amounts of anti-biotics and growth hormones, which people end up eating and consuming. Since they are mass producing the animals, it is easier and more common for the farmers to artificially inseminate the females or rape them instead of them being impregnated naturally. If you have ever seen that process, it is basically bestiality. They also rape the male too to get the sperm. They are raping and sexually assaulting these animals to make more animals and to milk them. It makes me cry. Thank you so much Beth for trying to understand all that and their pain and trying to make a difference for them."

"I'm trying and will be vegan. I believe I already am. I feel like I got it and will continue for good this time. No excuses."

Emerald got up and gave Beth a hug. At that moment, a few customers came into the store. Beth went up front, and Emerald asked the customers if she could help them with anything. After they looked around and Beth checked them out, Emerald went to the bathroom. After Emerald came back from the bathroom, Emerald went up front, so Beth could go to the bathroom. After Beth was done, they sat back down and continued their conversation.

"I don't know why people are so much in denial about the horrors of abusing, neglecting, and killing animals for food and products," Beth said. "And all the resources it takes to grow and farm them. And the waste they make is enormous."

"It's very concerning. Most of the food that we grow is for these animals, and so much of the agricultural land that we have is taken up by these animals and the food that we grow for them. It's so unsustainable and creates so much pollution that it's not funny. The waste is outrageous. People are definitely kept in the dark in regards to the feed lots or CAFOs, poultry houses, unsanitary farming practices, the slaughterhouses, the significance of the carbon dioxide and methane gases from animal agriculture on global warming and climate change, and the tons of waste and pollution they dump into the ocean and local water supplies. This waste is both the chemicals they use to farm the animals, the leftover parts after they kill the animals, synthetic fertilizers, and all their urine and defecation. That's a lot of shit and piss. The other issue that they keep people in the dark about is the deforestation that occurs for the animal agriculture industry. Deforestation is significant enough without this industry. Since the companies don't have to reforest, all the killing of trees significantly reduces the number of trees and other plants killed in the deforestation process. Trees and plants convert carbon dioxide into oxygen, so we end up with a lot more carbon dioxide in the air than if we had more trees. This problem contributes to global warming and climate change. They also end up killing many different species of animals and plants, which reminds me of the overfishing problem too. We are also depleting the oceans and fresh water sources of fish and sea life. So many species have gone extinct from all this devastation, greed, and irresponsibility."

"That is so depressing Em. It's heartbreaking."

"Eventually, most of the food that we grow will just be for the animals that we are growing to eat. Since our population is increasing, the number of animals needed to abuse for dairy and murder for food and other products will also need even more land to be on, so that will decrease our available agricultural land even more. We could be using that land for lots of other things that are healthier and more sustainable. This animal agricultural demand will also continue to significantly increase pollution, waste, new viruses, and diseases into the environment. All our major flu and viral outbreaks are directly connected to people killing and eating animals. It's just a matter of time before we have a significant pandemic that kills millions due to our abuse and killing of innocent and defenseless animals. That's karma. We already kill over a billion animals a week. That's an insane number. Imagine if another more aggressive being grew, killed, and ate a billion humans a week. We wouldn't be okay with that. If we keep it up, think about how much more fossil fuels we will have to use. Think about how much more deforestation will occur if we keep having more babies. I don't want to imagine what things will be like even in a few years."

"I have even heard that the genetically mutant corn that they feed the cows and other animals is causing these animals to get diseases, which are spread to humans when they drink the dairy and eat the dead animals. I heard that the cows are not biologically made to process corn, so they have to give them and other animals medications and anti-biotics to stop the diseases before the humans consume them. People already use enough anti-biotics on their own, but if they are also getting them from the animals' milk and the animals they eat too, that is just a recipe for disaster.

Just like the insects and the weeds that are getting bigger and stronger from being resistant to the poisons that they spray on them, viruses and bacteria are getting bigger and stronger too as we keep using more medications to fight them. People are also having to use stronger medicines and anti-biotics to fight these super-diseases that are becoming resistant to our pharmaceuticals. That's the definition of insanity too."

"It is insane Beth. It's so sad what we do to the animals, the earth, and to ourselves. All because someone wants to get rich. You would think that people would be suspicious of that by now. People have been conned out of their money for tens of thousands of years and maybe even hundreds of thousands of years when they used something else other than money as currency. You would have thought that we would have figured out the scam by now that people who want money are not focused on honesty, safety, and sustainability. They do not have the consumers' best interests in mind. It's all about getting paid. The negative consequences and effects of their practices, manufacturing, and products is just a minor inconvenience to them and a part of the con. To them, it's worth the disasters for the money. The company's goal is to make a profit. It's not to be good. Companies, corporations, businesses, and organizations that focus on making money are inherently evil and unsustainable. They will do anything and everything they can to make a profit. Look at the fossil fuel industry. Eventually, the earth will have very little fossil fuels to give. Are we going to have 100 percent of the land on the earth with a drill or mine in it to get every last drop? It's ridiculous. Geothermal energy and using the warmth from the earth is an excellent source of energy that is infinitely abundant. The sun is a million times better source of energy, and it is also very abundant. It doesn't have all the pollution tied to it either. Unfortunately, the businesses can't patent the sun. Everyone has access to it, so they will ignore it for now as a viable source of energy. What are we going to live on top of the drills while we are dying because of the amount of pollution everywhere?"

"If they have it their way, yes. They don't care about us Em. There's the fracking too. The drilling and mining were one thing, but all this fracking is just as bad. They waste so much water and pollute everything in their path trying to get natural gas. They are even causing earthquakes and affecting the fault lines and the tectonic plates. That's not cool at all. The extreme levels of pollution, poisons, and toxins in the drinking water is concerning. It was already bad enough, but then the consumer destruction agency over these energy companies thought it would be a good idea to let them pollute even more. You know. So, they can get rich too off our earth's misery. We could have easily switched over to using 100 percent renewable energies by now. It seems like we are using even more fossil fuels instead of less. That is backwards. I'm starting to believe if the politicians and companies aren't greedy and corrupt that they are mentally challenged."

"I'll say it Beth. They are retarded. We don't have to be politically correct with them. They are fucking retards because calling them mentally challenged is offensive to mentally challenged people. They are evil and retarded."

"They are Em. That's the point though. They are going to leave this world in ruins, so their children and the other generations will suffer. All so they can be rich today. It's fucking bullshit. They are not pro-life. They are pro-death. They don't care about fetuses, they don't care about children, and they don't care about anyone except for themselves. It's a fraud. There are so many options. They could be utilizing solar, wind, tidal, wave, and geothermal energy sources. Between all of those, it's enough to fuel the entire world without using one spec of a fossil fuel. It should be illegal to use fossil fuels. They make it illegal to use certain types of drugs because they don't want you hurting yourself, or they make it illegal to speed or steal, but it's okay and legal to use fossil fuels that destroy the earth, kill people, and make people sick. It's not hard to do the right thing. It's going to be very difficult for the future generations to fix these problems that we are causing, or it may even be impossible. They are going to be cussing us for eons and maybe longer. If they aren't all dead. Why wait until everything is completely destroyed or there is a crisis before we have to change for the better?"

"That is a good question. All this destruction is real. Money is not real, but the powers that be are so blinded by the money. They have become incompetent and dangerous. We have to revolt and take the power back and do away with this capitalistic society that is based on false and fake values. They will just keep using excuse after excuse to continue their devastation and corrupt ways, so they can get paid. Some are even saying, "We can just move to another planet." We are even already putting billions towards finding another planet to live on while we are currently destroying the one that we are on. How fucking upsetting and stupid is a statement like that? Wouldn't it be easier to just use the billions on fixing the planet that we are already on? That is so upsetting to poor people and to people who are hungry and starving. We can't help the people that are here on this earth, but we can allocate billions to finding another planet to live on instead of just fixing the problems that we have caused. It's not hard to tell the companies that they can't pollute anymore and have to use renewable energy sources. That's easy. Putting money and resources into moving us to another planet, that is hard and very challenging. Someone is getting paid off and getting rich from that decision too."

"That's great Em. Well said. I agree with you. It is so much easier to take care of this planet and the people on it rather than try to find another planet for us to live on."

"What about the government allowing the fossil fuel companies to take people's land illegally?"

"That one makes me angry too."

"I love that they call it eminent domain. No matter what you call it, it's stealing. It would be one thing for the government to take it for something useful, such as a park or wildlife refuge, but they end up stealing land for their destructive corporations that pay them billions to let them destroy the earth. They even may need it for a road, which is upsetting too since we should be using electric hovercrafts or electric flying cars by now. We shouldn't have roads on the ground, and the fact that we drive around in these barbaric and disgusting pollution mobiles is an abomination too. We should be ashamed of ourselves. It's like when they used animals to pull a cart for people to ride in. Oh wait, some people still do that too. What a fucking joke we are. We have to be the stupidest species ever to be on the earth. The sad thing is that we have all the potential in the world to be the smartest creatures on the planet, but we do the opposite instead because of our weaknesses for power and money."

"We do have a lot of potential and could be in a lot better place Em. If the government can be authoritative like that and take our land, we are not free. Like you said, it would be one thing for them to be using the land for something like preservation purposes, but they are taking it for companies who only want more money and don't care about destroying everything in their path. It's amazing that not one politician stands up and tries to stop that unethical and immoral act. I'm sure a progressive said something, but they didn't try hard enough to stop it. I would have made a ruckus and started a brawl."

"The other crazy thing is that the traditionalists are so anti-socialist, but they are the ones driving that socialist ship. During their campaigns, the traditionalists complain about wanting a smaller government and that the government should stay out of our lives. Then, when they get into office, they use the government to be authoritarian and a dictator to take things from citizens to help make their companies more money. They lied to get elected, and then after they get elected, they do the exact thing they were condemning. What a bunch of hypocrites. They don't care at all about the citizens. It is all about their companies and their pocketbooks. They just use the government for their own selfish and greedy reasons. A lot of progressives do that too, but it is not as many."

"Don't forget what it's like when the people protest Em. Since the government and the law enforcement let the companies do whatever they want to do, the people have to stand up to the businesses and protest their wrongdoings. We have a right to protest and a fundamental right to free speech. We should be able to let everyone know when an injustice is occurring, and just because something is legal and the companies were given permission to do something by corrupted and paid-off crony judges and government officials doesn't make it okay. We still have to protect and stand up for ourselves. It is absolutely disgraceful that the companies are able to get the government to use the military and the law enforcement to protect the evil companies that are wreaking havoc on people, the society, and the planet with their destructive and polluting ways. They are a menace to society, but when we protest that and try to stand up to them, there is the military and law enforcement there to protect the companies and not the people. Even when it is a peaceful protest, the protestors will get attacked, abused, and arrested. That is a crime against its people. Those are very shameful days for a so-called democratic and free society, and it happens every day. Right now, there are people getting censored, oppressed, and abused by law enforcement and governments because they are trying to stand up to the destructive companies and the corrupt government. Those are the true citizens. They are the true patriots and fighters for democracy and freedom. They are our heroes, but unfortunately, they are labeled terrorists, attacked, abused, arrested, and found guilty of crimes. What the fuck is that about? I am proud of anyone who stands up to the evil corporations and our tyrannical government. Our dictator needs to be forcefully removed. Sorry, I'll calm down. It's all very upsetting."

"It is upsetting Beth. I'm right there with you. You don't have to apologize at all. We are not living in a democracy, and we are not free. If people believe they are free, they are stupid. They are not seeing what is going on. What you were talking about with the government letting companies do whatever they want to do at the expense of the people and then using the military and law enforcement to protect the companies while attacking the people who are speaking out and protesting is martial law to some extent. It is definitely authoritarianism, fascism, and a dictatorship. If the government cared about its people, it wouldn't do most of the stuff that it does. It definitely wouldn't let the companies run wild and take from us and hurt us. Hell, they even kill us with chemicals, toxins, and poisons and aren't held accountable. They might get a fine, but that's about it."

"It's not okay. The military and law enforcement are supposed to protect us. They are supposed to protect its people and the citizens. It makes me so mad."

"I know. I've had to do a lot of meditating and deep breathing to refocus my energy on myself to stay calm and not get so upset."

"We have to Em. If we go crazy and lose it, they win."

"We will overcome Beth. Good will always win over evil. It may take time, but we will succeed. We are going to have to deal with the media and advertising issue though. It is so sad that companies are allowed to manipulate and lie through the media with their advertisements, especially with false and misleading claims, flat out lies, or the use of entertainers and celebrities. The gullible and stupid consumers have to take some responsibility too, but you have to hold the abuser and offender accountable first and foremost."

"Yes, I wish I could whip the entertainers and celebrities with a rubber hose, as violent as that sounds, for selling their soul to devil and not having enough dignity to say no to greed and money. They need to do what is right. Instead, they take money over values, morals, and ethics. They know people, especially the vulnerable youngsters, look up to them and will do as they do. Whether they want to accept it or not, they are role models and idols for a lot of people. It is their responsibility to act accordingly and be professional and appropriate. If they are supporting unhealthy and destructive goods and services that companies are paying them to advertise, they are responsible for the negative consequences and effects that those companies and their goods and services have on the people and the environment."

"Yes Beth. It's so wrong. I have even quit listening to artists and bands who sell their music for commercials and advertising of certain evil companies that I disagree with. It's horrifying and makes me sick. They are the worst of the worst. You wouldn't think a lot of them would need the money, but there they are advertising a horrible and awful product or supporting a destructive and evil company. Those celebrities are wretched and despicable. They deserve the worst too. Karma will get them eventually because that is not what they are supposed to be doing and they are putting a lot of negative energy out into the universe."

"I hope it will Em. I hope it wakes them up, so they can change for the better. So many people need to wake up. People are so brainwashed and programmed with the illusion of money and its power. They say, "But if you can make money at it, and it's legal, then it is okay." No, it's not okay, and I guess some don't even care if it's legal. You have to quit lying to yourself and stop chasing these false dreams and ideals. So many people have gotten so sick and died over sugar, foods with trans fats, foods with chemicals and preservatives added to them, genetically modified foods, medications, alcohol, tobacco, dairy and egg products, dead animals that they eat for food, foods with wheat and gluten, foods with other allergens, vaccines, asbestos, products with plastics and lead, and foods sprayed with herbicides, fungicides, larvicides, and pesticides. Who knows what else? We even have had so many people get sick and die from jobs that make these products and not to mention the poor miners in the fossil fuel industry, the farmers in the genetically mutant industry, and the farmers in the conventional farming industry that get exposed to the poisons from spraying their crops with all those poisons."

"Don't forget how many people have gotten sick and died from the stress of being worked all week. People are too exhausted to exercise, they don't sleep well, and they have a difficult time eating right. In addition, suicide is one of the top reasons people die. They are just sick of all this shit. You also have other vile, abusive, and disgusting industries. Prostitution is legal in some places, and they do advertise as escort services. There is also pornography. So, you have some industries where people are legally getting raped, trafficked, and sexually assaulted. All for money."

"We have mentioned a lot of horrible businesses and industries Em. I know not all companies are bad, but there are definitely a lot."

"I think that's our point. Just because things are legal doesn't make them okay. If certain drugs were legal, people would be selling them to get rich. If they legalized heroin tomorrow, would you sell it to get rich? You would make a killing, but would it be worth it?"

"Absolutely not. Making people sick and killing people, so you can get rich, is never okay. Some countries and their governments are legalizing certain drugs, such as marijuana, to get rich. Citizens are opening up businesses all over to make money off this drug. It has so many negative side effects too. People are using people's addictions and weaknesses to get high without any regard to the problems. Marijuana has been proven over and over again to cause cancer, anxiety, depression, paranoia, lack of productivity, attention-deficit symptomatology, and memory loss. It may have some benefits, but it's not worth it. There are better alternatives. So, yes, I think a lot of people would sell heroin if the government said it was okay."

"As long as it makes money Beth, they definitely would. You have the evil lottery and gambling industry too. As long as it tastes good and makes them feel good, they will sell it and buy it. It doesn't matter what the consequences are. Excuses, excuses. That is why it is important to have regulations and a responsible government to make sure the citizens and society are safe."

"People are so dumb. The companies use the media to lie and psychologically manipulate people about their products. They even try to make the products seem sexy and attractive when they wouldn't be. They use scantily dressed women and men to make them more attractive. They try to convey a sense of urgency or play on people's fears and desires to make them think they need the products. They make people think that everyone else is using the products. Back on the celebrity factor, people have some trust towards celebrities, so if a company is able to pay a lot of money to get a celebrity to advertise for them, the consumer thinks that the product is safe. They also advertise in a way to make some products seem like they do something that they may not necessarily do. I think prescription medications and a lot of services say they do one thing or make it seem like they are going to do something, but they don't, or it doesn't work like that for everyone."

"Using sex to sale a product upsets me."

"Yes, sex sales Em."

"That's how immature, juvenile, and gullible people are. Guys definitely think with their other head. They are a disgrace to rationalism and intelligence. Tell me why again that there are so many more men politicians and business managers than women. That's a cruel joke right. That's not real because men do not make good decisions. How did this disaster happen?"

"For the most part, yes, men are the worst decision makers. Unfortunately, some women are like that too, but it is mostly men who are hormonal and emotional. The only proof we need is all the issues that we have been talking about. Men have driven this country and world into the ground with their awful decision-making abilities. Look at all the fights they get into and all the battles and wars that men have led us into. That is proof of how immature, emotional, and unstable they are."

"The poor kids too. A lot of the marketing and advertising is really geared towards kids and adolescents. Get them while they are young, dumb, vulnerable, and gullible. They target young adults a lot too. Smart, mature, and intelligent adults, who are mainly over 40 years old, know when to say no and will say no, so that doesn't appeal much for predatory companies to spend their time, energy, and money on. They are intentionally trying to target kids, people who don't know any better, and people who are uneducated. On a side note, the traditionalist politicians use that strategy too, especially towards uneducated and ignorant voters. If they can get them hooked on something, in the habit of buying and using something, to think that they need something, or to think that they are cool if they have something, the products become a part of their being and their personality. The companies know exactly what they are doing. The parents need to be more responsible and screen these advertisements from them."

"I like that Em. They are predatory. Yes, it's basic psychology. The younger you are when you start consuming something, the longer you consume it or the harder it is for you to stop consuming it. It becomes a habit. Consumerism and materialism are or can be addictions, and we all know food and sugar are addictive. The repetition of the information, advertisements, and commercials sucks people into buying too. Just like a politician who lies over and over again to the point that you actually believe the lie. It's the same strategy, but a different game."

"Let's stretch our legs and walk around a bit."

"Sounds good."

Emerald and Beth took a break to stock some shelves and help some customers who came into the store while they were stocking the shelves. Beth went up to the front while Emerald helped the customers and stocked some shelves. After the customers were checked out and left, they sat back down and continued their conversation.

"Advertising and marketing are very insidious practices," Emerald said. "It's crazy that they spend billions on advertising and marketing strategies. Those companies and people are horrible. That money could be utilized for so much good. It's a waste. It's the same with all the money that politicians raise for their campaigns. It's a waste. You could use that money for so much good, and they don't. Absolutely disgraceful."

"Don't forget the product placement in stores too. They spend lots of money every year researching and figuring out how to manipulate people into buying stuff on the whim that they don't need. There's a bunch of psychology behind those strategies. They put needed or high purchase items in the back of the store, so people have to walk all the way to the back of store while being manipulated by all these other products on the way to the back and all the way back to the front. They also put these cheap unhealthy and unnecessary products at the front or near the check-out counters, so you will just quickly grab one or two or more. The kids are very gullible to that unhealthy and unnecessary stuff, especially the candy and junk food. Parents need to be assertive and say no, which is the best way to teach the kids self-control and restraint or even delayed gratification."

"You have to be an awful and good-for-nothing person to be in marketing and advertising. Depending on what they are lying and manipulating about, a lot of them deserve to die a slow and painful death or deserve to just be tortured for the rest of their lives."

"That's harsh Em, but I have to agree with you. You did say a lot and not all. It depends on what they are advertising. As we have already concluded though, there are a plethora of evil companies out there selling calamitous products. The media is just as bad too. The media and the advertising and marketing companies have to take responsibility for being a medium to assist these companies in making people sick, killing them and animals, and destroying the earth. It makes me so proud and happy when media and marketing companies stop working with a company or stop advertising for them because the company is involved in a scandal or was accused or found guilty of a crime. They should have done it a lot sooner, but at least they finally pulled the plug. I know they are just looking out for themselves and their bottom line though."

"It is hard for them to say no. They keep it going. They keep the proverbial money machine rolling. As long as people get paid, morals and ethics go out the window."

"That reminds me Em. I was thinking the other day about all the horrible industries in this country, and I can see some need for them as long as they are regulated and ran properly for the benefit of the people and not the rich and wealthy. Since they are not regulated very well, are not ran properly, and only care about money, they have become malevolent and destructive. Some good examples are the healthcare industry, hospitals, nursing homes, animal agriculture, conventional farming, the financial industry, the energy industry, and the insurance industry, which works with the healthcare industry to rip off the citizens."

"You are correct Beth. We do need most of these industries to some extent. Maybe not the animal agriculture and insurance industry. Conventional farming needs a lot of help. We can just replace that with organic farming. These industries are just not working for the people. They are working for themselves to get paid and to make a few people rich. If the energy sector would move away from being unsustainable and stop using limited and polluting fossil fuels and move over to all renewable energy sources, it would be producing and doing something great. Coal is dirty and disgusting. You are a moron and evil person if you say that coal is clean or there is clean coal. You have to be blind or corrupt to say that coal is clean. It is absolutely filthy, and the money from it is just as dirty. There is no excuse at all for these businesses and industries to keep doing what they are doing. It would be so easy for them to change for the good and to probably still make a lot of money in this sick capitalistic society. However, money is not a reason to make people sick, kill people, and destroy everything. You have to first and foremost be focused on not doing harm to people, the animals, and the earth. If you can't achieve these goals, you shouldn't do what you are doing just to make money. If your only goal is to make money, I feel sorry for you and the misery that will eventually come to you. The government expects people to be giving back to society, and if they don't, they are not given extra privileges and extra money to harm everyone around them. So, why does our government allow the businesses to harm everything around them and get extra privileges and become filthy rich off pollution and the negative effects onto society? More hypocrisy, I guess."

"That's deep Em. I haven't thought much about comparing what the government allows for individuals versus companies when it comes to how each one is benefiting society. It definitely makes you wonder and see the dichotomy. Businesses have a huge impact on everything around them, so they should definitely be held to a high if not higher standard. The disastrous fossil fuel and animal agriculture industries concern me a lot. We have to transition to all renewable energies and plant-based foods to survive the catastrophes of global warming and the pollutions and toxins that we have put into the air, the water, and the land. There is no reason we shouldn't be running on mostly renewable energies by now, and there is no reason we shouldn't be growing cleaner, healthier, and more nutritious fruits and vegetables over abusing and killing helpless, defenseless, and voiceless animals. Plants make excellent meat or dead animal alternatives, dairy or animal sex abuse alternatives, and egg or animal embryo alternatives. Plant-based meat alternatives are fucking delicious. It's amazing. They taste so good. People who abuse and kill animals for food wouldn't even know the difference."

"Fruits and vegetables are significantly more nutritious too. We wouldn't need that much land and resources either, and the reduction in pollution and waste would be very significant. We would also be able to feed so many more people by doing away with animal agriculture. In addition, if we switched over to almost 100 percent renewable energies and plant-based foods, we will be able to stop and even reverse global warming. It would take a little bit of time, but we can do it. We would have to focus on organic farming though. It wouldn't work with genetically mutant organisms and the use of poisons, herbicides, fungicides, larvicides, and pesticides, which are causing or have already caused an epidemic and so many major environmental and health crises."

"We would save so many poor, helpless, defenseless, and voiceless animals too. That would be great Em."

"It would be great. There is something wrong with someone who has alternatives for food, but instead, they still choose to abuse, torture, and kill animals. Not if it's a cat, dog, or a horse though. For some reason, those animals are special and protected even though they are no different than the animals that they abuse and kill. You can't love one type of animal and then kill and eat another type of animal. That is speciesism and is another form of discrimination."

"I like to call those people psychopaths. They are hypocritical psychopaths."

"Absolutely, they were the same people who had slaves and would say things like, "We've always done it like that," "That's just the way it is," "That's the way I was raised," and "Everyone else does it." It's a very careless, dangerous, ignorant, and stupid way to think. You have to think for yourself, use common sense, and use compassion. If you don't, leaders and companies use you to do some iniquitous things. That's how right-wing, traditionalist, and fascist governments and countries are able to commit genocide and kill innocent people with division, hate, and discrimination. A lot of the citizens just go along with it and no one questions whether they should be hurting, abusing, and killing others or the animals. It's happened before, and it will keep happening."

"Unfortunately, yes. You are right Em. I hate to say it."

"Now, the healthcare industry is in a good position to do a lot of good. They could provide a lot of useful services, and some do. However, instead of them helping others, they make them sicker and don't' educate people on healthy behaviors and habits, such as exercise, healthy plant-based diets, nutrition, meditation, relaxation techniques, enjoying nature, and fun activities."

"I agree. It seems like the goal of the healthcare industry is to medicate, medicate, and medicate some more instead of curing and even preventing illnesses. It's like the doctors and health professionals don't think people want to feel better or change their ways, so they aren't upfront or honest with them. There may be a business strategy to that as the doctors and health professionals may think the patients won't come back to them, but I don't think that's true. If you help someone feel better, people will flock to you. Instead, they get them addicted or hooked on drugs. These drugs or medications may help with one problem, but they cause a few more, so they have to prescribe more medications to help with those. Then, those other ones cause more problems. It's a dangerous way to treat people."

"It's neglect and abuse Beth. The doctors and the other healthcare professionals should be ashamed of themselves, but since they are getting paid and some are getting filthy rich off keeping people sick, they don't care. They are able to look the other way. I know there are some good doctors and healthcare professionals out there, but in our country, it's the exception and not the rule. I love it when a doctor says that they are no longer prescribing medications and that they are focusing on alternative medicines that involve the strategies that we already mentioned that actually cure and prevent diseases."

"It's so sad too when you hear about these alternative medicine doctors getting ostracized, disparaged, and excommunicated from the medical community for actually helping people without using drugs, surgeries, and other topical approaches that don't cure or prevent illnesses."

"Some of these doctors have even been murdered, especially the ones who encourage the no sugar added diets, all organic fruits and vegetable diets, and the diets that include fruits and vegetables that are considered superfoods because they are loaded with lots of vitamins, minerals, and antioxidants. They are murdering them because these diets prevent and cure cancer and a lot of other diseases, but it's suspicious that these diets are never the fad, popular, or commercialized diets. There is so much evidence and there has been so many studies done that prove that these diets cure and prevent cancer and so many other diseases. It's even more suspicious that these doctors are said to have died because of an accident or by natural causes. The other doctors don't die like that, and the general population doesn't die like that. Very concerning indeed."

"That's crazy Em. That's when you know they were murdered. I've heard them say that they even committed suicide when they were so outgoing and social. Their family members even reported that they did not have a history of depression or suicidal ideation or attempts. It is very suspicious and makes you wonder if the insurance companies, private companies, or the healthcare companies are behind the murders. They probably are. You also have the disgusting, evil, and profitable non-profit agencies that make billions off people getting cancer, heart disease, diabetes, and other diseases that are easily curable and preventable. These non-profit agencies are just as bad as the healthcare industry with making sure that people continue to get and stay sick. They just keep accepting billions in donations while they do absolutely nothing to prevent and cure these diseases. However, the executives get to fly private jets and have expensive cars and houses. Just like the preachers and the politicians."

"You are right Beth. Those non-profit agencies are a scam. They will even provide and serve cancer-causing and disease-causing foods at their events. They are really just pushing drugs for the filthy rich and despicable pharmaceutical companies, who actually pay the non-profits and the healthcare and insurance companies to market their ineffective, unnecessary, and sickening drugs and treatments."

"We already have a cure for cancer, but those so-called anti-cancer and cancer-curing non-profits don't talk about cancer prevention and cures. There are also the other evil non-profits who scam people out of their money by saying they are trying to find cures for these diseases, such as heart, respiratory, stroke and cerebrovascular, Alzheimer's, diabetes, kidney, influenza and pneumonia, tuberculosis, and cholera and dysentery. They say they are searching for a cure, but they do everything opposite of finding or providing a cure. They don't talk about foods and beverages with added sugar being the top cancer causers. They don't talk about the need for exercising and eating a healthy plant-based diet. They don't talk about the need to meditate and find inner peace to reduce your stress. They don't talk about avoiding genetically mutant organisms and foods that are sprayed with poisons, herbicides, fungicides, larvicides, and pesticides that all cause cancer. For the cancer-causing non-profits, they do, however, talk about people with cancer needing to have chemotherapy and radiation therapy, which both of these treatments cause cancer and death. They don't tell you that you have a higher success rate if you don't take drugs and don't do the barbaric chemotherapy or radiation therapy. You have an even higher success rate if you actually start exercising and eating a healthy plant-based diet. It's very upsetting. Still, people donate billions to them every year, and they don't use the money to cure or prevent diseases and cancer at all. They use it make themselves rich and make more cancer and illness causing drugs. A manager or executive of a non-profit agency shouldn't be a millionaire and making that much money. It's like a preacher from a church who is a millionaire. It's a scam. Wake up people. You have been fooled, and you are all morons. It's the same as the genetically mutant organism companies suing the organic farmers and making them go out of business."

"Well said Beth. It's outrageous. What about the greedy hospitals who sue the parents of sick children to force their kids into bullshit treatments, such as the barbaric chemotherapy or radiation therapy and other unnecessary and dangerous treatments and surgeries, because the parents don't agree with the doctors, the hospitals, and their money-making methods? Then, when the parents tell them that they don't want their kid to undergo those sickening, ineffective, and sometimes deadly treatments, the hospitals sue them and then pay off the judge to court order the kid into child protective custody to force the kid into these horrible treatments. Those poor kids and the poor parents. It makes me sick."

"That is enraging. I hear that all the time. A lot of the time, the kid ends up dying because they received the barbaric chemotherapy, radiation therapy, or some other unnecessary surgery with or without the parent's consent. However, the doctors and hospitals don't receive any consequences. They say, "We told you that death was a part of the consequences of the treatment." For the kids that were court ordered to go through with the deadly treatment, the parents didn't want to do it to begin with. Now, their kid is dead. The hospitals, doctors, and insurance companies don't care because they got paid anyway."

"It is enraging Beth. Let's not forget that while all this murdering and sickness is going on that the government, politicians, the consumer destruction agencies, and the law enforcement are just letting the companies run wild and commit these heinous acts. They are literally allowed to get away with murder and are getting away with murder. But hey, let's arrest and sentence the illegal drug dealers and put them in jail. Most legal drug dealing by licensed medical doctors is worse than the illegal drug dealing that goes on. Just because it's legal doesn't make it okay."

"Well, if we can't prove that they are actually hiring people to kill good holistic, natural, or alternative medicine doctors, these companies are still killing people with pollution, unhealthy food, sugar, meat, dairy, eggs, alcohol, drugs, tobacco, chemicals, poisons, fluoride, vaccines, prescriptions, unnecessary surgeries and treatments, the barbaric chemotherapy, plastics, and genetically mutant foods. The consumers may not die immediately, but they will die eventually from consuming these products, which makes it convenient for the companies to say the death was not directly related to their products because they didn't die right away."

"Absolutely! I like the way you think Beth. I forgot how informed and aware you are. It's nice to have an intelligent and deep conversation with another wise individual besides Mary."

"Thanks Em. I truly appreciate that. There is still a lot to learn though. Lots and lots, and I think that's what makes us so smart is that if we are given new information that contradicts what we know or believe, we will assess the new information and change our beliefs while not throwing a fit or denying it like an immature child or adolescent. Oh wait, that's what our elected politicians do, and they are supposed to be grown adults. When someone calls them out on their shit, they immediately get defensive and start calling the other person names or making up lies about them."

"You mean, like the traditionalists mostly do with scientific evidence or when they are called out on their corruption, obstructions, abuses of power, crimes, infidelities, and lies."

"To be fair, some progressives throw fits too, but yes, it's mostly right-wing traditionalist and religious people. I guess the progressives mostly throw fits because of the injustice and outrage from the inequality and all these horrible issues we have been talking about today."

"That is so true Beth. I'm just glad that I have made some lifestyle changes from not buying into the brainwashed and unnecessary educational system that we have and not trying to slave away at a meaningless and most likely stressful job for 40 hours or more a week. It's horrible how many jobs have these low slave wages where you barely survive paycheck to paycheck and so many promote and support sexism, racism, sexual harassment, nepotism and favoritism, verbal abuse, ageism, religionism, and heterosexism. On top of all that, the managers are mean, abusive, dictators, greedy, biased, and authoritative. The companies would have definitely been more successful if they understood equality, encouragement, cooperation, motivation, quality, employee and customer engagement, and all the benefits of keeping employee turnover at a minimum."

"Totally. It's common sense that you have to treat your employees really well to have a great company. Not all employees are great, but they can be taught and coached to be better instead of punished, disparaged, and abused to where they end up quitting."

"Then, when the department or the company doesn't do well, the inept manager blames the employees instead of taking responsibility for what they were responsible for in the first place."

"If you can't take responsibility, you shouldn't be a manager, supervisor, or leader. You shouldn't be a politician either. Never trust anyone who blames someone else. If someone is blaming someone else, especially if they had the job before them, they are basically admitting that they are irresponsible and inept. If you are not taking responsibility, you can't be surprised when things fall apart, fail, or break. It's not surprising some of the awful things that companies do to make a profit at the expense of the employees, the consumers, and society. If they can't take responsibility anyway, we can't expect them to act morally, ethically, and justly. You don't have to blame people to do your job. If things are messy or broken when you take over as a manager or a leader, just fix it. Don't spend time and energy blaming, disparaging, and lying."

"You nailed it Beth. That is definitely part of the problem. Don't forget at the expense of the poor animals and the earth too."

"You also have the low wages, lack of benefits, long hours, too many days worked in a row, inequality of pay and positions, pollution, child labor, huge executive and management bonuses, and government subsidies to already very profitable companies that don't need any more money. You also have companies who move jobs and factories to other countries to pay less wages, avoid taxes, increase pollution, and have less regulations that lead to increased risk, safety concerns, and unsanitary working environments."

"That is a great list. Yes, very upsetting. I think it's so disgusting and hypocritical for politicians, who are mostly traditionalist, to say they are going to create more jobs and help the economy, but they are the reason there are less jobs and the economy is hurting because they send their companies' jobs and operations to other countries to avoid taxes, have less regulations, and pay the workers a fraction of what they pay them here. They also get to hire children in other countries who don't have child labor laws like we do. Still, their supporters still vote for them even though they know that they do those things. What the fuck is that about? Their supporters know the politicians don't care about the economy or anyone but themselves, ruin the economy, avoid taxes, pay slave wages, discriminate, move jobs to other countries, abuse their employees, make horrible and destructive products, pollute the environment, and don't give back to the community or society, but they still vote for them anyway. Some may not know all these truths, but you have to be an idiot to not know, and you have to be an idiot to know and still vote for them. It's madness. In that case, do you blame the greedy politicians, or do you blame the idiot followers? I ultimately blame the politicians and leaders, but I also blame the idiots."

"Me too Em. You do have to hold the leaders accountable, but yes, the followers have accountability too. For the elected officials, they put them in office, so they have to take responsibility. But, like their leaders who don't take responsibility, do you really think the citizens who voted for the irresponsible politicians are going to take responsibility? Hell no. They are going to blame the other party members even though they didn't do anything wrong. People have a hard time taking responsibility. That's the downfall of human beings. It will end us. It's like when the political party that has the most power causes a recession or depression. They blame the other party even though the other party isn't in control, and their followers believe them. Or, the ultimate leader blames that guy that had the job before him even though he hasn't had the job for years, and his followers still believe him."

"It's bullshit. Take some responsibility. What about all this political and legal talk that companies, businesses, or corporations are individuals and have rights?"

"That's crazy talk Em. Fuck that shit. That's more fuel to the fire. Absolutely enraging. Companies do have more rights than citizens now thanks to the corrupt government and politicians. If they didn't, they wouldn't be able to do most of the things that they do."

"You mean like rob, discriminate, cheat, steal, abuse workers, evade taxes, kill, pollute, and destroy the environment."

"Yes, definitely. Individuals and citizens aren't allowed to do those things, so why do companies get to get away with all those awful things? In addition, when individuals get into a financial bind, the only social programs for them is to declare bankruptcy, obtain very limited and short-term financial social welfare services, and/or start a debt management program. Some of these programs and services may help a little, but they still have to pay a lot of the money back. For individuals, a lot of loans, such as student loans, are not forgivable through bankruptcy, so they still have to pay those high debts back."

"Education should be free or very affordable anyway. It is insanely expensive, especially since they get government funds, but that is what is wrong with the healthcare industry too. Post-secondary or higher education is a scam anyway."

"Yes, it is, but when companies get into a financial bind, they can file bankruptcy and pay a little back and just start all over again like nothing ever happened. Individuals get stuck with very poor credit and civil judgments and still have to pay back a lot of money. These actions, court, legal judgments, and poor credit ratings make it hard for them to get a good paying job too. Businesses don't have a lot of those negative effects. It's like they get a free pass for fucking shit up. It should be the opposite. They should be held to a higher standard due to the significance and the impact that they have. They should have to dissolve and be forced to fail and shut down because of their wrongdoings. Managers and owners should have to do jail time for their crimes and not just have the company pay an insignificant fine."

"That's true Beth. Lock them up. A lot of individuals didn't ask to lose their jobs and get into a financial bind. Companies cause their problems. It's their fault they fail. You also have the bigger agencies who do illegal acts and get into a financial bind. They even cause the recessions and depressions. Then, they get bailed out by the politicians and governments even though the citizens don't support that corporate welfare at all."

"Which again is socialism, but the traditionalists totally support it because the bailout from the citizens and the taxpayers goes right through their companies and into their pocketbooks. It's like they do it on purpose, so they can scam us all out of billions. Why wouldn't you do it if you could? If you could get billions from the government for committing crimes and not taking care of your business, why wouldn't you do it? It's the ultimate scam. The only ones who get hurt are the citizens. The company owners and managers all get paid. The politicians all get paid. Unfortunately, the citizens don't get paid and go deeper in debt. The government's debt is the citizens' debt. It's still socialism that the hypocritical traditionalists support. The progressive politicians support it too, but at least they aren't anti-socialism or hypocrites. Some of them are just thieves."

Some customers walked into the store, so Emerald went up front and Beth helped the customers. After some time, Emerald checked out the customers. Emerald and Beth sat back down and continued their discussion.

"It is crazy how much they give to the companies who don't need it," Emerald said. "We are talking about billions. Yet, when citizens are starving and living in poverty, the government and politicians are like, "We can't give money out like that" or "We don't have the funds to help you." That's enraging too. You just gave billions to companies that made billions last year, but because of their own wrongdoings and crimes, you give them billions more. No one goes to jail or gets charged with a crime, but you don't have any money to help the citizens and people who are starving and living in poverty that gave you that money to begin with. Tell me how that makes any sense. The rich help the rich, the poor help the rich, but the rich won't help the poor. That's a very concerning and disturbing truth. If the companies want to be treated like individuals, they should be treated like individuals. People don't get bailed out, so companies shouldn't get bailed out. People get arrested and convicted for committing crimes. People don't just get fined for major crimes. The owners and the managers should get convicted for committing crimes and violating regulations. They shouldn't be just fined with fines that are easily paid because they make billions. If their products make people sick and die, they should be held accountable for that. The owners and managers should be convicted of these crimes and should have to go to jail. If an individual was intentionally making people sick and killing people, they would go to jail. Business managers and owners should be convicted and go to jail too. They should even be charged and convicted for crimes that are unethical and immoral because they should be held to a higher standard due to the significance that they have on society, the economy, and people's lives. They shouldn't get to wipe their hands clean because the politicians own the companies or were paid off by the companies. If that is the case, which is easily traceable, the politicians should also be arrested, convicted, and sent to jail. You are guilty by association. That's how individuals are treated, so that's how companies should be treated."

"You go Em. That sounds like a great plan. Let's get it going. That is one of the biggest infections in this country. It's not okay that companies get to get away with what they do, and it's definitely not okay that the politicians let them do it because they are getting paid. That conflict of interest and bribery has to stop. The citizens want the businesses to fail. The companies need to fail and go out of business. Even if that means jobs are lost and the economy gets negatively affected. You sometimes have to feel some pain before you get better. You don't need to be or should be working for those criminals and awful companies anyway. However, we could set up some assistance and programs to help the employees find other jobs and use the leftover money and resources from the despicable company to assist with them transitioning to another job. Nevertheless, these corrupt and evil corporations need to be deleted and wiped away. We need to get rid of them. We will recover for the better, and it's better than this cycle of insanity continuing again and again. A lot of these companies are not being ran properly because of the corruption and greed. They have to pay for their misdeeds."

"It's almost to the point where citizens should be voting for the issues and not the politicians. The citizens should vote on the laws, and the politicians should just be administrators. The politicians should only do what they are told, and they should not be allowed to make decisions. They have broken our trust time and time again. Therefore, the system has to change. They fucked it up. Or, we could just do away with them and have just a few elected administrators. A good and just society doesn't need these fake, dishonest, and corrupted politicians and leaders."

"We should figure out how to do that Em."

"If businesses aren't being ran properly anyway, they should be put out of business. The owners, politicians who accept money from them, and the managers should go to jail and never get to do those jobs again. It's not okay for them to keep hurting the people and the society. It's wrong. Fuck them. Sorry, I'll calm down."

"No worries Em. It is upsetting. We should all be pissed off at them and the people who support and protect them."

"What about the whole monopoly thing? We have laws against monopolies, yet we currently have companies that have a monopoly in their markets. Even if it is two or three companies, that can still be a monopoly, especially if they control the prices and if no other businesses can enter that market or compete with them. The government and the politicians, especially the ones who own or have interest in those companies or receive bribes from those companies, let them control and own most or all the market share. If a company is able to compete with them, the corrupt politicians will let them buy and acquire or merge with the company to keep the monopoly going."

"To me, it just keeps going back to the conflict of interest issue. We have already concluded that the companies will do whatever it takes to make money at the expense of the people, the society, and environment. They are inherently evil due to their number one goal of making money. It is up to the people to force the corrupted politicians and the government to deal with the corporations differently. The only way to do that is to not allow the politicians to have ownership and interest in the companies, and we cannot allow them to receive gifts, bribes, or money from these corporations and individuals that own or have interest or are employees of the company."

"I agree Beth. Yes, indeed. They also say that it is a free market economy, which allows for businesses to determine prices based on competition, but this process doesn't make sense and allows for greed and corruption, which is evident with high prices, poor quality products and services, inflation, and monopolies. The numerous recessions are evidence too. Not to mention that some bigger corporations have different goods and services, so they have a larger budget and can offer lower prices while a small business is not able to compete with them due to them needing to have a higher price to even make a small profit. The small businesses can't compete with the unfair free market system. Since corporations cannot act ethically and morally in so many other ways, they should not be allowed to have control over prices. They even engage in price gouging during times of crises, such as natural disasters and recessions, which is supposed to be illegal, but the government and politicians let them do it anyway. The companies who have a monopoly or a patent on a product, which is a monopoly in and of itself, set prices way too high. Pharmaceutical companies do that with prescription drugs, which is very sad if someone who is poor needs those medications to get better or to stay alive. They end up dying because they can't afford the medication. That is not okay. The pharmaceutical company should be charged with murder. Just because your poor doesn't mean you should have to die because you can't afford a medication, treatment, or service to help you. Patenting products should be illegal. A free market society should be just that, free."

"Totally Em. I think the only other thing, which I'm sure there are a whole lot more, that I can think of off the top of my head that is atrocious in the world of business is the pyramid scheme of the financial and insurance industries, which includes both the public and private companies. The government made one of its biggest mistakes a long time ago by allowing banks to be private companies. To add insult to injury, they approved a separate and private central bank and institution to handle its money and have control over making money, which is made out of thin air, and the interest rates, which significantly affects the economy. They even gave them power over the evil and corrupt private banks. That has to be one of the stupidest fucking decisions ever made. It's up there with slavery, animal agriculture, declaring and fighting in a war, discrimination, inequality, poverty, allowing companies to bribe and give money to politicians, and having a high military budget. It kept and made a lot of people filthy rich, but it was not in the best interest of the people or the country. This mistake will haunt and destroy so many countries and neglect and abuse the citizens of these countries. We will always have fake booms, which is just an illusion that the economy is doing well, and the real busts of the economy due to the lack of control that the citizens and government have over their finances and the economy. They pyramid scheme is in the fact that you have a few people who get really really rich off this scam, a few who are doing okay, and most of the population who are living paycheck to paycheck or are poor. It's insane that so many people can't see the scam and the pyramid scheme."

"That sounds about right. Both the financial and insurance industries are pyramid schemes. A lot of corporations are set up that way too. The majority of the workers don't benefit very much or at all from the company. It's obvious that the rich and the rich politicians set it up this way. They knew what they were doing. It's interesting that an individual, who even has little debt and good credit, can have a very difficult time getting a loan or funds for something, but the government and companies, who are both riddled with debt and problems and are over spending and not living within their means and could be considered high risk, are able to get millions and billions in loans and lots and lots of money. I mean, how can you be millions, billions, and even trillions in debt and keep getting more loans to pay off the loans that you can't pay off? It's insane and irresponsible. A bank wouldn't let an individual have a loan if they couldn't pay off the last one. There are going to be consequences to that. You have to pay off your debts and cut your expenses. You have to have at least a balanced budget where you are not overspending while maintaining little to no debt. I'm starting to think that the people running our country are mentally challenged. Actually, they are retarded because I don't want to offend or compare them to the mentally challenged people out there."

"They are retarded. Fucking retarded, but I know they know what they are doing. It's a con, so the people are really the retarded ones. The powers that be are just greedy psychopaths. The crazy part is that the economy is so big and has so many problems, but there is no accountability. When everything goes wrong, the companies and the people who caused the problems are practically rewarded for their wrongdoings. They are given bonuses even when they fire and lay off employees due to the failures of the company, its owners, and its management. They are given tax breaks and government bailouts to help them through their difficult time that they caused due to their greediness and corruption. They are even allowed to keep their jobs and do not get charged with any crimes even though they are committing a host of financial crimes, especially fraud and tax evasion. That wouldn't happen if the politicians actually worked for the people and not the companies. It's like a slap in our faces that most of the population is struggling so much, but the second the companies have a hard time, the government and politicians bend over backwards to assist them financially. Hello. There are millions and billions dying and living in poverty who need help every day. Right now. This very second. But you aren't going to help them out. So, you are telling me that there's not enough money to help people and provide for the people, but we can find all the money in the world to create social welfare programs for the rich and their companies. With the way things are going, a depression of all depressions is inevitable. Something has to drastically change to avoid or prevent a major economical and societal depression at this point. I hope it does all come crashing down. Then, the truth will really and finally be exposed to the brainwashed and programmed that all this capitalism is just a scam."

"How so Beth?"

"Well, the financial and insurance industries don't actually make anything of substance. Unfortunately, those industries contribute significantly to the economy. At least in terms of numbers. You also have the information and marketing or advertising industries that don't really make anything either, but they also significantly contribute to the economy. Therefore, you have a lot of money going into and through these industries that aren't producing anything of practical value or usefulness. You could even argue that some of the goods that we make aren't really that useful or valuable and are even harmful and are causing a lot of negative consequences."

"Totally, like drugs, alcohol, tobacco, prescription drugs, and so many foods that are very unhealthy for us. Especially, the animal agricultural industry. I'm not even sure if a lot of technology is actually useful or good for us, and that is a huge industry too."

"Exactly Em. We don't need all these things. We may want them, but they do more harm than good. Our money needs to go to things that are helping us, so when a significant amount of our money and economy is going to industries that are basically worthless from a societal point of view, you are asking for a disaster to happen with the economy. Not to mention that the people running these businesses are unscrupulous as all get out. They don't care about anything but themselves and making money. They would sacrifice the entire world to make a buck. They are okay with death and destruction to get rich, and that is a fact. Look at what most industries are doing to the environment and climate. It's catastrophic. If anything is going to destroy us, it is pollution and the earth's violent response to our irresponsible and abusive ways. If the greedy politicians, businesses, and rich don't send us into another recession or depression, the inclement weather from global warming and climate change will. The amount of pollution that we create is absolutely appalling. There is no reason we can't switch over to renewable and sustainable energies."

"There is no reason at all. Well said."

"The pollution and global warming are one thing, but since the government and corporations have been allowed to borrow, borrow, and borrow some more and since a lot of these industries don't make tangible goods or things that we actually need, we are suffering. A dark and ominous cloud has formed over us. You also can't keep creating money out of thin air and expect that there won't be any consequences in the future to our monetary economical system. There is something diabolical about the central banking system that many people ignore. If the people don't revolt soon, like they should, we are headed for an economical and societal disaster. The wealthy, the businesses, and the politicians can make changes now, but they procrastinate, make excuses, and just don't do it. Eventually, the wealthy will stop buying and investing because they will want to save their money, the banks will lend to people who can't pay the loans back and then they will stop lending money, the corporations will start laying off and firing people or lower their wages and benefits, the corporations will start raising their prices and contributing to inflation, the banks will keep making risky investments that will turn into bad investments with people's hard earned money and savings, the corporations will sacrifice the employees' wages and benefits and their employment with the company to give themselves bonuses and raises, and the consumers will stop buying and contributing to the economy."

"That's the domino effect Beth. So, who's to blame? The wealthy, the government, the corporations, the politicians? Nope. They blame the citizens and people for them not making sacrifices and not continuing to buy and do without certain things. It's never a good idea to allow a few people to own and have most of the wealth in a nation or in the world. It's a very very bad idea. It's like some tattoos that people get. Those are bad idea tattoos. They know they shouldn't do it, but it seems okay in the short term, but it will have negative consequences in the future. It makes sense to the already wealthy people, who unfortunately make the rules and the laws, so income or economic inequality is basically corruption and greed in its finest form. It makes you wonder if people should only legally be allowed to have a certain amount of money. I mean who needs billions. Who needs tens or hundreds of millions? I know it sounds ridiculous to say you can only have a certain amount of money but look at what economic inequality is doing to the majority of the population, to the country, and to the world. Why do a few people get to live well at the expense of most? There is no reason that anyone should be suffering or living in poverty. I'm sure there is an amount that is still very excessive, such as tens of millions, that people could still live really well and give the rest to charity or back to something."

"I don't know what that amount would be Em, but it could definitely still be a lot. Most people can't imagine having tens of thousands in savings let alone a million in savings. That would significantly change most people's lives and their statuses of living."

"I agree. We could even cap it at 10 million. Just to give the wealthy a little room to feel like they have something. That's the problem though. The only ones that would have a problem with that regulation or law would be the wealthy. Since the wealthy pay off and bribe the politicians, that regulation would never happen. Tell me how that is okay or fair. It's not. That is the problem with democracy, and it will be the end of us. The politicians don't do what the majority of people need and want. They do what is in the best interest of them, the rich, and the corporations. Some even just do what is in the best interest of their church or religion even though that is illegal. Eventually, things will fall apart or get even worse. They already are. We have given lots of evidence and proof today that what they are doing is not working. Look at the horrors all around us, and the mess that we have made. Every day, people are sick, dying, and living in awful conditions because the rich run this country, they bribe the politicians, and they are the politicians."

"I can't even imagine having a million. Let alone 10 million. I can think of so many wonderful things to do with that money to help the earth, people, and the animals. It is sad that the wealthy don't help others more and do more with the money they have. It's like bragging rights. There is no point in being wealthy if you aren't doing good with the money."

"True that Beth. Instead, the rich, the corporations, the government, and the politicians just hoard it and use it for wicked and destructive things. And now, we have so many more environmental factors causing problems for companies and people."

"What do you mean?"

"Well, like you were saying, all these natural disasters from global warming and climate change. The pollution from animal agriculture, deforestation, and fossil fuel use has a significant effect on the economy. You have the destruction of homes and buildings, energy crises, devastation of agriculture land, loss of jobs, loss of products and resources, increased prices from extorting companies, increased borrowing by the government to pay for the disasters, and insurance scams and other fraudulent acts during these times. The insurance companies make me sick. They are so greedy. They take, take, take, and when it's time for them to pay out, they do very little or nothing at all. It's a scam. You would think if you were a business owner that you would accept global warming and climate change. It is a true liability and is or will soon affect your business. Since we are playing an omnipotent being and significantly affecting the weather, which is bringing destruction from the different weather-related systems, everyone's finances and assets are being hurt. Everyone. The people, the government, the politicians, and the businesses."

"I can see that. Great point Em. It definitely affects the economy, but there are lots of things that we can all do to prepare and intervene. The first step is acceptance. The second step is to take action. Since there are so many traditionalists lying and denying the truth of global warming and climate change, we may have to force action due to the greed and corruption of the businesses who are making a lot of money off the pollution and contribution to global warming. They deny it while causing it at the same time. They know it's real, but they just want to milk the natural resources and make as much money off the pollution as they can before something happens or someone stops them. As much as I hate force, sometimes you have to revolt and overcome tyranny and corruption through aggressive means. You don't want to be a part of history where you were the people who were getting oppressed, neglected, abused, and even murdered because you did nothing and allowed your authoritarian and tyrannical government, who was powered by the rich and corporations, to control and abuse you. Silence, apathy, and conformity are all consent. We have to finally stop them and make them do what's right."

"We'll see Beth. It makes me afraid of the future."

"Totally."

"People need to wake the fuck up and get a clue. They need to spend their money smarter, support local and small businesses, support businesses who are trying to be green and use renewable energy sources, work for these better companies instead of larger immoral companies, listen to scientists over paid-for politicians and corporation advertisements, research politicians before they vote for them and find out which corporations are giving them money and what they have supported or voted for, vote for politicians who are poor or middle class, vote for politicians who are qualified and educated, support local organic farmers, and buy healthy organic and plant-based foods."

"Those are great Em. I feel like we really accomplished something here today."

"I hope so. I am trying to remember all these conversations that I'm having with everyone. I might write a book one of these days. I have really enjoyed this conversation and have loved talking with you today. I'm glad we got to spend some time together."

"Definitely. I had a blast. I felt like we just got here. It's been a few hours. Wow."

"Well, let's close up shop. We should do this for Adam and Don more often."

"That would be fun. Let's do it."

"If you want to hang out, let me know. I'm sure Mary would like that. She hasn't seen you in a while."

"That sounds great. I feel like my after-work time has been filled up with the guy I'm dating. It's good though. He is nice."

"Good luck with that. I'm so glad I don't have to do all that dating crap. It's exhausting when you get older."

"Yes. You are lucky. Well, I'm out. I'll see you in a couple of days."

"Sounds good Beth."

Beth and Emerald hugged.

"Love you girl," Beth said.

"Love you too," Emerald said. "Take care."

Beth left the store.

Emerald locked the door behind Beth. She went to the back room and used the bathroom. She grabbed her bike and turned off the lights on the way out. She unlocked the door again and walked out of the store with her bike. She turned around and locked the door behind her. The sun was almost setting, which was awesome for her as she was usually in bed before or getting ready for bed during the sunset. Her head was spinning from the conversation that she had with Beth. She couldn't believe all the issues that they talked about regarding how corrupt the government was and how much they let the corporations do whatever they want. It made her sad to think about how many problems were being caused because people were more focused on money and immediate gratifications than being ethical and moral.

Emerald couldn't believe that a lot of these people actually say they are religious and are good people. In reality, they are not good people and are not really religious. They only say that as an insurance policy because they believe that if they don't believe in a god and their religion that they will not be saved and will be damned to a fictional place of horrors. However, their actions and evil ways will be the deciding factor in their fate and will determine their karma. They are really just hypocrites who only care about themselves and don't care about the destruction they are causing. They act like they are all high and mighty, but they are sinners. Their selfishness and greediness are more important to them than helping others, the animals, and the earth. They say they care; they say that they are good people; they say they are going somewhere beautiful and amazing after they die; they say that they are saved; but they are everything that they say they are not. That's why they are hypocrites because they say or believe in one thing and do something else. They say they believe in goodness, but they do and support things that are nefarious and destructive. They don't care about the things that matter and are awful and horrible people because their religion has told them that they will be saved as long as they believe in a fake and illusory god and give the church money, so they use that as a pass to basically murder the current and future generations, slaughter and abuse animals, and destroy the earth.

Emerald rode over to the park to watch the sunset. She got off her bike and just stood on the edge of the sidewalk as it started to drop into the horizon. She thought it was absolutely gorgeous. There were some clouds, so they were creating some wonderful reddish and purplish colors from the sun light. The sun itself was a rich amber color, which was breathtaking to Emerald. While she was watching the sunset, she started to think about the song she was working on and how she could incorporate some of the issues that she talked about with Beth. She took a bunch of deep and long breaths and just soaked the sun and the beautiful lights and colors into her being. She felt the connection with this amazing star that gave life to everything around it. Ironically and eventually, it will also be the doom of everything. It was mind blowing for Emerald to try and grasp or think about millions and billions of years going by, especially since we are only alive for about several decades. It was even crazy for her to try to take all those years in and make something out of them.

Emerald thought the sun was our savior and that we should respect the sun, what it has created, and what it has given us. The sun got lower and lower. She watched it get smaller and smaller as it went below the horizon. She got back on her bike and started riding back home. As she peddled home, she thought more about her song and some of the lyrics that could go with it. She got home and put up her bike. She went into the living room and grabbed the guitar and her song notebook by the sofa. She sat down on the sofa and made sure the guitar was in tune.

She took a moment and tried to think of and feel the frustration and the outrage of the oppressed and abused. She thought of the women, minority populations of the different cultures, slaves, gays, the poor, intersexed, lesbians, transgendered, transsexuals, bisexuals, asexuals, allies, queers, questioning, children, natives, vegetarians, vegans, disabled, animals, environment, and the beautiful and wonderful earth. She thought of anyone or any animal that has been abused, neglected, bullied, and taken advantage of. She knew there were more she wasn't recognizing, but she wanted to get back to the song.

She played the notes that she thought of earlier even though she imagined them with some distortion and with a wah pedal. The acoustic guitar would be fine for now. She didn't think the song needed a bridge between the verses and chorus like a lot of popular songs try to do. She thought it was unnecessary to add a bridge, which would make it sound forced or fake like a lot of popular songs sound. She imagined the sound in her head with the sinister doom rock tone. It was a very assertive song with a powerful message. It almost felt angry to her. She wanted it to be an anthem for a revolution.

The Reclamation

Intro Riff: (Starts on D string with a wah pedal)
E, D, E, F, E, D, E, F, E, D, E, F, E (hand over all strings, chicka chicka
sound, down then up and down then up)
Play riff again.

Verse 1:
(Play intro riff during verse)
You have been programmed to be a zombie
Open your eyes to the lies and you'll see

Chorus:
(Play following chords with chorus words: E, F, G, E, F, E, D, E)
It's the reclamation (then play in like a flamenco style: E, D, E, F, E, D, E,
F)
It's the reclamation (then play in like a flamenco style: E, D, E, F, E, D, E,
F, E, D, E, F, E)

Repeat Intro Riff

Verse 2:
(Play intro riff during verse)
You're under the spell and the control of the few
It's time to rise up and tell them to fuck you

Repeat Chorus

Bridge to solo
(Play following chords with bridge words: A, B, C, D, E, F)
We have been down far too long (then play in like a flamenco style: E, D,
E, F, E, D, E, F)
It's time to stand up and be strong (then play in like a flamenco style: E,
D, E, F, E, D, E, F)
We're taking back what is ours (then play in like a flamenco style: E, D, E,
F, E, D, E, F)

We will leave with our scars (then play in like a flamenco style: E, D, E, F, E, D, E, F, E, D, E, F, E)

Solo with the flamenco style and then just faster guitar solo.
Then, drum and bass instrumental jam.
Some parts of it have a native chanting in a melodic and emotional way.

Back to Intro Riff

Verse 3:
(Play intro riff during verse)
Look what you've lost through your conformity
Take back what's rightfully yours and be free

Repeat Chorus

Episode 6
The Lines That Divide Us

The differences that we see cause so many of our problems.
Thinking you are different or better than someone else is a pathological mental illness.
Diversity is beautiful and beneficial, but the illusion of separation with the attitude and practice of discrimination is ugly and harmful.
Equality and cooperation will solve the most challenging and difficult situations and problems while discrimination and competition will pollute and destroy everything.

A few days later, Emerald woke up really early from a bad dream. It was so intense that she got startled and sat up in the bed. She even felt a bit warm. She had to take a moment to orient herself to where she was at. Mary even woke up.

"Are you okay?" Mary asked tiredly.

"I think so. I just had a bad dream."

"Do you need to talk about it?"

"No, my dear. I'll be okay. I think I'm going to go write it down though. Very weird."

"Sounds good. I love you."

"Sweet dreams my beautiful. I love you too."

Emerald leaned over and kissed Mary on the cheek. She got out of bed and quietly left the room. She gently closed the door behind her. Since it was so early, she wasn't hungry just yet, so she used the bathroom and then went into the living room and grabbed her dream journal. She flipped a lamp on, sat down on the sofa, and opened the booklet with the pen that held her place with where she was at in the journal. She started to write about her dream.

She wrote about being in a building with lots of hallways and doors. It was like a hotel, but she was not for sure if it was or not. She didn't recognize the place or the surroundings. There were no windows, so she couldn't see outside of the building. She felt uneasy in the dream like she wasn't supposed to be there. She started walking down the hallway to see if she could find an exit or to see if she could find out where she was. All the doors in the hallway were closed, which made her feel trapped. She heard one or two people shouting behind her. She was not sure what they said. She started to get anxious, worried, and scared. For some reason, she was afraid of them, so she started to walk faster. She found an elevator at the end of the hallway. She pressed a button for it to come to her, but it seemed like it was taking forever to get to her floor. It finally arrived, and the doors opened. She walked into the elevator, and the doors closed. She felt some relief. She then heard some banging and started to get nervous again. She didn't feel like she was in control of the elevator. It started to move without her pressing any buttons or telling it where to go. She had no idea which direction it was going. She thought it was going down, but she was not for sure.

The elevator finally stopped, and the doors opened. She was scared at this point to see what was on the other side. There was a man and woman standing and waiting outside of the elevator. It was another floor and hallway. They both walked into the elevator but didn't say anything. Emerald didn't feel immediately threatened by them, but she was suspicious of them as they didn't seem to be friendly. She tried to talk to them, but her words were jumbled and unintelligible. She couldn't talk right. She has had dreams like that before, but this one was really challenging for her to say what she wanted to say in the dream. She felt like either her anxiety and fear were keeping her from talking right or there was something wrong with her physically in the dream. Every time she tried to say something, the words didn't make sense. She was trying to ask them for help, but she couldn't. She just made incomprehensible noises or mumbled sounds. The couple just stared at her.

The elevator started moving again. It stopped on another floor, and the doors opened. The couple walked out. Then, the woman looked back at Emerald in a serious kind of way. The woman turned her head back to look forward, and they kept walking. The floor was just another hallway in the building. Emerald was scared to leave the elevator but thought she should go with the couple. She couldn't move though. The doors closed again. She felt helpless and paralyzed. She was not sure if the elevator started to move again, but she heard the banging again. It was not a normal sound that a machine would make. It was like someone was hitting something to either break or get into something. It was very frightening to Emerald. At this point, she tried to scream at the top of her lungs. Since she couldn't talk or ask for help, she hoped someone would be alerted by her scream. Unfortunately, she couldn't scream or yell either. It was like a whisper. It was a very low and raspy scream. She kept trying to scream louder, but she couldn't. Then, she felt something, or someone grab her from behind on the left arm. She didn't see anything, but she couldn't move. She almost didn't want to look. She didn't want to see what or who it was. She felt safer not knowing, but it started to pull her backwards. She was extremely frightened, so she started screaming again. She finally woke up.

Emerald put the pen into the dream journal between the pages and closed the journal. She set it down on the table in front of her. She thought about the dream, how it felt, whether there was anything to learn from it, and what it might have meant. While she was dreaming, Emerald felt very anxious and afraid. It was scary to her. She didn't feel like she was safe or had any control. She hasn't had a bad dream or nightmare in a long time, so she was not used to feeling those feelings. Overall, she has been feeling really good and confident, so she was surprised that she would have a dream about someone coming after her or trying to get her. She tried to do some self-reflection to see if she is worried about anything. Other than her legal issues and getting done with her probation, she couldn't think of anything. Even though the legal issues have been stressful, she has felt excitement about getting off probation and getting her record sealed. However, she was traumatized from the drug addiction, the way she treated herself and Mary, the arrest, and the court process. She wondered if she was still recovering from all that craziness. She wondered if her mind, body, and spirit were still healing from the abuse that she inflicted onto herself. She still felt very guilty about so many things.

To her, the dream was so real. It was so real that she woke up confused and disoriented. She couldn't tell if she was still dreaming when she woke up. It was very vivid too. Emerald sensed not only the emotional feelings but also the physical feelings. The sights and sounds were very stimulating to her. She even felt the floor as she walked, which she normally didn't feel. If there was an odor or taste, she probably could have smelled or tasted something. While she was thinking about the dream, she still felt like she was in it and experiencing it.

Emerald thought about whether dreams had any real meanings to them. She would like to think that they do, but she was still pondering that debate. She thought it was difficult and a challenge to surmise or obtain the meaning. Even if you gather some meaning from the dream, it was still a guess and very subjective or biased. However, she knew for a fact that bad dreams and nightmares seem to happen when things are not going well in your life or you are sick, especially from abusing drugs and alcohol. Those types of dreams seem to be a direct result from stress, exhaustion, injuries, illnesses, physical or emotional trauma, or problems with work and relationships. She abused herself for many years with drugs and dishonesty, so it was not surprising to her that she would still have some awful dreams once in a while. Even though it has been about 10 years since she quit the drugs and started taking care of herself, her mind, body, and spirit hasn't forgotten all those problems. It may take another 10 years for her to be fully healed. Nevertheless, she felt a whole lot better than a few years ago.

She tried one more time to try and understand the dream. It was the only dream that she could remember last night, which was weird and rare. She usually remembered at least two and sometimes up to five or six. About once a month, she didn't remember any dreams due to not sleeping well or waking up a lot. She also thought it was weird for her to have dreams where she saw people that she has never met before and was in places that she has never been before. She had no idea where those dreams came from or how she got those ideas. She has been to a bunch of different hotels, so that wasn't too surprising. Hotels were somewhat confining to her, and she felt like people just walk by and ignore problems without helping. Her subconscious mind could have remembered that. Emerald has accepted that bad and negative people are out in the world, so she was suspicious and distrusting of people when she was out in public. She also thought that when she was on drugs that she was screaming and yelling for help without actually screaming and yelling for help. Her self-destructive behaviors were the screams and cries for help.

Emerald asked out loud, "Who knows? What difference does it make?"

What was important to her was that she was aware of how she was. She knew she needed to keep taking care of herself. She concluded that her mind, body, and spirit were still hurting and still traumatized. She needed to keep taking care of herself, so she could continue to heal and get to a better place. She accepted that she could have died and that she could have killed herself while she was on drugs. She was killing herself. She wondered how much physical and mental damage she actually did. She must have really done a number on her organs and other biological systems. She knew she really hurt her brain, heart, liver, kidneys, and digestive system. She may have even had some serious diseases and even some cancer. She hoped that she reversed those problems with all her efforts. She needed to keep doing what she was doing and stay on the right track. She owed it to herself and Mary. Emerald and Mary deserved to be happy. She used to have bad dreams all the time while on the drugs and for a while after she got clean. They have definitely minimized through the years.

Emerald thought about the dreamworld and whether it was actually another dimension or another plane of existence. It was a very odd experience. Emerald didn't know why we even needed to dream anyway. She knew we needed to sleep and rest ourselves, but the dreams seemed to be very unnecessary for that process. Dreams were very enigmatic. If the dreamworld was like another dimension, she wondered whether or not she was even supposed to be in some of these places that she was dreaming about. She thought that bad dreams and nightmares could be a result of us being in a dimension that doesn't want us there or being in a dimension that we are not supposed to be in. So, we experience all these intense feelings of anxiety, pain, and fear. She also thought that the dream could actually be someone else's dream and that was why it didn't feel like she belonged or was supposed to be there. So, the anxiety of someone or something chasing her was actually the dream trying to get her out of the dimension or someone else's dream. She thought that they did their job because she woke up and left the dream. She thought it would be so cool if dreaming was how we traveled inter-dimensionally or connected with other people's subconscious minds while they were sleeping too.

At that moment, Emerald thought of a cool invention or idea where there could be some kind of technology that would be like a dream collective. A lot of people would need to use it for it to be effective though. Every day, millions or billions of people could write in what they dreamed about and the technology would match or connect your dream or dreams to other similar dreams. The technology could use keywords or phrases to match up similar dreams. Voluntarily, of course, you could communicate with others who had similar dreams and whether you were connected with them in some way, either in that same moment you had the dream or in some other way. Emerald thought it would be amazing to find out that you actually had a very similar or the exact same kind of dream with someone you have never met and who was really far away or on the other side of the world. She thought it would be even more amazing if you saw pictures of these people you never met, and they were the unfamiliar people in your dreams. In addition, it would be crazy if the places that they were living were the unfamiliar places in your dreams. As great of an idea as Emerald thought this dream collective would be, she didn't think enough people would use it to make it effective or people would abuse it through lying and dishonesty. She thought it had great potential though.

She felt she spent enough time this morning pondering her dream and the amazing dreamworld and subconscious mind. It took her about an hour to do all that processing, which was longer than usual. Overall, she was glad that she was journaling her dreams. She felt like it was helping her remember her dreams more, find some meaning in some dreams and her life, describe things and express herself better, be more aware of lots of different things, and develop and grow as a person. Even if the dreams were meaningless, Emerald was still using them to her benefit and creating meaning out of them. She tried to imagine all the dreams that she couldn't remember, which was probably more than the ones that she did remember. Emerald forgot a lot of them when she woke up or got around. She wondered if there was a reason that she remembered some and not others.

Emerald was hungry at this point, but she used the bathroom and did some light hygiene before she made some food. After she was done in the bathroom, she went into the kitchen to make some breakfast. She made her raw, vegan, organic, and whole foods shake. She puts some greens and some diatomaceous earth or silica in it. She loved how many vitamins and minerals were in it. It made her feel so good. She thought it tasted really good and delicious. She finished drinking the shake, and then drank some veggie juice. She remembered another dream, so she grabbed a couple more things to take back into the living room. She made a glass of fruit juice and grabbed a banana, an apple, some nut butter, and some of her amazing and fabulous home-made chocolates. She thought her chocolates were absolutely divine and decadent. She looked forward to eating them every morning. She thought they were very delicious. They were very healthy and good for her too, which was the best part about them. Emerald was so proud of herself for not eating out and avoiding processed foods with added sugar, preservatives, stabilizers, gums, genetically mutant organisms, and poisons sprayed on them. Emerald loved that she only ate foods that were 100 percent organic fruits and vegetables or only had those ingredients in them. She definitely felt the difference and noticed how much better she looked and felt with her plant-based diet and being vegan. It made her feel sorry for people who lack self-control and poison and hurt themselves with food.

She placed her glass of juice and food on the table in front of the sofa and sat down. She grabbed her dream journal again and ate and drank while she journaled the other dream that she remembered. Since she forgot this dream, she thought it was weird how some dreams come back to her after she wakes up. She tried to think if something triggered it back to her memory or consciousness. Sometimes, she was able to identify a clear trigger. However, other times, she couldn't figure out why the dream came back to her. Sometimes, meditating and exercising caused her to remember the dreams that she forgot. She thought most of the triggers were internal or with her thoughts. Some of the dreams were related to certain places, people, and events, so when she thought of those things, she would remember the dream. It was weird to her that she would think about some of those things that she dreamt about the day after she had the dream because she didn't think about a lot of those things very often. It was like the dream either predicted the thought or her conscious and unconscious were working together to produce those thoughts to help her remember the dreams. However, she felt like some of the dreams that came back to her seemed very random because she couldn't identify or figure out the trigger. She wondered if the focus on the other dreams that she remembered pushed the other dreams out of her consciousness or awareness.

For this dream, it was her making breakfast or thinking about the food that triggered it. She started writing about the dream. She didn't remember a whole lot about the dream but that she was in some unfamiliar building. There were a bunch of unknown people. She was in a restaurant. She was sitting at a table with some other people that she didn't recognize. A guy brought her a bowl of pasta. Even though she hasn't eaten pasta in over five years, she took a bite of it. She wasn't for sure if it was plant based or not. There was a woman sitting next to her. The atmosphere was cozy. The lights were dim. Emerald felt relaxed and comfortable. She remembered that she had a thought in the dream that she shouldn't be eating the pasta, but she did anyway. She felt like she actually tasted the pasta. She could feel the texture of the noodles and taste the spices from the sauce. She couldn't remember anything else from the dream.

She didn't put as much thought or energy into deciphering this pasta eating dream as the scary hotel one. However, she wondered if the pasta dream actually had more to give her than the other one. She hasn't missed eating pasta and hasn't thought about it in a long time, so she didn't think the dream had a literal meaning. She didn't think dreams had literal meanings anyway. She remembered eating pasta a lot though before she gave it up, so the dream could have been from a memory. Her subconscious could have been accessing her old ways or habits. Emerald thought it was weird that she would sometimes do things in dreams that she wouldn't do in her conscious or real life. In the dreams, she felt like there was some pressure or just lack of ability to control herself and do want she wanted or needed to do. She didn't feel like she was in control of herself in a lot of dreams. She felt like she was an observer within herself or whoever she was looking out of in the dream. It was almost automatic. It was like she was watching someone else guide her, so it just felt like she was that person.

She wondered if she was able to look into a mirror while she was in a dream. She couldn't remember ever looking into a mirror in a dream. She wondered if the reflection would actually be her or if it would be someone else, an animal, or an alien being. It was a huge assumption to think that she was the person in the dream that she was looking out of. She couldn't remember ever actually seeing herself in a dream, so she was not for sure that she was really her in the dreams. She wondered if she was another being or animal. She could have been an alien. Emerald tried to remember what else might have happened in the dream, so she really tried to focus on it for a minute. Sometimes, if she spent more time focusing on the dream or giving it her attention, she would remember more of it. She thought she might have gotten up from the table after a couple of bites of the pasta and went somewhere else, but her memory of the dream was very hazy. She wasn't for sure what happened after sitting at the table.

Emerald stopped thinking about the dream and decided to meditate. She washed out her dishes and used the bathroom again. She went back to the living room and grabbed her mat to meditate. She placed the mat on the floor and sat down crossed leg on the mat. She made sure her back was straight. She took several slow deep breaths and then did several Om chants. She tried not to be too loud, so she didn't wake up Mary. She finished chanting and focused her attention over various parts of her body to help her become more aware of and be able to use the clandestine energy sources within her. While she was giving each part of her body her focus and attention, she would think about a mantra for each one. For the top of her head, she thought, "I understand." For her forehead, she thought, "I see." For the throat, she thought, "I speak." For the heart, she thought, "I love." For the abdomen, she thought, "I do." For the groin, she thought, "I feel." For the base of the spine or bottom, she thought, "I am."

She started her focus with the top of her head area or the crown chakra, then her forehead area or the third eye or mind's eye chakra, then her throat and neck area or throat charka, then her heart and chest area or heart chakra, then her abdomen area or solar plexus chakra, then her groin area or sacral chakra, and then the base of her spine and bottom area or root chakra. She then started at the bottom and then went back up through them again. She tried to focus her awareness up and down her spine a few times. She tried to not think while letting her mind and body relax. She wanted to just be in a state of being.

Emerald was trying hard to understand the concept of not resisting while letting go, but her mind seemed to be very demanding at times with her thinking patterns. She knew thinking was just like any other habit. She had to keep practicing, so she could control it or not let it control her. She wasn't sure if controlling it was the right way to say what she was doing as she understood that her thoughts were just a response to stimuli and didn't define who she was. To Emerald, thinking was a sense like seeing and hearing. As with any sense, you can choose to decipher it or ignore it. Most people are brainwashed and programmed to believe that who they are is how and what they think, but Emerald didn't believe that. Most people think the way they do because of what they were taught, which is how someone else wants you to be. Emerald wanted to be who she was before thought and before the brainwashing and programming. Then, she focused her attention on her heart and her breathing. She felt the beating of the heart while feeling her gentle breath go in and out of her. She kept her attention and focus there for a long time while letting her thoughts come and go as they wished.

She came to after about an hour and felt like it was time to end her meditation session. She took one last deep breath and stood up. She folded up the mat and put it back by the wall. It was very cloudy this morning, but it wasn't too cold. Emerald was upset that she wouldn't be able to watch the sunrise, so she decided to stretch and go for a run outside. She stretched as much of her body out as she could. She stretched out her neck, arms, back, legs, and ankles. She went to the bathroom again and wrote out a note for Mary. She wrote, "Great Morning Beautiful. I hope you are sleeping awesome. I'm out running. Miss and Love You. Em." She drew a little heart under her name.

Emerald left the apartment, took a deep breath when she got outside, and started running. It was still dark, so she brought a pulsating light that she wrapped around her wrist. She decided to go the long way, which went south of their apartment to the country and back over to the park. She had to turn off on a road to get to the park though, or the road would keep going away from the park. There was a hill down the road that she liked to run up. It gave her a good workout. For some reason, while she was running, she thought about her meditation and getting into that place of oneness and completeness. She really liked running outside because she got to look around and see the vastness of the sky and the environment. People in automobiles didn't get to experience that view as much, and a lot of people on their bicycles could enjoy it, but a lot of them didn't. She also liked to get some fresh air by running outside. It was refreshing and invigorating to her.

Emerald thought how small we really were in the vastness of space and within the universe. She felt like we were just a speck or a small piece in this cosmic playground. She felt sorry for all the people who rush around and act so busy while they chase a false dream and lie from the manipulations of rich people, companies, politicians, and the government. It upset her how they keep people focused on material gratification, food, religion, employment, money, drugs and other addictions, immediate gratifications, trivial entertainments, and other short-term wants, so the people can't or don't ponder these questions. People end up focusing on meaningless and trivial things, so they can't figure out and understand who they truly are.

"Who are we?" She asked out loud. "Who am I? What are we doing here? What is my purpose?"

Emerald wondered if those were trick questions and whether some people think about them because we are curious. She wondered if they were supposed to be asked or if there was even an answer to them. She knew there was something to pondering those types of questions and felt more intelligent by spending time thinking about them. To Emerald, it definitely wasn't intelligent to spend time thinking and focusing on trivial matters, such as sports and certain types of entertainment that focus on celebrities' or other people's lives, electronic games, media shows, and programs. She felt sorry for the people who spend time focusing on these entertainments or have full-time jobs in these fields. She couldn't imagine living in their meaningless existences as they contribute almost nothing to their lives and the lives around them. Sure, people get entertained in those ways, but it's pointless and a complete waste of time. There are so many more intelligent, positive, and progressive ways to be entertained, such as the different arts, creativity, imagination, nature, exercise, meditation, gardening, music, and reading.

She thought of herself as a philosopher of sorts. She knew pondering existential questions definitely separates higher intelligent beings from others. People who are brainwashed and programmed, not open-minded, and not awake would answer a question like "Who am I?" by saying, "I'm a human" or "I'm a mammal." They might even say their name, where they come from, their family name, their school mascot, their religion, their nationality or ethnicity, their political party, or some other category or group. Even though most people would answer using those descriptions, none of them are correct. They are all masks and fake identities. Emerald knew that the deeper and more intelligent answers come from spending decades of self-reflection and self-realization due to how brainwashed and programmed we are. Most people have no idea who they really are other than what other people have told them or made them to be.

"I am everything," Emerald shouted. "I am energy, and I am love."

After years of being lost and ignorant, Emerald figured out that the same thing that makes up the sun and the stars makes up her and everything around her. The same thing that makes up the most disgusting things makes up the most beautiful things. The same thing that makes up the most boring and dull things makes up the most fascinating and most interesting things. It's all how you look at it, but you have to see past your own deceitful eyes and what you have been told to believe. The best thing that you can do to get closer to being awake and connected to yourself and the universe is to question everything that you were ever told, especially about the past, religion, and politics. It's never a good idea to blindly believe what you were told growing up. Our parents lie to us the most. It's not necessarily their intentions to lie. They may not know they are lying due to being brainwashed themselves. You are not who you are told to be. You are not your name or where you are from. We are a whole lot more than that. No matter what you believe, you can't deny how much other people, society, and your senses have influenced what you believe and who you are. Unfortunately, these sources are very distorted, limited, and misleading. Sometimes, they are just plain wrong.

Emerald accepted that our senses are very limited too. Compared to how much information is out in the world and the universe, we are only exposed to a small fraction of this information. We also don't retain that much of what we are exposed to, and with the information that we do retain, we distort and misinterpret it to fit it into our beliefs and uses. While she continued to run, Emerald thought about how many things that she thought was true growing up that she didn't believe in anymore. She also thought how many times society has changed its view of so many things. That's what makes some people more evolved and more intelligent than others. You have to learn from your mistakes and not hold onto old beliefs when new evidence and facts contradict what you believe. It is so important to change when faced with new information that disproves the previous information. Emerald loved to be proven wrong or to learn something new. That made life exciting to her.

Emerald started to really push herself on her run. She started to pick up the pace and run a little faster. She needed the momentum to get up the hill, which she was almost there. Because she was trying to run faster, it was getting harder for her to think rationally about these existential and philosophical issues. Her attention kept going to her breath and legs. She felt satisfied with her contemplation anyway and the conclusions that she came up with. She strongly believed that she was everything and was connected to everything. She knew for a fact that she was energy, and she was trying her best to use this energy for good and love. She was pleased with herself for continuing to meditate on feeling and being connected to everyone and everything. Emerald thought there was something magical and mystical about this connection even though it was a scientific fact.

This realization and connection made her feel amazing and invincible. She felt like she was the universe and the universe was her. She saw everyone and everything for who and what they truly were, which was energy. Everyone and everything are working together in lots of different vibrations and frequencies. We are all in this together, and you can either go with it and cooperate and accept it, or you can deny, fight, and resist it, which a lot of people do.

Emerald finally got to the hill, so she decided to take a couple of deep breaths and fire herself up. She ran up it as fast as she could. She liked challenging herself by pushing her physical and mental limitations. She came up with a philosophy that you can never do better or more if you don't try to do better and more, so she wanted to always try to do better and more. She also stated this philosophy as if you only do what you think you can do, you will only be able to do that much, or if you only keep doing things the same way, you will only be able to do it that way. She felt like she was running really fast, but it was most likely a lot slower than she thought. If she was watching herself, she probably would think it was in slow motion. She felt her heart beating really fast, and she was breathing really hard. She finally got to the top and stopped. She rested for a minute, so she could catch her breath. She stretched her legs and back out. She also checked her shoelaces to make sure they were still tight. She took a couple of deep breaths and then let out a good yelp.

She shouted, "That's how you stay in shape!"

Before she started running again, she saw some of the horizon on the east start getting lighter from the sun. She looked at the strange contrast of light and dark form the eastern sky to the west. She felt the connection and cooperation of the polarities. She took a couple of deep breaths and felt a sense of gratification and appreciation. She started running again. She ran over to the park. She could really see the clouds now as the sun started to lighten up the sky. It was very cloudy, but there wasn't any rain. She didn't think it was going to rain. There was a little breeze, so that was nice for her to feel with her physical exertions. There were a few cars out but not as many as she thought there should be on a weekday. While she continued to run, she started feeling a rush of energy through her body, which she loved and enjoyed. It was like a second wind to her to keep her going. She felt energized. It made her think how electric our bodies are without us realizing it. We actually have electricity running through our bodies. It doesn't seem like it, but we do. Emerald was reminded of this fact a lot more since she got healthy and started exercising. She was able to feel and sense her body a lot more.

Emerald thought how horrible it was that she used to be so out of touch with everything, especially her body, when she was on drugs and not taking care of herself. She didn't care about anything except getting the drugs and getting high. She was still upset with herself for falling into the drug trap and focusing so much on false and fake feelings from an external source. However, she was glad that she was able to snap out of it and wake up before it was too late. She could have easily overdosed and died, or she could have had an accident and ended up with a permanent injury or damaged an organ or something in her body that could have negatively affected her for the rest of her life. She could have also lost Mary for good or ended up in jail or prison for a long time. Things could always be worse, so Emerald felt a lot of gratitude and was thankful things were not worse. She made sure to use that negative energy and that difficult time as a positive. It was important for her to learn from her mistakes and change. She was grateful that things weren't worse and that her health was still good. She was so happy Mary was still a part of her life. In a way, she thought that she had to go through all that pain and misery to be who she is today. As weird as it sounded, she was grateful for her addiction.

Emerald felt like she was finally able to realize the truth. She accepted that we have been lied to so much by so many people. There are so many people, companies, and organizations in the world that just want to manipulate and deceive you. They want to control you, get your money, get other things from you, or get you to do things for them. A lot of people, such as some parents and teachers, don't even realize they are lying to you, and a lot of people don't even realize they are being lied to. People trust other people to tell them the truth, so it's horrible for Emerald to hear parents, teachers, preachers, and politicians intentionally and unintentionally lie to people, especially children. Emerald thought that if adults let people lie to them and they believe the lies, they are just idiots and morons. Unfortunately, there are a lot of idiots and morons in the world. Just because something sounds good or is what you want to hear doesn't make it true. Emerald knew that it was important to keep questioning what she was being told. That made her smart and intelligent.

Most people are living a lie right now. They believe they are something that they are really not. If you believe you are who you are because of your job or how much money you have, you are very ignorant and misled. You are lying to yourself. It doesn't matter if you have a horrible or great job or if you have no money, very little money, or more money than you know what to do with. If you let those things define who you are, you are closed-minded and asleep. You have a lot to learn about life and are missing out on so much. If you had a choice, which you do, and more control, most people would not be doing what they are doing, especially when it comes to work and having a job. However, you would probably not be engaging in a lot of habits and behaviors that you do. You would probably not be in some of the relationships you are in, especially with the friends and family members who hurt you. You would probably be doing lots of other activities or have other interests. We do most of the things that we do because we were told to do them not because we choose to do them. It's interesting how the environment and our society have such an enormous impact and effect on us. Emerald thought that a lot of people probably didn't think about these things or didn't realize the control they had given up. People think they have control over their lives and that they make choices. Emerald knew that was an illusion and a false sense of responsibility.

She was getting closer to the park, so she decided to speed up and run faster. By the time she got there, her heart was beating really fast and she was breathing very heavily. She finally got to a bench she liked to sit at and stopped to catch her breath and rest. She walked back and forth a few times around the bench. She took several deep breaths, so she could catch her breath and calm down. It was somewhat humid, so she was sweating a good amount. She held her hands over her head a couple of times to let the blood flow down from her hands and arms. She stretched out her back and legs again. She sat down on the bench.

"That's how you stay in shape," Emerald said. "No excuses. Know thyself. I am the creator of my universe."

She sat on the bench for a few minutes. She heard some traffic, but she tried to focus on the calmness of the park with the wind rustling the trees and creating some ripples in the water. She heard some birds chirping and some squirrels running across the grass and onto the trees. The night was turning into day. She felt the energy of the sun creating the light all around her. There were a few people running, walking, and riding their bikes around the park. She liked that others were trying to be healthy and enjoy nature too. Emerald felt a sense of relaxation and peace even though she just got through running really hard. She felt relief and satisfaction from the run. She was proud of herself. She then saw an older lady approaching her.

"Emerald is that you?" The unfamiliar lady asked.

Emerald stood up and tried to focus on her face and remember her, but she wasn't sure who she was.

"Emerald, it's me. Dr. Robinson."

"No way. Hi, Dr. Robinson."

"Please. That was 20 years ago. You are a certified adult now. Call me Abby. I just didn't think you would know or remember my first name."

Emerald shook her hand due to being sweaty, but she wanted to hug her.

"Well, I almost couldn't remember you," Emerald said. "Your hair is much longer, and you look a little different."

"It's probably the lack of dress pants and fancy shirts."

"Definitely. I can see that. You look good though. Very relaxed."

"As do you."

"Sorry, I would hug you, but I'm very sweaty."

"It's okay. I completely understand. Thanks for not getting me soaked."

"Wow. How about that? Running into my intro-to-philosophy teacher 25 years later. I would have never guessed."

"Isn't it weird having things happen like that? It's so nice to see you again."

"You too. How are you?"

"I'm doing great. Retired and doing whatever I fucking feel like."

They both started laughing.

"I love it when older people use profanity," Emerald said. "It's so refreshing."

"Definitely. I get to do whatever I want to do, go wherever I want to go, and say whatever the fuck I want to say. If someone doesn't like it, I just tell them to go fuck themselves."

Emerald started laughing again.

"Absolutely," Emerald said with a smile.

"As long as I'm not hurting anyone, who cares?"

"Totally. I agree."

"You know the only reason that I recognized you was that amazingly awesome and unique name of yours. I guess there was something about your face too. You were always so curious yet attractive."

"Thank you?"

"It's definitely a compliment Emerald. I wasn't going to say hi to you. I usually don't say hi to former students. I value my time now, and I try to be very selfish with my time. I could spend hours talking to former students. Some are a waste of time with their brainwashed and ignorant ways. I still see the occasional student walking around. I taught for almost 40 years, so I met a lot of people. Unfortunately, I remember a good amount of them and their names. Once they open their mouths and start talking about this and that, I cringe with disappointment and sadness. You would think they would have learned something in school or from somewhere. It seems like people only care about money, the stuff they have, and what kind of job they have. If I hear someone else start talking about sports or the weather, I'm going to slap them in the face. It's so sad. I got better things to do with my time. We are only on this earth for a limited amount of time in this body. I want to enjoy it before I turn into some other form of energy. Then, I'll enjoy that part of my life."

"I appreciate you reaching out then. That makes me feel privileged."

"You are welcome. You were one of the smarter ones. Even way back then. You still had a lot to learn and didn't know that much, but you were curious and asked questions. That is what you have to do when you are young and inexperienced. You have to learn and ask a lot of questions. Shit, you actually need to keep doing that your entire life. It can be fun and spontaneous running into people from our past, but a lot of people can be annoying. And, I don't like all these closed-minded bigots around here. They might seem nice, but after talking with them, I have no idea what happened to them. I don't think they learned anything in philosophy. If your idea of living is to judge and hate, you obviously don't understand what it means to live and enjoy life. If I would have known that they would have ended up like that, I would have flunked them right then and there or did something different. They were probably already a lost cause, but who knows?"

"A lot of people are raised to discriminate and hate others. I know what you mean. I agree. You should pick and choose who you say hi to. That can be very time consuming. I bet you have a whole technique and everything when someone comes up to you that you don't want to talk to."

"Oh yeah. It's called the short and sweet, but I run into some where it becomes the long and mean. I hate being rude too, but you have to with some people because they don't listen and communicate very well, especially with nonverbals."

"Well, I'm glad you stopped and said hey Abby."

"How are you doing lady?"

"I'm doing fabulous. Trying not to work too much and enjoy my life as much as I can. I've had some ups and downs, but I'm in a pretty good place right now."

"That is good to hear. You deserve it."

"I'm just out for my morning run. Trying to get it in before the weather starts to get too nasty and too cold. I'll probably still run outside, but it won't be as enjoyable."

"The seasons are changing."

"It's funny running into you."

"Why is that?"

"I was philosophizing on my run this morning."

"Really. What about?"

"A couple of things, but mainly the who or what am I questions."

"That's a good one. What did you come up with?"

"I am everything, which is energy."

"Very good and deep." Abby said with a satisfied smile. "It's so true. You know philosophers have been saying that or something like it for many eons, and I mean tens of thousands of years and maybe even hundreds of thousands of years. Yet, here we are today with so many people who have no clue who they are and what they are. Unfortunately, they got brainwashed by a popular religion that distorted and lied about the information that they had a long time ago. Now, so many people believe they are their body and some imaginary soul and that some apparition of that body or imaginary soul will continue after they die, which is total horseshit."

"You are correct. And, all they see are differences."

"Exactly. Hey, I was planning on getting lunch in a couple of hours. I know you are out running, but I'd love to catch up with you some more. If you think you can tolerate a foul-mouthed elderly woman. I haven't got to talk about some of this stuff in a while. If you are interested, you are more than welcome to join me. No pressure if you don't want to or can't."

"Actually Abby, that would be fanfuckintastic. I wasn't sure what I was going to do later anyway after my lady went to work, so that would be perfect."

"Lady? Good for you Emerald. That makes me so happy. I can't wait to talk to you some more. Meet me at the Veggie Café at 11 a.m."

"Awesome. That is one of my favorite spots. Or, it used to be anyway before I stopped eating out. That sounds great. See you then."

"Enjoy the rest of your run."

Emerald shook Abby's hand again, and Abby walked off. Emerald thought how cool it was to run into Abby after all these years and when she was pondering some deep stuff this morning. She quickly remembered that she has actually been pondering some deep stuff for a while now. It was getting frequent too. She still thought it was very synchronistic that she ran into her in this moment of her life. She tried not to downplay what could be a meaningful coincidence because it did happen and was happening.

Emerald stretched out her back and legs a few times before she started running again. She took a deep breath and started running. She decided to run around the pond before heading back home. She started thinking about what she could ask and talk to Abby about. She thought it was wonderful to have the opportunity to sit down and have a one-on-one conversation with a philosophy teacher. She started to get excited. It was going to be way better than being at school or in a classroom setting where you have to share the teacher's time with a bunch of other students, who probably didn't want to be there anyway even though the subject matter that the teacher was talking about was very interesting and fascinating. A classroom setting is less engaging than a one-on-one setting. Emerald was going to have more time to speak her mind instead of being distracted by a bunch of dumb questions or ignorant comments. She was also looking forward to what Abby would say.

After thinking about it for a bit, she decided not to think too much about what she wanted to talk about or ask. She really just wanted to see what would come up organically and what would just happen automatically. She was trying her best to let go of some of that control in her life instead of trying to make or force things to happen. She wanted to embrace the chaos and the unknown more and just go with the flow. Since she was going to have the chance to talk with Abby, Emerald wanted to bring up the concept of oneness. Besides pollution, animal agriculture, poverty, inequality, and the many different types of discriminations and abuses, she thought one of the biggest problems facing humanity and society was the illusion that people are different. It wasn't just about people thinking they were different from each other but also people thinking they were different from animals and the earth and really everything. She felt good about that topic being the focus but wouldn't be too upset if something else overshadowed it.

Emerald tried to enjoy the rest of her run. She focused on how good her body felt and how much easier it was to exercise now. She felt strong and had a lot of stamina. She used to get really tired really fast, but it took a lot to wear her out now. She thought about the energy coming out of her and the energy that she was getting from all around her. She knew there were so many other things at play in the universe. She felt good about her realization that she was part of a larger system. She wanted to make sure that she was adding to it and contributing to it in a positive way. That was very important to her. It made her feel good. She wanted to keep progressing and not get complacent and apathetic like a lot of people do. To Emerald, that was a disease. She couldn't believe that most people are the cause of their own suffering, their own pain, and their own sicknesses. She got home and walked in the door. Mary was in the front room eating and listening to some psychedelic space rock music.

"Hi my love!" Emerald shouted.

"Hello my cutie."

"Good morning."

"Good morning to you."

Emerald walked over to her, and they kissed. Emerald wanted to hug her but didn't because Emerald was sweaty.

"You sleep good?" Emerald asked.

"It wasn't too bad. It was enough. You?"

"A little rough at times but not going to complain. It could have been worse."

"It always can."

Emerald went to use the bathroom and came back out a couple minutes later.

"Guess who I ran into at the park?"

"No idea. Anu?"

"That's funny, but no. Good guess though. I wish. That would have been awesome. My freshman year philosophy teacher from college. Dr. Abby Robinson."

"Interesting. So, that was a good guess."

"Yes, it was. We are going to get lunch at 11. What time do you have to leave for work?"

"Not until noon. Damn. I thought it was earlier than that. Do you want to go with?"

"No, that's okay. I think I'm going to get a bike ride in here in a bit. I'm sure you are ready for a shower and some food. I don't want to be a third wheel or a distraction anyway. I know how you love philosophy. You should get to pick her brain all you want. We can talk about what you all talked about later."

"Sounds good babes."

Emerald bent down and kissed Mary on the lips.

"I love you sweetie," Emerald said.

"I love you too darlin."

Emerald did another round of stretches while Mary ate. Then, Emerald went to the bathroom and took a shower. While Emerald was in the shower, Mary yelled at her that she was leaving and that she loved her. Emerald shouted that she loved her too. She heard the door close as Mary left to go on her bike ride. Emerald got done with her shower and did some hygiene and made herself up. She went into the kitchen and made some food. She made a mixture of nut butter, seeds, stevia, mulberries, goji berries, cinnamon, cacao powder, spearmint, and a banana. She made some juice and a glass of water and grabbed an apple to eat too. She sat down on the sofa and ate while she listened to the music that Mary had on. She grabbed her journal to write about the morning and meeting Abby. She then grabbed her song booklet to go over some of her songs. She had to turn off the music that was playing though as it was too distracting for her to focus on her own songs. She changed some lyrics on a couple of songs and added some ideas for some changes in a couple more. She got done eating and just grabbed her guitar to go over a few songs. After a while, she put the guitar down and washed out her dishes in the sink. She went to go floss and brush her teeth. Mary walked back in the door after Emerald was done with her oral hygiene in the bathroom. Emerald walked over to her.

"Sorry that we didn't have more time together," Emerald said.

"Me too baby doll, but we both have tomorrow off together. I can't wait."

"Shit. That is true. I'm totally looking forward to that then."

"I hope you enjoy your visit. I'm sure it will be interesting. I can't wait to hear about it. You can fill me in tomorrow."

"Sounds good."

They hugged and kissed again.

"I love you," Mary said. "Enjoy."

"I love you too my everything. Have fun at work."

"Will do."

"Bye, my love."

Emerald grabbed her bike and left. She rode to the café and got there a few minutes early. She parked and locked up her bike. Emerald walked into the café and saw that Abby was already there. She had a table in the corner away from everyone. Emerald thought that was perfect, so they could talk more in private. She walked over to Abby and sat down.

"Hello there," Emerald said. "Fancy meeting you here."

"Yes, indeed. I thought you looked healthy enough where you might eat at a place like this."

"I used to. I don't eat out anymore, but they do make an organic raw juice that I will drink."

"Nice. What made you stop eating out?"

"Mainly, not trusting people to make my food right, but there are also the issues of how expensive it is to eat out and how horribly made and unhealthy the food is when you eat out."

"Interesting."

"There are a couple of local places where I know the staff, who I trust, but a couple of years ago I went all organic and raw. I have been a vegan for over 20 years. You can eat okay as a vegan, or I should say plant based, in a lot of places, and you can eat a few things that are raw. However and unfortunately, there are no restaurants around here that are 100 percent organic or even a quarter organic. For some crazy and ridiculous reason, people love their poisons and genetically mutant organisms, which make them so sick and will eventually kill them. So, it's best that I just make all my food myself because you still have a lot of people in the food service industry who don't fully understand the vegan term and plant-based, organic, and raw diets. Some don't care either, and some even despise vegans and sabotage the food due to their own insecurities and mental problems."

"That makes sense."

"Then..."

"Oh, there's more."

"I also stopped eating anything with added sugar, and if I do eat something that is packaged or pre-made by a company that is raw and organic, the ingredients have to be a fruit or a vegetable. I won't eat any preservatives, additives, dyes, gums, stabilizers, or chemicals. Mary has a serious gluten allergy too, so I went gluten free for her a few years ago. That restricts my diet somewhat too, but that wasn't too hard for me to do. I didn't eat a lot of wheat and bread anyway."

"That is something else Emerald. What a diet that is. I don't think I have ever heard of anyone being that restrictive with their diet. I commend you. That is awesome and takes a lot of dedication. Good for you. You look great too. You have to be in your forties now, and you look like you are in your late 20s or early 30s. I'm jealous."

"Thank you, but I just want to feel good. I owe it to myself and to Mary but also the animals and the earth. I have to make up for most of the people not giving a flying fuck. I also didn't take care of myself for the longest time and got really sick. I told Mary that she deserves someone who is responsible and healthy and chooses life and happiness over death and sadness. I probably don't need to exercise as much as I do, but I like the feeling, the extra strength, and the way that I look."

"Even though you have such a strict diet, you probably don't have to worry too much about what you eat or how much you eat."

"Not at all. I do eat a lot. It's different than a lot of people. I eat a huge and high caloric breakfast every day. On the days that I exercise, which is most of the week, I eat a high caloric lunch too. I usually don't eat anything after noon. I also eat a lot of fats, which people don't understand. A lot of people stay away from high fat foods, but they are confusing high fat processed foods with good fats that are found in nuts, seeds, coconuts, olive oil, and avocados. You need those fats and can eat a lot of them as long as you are exercising too. They do have a lot of calories, so if you are not exercising and eating a lot of those, you will probably gain weight. Even if you aren't exercising, you need those fats to some degree. I like to say that I am vegan and organic for the animals, the earth, and humanity, but I am raw for my health. You lose a lot of nutrition by cooking your food. In addition, the enzymes, antioxidants, vitamins, and minerals get lost when you cook food. You need the enzymes to help you digest food, heal, and metabolize vitamins and minerals."

"That's wonderful Emerald. I'm so glad that you are taking care of yourself. You sound really knowledgeable about nutrition, which a lot of people could care less about. I don't think a lot of people even care about their health. They just eat whatever they want, whenever they want, no matter how sick and fat it makes them. It's kind of sad when you think about it. I've actually been a vegetarian for several years now. I still eat dairy, honey, and eggs. It's more for my health, but I don't like to contribute to killing innocent animals either. I think it's better for the environment too."

"That's cool. It is better for so many things. My lady, Mary, has been vegetarian for a long time now. I think she eats a plant-based diet most of the time, but she still eats honey and some dairy here and there. I don't think she will ever part with some of her leather shoes though. She has this thing about shoes. They do something to her, which I think is the brainwashing of the advertisements and the companies. Materialism is a very destructive force and devastating way of being."

"That's interesting. I can see that. I guess if I thought about the animals more and the future of the earth and humanity, I would go vegan. It's never too late to change and make a difference. After talking with you, I feel motivated and encouraged to be vegan."

"Go for it. It's never too late. I wish I was born and raised vegan. The animals deserve it, you deserve it, the earth deserves it, and our future deserves it."

"Well, that makes me so proud that you would put aside your tastes and desires and the way that most people are raised with our cultural and societal traditions and beliefs to have a diet like that."

"Diet? It's a lifestyle for me."

"Yes, sorry. Lifestyle. You did say vegan and not plant based."

"Totally."

The male server came over to the table.

"Good afternoon my fine folks," the server said. "Sorry for the wait. My name is Art, and I'll be taking care of you today. What would you all like?"

"I'll take a glass of the delicious veggie juice, and that's all," Emerald said.

"Great choice," Art said. "And you?"

"I'll have the same with the soup and salad combo with raspberry vinaigrette. I'll take a water too."

"Sounds good. I'll be back in a few with your lunch."

Both Emerald and Abby said thank you.

"I was thinking on my run home how weird it was to run into you since I was philosophizing on my run this morning," Emerald said.

"What's even weirder is that I had a dream about teaching last night. You would think that I would have lots of dreams about teaching, but it's not that often. And, that's only the third time that I have walked at that park, and there you were."

"How strange is that? As much as I go down there, it was probably a matter of time before you ran into me."

"It's a little strange. Well, you know I kept on teaching for the rest of my career, but I'm retired now and having fun doing whatever I want. How has your life been going?"

"It's a lot better now. I had some rough spots."

"Oh? I'm so sorry to hear that Emerald. I guess we all have our ups and downs."

"Well, you may not like the sound of this, but the smartest thing I did was quit college after my freshman year. After all these years, I'm still proud of myself for that decision."

"I can go either way on that one. I think it depends on the person, the intentions, the major and course of studies, and how much debt is acquired."

"Absolutely. I love to read Abby, so I was concerned about not being able to continue my education after the brainwashing and mindless high school experience. At first, it did interest me to be disciplined and learn some more, but I realized that I was doing it because I thought I felt like I had to. It was more for money or a prestigious job. So, there I was listening to things that didn't interest me and things I didn't think had any meaning or purpose for me. Not to mention the poorly constructed curriculum. College is almost exactly like four more years of high school. It's ridiculous. You have the half-ass education, mandatory subjects that you have to take that you don't want to take and don't care about, some awful and confused teachers, the counterproductive tests, the discriminatory and abusive athletics and sports, the popularity contests with the societies and cliques, and the drugs and alcohol. I can't leave out the hormonal men too and them sexually harassing, sexually assaulting, and raping the women too. Actually, some of the fraternities actually sexually assault and rape their pledges too during the hazing periods, but they refuse to admit that they are gay and/or criminals. Unfortunately, a lot of these rapists are in very high positions within companies and the government."

"Can you believe so many are judges too? It's so upsetting to find out so many judges and politicians are sexist, racist, bigots who have sexually assaulted and raped women when they were younger. Some even did that in high school. Most likely with underage girls. So, they are pedophiles too. For them to be called "Your Honor" is a dishonor to us all. It doesn't matter if you aren't found guilty in a biased and discriminatory court of law, especially since most high-profile cases don't even go to trial. A lot are even thrown out before the case begins because the victim was threatened to recant or to not testify. If you have a sexual assault and rape allegation, you should not be allowed to be a politician, corporate executive, or judge. Women don't lie about being raped. Men lie about raping women."

"Absolutely. You are so right Abby. Thanks for saying that. It's sad to say that I actually believe that a lot of men in these powerful positions are rapists and abusers. It's not okay. That's how out of control rape is at colleges and within our society. I guess in high school too. The schools and their administration just cover it up with the help of law enforcement and the legal system. Our patriarchal and misogynistic society just covers it up. They don't confront and deal with the sexual harassment either, which is a symptom to sexism and precursor to the rape and sexual assaults. Of course, the general society tries so hard to deny it and cover it up too. Nobody wants to or likes to talk about rape and sexual assault. It's a very graphic and emotional topic. They definitely cover it up if it's a popular male, such as someone who is related to someone who is rich and famous, such as businessman, celebrity, politician, or judge. They also let them off the hook if they are an athlete too. After they get caught and are accused of raping some poor girl, their families and businesses spend lots of money slandering her by trying to discredit and blame her. They also threaten her and harass her. They try to convince the public that she is making it up or that it's her fault. Then, the stupid public believe the lying advertising and marketing strategy. You know. Because so many people are stupid. Instead of using reason, they believe what they are told by people who don't know anything about anything. And, it's really upsetting when the rape victim ends up leaving the school because the school took the side of the rapist. She gets raped, and she is the one who ends up leaving the school while he gets to finish school and ends up becoming a judge, lawyer, politician, or corporate executive. How fucked up is that?"

"It's very upsetting. Sorry that we are focusing on such a serious topic Emerald. I'm sure there are other things that you and I can talk about."

"No problem. It came up for a reason. It is a very real problem that needs to be addressed. All I know is that offenders, who are mostly men, and rapists, who are mostly men, lie about what they did or do to women. Victims and women don't lie about being abused and raped. Those are the facts. Like you said, it doesn't matter if the men aren't found guilty in a court of law by a biased jury and corrupted judge. What matters is that men aren't held accountable for their crimes and misdeeds and so many people are in denial about how many men, especially rich and popular men, sexually abuse and rape women and sometimes underage girls and boys. It's an epidemic that needs to be dealt with in this patriarchal and misogynistic society. I guess it's more upsetting that there are women who take the men's side because they were never abused and don't understand these problems and issues. Or, they are just as sexist towards women as the men are. It's so hard to believe that so many women have been oppressed and abused by men for so long and brainwashed by religion and society that they are okay with men continuing to abuse us. It's awful and horrible. It's not okay. Who would lie about being sexually assaulted or raped? Really?"

"It's very rare. The ones that do usually recant pretty quickly, but even a lot of those were telling the truth but were threatened or abused by the offender to recant or not testify."

"Exactly Abby. You lie about raping not about being raped. What do most criminals say when they are accused?"

"I didn't do it."

"So yes, I was happy to get out of that cesspool of immaturity, incompetence, disorganization, sexism, discrimination, and abuse. Even their primary focus on athletics, which was the same in high school, is appalling. It's called school and not sports for a reason. It's called academics and not athletics for a reason. Athletics should be separate institutions from the academics. It's ridiculous you have athletes who are getting the same degrees as everyone else, but they don't get any homework or have to take tests. They get to pass all their classes and get a degree without doing the same work. You wonder why most of them are complete fucking idiots. If you aren't teaching them, they aren't going to learn anything. Not to mention that they weren't too bright to begin with."

"That's a good point Emerald. I agree."

"So, I left school and decided to just work some odd jobs here and there. I worked full time for a while, but I hated it. I don't know how people slave away all week so someone else can get rich off your lack of freedom and misery. It's a game and a scam. Capitalism is a true pyramid scheme.

There are some jobs out there that are tolerable and some that are rewarding both emotionally and financially, but they are the exception and not the rule. And, there is no job that is worth making a lot of money at if you are killing others, making people sick, polluting the earth, and murdering innocent, defenseless, and helpless animals. Unfortunately, so many companies and jobs participate in all that devastation and destruction. On a good note, I did end up meeting the love of my life shortly after I quit school."

"That's fabulous Emerald. I'm so happy for you."

"Unfortunately, it wasn't too long after that where I had an accident and eventually got addicted to pain pills and other drugs and alcohol. I started lying to Mary and almost lost her. I got arrested for doctor shopping, but I finally got clean and straightened my life out. Life is almost awesome. I have one more year of probation. Then, I can seal my record."

"That's great."

"I'm glad I got caught though. I'm better for it."

"Good. It's great to look at things in a positive way, especially the past and mistakes. Unless you are having problems now. Then, you have to face that shit. We have to face our fears and the pain. We have to take responsibility."

"Totally. I try to live every day now like how I should have lived my life. I try to take care of myself every second. It's so very important to take care of ourselves. It's the most selfless thing you can do as funny as that sounds."

"Yes, it is very important."

"I want to feel awesome and amazing as much as possible. If I do get sick or stressed or frustrated, I want to bounce back as quickly as possible."

"That's really smart Emerald. You are inspiring me. I'm so proud of you."

"Thanks Abby. I appreciate that. I always respected you. Philosophy is a passion of mine, so for you to be a philosophy teacher and most likely a philosopher makes me really look up to you. I always loved going to your class, listening to you, and learning about the different philosophers and their ideas, even if I disagreed with them. I still can't get around running into you today though. I was running this morning and really pondering our connection to everything and how society, our senses, and our thinking really fool us into seeing differences, which creates this separateness or distance from others, animals, the earth, and everything.

It's almost pathological or can be pathological. It's like a sickness. Our ego and self-centeredness are our demise. Look at all this division, hate, violence, fighting, war, and lack of empathy and caring for others, the animals, the earth, and the environment. People don't even take care of themselves, which is probably the root of a lot of our problems. It's insane. You think most people would eventually say, "You know what, it would be a lot more constructive if we all just cooperate and help each other instead of thinking that we all have to compete and fight over things." And, I feel so sorry for the poor and helpless animals, the earth and its environment, the children, and the future. It doesn't look good with the way that the rich, the governments, the politicians, and the companies are doing and running things."

Art came back over to the table with their food and beverages.

"Here you go ladies," Art said. "Again, sorry for the wait. We are short staffed this afternoon."

"No problem at all," Abby said.

"Anything else for you?"

"I'm good," Emerald said. "Thank you."

"Looks great," Abby said. "Thank you."

"Just yell at me if you need anything else."

"Will do," Abby said.

Art walked away. Emerald drank some of her juice, and Abby ate some of her salad and soup.

"Yummy," Abby said. "The salad and the soup are really good. Very tasty."

Abby took a sip of her veggie juice.

"That is really good too," Abby said. "Wow. So much flavor."

"It is good. You can't beat cold-pressed and fresh juice. So, what is your take on all this division? It almost seems like the powers that be are doing it on purpose."

"Well, Emerald, there are a few things going on there. You got a question of moral and ethics, sociology, social psychology, and biology. All with a splash of metaphysics. First off, I'm so happy you would love to have a deep conversation with me and that you are pondering these challenging and important issues."

"Yes, Mary probably gets exhausted with my constant philosophical, political, and religious debates, but she seems interested and can dish out some great perspectives."

"That's fabulous. You don't know how many couples that are out there where all they talk about is trivial shit, such as the sports and weather or their programs and shows they watch, instead of trying to figure out who they are and what really matters or what is important in their lives and this universe. Or, should I say universes?"

"That's funny. Yes, there is a lot that we don't know. It's important for us to keep an open mind and continue to learn. After my drug problem, I knew there was more to work and what family and society were pushing or forcing us into being and doing. I think that is why a lot of people seek out religion and even drugs. People also get sucked into other addictions, food, and consumerism or materialism. They are vulnerable and gullible. They feel lost and unfulfilled. Religion and drugs are dangerous paths to go down. The other addictions and the trivial or short-term gratifications are just as dangerous too. Drugs are so destructive, sickening, and deadly. They are not real and a bandage for your problems. They don't solve anything, and they make things worse. In addition, religion is a lie and a manipulation to not only get your money and time but also fill you full of lies that aren't true."

"Trust me Emerald, I have met a lot of people. Most people don't take the time to properly and thoroughly think about what matters the most and what is really important. It's unfortunate that the people who do run into me don't ask me deep questions or want to talk to me more. Not that I would want too much of that, but it would tell and show me that I taught them something or that they learned something. I am a wealth of knowledge, but I guess that is their choice. However, it also tells me how superficial a lot of people are. We live in a trivial and superficial world. People are definitely disconnected from themselves and others. People are definitely divided in lots of different ways. People are in their cages and bubbles. They are rushing and racing around to the next false sense of being. They feel pushed and pressured to be a certain way and to do certain things. It is so fake. You have to stop. You have to ask questions. You have to analyze. You have to find yourself and start thinking about how to be happy and healthy. More importantly, you have to use your imagination and create. That's why I love philosophy. I can see that is why you do too. It helps us to find the answers, to find the truth and what is real, and to figure it all out."

Abby ate some more of her salad and soup.

"It feels great too," Emerald said. "I get some sense of satisfaction and some energy from thinking and talking about these things. It energizes me. I feel connected to everything just thinking about how we are being manipulated and forced into being disconnected from everything."

"Yes, this concept of non-dualism that you are thinking and talking about has been thought about and debated for thousands of years. It wouldn't surprise me if the idea is tens of thousands of years old. Some call it monoism or monism. It's not just a philosophical concept, but it is a theological and spiritual one. Physicists and other scientists are even chiming in on the debate."

"That's interesting. I can't imagine that a lot of religious people, who aren't necessarily spiritual, believe that we are all one or there is a connection that we have to everything. They seem very bigoted and discriminatory towards others and the things around them."

"To some extent, just because some theologians philosophize and contemplate deep issues doesn't mean they believe in it, and if they do, there are limitations as to how far they go down that enlightened path or hole. I think religion started out as a good thing. I hope it did anyway. Religion used to be about morals and ethics and that we are all in this together and that we should help each other and respect everything around us. It's interesting that philosophy is the field that focuses on all those concepts now and not religion. Religion used to teach that there was a connection to everything. Some religions today still believe in some or all of that. They are just not the popular ones, which focus more on money, power, government influence, disparaging others who don't accept their beliefs, and dividing people. The most popular religions, excluding the philosophical ones, are absolutely atrocious and disgusting. They are pure evil. All they do is whine, complain, steal, hate, fight, and kill. The followers have to take responsibility for being manipulated and lied to, but the real monsters are the church, the preachers, the rich, and the politicians who spread the lies and the hate and start the wars and fighting."

"That is so true Abby. It's not okay and totally wrong, but it's true."

"At this point, if the religions and religious people tried to listen to and accept that we are all one, it would challenge and even disprove their beliefs and religion. They would have to admit they are wrong and that their religion is saying the same thing as the other religions. They would have to accept that their religion is connected to other allegedly different or opposing religions and belief systems. In reality, they are just using different words, and the preachers are misconstruing and lying about the meanings of the ancient scriptures for their own benefit or for some other greedy reasons. Or, things were changed and lost in translation."

"Yes, the translation issue is huge. Lots of believers in religion don't understand that what they are being told to believe is not what was originally taught or said in the original or ancient scriptures."

"That's the difference between philosophy and theology though. Philosophy is a science that can evolve, change, and grow based on new information and disproving and proving ideas. Philosophy is based on ideas and concepts based on evidence and proof. Philosophers aren't afraid to change their minds and ideas. They spend time proving and disproving theories and hypotheses like a scientist would. They try to use logic and rational arguments to make conclusions. Religion doesn't do any of that or very little. It's whatever the authorities and elderly or senior members of the church say it means. It's based on their, mostly men and rich men on top of that, opinions and not evidence or proof. Unfortunately."

"Yes, unfortunately. I can see all that. That makes sense. Theologians and religious people do seem to hang on to their beliefs no matter what. They are very obstinate and incorrigible."

"They are Emerald. The good news is that a lot of people are leaving their religions as they recognize and realize what they are being told is not correct, not accurate, or just a flat out lie. There is a mass exodus from religion going on. People are tired of the patriarchal churches, the inequality, the bigotry and hate, the discrimination, and the constant badgering for you to pay them or give them money. The religious leaders and churches even use threats that you won't go to some after-life paradise if you don't pay your dues to the church. That is a fucking travesty and an awful lie. It is pure evil to threaten people like that. They are definitely preying on people's gullibility and vulnerability, but people are starting to see the manipulation and the lies and understand that they can still be good and saved without being a part of the religious institution."

"Also, the hate mongering is not attractive and a turn off for a lot, especially the younger generations. A lot of them can see right through that shit."

"Exactly. You can't in one breath say that your religion or prophets are preaching love and peace but in another express damnation to those who disagree or who don't want to live a certain way or engage in a lifestyle that you denounce. It's very hypocritical, and it basically discredits your own beliefs and what you are saying."

"Especially if you are using fear and intimidation, which is evil in itself."

"You could say that Emerald. Yes, it doesn't make sense from that perspective. Are you against evil or are you for it? Hate, discrimination, and violence are evil. If they are trying to manipulate people to keep them on their side and from looking elsewhere for answers, fear does work, but it's not okay. Fear is abhorrent and wicked. I understand that they are trying to control people, and it is scary for people in power and authority to allow their followers to ponder and believe in oneness, harmony, collaboration, cooperation, non-dualism, and monism. However, you are doing it in the wrong way by using threats, intimidation, hate, and fear. You are sinning. You are being hypocritical, and that is a problem."

"I would accept and follow a religion that totally focused on oneness, harmony, peace, love, and cooperation. That's what life is all about. It's crazy that so many religions and people think it's okay to hate, discriminate, and abuse and neglect others. Furthermore, religions should never use fear, discrimination, hate, and dishonesty to control and manipulate others."

"I agree. I would follow a peaceful religion too that had all those characteristics. Unfortunately, it's better and easier to just believe in and practice those things and not worry about having a religion, especially since the religions that are closest to following those positive characteristics and practices still have these wild and mostly erroneous ideas about the past, the future, where we came from, and where we will go after we die. It's also not good to believe in a popular religion that has questionable and erroneous teachings and methods. Just because the majority or a lot of people believe something or believe in something doesn't make it true. However, you can blame religion all you want for our problems, but you also have to take a psychological and biological view, which supports the human instinct or learning style to create duality, polarity, opposites, and differences. Unfortunately, it seems that our minds and bodies are prone to creating differences."

"I can see that Abby. We do seem to sway towards duality due to how we are made. It's so easy for us to see the differences but not the similarities."

"It's somewhat biological and instinctual, but it is mostly taught and learned. We have the psychological and biological ability to see oneness, similarities, unity, and non-dualism, especially once we start waking up from the illusion and start questioning how we were raised and what we were taught. Then, we start to see the similarities and the reality or truth that we are all connected and made up of the same exact things. More importantly, we are all in this together. We have to share, cooperate, and work together no matter what we believe. We have to help each other and protect each other. Not just people but also the animals and the earth. They are connected to us too and a part of us too."

"I like that Abby. Well said."

"Our view of division is a huge thinking error and a fallacy of our linear thinking, vulnerabilities, and gullibility. We tend to easily separate and divide things. It's easier and simpler for the mind to process information by creating categories and differences. It also makes us feel special to be different than others, which strokes our egos. Unfortunately, it's an illusion that leads to separation, hate, and a lot of emotional issues."

"The biggest problems with creating differences and divisions are fighting, abuse, killing, hate, war, discrimination, inequality, poverty, and pollution."

"Yes, indeed."

"So many people and animals have had to die and so much of the earth has been destroyed in the name of differences or the thinking like "That doesn't matter," "That's not important," or "That is beneath me." It's very selfish, apathetic, and narrow or closed-minded."

"Now you are getting it Emerald. It also doesn't help that our senses, especially our eyes, are so limited. Most of the universe and the world is not exposed or shown to us. Our eyes are very deceitful. Our eyes are great and amazing, but we put a lot of trust into our eyes, our other senses, and our brains. We are hoping that they are getting all the information that is out there and interpreting it all correctly. That is not the case though, and it's far from the case. We miss out on most of the information and events that are happening."

"Great point Abby. In addition, our brain or mind is also distorting this information based on our own beliefs and what we have been taught."

"Absolutely. You can ask two people to look in the same direction, and then ask them to tell you what they see. They will both describe to you some similar things but also some different things. It's amazing how people interpret things so differently. If people's belief systems are different and they were raised differently, they are going to view things differently and have different beliefs."

"Makes you wonder about eyewitnesses testifying in criminal trials."

"Totally, a lot of innocent people have been convicted and sent to jail for crimes that they didn't commit due to eyewitnesses thinking or believe that they saw something when they didn't. Their prejudices and biases come out in these situations too. That's how a lot of minority people get convicted of crimes that they didn't commit. The eyewitnesses were really just racist and wanted to see the minority in jail even though the accused didn't do what the accusers said they did. The racist and biased prosecutors influence the witnesses too with their erroneous suggestions and theories. It gets worse when people are allowed to start using adjectives and other descriptions. That's when things really get carried away, and the imagination of the person really comes out."

"Don't forget "The one that got away" or "You should have been there" quotes."

"Those are classics Emerald. People tend to exaggerate a lot for bragging rights and for ego sake. Just with the eyes alone, we see differences on a fundamental level, such as colors, shapes, and sizes. Then, with our mind and beliefs, we start critiquing, criticizing, discriminating, and judging. However, we also favor or like things too because certain things are attractive to us, but that doesn't mean we recognize them as similar. We might feel connected to attractive things, but that can be an illusion too, especially with our hormones. Some of that is based on our experiences, but a lot is still based on what we have been told or what we think is expected of us. There are biological and chemical issues going on there too."

"I was talking about that recently. So many people think they are free because they have a choice and think they are choosing what they like, but they are really not free. They were made to choose what they think of as a choice due to being manipulated and controlled. They just don't realize that they are doing someone else's bidding. They are brought up that way or taught to do that. They are also pressured to do things that they think they are choosing to do. They think they should do it because everyone else is doing it. They are programmed and brainwashed. If they were living somewhere else or in a different culture or raised by a family or society with different beliefs and practices, they would see things differently and make different choices. Then, they would be arguing that those choices were made of their own choosing."

"Great example Emerald. Our minds are very deceitful. Do we have control over it, or does it have control over us? How much stuff do we do where we don't know why we do it? Can we stop it and do something else if we wanted to? And, to top it all off, for simplicity and brevity, we make assumptions, generalizations, and judgments. We love to do all these quick responses, which some are programmed, so we can save time. Jumping to conclusions and generalizing are very common with our thinking. However, that type of thinking with other thinking errors and defense mechanisms can be very dangerous and lead to mistakes, biases, and the horrible ways of bigotry, racism, sexism, ageism, heterosexism, classism, speciesism, and so on."

"That's cool Abby. Thanks for including speciesism in that list."

"You got it. Just for you. I knew you would like that. It's true though. The way we treat helpless, voiceless, and defenseless people says a lot about people, but that is also true when it comes to helpless, voiceless, and defenseless animals. It doesn't matter the species. What matters is the lack of empathy and the harm that is inflicted onto them."

"Don't forget the earth. It's a living organism too."

"You know it, but there are so many different forms of discrimination, especially if your parents, friends, groups, religion, preachers, political leaders, and culture support hating certain people and other things, such as animals."

"Some of that makes me think of how horrible the whole school spirit or patriotism programming is. It really upsets me. It's like brainwashing and manipulating people to hate others that they don't even know or who they have never met. They teach us at a very young age that our group that we are closest to or a part of is our group and that we should fight, battle, hate, distrust, and compete with others outside of our closest groups, especially others from other places or geographical locations. You are teaching kids and whoever else to despise and loath and even hate others because they were born somewhere else. We don't have a choice where we are born, so why do you hold that against them and why do you think you are better than them or why should you fight or compete against them? That's stupidity and bullshit. Sometimes I think that is what they are really teaching us in school. They are teaching us to fight and compete, which leads to conflict, discrimination, inequality, abuse, war, death, and destruction."

"So true Emerald. I agree. Athletics and competition make a lot of money, but they don't think about or consider the psychological and societal ramifications of what they are teaching the kids. Or, they don't care. It's the same with companies getting rich off products that make people sick, kill people and animals, and pollute and destroy the earth."

"That's fine if you want to engage in that immature and childish sports rivalry attitude as an adult, even though you were brainwashed to think that way, but teaching poor kids who don't know any better is child abuse. You are teaching them to judge and to hate. It's not okay. It's so wrong."

"Yes, it causes a lot of problems."

"Outside of learning discrimination, separateness, and hate in school and through sports, the politicians and religious leaders are awful at contributing to these disgusting acts too. They should be ashamed of themselves. They act like a bunch of kids most of the time by putting others down and lying about others to make you afraid or suspicious of them. They use our differences to create hate, fear, and paranoia. I'm not even going to get into the immigration phobia scam where the politicians use fear and discrimination to create illusory borders and scam the citizens out of billions to build walls, which are conveniently built by the construction companies that are owned by the politicians, their friends, their cronies, or their family members. Cronyism, favoritism, and nepotism should all be criminal behaviors. Nothing every good comes from building walls and creating borders. Then, there is the question of whether they are really trying to keep people out or are they trying to keep us in."

"That is the question. It's all very provocative and counterproductive Emerald."

"Actually, I believe that any competition is inherently negative and unhealthy. I think some are able to use it in a positive way, but that is a rarity. However, they could have done something constructive, cooperative, and supportive to achieve their goals. They may have gotten what they wanted out of the competition, but the other party that they were competing against did not, so it will always have consequences. Through cooperation, both parties win and grow instead of just one."

"Well put Emerald. You are really impressing me with your train of thought and intelligence. I knew you were smart but damn. You go girl.

I've always liked a little competition, but I can see where you are coming from. Competition does seem mostly one sided and very limited. It can definitely cause a lot of issues and problems. I can see that it definitely does more harm than good."

"It does, so the political competition easily becomes disastrous. Not just for the candidates and politicians but also for the society and the citizens. To get your attention and to shock you, the politicians with their political divide play on people's fears, insecurities, prejudices, and hate. They want you to feel separate and different, so you will take sides and be loyal. It's a total manipulation just so they can get elected and then rob you blind. Slandering others and committing libel for the purpose of campaigning for elections should be considered treason and should be illegal. I know it is illegal to some degree, but it's left up to the victim to sue and hold them accountable. That can be very expensive and time consuming. If there is proof of a crime, you shouldn't need the victim. Defamation is a serious and negative act. It definitely affects the country and its citizens because you have so many vulnerable and gullible people who believe the lies that the candidates and our leaders spout off. Therefore, I think the judicial branch of the government should have responsibility with holding lying and dishonest politicians and companies accountable without the support of the victim. If you are running for a public office, everything you say and do is a reflection of the country, the nation, and its citizens. If you are spouting off untrue negative comments about your opponents or other people, you need to be held accountable for that. Politicians are intentionally dividing their own people. This division could easily turn into a civil war, which causes people to die over greed and selfishness. That is why it is treason, but they also use the non-issues to separate and divide people."

"Non-issues? What are those Emerald?"

"Those are valid issues but not in the sense of what the politicians can do anything about. So, the politicians mention these controversial issues to spread hate and fear. They create emotional responses from people. A lot of greedy and manipulative politicians have lip service and certain bullshit talking points that distract from the fact that they don't know what they are doing. My theory is that they don't know how to deal with the real issues that they have some control over dealing with, so they manipulate people to take their side and vote for them due to their position on these non-issues or distracting issues. These issues would be like gun rights, terrorism, homosexuality, global warming and climate change, gay marriage, immigration, abortion, and welfare. There are others but those are some major ones. Avoidance and slanderous remarks about others are also non-issues as they don't address what the politicians are going to do about the actual problems, such as inequality and discrimination, poverty, political bribes and lobbying, pollution, the over-budgeted military, impacts of global warming, gerrymandering, obtainment and use of fossil fuels, the country's enormous debt, domestic terrorism by the citizens, not labeling poisonous and genetically modified foods, the sensitive and shaky economy, corporate corruption and corporate welfare, healthcare, and so on."

"I see what you are saying. Those are definitely the real issues that need to be dealt with over those other controversial issues. There might be a better term than calling them non-issues, but I don't know what that would be off the top of my head other than calling them controversial issues or distracting issues. A lot of those non-issues are manufactured, but some have serious issues that come out of them, such as the need for more gun control due to the ease of access for kids, criminals, and emotionally unstable individuals to obtain weapons. Either way, they do use those non-issues as distracting techniques or avoidance tactics to keep the attention off their own misdeeds and the lack of ability to discuss the real problems and how to actually deal with the real problems. I agree with you. I don't think a lot of them know how to deal with those real issues either."

"Exactly Abby. That's a real issue that needs to be addressed too. It's not okay that most of our politicians are completely inept and incompetent. Just because your daddy gave you or left you a shitload of money doesn't mean you have any business being a politician, a business manager, or a business owner, and if you are trying to get rich or richer by being a politician, you deserve some bad karma for that goal and definitely don't deserve to be a politician. It's horrible that the politicians, the candidates, and their groups or associations just spout off words that people have emotional attachments to, and they have no idea what they are doing and how to fix anything. Maybe we should call them emotional issues instead of non-issues. Nevertheless, they definitely have no plan or no realistic plan to prevent or reduce crime, drug abuse, other addictions, poverty, inequality, homelessness, hunger, waste, and all other real issues that I mentioned earlier."

"You are right. They don't really talk about dealing with those real issues. That issue needs to be dealt with. If they do mention them, they don't have practical or realistic plans to address them."

"They manipulate, lie to, and divide the citizens. While we are all fighting with each other over those emotional or non-issues and our differences, they are robbing us through their taxes, corporations, and businesses. They pass laws that only help the rich and the companies. They don't cut taxes for the middle class and poor, but they cut taxes for the rich and the corporations. It's a bunch of bullshit, and people just let them keep doing it. Gays getting married doesn't hurt you. People from different religions aren't hurting you. People, who are called terrorists by our political terrorists, living on the other side of the world aren't hurting you. Mothers, who were raped or sexually assaulted, who are in relationships with abusive and horrible men, who are addicted to drugs, who can't take care of a baby for whatever reason, who had their birth control fail, and who want to legally choose to abort the fetus, aren't hurting you. People, who want the society and schools to be safer by keeping guns out of the hands of kids, criminals, and emotionally unstable people, aren't hurting you. Immigrants aren't hurting you. The politicians, the rich, and the government do hurt you. Every day they hurt you, but people would rather fight about the people and groups who aren't hurting them and vote for and support the people who are actually hurting them. It's fucking insane and absolutely crazy. It's also so very very stupid. We are surrounded by idiots. Sorry Abby. I'll try to calm down."

"You don't have to apologize Emerald. It is very upsetting. That's a part of being awake and realizing the truth. The truth is not always attractive or nice to see. Some of it is downright disgusting. We are alive when we feel, even if it is pain. It's good to feel, even if it is upsetting. It means that something is wrong, so we have to recognize those feelings and then do something about it. The worst thing we can do is become apathetic, compliant, complacent, helpless, and/or hopeless. There are so many people who choose to become addicts to numb the pain instead of dealing with it. In a sense, the government and politicians and the corporations love that people are addicted to drugs and so many other things. Addicts become compliant, apathetic, and complacent that way. That is even the problem with milder drugs, such as sugar, processed and poisoned or GMO foods, foods from animals, tobacco, caffeine, and marijuana. Besides all the negative side effects and health problems they cause, they still keep us in denial, apathetic, and compliant. We also can't leave out shopping, consumerism, and entertainment, especially sports."

"Yes, they do. People are also so selfish and self-centered with their possessions. They get so caught up in consumerism and greed. They are so blinded by money and material things. People hoard shit that they don't need and store it, but if someone else steals it because they need it, they get upset even though they were never going to use it anyway. Imagine all the good that we could do with letting others have the crap that we have that we don't want or need. These are grown adults acting like kids who don't want to share. "It's mine," "You can't have it," or "You can't play with it." They also get paranoid and neurotic. They would even kill to protect their trivial things. People have killed others for trying to steal their shit or being on their so-called property. Unfortunately, they mainly get defensive like that when the other person is not like them or looks different than them. You know. Because they are racist bigots. They end up projecting their fears onto people who look and/or act differently than they do. In reality, it's all an illusion. It's all in their head. The real problem is that they don't like themselves and who they are. They are afraid of themselves."

"Very true Emerald. That was a good train of thought. That is the point. We see ourselves a certain way, and when others who we see differently try to interact with us, we become uncomfortable and nervous, which leads to fear. Then, we project our own insecurities onto them, which can be disastrous for them due to the abuse and violence that may come out of these people."

"Yes, it could get deadly. That makes me think of the language issue too. These insecure people use names and labels, so they don't have to think about the other people that they are discriminating against as actual people or human beings. It's the same as the animal agriculture business calling dead cows names like beef and hamburgers or calling dead pigs names like pork and bacon. It's a manipulation and lie to not call it what it is or see it for what it is. They are abused, tortured, and murdered dead animals that had a family, thoughts, and feelings. When you call people names and use labels, it dehumanizes them. It has a blinding effect, so they can separate or distance themselves from them, even though they are the same. Whenever we are named and labeled, it puts us into different categories and groups to differentiate us from other things and beings. It's faulty thinking, especially if the names and labels are derogatory, disparaging, dishonest, and stereotypical. Never trust someone, especially a politician, who uses names and labels to put other down. It's a trick, and the people who feed into it are complete idiots. I know I'm engaging in name calling right now, but I'm not in a leadership role who needs to be a role model."

"Your cool. It's not a put down if it's true, and we are having a private and honest conversation. It's also an intelligent one. They are idiots. However, we do have to use names to some extent, especially for communication purposes, but you are right. There are lots of names and labels that have a negative and unhealthy impact on people and the society. These names and labels can actually influence the groups that you are using them towards. It's a fact that if you call a child a name or tell them they are something, they will grow up to believe that they are what you called them. This process can be bad or good. If you call them stupid, they will grow up thinking that they are stupid. It's verbally, emotionally, and psychologically abusive. You do have to be very careful with names and labels. It does influence and cause polarities."

"I can see that Abby. We do need names and labels to communicate effectively. We just need to be careful with how we are using them. I'm glad a lot of people can't hear me then because I just called a bunch of people stupid for believing their lying politicians."

"I think you are okay. They didn't hear you, and there is truth to what you are saying because the politicians are lying and being hateful. In addition, the followers of these evil politicians should know better, so they are idiots."

"I'm glad you understand that Abby. It is different when you are in a position of power and abusing this power by using your platform to express division and hatred through public media outlets. Being negative and mean to others is never okay. It's not okay to call people names to their faces."

"If our parents, family, friends, and/or society have labeled us in some way, we can easily take on these labels, and they can shape our personalities, behaviors, and attitudes. We can be told what to be and how to be."

"There is a control issue with that statement. If we have been manipulated and have taken on labels, that may not really be us. We think we are a certain way, but we are not. We were told to be a certain way. Originally, we were told to be a certain way, but after we realized that we were shaped by what those people told us, we should know better. We can actually choose to not be that way and change ourselves. It may take us time to think, feel, and act differently, but we do ultimately have that power. That choice is ours to make. We just didn't realize that when we were a child or when we were young. I would even say that most adults don't realize that truth. They think they are the way they are and that there is nothing they can do about it. They think they have an unchangeable personality and attitude. They don't have to be that way, especially if it is negative and unhealthy. It's never okay to hurt and abuse yourself, others, animals, and the earth. It doesn't matter if you were raised that way. A lot people use the fallacious and bullshit genetic or nature argument to avoid taking responsibility. They are just lying to themselves, so they don't have to change."

"You said it Emerald. The choice is ours to make. We can determine our personalities and attitudes, and we definitely have control over our thoughts, feelings, health, and behaviors. If you don't think that, you are very irresponsible or just ignorant. It would take a lot of self-reflection to change, but it can be done. You have to finally see that you are wearing a mask that someone else put on you and that you keep choosing to wear that mask."

"Masks. Plural."

"Sorry. Yes, masks. We wear many different masks. So many people are fake and try to be something that they are not, especially around different people and in different situations. We even wear different masks for ourselves. They are not all bad, but they can be. We can have so many different identities."

"Work, family, friends, society, religion, politics, gender, sexual orientation, race, language, various groups and associations, language, nationality, and so on."

"Good list Emerald. There's a lot. It's crazy how we focus on our differences, but we are like 99.99 percent similar to everything, especially on a molecular and atomic or quantum level. We are all atoms and what the atoms are made of."

"Absolutely. There are similarities that we don't even know of yet. There are microscopic and quantum substances that make up what we think are the most basic and smallest pieces of matter. We have no idea what else is to be discovered. It is exciting and hopeful to find that we are all connected and all working as one. You are me, and I am you. We can either work together or work against each other. The important thing is that we are made from the same things, so we should put aside any illusory differences and collaborate and cooperate. More importantly, we should share and help one another."

"Once again Emerald, your insight and understanding amazes me."

"I wish more people would have this conversation Abby. We are made up of the same stuff and are connected. The problems that we are having are rooted in inequality, division, and discrimination. People are believing a lie that they are different than others, they believe in so many things that aren't true, and they are chasing false and fake goals or dreams. We are all one. We need to help and support each other, the animals, and the earth."

"I love it. So true. Hopefully, the majority will see that sooner than later, instead of how it is now."

"Hopefully, we can keep spreading the message and slowly but surely wake everyone up from their denial and programmed and brainwashed way of life."

"Great discussion Emerald. It was so nice to see you again and to have this very intelligent and enlightening conversation with you. I enjoyed it immensely. Here's my contact information if you ever want to get together and chat again. No worries if you don't."

"Thank you so much. I will definitely reach out to you. I love talking to open-minded and intelligent people and discussing what needs to be done to deal with our issues and problems. I want you to know though that the pleasure was all mine. Thank you for taking the time to talk with me. It means a lot that you think I am smart enough to discuss some of these topics with you."

"Well, I gotta go. This old lady has a date tonight. If I don't hear from you, keep doing what you are doing. You are getting it. By the way, I'm paying for your juice."

"You don't have to do that. Thanks. I really enjoyed our talk and the company. Thanks again. Take it easy."

They both got up from the table. Abby left some money on the table. They both hugged and said goodbye. Abby waved at Art and left the café. Emerald went to the bathroom, thanked Art on the way out, and exited the café. She grabbed her bike and headed back home. On her way home, she thought about some of the things that Abby said and some of the issues and problems that they talked about. She had so many more things that she wanted to discuss with Abby, but overall, she was satisfied with what they did cover. Emerald couldn't believe that so many people, especially grown adults, are so gullible. They let themselves get manipulated with hate, fear, consumerism, drugs, other addictions, materialism, entertainment, and discrimination.

She got home and walked into the apartment. Mary was at work, so Emerald had the place all to herself. She put up her bike and decided to go ahead and work on a song. She liked to use the energy and the feelings from some of her deep and controversial discussions to create her music. She grabbed her electric guitar, the guitar processor, and her small amplifier. She plugged everything in and made sure the sound was not too loud. She was working on another doom rock song. She thought it could probably start off with a bassline. She has had the melody ringing around in her head for about a year, but she was having a hard time completing the entire song. She already knew what she wanted to say, so the lyrics were going to be easy. She called the song, "Inside of You." After the introductory bassline, she wanted like an instrumental bridge before she rocked out with the wah pedal on the riff. She imagined the drums and the bass guitar jamming right along with her guitar work. She didn't think the guitar needed a lot of distortion but maybe a little. Emerald started playing and singing.

Inside of You

Intro Bassline: (On low E string)
A A A G G G Bflat, Bflat, Bflat, A, A, A, G, G, A, A
A A A G G G Bflat, Bflat, Bflat, A, A, A, C, C, A, A
Repeat both lines

Instrumental Bridge:
A (hold for 1 bar), Bflat (hold for ½ bar), C, C, Bflat, A, A (Play 3 times total)
On last one: A (hold for 1 bar), Bflat (play 8 times), C (play 8 times)

Riff for Verse and Chorus (play with wah pedal):
A, G, Bflat, A, G, A
A, G, Bflat, A, C, Bflat
Repeat both lines

Verse 1:
(Play Riff)
Outside you've constructed, a polluted world that's
Been distorted by your, brainwashed mind and now you've
Come to the conclusion, that you're a delusion
Now it's time to, open up your fucking mind

Instrumental Bridge

Chorus:
(Play Riff)
The war is inside of you
Peace is inside of you
Answers inside of you
Why can't you see the truth?

Instrumental Bridge

Verse 2:
(Play Riff)
Inside you're conflicted, with what's real and what is
In your head that you don't, understand and now the
Truth eludes you but you're, going crazy now it's
Time to wake up and, open up your fucking mind

Instrumental Bridge

Repeat Chorus

Instrumental Bridge

Guitar Solo

Play Riff

Verse 3:
(Play Riff)

Reflecting upon your, self is what you have to
Do to find the real, you so you can e-
volve into the being, that is your meaning
All because you, opened up your fucking mind

Instrumental Bridge

Repeat Chorus

Instrumental Bridge

TO BE CONTINUED…

About the Author

I have spent most of my career in human services and have a Bachelor's Degree in Psychology, a Master's Degree in Counseling, a Master's Degree in Business Administration, and completed two years of a PhD in Public Policy and Administration before running out of student loans. During my extensive career helping others, I learned that so many people are in denial about what they need to do to take responsibility and be happy. Most people blame everyone else for their problems and refuse to do what they need to do to be healthy and happy. Some people are able to overcome this blockade in their lives, but others become really sick and die a miserable life. As a vegan for over 20 years, I know that we must accept the realities of what we are doing to ourselves, others, the animals, and the earth. We project our pain and hurt onto ourselves and everything around us. If we were okay and at peace with ourselves, there wouldn't be a reason to hurt ourselves, others, the animals, or the earth. Therefore, I have made it my life's work to take care of myself first and foremost while spreading this enlightenment, health, and positivity onto everything around me. I need to feel good in a healthy way and be happy every second that I am alive, so I can project this goodness outside of me. I hope it makes a difference. Life is too short to be unhappy, miserable, sick, a slave, angry, and hurtful to yourself, others, the animals, and the earth. Peace and Love! Forever and Always!